I0614056

SKIES WILL BURN

Book Four of The Dragons of Mother Stone

MELISSA MCSHANE

Night Harbor Publishing

Copyright © 2022 by Melissa McShane

ISBN-13 978-1-949663-68-6

All rights reserved

No part of this book may be used or reproduced in any way whatsoever without written permission except in the case of brief quotations embodied in critical articles and reviews.

This book is a work of fiction. Names, characters, businesses, organizations, places, events, and incidents either are the product of the author's imagination or are used fictitiously. Any resemblance to actual persons living or dead, events, or locales is entirely coincidental.

Cover Design by MiblArt

Night Harbor Publishing

www.nightharborpublishing.com

For Rhys,
battle consultant and enthusiastic reader

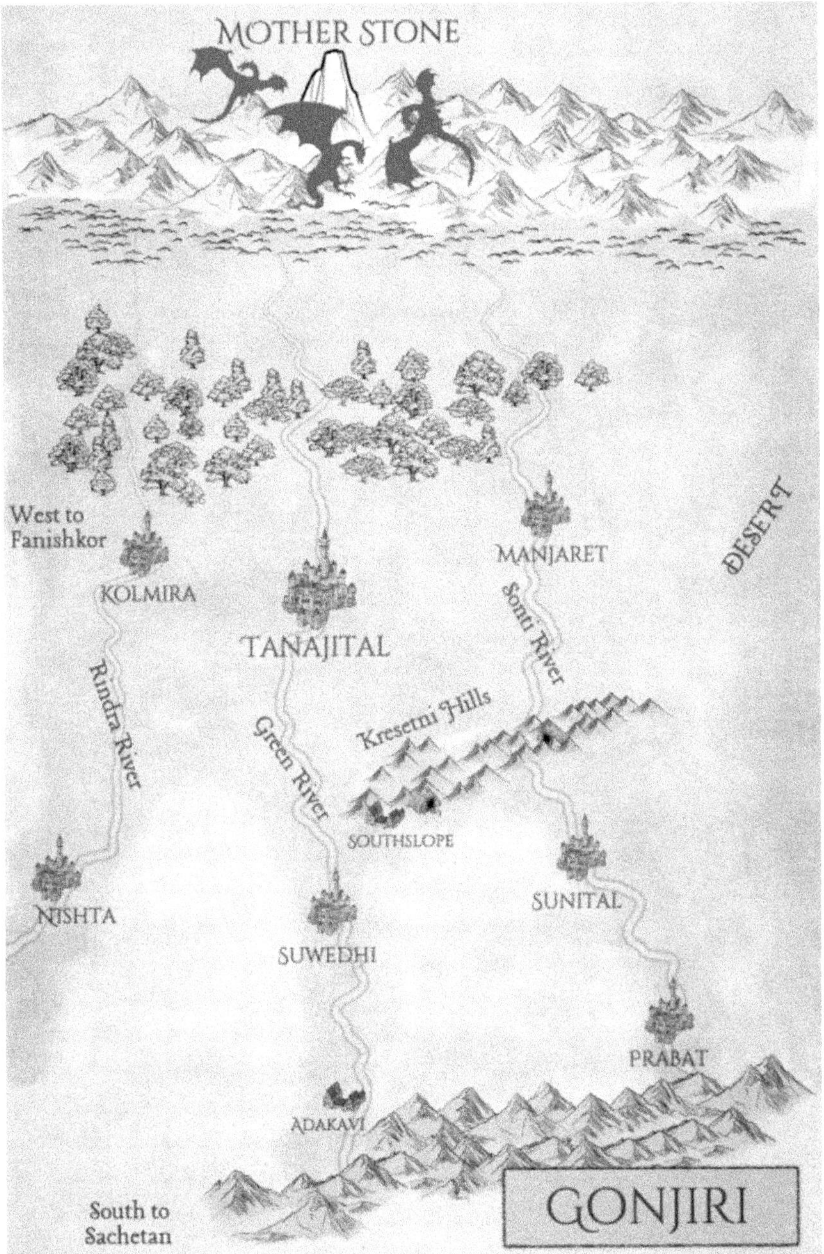
MOTHER STONE
West to
Fanishkor
KOLMIRA
TANAJITAL
MANJARET
DESERT
Somti River
Rindra River
Green River
Kresetni Hills
SOUTHSLOPE
NISHTA
SUWEDHI
SUNITAL
PRABAT
ADAKAVI
South to
Sachetan
GONJIRI

AUTHOR'S NOTE: ABOUT DRAGONS

Dragons have six fingers on each hand, and the number twelve is semi-religious to them. They measure the passage of time in twelvedays as well as seasons and years, and frequently count by dozens as well as more conventional base ten numbers (thanks to having ten toes on their feet).

Dragons measure time of day by the position of the sun: dawn, morning, mid-morning, noon, mid-afternoon, late afternoon, dusk/sunset. Time of night is measured by relation to midnight: dusk/sunset, evening, late evening, midnight, the dreaming hours, pre-dawn, dawn.

Dragons take approximately thirty years to reach adolescence and are considered adults at age fifty-five, though it can take another ten to fifteen years for a dragon to achieve her full adult size.

Dragon time and distance measurements are inexact and based on the average dragon body. The basic unit of time is the heartbeat, or beat. A dragon's resting heart rate is about twenty-five beats per minute, so a single beat is the equivalent of two and a half seconds, a hundred beats is a little over four minutes, and a thousand beats is almost forty-two minutes.

An adult dragon is approximately the same length and height (not including wingspan) as a double-decker bus, but slimmer. Their basic unit of distance is the dragonlength, which is somewhere between twenty-five and thirty feet long (counting from tip of the nose to tip of the tail). For smaller distances, they use the handspan, which is approximately twelve inches long. For long distances, they are more likely to measure by the length of time it takes to fly somewhere rather than how far it is in dragonlengths. A dragon standing erect is sixteen to twenty feet tall.

Adult dragons weigh between 4000-5000 pounds. An active dragon will eat, on average, 250-300 pounds of meat per day, plus a quantity of stone equaling another 8-10 pounds (sometimes less depending on the "richness" of the stone). Dragons generally eat twice a day, though in lean times a dragon will gorge herself on available food and then not eat again for several days.

An adult dragon can fly up to 120 miles per hour.

CHAPTER ONE

Lamprophyre sat back on her haunches and restlessly flexed her wings, sending a cooling draft over her body. At nearly noon on the first day of winter, the sun's rays weren't as punishingly hot as they would be in a few twelvedays—a few *months*—but the day was still unusually warm, warmer than was comfortable for a dragon. It hadn't rained in several days, and the dragon embassy courtyard smelled of dust and, faintly, the roast pig Lamprophyre had had for breakfast. It also smelled, closer to hand, of leather and the oily tang of warm metal. Such ordinary smells with such extraordinary meaning.

She lifted the tangle of leather straps and metal buckles in one hand and eyed it narrowly. Wide leather bands connected to an oddly shaped piece of leather, stitched to curve up on both long sides in an oblong cupped shape. Thinner bands hung off the tapering ends of the oblong, attached to fat metal triangles barely big enough to fit all her fingers through. Buckles swung and tapped against each other, making little *tink* sounds that contrasted with the soft purr of leather rubbing against leather.

"I don't know about this," she said.

"It was your idea, Lamprophyre," Rokshan said.

"Yes, but I didn't know it would look like this. And *this*—" She tapped a finger against the leather oblong. "Did it have to look so much like a saddle?"

"It's the only way to connect all the harness straps and keep them from crippling me," Rokshan reminded her. "Look. If you don't want—"

"I do. I'm sorry. It's just, now it's ready, I feel so foolish putting it on. Dragons aren't draft animals."

"You could think of it as a kind of clothing," her clutchmate Flint offered. "Utilitarian clothing."

"Dragons don't wear clothes, either." Lamprophyre sighed. "All right. Help me get it settled."

The...saddle...went first, fitted snugly into the notch above her shoulders by Flint. It was heavy and awkward enough it took a dragon to manage it. Then the straps under her arms that buckled securely across her chest. The iron buckle rubbed uncomfortably across her scales, but it wasn't painful, so she didn't say anything. Next, the straps above her arms that crossed over the base of her throat. Those were more comfortable, though they would have choked a human; dragon hide was stronger than that.

She cinched the buckles tight and twisted her torso to make sure the straps were secure. The metal triangles, the stirrups, bounced lightly off her sides. The harness actually wasn't that awkward, no worse than human sandals had been, and she'd endured those.

"All right, climb up," she said to Rokshan, crouching so the left-hand stirrup scraped the hard-packed earth of the courtyard.

Rokshan settled himself in his accustomed seat. "Oh," he said in a breathless voice. "That's, um, very snug now."

"Does it hurt?" Flint asked.

"Not hurt so much as compress. I think the saddle needs to be of thinner leather."

Lamprophyre twisted to look at him, but as usual saw only her own shoulder. "Should we have them make a different one?"

"I've waited two weeks to race with you, Lamprophyre. I'm not putting it off because of a little discomfort." Rokshan fitted his feet into the stirrups. She felt the brush of leather against her skin as he fastened the hip straps. "They can make another one after we try this out. There might be other adjustments to make."

Lamprophyre shifted the buckle of the chest band. "Good point. Are you ready?"

Rokshan patted her neck. "Ready."

Lamprophyre nodded at Flint, who launched himself into the sky and winged his way southward toward the warehouses where the rest of the clutch lived. She drew in as deep a breath as she could manage against the chest band and followed Flint.

Flying wearing the harness didn't feel any different than it usually did, except for how the buckles pressed against her scales, rubbing lightly. On anyone but a dragon, that would result in painful sores over time, but no dragon's hide could be damaged by something as soft as iron. It was annoying, but no more than that, and Lamprophyre could bear a little annoyance.

They flew in silence across Tanajital, not needing to speak. Rokshan's presence on her shoulders was a pleasantly warm ember, constantly reminding her he was there. Occasionally the reality of it struck her: she, a dragon, was pair-bonded to a human she loved more than anything, and then she felt warm all over and not just from her mate's presence. Their bond had continued to strengthen over the last two twelvedays until now she could tell where he was from halfway across Tanajital.

She felt him run his hand over the base of her neck, below the sensitive spot at the back of her head. They weren't the same species, and couldn't share physical intimacy, but his touch meant so much more now that she knew he loved her.

Dragons rose into the sky ahead, orange and red and green and silver, and came to meet them as Lamprophyre approached. "So it works," Coquina said. "It's surprisingly attractive."

"You think so?" Lamprophyre asked. She'd felt so awkward with all of them staring at her that Coquina's response was a surprise.

The drifting surface thoughts of the clutch showed they were all in agreement with Coquina. "It looks like jewelry," Dolomite said. "Very plain jewelry. I realize that doesn't make sense."

"We could make them brighter," Bromargyrite said, himself a beacon of brilliant orange and yellow. "If it's a success."

"There aren't many people we'll want to have ride," Orthoclase pointed out. "Just Rokshan and Melika and maybe Lokun."

"And it's not as if you need riders," Rokshan said. "This is purely for humans' benefit."

"Then I suppose it's time to test it," Lamprophyre said.

They flew low across the city to give the residents of Tanajital something wonderful to look at. Lamprophyre loved how the city's voice, a low, rumbling hum, grew higher and more excited whenever the dragons appeared. People stopped in the street and pointed, held their children up for a better view, and a few of them even cheered. How different from the first days almost a year ago, when Lamprophyre's appearance had started more than a few riots. Rokshan had said, back then, that it was human nature to quickly grow accustomed to the strange until it became normal, and then normal became taken for granted. Now, she knew from talking to the people who came to the embassy for the free soup, most citizens saw the dragons as part of the city.

They crossed the Green River and flew on a few dozen dragonlengths to the tall wooden structures, red as the floor of the coliseum, that marked the racing course. If Lamprophyre had to attribute dragons' success at making Tanajital love them to anything, this would be it. Rokshan's idle thought that humans might enjoy watching dragons race had turned into this semi-permanent collection of obstacles and the two tall spectator stands on either side. A third stand, topped by a green and gold canopy, gave the royal family somewhere to sit when they attended.

The seven dragons of the clutch alit on the field. "How should we do this?" Rokshan asked. "Run the obstacle course?"

"I was thinking of a speed test first," Lamprophyre said. "Something straightforward."

"Then let's make it a true race," Coquina said. Her clutchmates groaned. "What?" she protested with a smile. "You might win."

"The odds are not in our favor, love," Flint said, elbowing his mate. "But it's still a good idea. We'll be there in case Rokshan falls off."

"Let's not use those words, all right?" Rokshan said. "I don't want the Immanence hearing and deciding to make my life short and exciting."

Lamprophyre pushed off and flapped until she was just above the spectator stands. "Everything will be fine. Tell me when you're ready."

Rokshan patted her neck again, then gripped her ruff firmly. "Ready."

Lamprophyre glanced to either side, where the other dragons had gathered. "Go!" she shouted, and seven dragons sent up a tremendous wind as they took off for the horizon.

Lamprophyre had never flown as fast as she could with Rokshan as a passenger. Now his knees gripped her shoulders firmly, his heels in the stirrups dug into her sides, and she gradually sped up until she had to close her nictitating membranes to protect her eyes from the wind.

Coquina was already well in the lead, with Porphyry close behind. Flint and Bromargyrite flanked Lamprophyre, and she had just realized they were doing it on purpose when Orthoclase pulled ahead and Dolomite dropped to fly beneath her. She loved how much care her clutchmates had for Rokshan, how he was one of them for all he was human.

Below Dolomite, the ground streamed past in streaks of green and brown and gray, with the Green River a glittering stripe to the left. The horizon lay low and steady in the distance, misty with an oncoming storm. Rain would be welcome after so many dry days. Ahead, Coquina and Porphyry had reached the lone tree that marked the end of their race course and were wheeling to return. Orthoclase had made up ground and was barely a dragonlength behind the leaders.

"Hold on!" Lamprophyre shouted to her rider. She thought about slowing to take the turn more gently, but what would be the point of the test if she didn't push her limits? So she sped up instead, aiming to the right of the tree, which was tall and slender like a giant finger pointing at the sky. Flint and Bromargyrite moved away, giving her room to make the turn—

—and she banked hard, wheeled on her left hind leg, and tilted nearly sideways as she circled the tree and headed back toward the obstacle course. Rokshan's grip on her shoulders and ruff tightened, and he shouted, a wordless cry of exhilaration that made Lamprophyre's heart leap. He hadn't shifted at all and the saddle hadn't slid. Lamprophyre shouted with him and sped faster.

There was no way she could catch Coquina or Porphyry, but she pushed herself as fast as she could go. Rokshan leaned closer, pressing against the sensitive spot and sending a pleasant tingle through her body. He'd finally gotten over his embarrassment at learning that spot was related to sex, at least when a dragon touched it, but he still avoided leaning against it. She wondered what had made him do it now.

She sped past the finish line, which was more a mutually-agreed upon spot near the spectator stands than an actual line, and shed momentum until she hovered over the royal stand. "It worked," she said, somewhat breathlessly.

"It did," Rokshan said. His voice was strained, and he continued to lean forward across her neck.

"Are you all right? You sound as if you'd done the racing."

"Wind took my breath," Rokshan gasped. "And I think my eyeballs tried to escape my skull. We'll need to figure out a way to protect me from the wind if we're going to fly that fast."

"I hadn't thought of that. Sorry."

"Don't be. It was amazing. And you were right. That's something I want to share with you, now and always."

Lamprophyre blushed. "Until you can fly on your own."

"Until then." Rokshan leaned forward and hugged her neck. Neither of them said what Lamprophyre knew they were both thinking, even without listening to his thoughts: the chances of Rokshan being transformed into a dragon were not good. They'd searched for an answer for weeks and were no closer now than they'd been on the day Lamprophyre had been turned back into a dragon from the human form she'd had for a twelveday.

She wanted it as much as he did, but with so much time passing with no success, she was ready to give in to despair and admit defeat. She had to remind herself frequently that twenty-five days with no success wasn't all that long, but her impatient heart didn't want to be reminded.

The rest of the clutch gathered around them, hovering in midair. "It worked," Flint said. "I can't believe it worked."

"What, you didn't have faith in your own creation?" Lamprophyre teased.

"Faith is one thing. Testing an idea in the real world is something else." Flint lazily flapped his wings until he was next to Coquina. "Now let's have you run the obstacle course and give it a *real* test."

"Or maybe not. Who's that?" Orthoclase asked. He descended slowly, half-turned to look in the direction of the city. Lamprophyre followed his gaze. A small figure ran toward them, one Lamprophyre recognized after a closer look.

"It's Rassika," she said, descending with the others. Rassika often ran errands for her, but those were always things Lamprophyre requested. For Rassika to be here on her own, or sent by some other member of the embassy household, something had to be wrong.

She listened to Rassika's thoughts as the girl drew nearer and found them worryingly single-minded, suggesting Rassika was in some distress: *find Lamprophyre, ecclesiasts here, hope I don't have to run all over Tanajital.* Ecclesiasts? The representatives of the human religion weren't officially at odds with dragons anymore, but that didn't stop some ecclesiasts from preaching to the heathen dragons, trying to convince them to worship the made-up dragon god Katayan. Lamprophyre didn't like the thought of dealing with ecclesiasts, however innocent their intentions might be.

She put a hand out to catch Rassika as the girl stumbled to a halt before her. “Don’t speak just yet,” she said. “Catch your breath. Nothing’s so urgent it can’t wait a few beats.”

Rassika shook her head, but she was bent over with her hands on her knees, sucking in air without speaking. *Hurry back Depik says, don’t know what they want, nothing good,* she thought.

“Is everyone all right?” Lamprophyre said when Rassika’s breathing had stilled somewhat. She knew no one of her household was hurt, but Rassika didn’t know dragons could hear thoughts, and that wasn’t a secret Lamprophyre felt inclined to share.

Rassika nodded. “’S not that,” she said. “’S ecclesiasts at the embassy. Want to talk t’ you, my lady.”

Lamprophyre exchanged glances with her clutchmates. They looked as concerned as she felt. “About what?”

“Dunno. Wouldn’t say. Just that they need to talk to the dragon ambassador and they’ll wait ‘til you’re back.” Rassika took one last deep breath and let it out slowly. “It was two of ‘em, my lady, and they di’nt have those people with ‘em, the ones with the ugly haircuts.”

“That’s unexpected,” Lamprophyre said.

“You don’t think they want us to leave Tanajital again, do you?” Bromargyrite said.

“Unlikely,” Coquina said. “The Archprelate likes us, and she wouldn’t allow anyone to persecute us even if we do follow a different religion. Though that doesn’t mean this isn’t a couple of ecclesiasts with their own agenda.”

“We won’t find out if we sit around here guessing,” Lamprophyre said. “I suppose I can go see what they want. Rassika, do you want a ride back?”

Rassika hesitated before nodding. Lamprophyre heard the traces of fear in her thoughts, but the girl was trying hard to suppress them, so Lamprophyre decided not to say anything that might reinforce those fears.

"I'll take you," Porphyry said, bending low to give her a leg up. He was a good choice, Lamprophyre thought, because he was a frequent visitor to the embassy and Rassika's thoughts showed she felt more comfortable with him than with the other dragons.

"Supper tonight at the warehouses?" she asked her clutchmates.

"We can make adjustments to the harness," Flint agreed. "You bring the cows."

Lamprophyre nodded and leaped into the air.

She decided not to hurry back. Not only was she slightly tired from the race, she didn't think it was a good idea to let the ecclesiasts think dragons would drop everything at their summons. So she flew at her usual pace and admired Tanajital's gleaming metal roofs. The smell of gold sharpened her appetite. Cow for supper would be especially delicious.

"I wonder if Dharan would be more willing to ride a dragon if he could be strapped in," she mused.

"Dharan would only agree to the harness if you promised not to fly anywhere," Rokshan said. "I don't think you appreciate his hatred and fear of heights."

"I actually do, because when I had a human body, heights scared me. It was knowing I couldn't save myself from a fall that made them terrifying. But I think I could have borne to ride if I'd had that harness." She banked left to avoid one of the looming towers. The hum of the city was quieter now, during what would in summer be a rest hour getting people away from the worst of the heat. At this season, it was just tradition to nap indoors. Lamprophyre thought humans ought to welcome the cooler weather and take advantage of it to be active, but humans didn't think like dragons did.

Ahead, the blue roof of the embassy came into view. It had been a customs house long before Lamprophyre had arrived in Tanajital, and now Lamprophyre thought of it as almost a second home. It was as cozy as her own cave in the mountains, spacious enough to fit two female dragons and always smelling of fresh air and the warm, musky scent of dragon skin.

Two yellow-curtained litters waited in the courtyard, bright blotches against the dark earth. Their bearers had set them down on the spindly legs attached to the four corners and stood stolidly beside each one, arms folded across their muscular bare chests. Lamprophyre had developed an understanding of human attractiveness while she was temporarily in a human body, but she still didn't see the appeal of humorously bulging muscles.

The ecclesiasts hadn't been smart enough, or foresighted enough, to leave room for a dragon to land in the courtyard, and Lamprophyre had to perch on the roof ridge beam so Porphyry and his small passenger could alight near the dining pavilion. Porphyry crouched very low to let Rassika climb down, which she did with alacrity, though Lamprophyre didn't hear any unusually frightened thoughts from her.

"I'll see you later," Porphyry said as he beat the air to rise even with her head. "I cannot wait to hear what all this is about."

Lamprophyre grimaced. To him, no matter what the ecclesiasts wanted, it would all be an amusing story to be told round a comfortable bonfire. To her, the ambassador, it would likely be an annoyance at best and an infuriating demand at worst. She flapped gracefully to the spot Porphyry had vacated and waited for Rokshan to climb down before unfastening the buckles and shrugging out of the harness.

The ecclesiasts had emerged from the litters the moment she set foot on earth and now stood watching her disentangle herself. Their attention made her uncomfortable, and she fumbled more awkwardly than she'd intended getting the saddle free of the notch. She finally dropped the harness on the ground and said, embarrassment sharpening her tone, "Yes? How can I help you?"

The ecclesiasts looked at each other. The man was thinking *Jiwanyil have mercy she's bigger than a house*, though his awed fear didn't show on his face. The woman's thoughts were less fearful: *convince her of Jiwanyil's cause, heard they were logical creatures.* That was interesting, and potentially bad. Lamprophyre was in no mood to debate religion with anyone.

"My lady ambassador, greetings from the Archprelate," the woman said. She didn't bow, but Lamprophyre already knew ecclesiasts didn't generally bow to anyone not another ecclesiast. "I am Ashta, and this is Nirav. We have an important matter to discuss with you."

"If it's about how dragons should worship Katayan, I've already heard that one," Lamprophyre said. Rokshan chuckled under his breath.

Ashta didn't react. "Dragons' relationship with the Lonely God is not, at present, our concern," she said. "I have been possessed of a prophecy relating to your people, however, and the Archprelate instructed me to bring it before you."

This news didn't make Lamprophyre feel better. "And what prophecy is that?" she asked, hoping she didn't sound as sarcastic as she felt.

Ashta tilted her head to look Lamprophyre in the eye. "Jiwanyil instructs me to climb the holy mountain Nirinatan," she said. "What dragons refer to as Mother Stone."

CHAPTER TWO

Lamprophyre sucked in a horrified breath. "Are you out of your mind?" she demanded. "Climb Mother Stone? *Humans* climb Mother Stone? That's..." A dozen furious words crowded her mind. "That's *blasphemy*."

"What God has decreed so cannot be blasphemy," Ashta said. "Of course I do not remember the prophecy I was possessed of, but I'm told it was unusually clear. Nirav?"

Nirav cleared his throat. "*The stone rises to greet the sky,*" he said, in a singsong tone that told Lamprophyre he was reciting. "*Humans rise to greet the stone. Upon her slopes will you find salvation.*"

His words struck Lamprophyre speechless. In the silence that followed, Rokshan said, "You understand dragons don't worship the way we do. Our prophecies don't apply to them."

"I disagree," Ashta said. "Jiwanyil's voice goes to all creatures everywhere, human and dragon, believer and heretic. The clarity of this prophecy—"

"Enough," Lamprophyre said. She let out a deep breath and a puff of smoke. "Whether or not Jiwanyil speaks to dragons, what you want is impossible. Even if Mother Stone weren't a holy place humans are forbidden to go, she's too deadly for anyone to survive on her slopes to find salvation or anything else. Even dragons have trouble breathing that high."

"We have faith in Jiwanyil's prophecy," Nirav said. "If he wants us to climb Nirinatan—Mother Stone—he will provide a way."

Lamprophyre looked at Rokshan, who shrugged. "You know humans won't disregard a prophecy," he murmured. "Maybe we need to find a compromise."

Compromise. Mother Stone. Lamprophyre shook her head. "I'm sorry, but I can't allow this," she said. "Imagine if...if dragons told you they'd received a prophecy that the Archprelate wasn't Jiwanyil's representative on earth and you should disregard all her teachings. You wouldn't feel obligated to obey, would you? Well, that's nearly the same as what you're asking. Mother Stone is sacred to dragons, and humans climbing her would be a serious affront to our faith."

Ashta's eyes narrowed in thought. "Then we're at an impasse," she said, "because we must obey prophecy, regardless of your desires."

"Forget desires." Lamprophyre drew in another breath that failed to calm her. "I'm telling you humans are forbidden to set foot on Mother Stone. If you disregard my instructions, we will consider it an act of aggression by Gonjiri against dragons. Is that what you want?"

"We do not fear dragons," Ashta said sharply. "We fear the wrath of God for failing to obey *his* instructions. Your words mean nothing beside that."

"Your Holiness, think carefully," Rokshan said. "It's not the duty of dragons to bend to allow you to obey prophecy. It's your job to figure out how to follow Jiwanyil's teachings in the face of opposition. And I assure you King Ekanath will not be pleased if ecclesiasts anger the dragons. Or did you think this wouldn't eventually involve him?"

"Prince Rokshan," Nirav began, but Ashta cut him off with a gesture.

"Then you are determined not to assist us?" she said to Lamprophyre.

"Assist you? Your Holiness, dragons will actively oppose you if you try this," Lamprophyre said.

Ashta's lips thinned in a hard, angry line. *Stubborn beast*, she thought. "Very well," she said. "Remember, we approached you in good faith. Whatever ill comes of this, it will be on your head."

"I'll chance it," Lamprophyre said. "Now, unless you have any more irrational demands, I'd like you to leave." At the moment, she didn't care about diplomacy, and Stones take these stupid ecclesiasts. Climb Mother Stone. Just thinking about it infuriated Lamprophyre.

Ashta and Nirav got back into their litters without another word and without looking back, and the bearers picked up their burdens and moved smoothly off into the street. Despite her anger, Lamprophyre couldn't help thinking, as she always did, how well trained the ecclesiasts' bearers had to be to maintain that even gait. They might have ridiculously large muscles, but in a group like that, they looked as beautiful as a running horse.

"That might not have been the best option," Rokshan said.

She turned on him. "And what should I have done, Rokshan? Let those ecclesiasts trample on what dragons hold most sacred?"

Rokshan didn't flinch. "The ecclesiasts have come to an accommodation with dragons challenging their beliefs in Katayan," he pointed out. "You could extend them the same courtesy."

"Rokshan—"

"I'm not saying give in. I'm saying accord them the same respect they've given you. You know prophecies are the true word of Jiwanyil—didn't it occur to you to wonder why he might want humans on Mother Stone?"

Lamprophyre's mouth fell open. "I—" She closed her mouth in a tight line the way the ecclesiast had. "All right. I could have been more accommodating. But I'm not sure how. Even dragons don't go to Mother Stone unless it's their death journey. The idea is just...it's unthinkable."

"I understand." Rokshan put a hand on her forearm. "Maybe this is something we should look into a little more deeply. It wasn't the best idea they had, coming here and making demands instead of explaining. It could be one of the High Ecclesiasts has a better understanding of the circumstances surrounding the prophecy."

Lamprophyre sighed. "All right. And I promise to be more openminded."

"You usually are." Rokshan stretched. "That saddle was more uncomfortable than I realized. It didn't occur to me that the padding might be a problem."

Lamprophyre followed him into the embassy. "So you'd rather have room for your male parts than softness?"

Rokshan shot her an ironic glance. "Yes, sweetheart, I'd prefer that. I thought we discussed what is and is not a polite topic of conversation."

"You're my mate. It's not inappropriate." Lamprophyre settled herself on the floor and furled her wings over her spine. Thanks to her friend, the prostitute Darsha, she actually knew many names for a man's male parts, but some of them embarrassed Rokshan and others made him laugh, so she stuck to the generic term.

"True, but it's still not something people discuss casually." Rokshan sat leaning against her side. "I think dragons have the right idea. Keep everything delicate inside where it can't be damaged."

"I don't know anything about dragons' male parts," Lamprophyre said, "but I imagine they're as invulnerable as everything else."

Rokshan laughed. "You could ask Flint or Orthoclase."

"Ask—" Lamprophyre blushed, and then she laughed as well, somewhat self-consciously. "Now *that* would be inappropriate. And we'd all feel very uncomfortable."

"It's nice to know there are things that embarrass dragons." Rokshan tilted his head back and sighed. "Racing is amazing. We just need to fix that harness, and then I have some ideas for warmer clothing that will let us fly higher than before. And I think a good scarf should keep the air from being blown from my lungs."

"You've given this so much thought. I'm glad it makes you happy."

"Well, that, and it takes my mind off the Fanishkor problem." Rokshan ran his fingers through his hair, a gesture that meant he was frustrated.

"Is there more of a Fanishkor problem than usual?" Lamprophyre asked.

"Yes and no. They haven't declared war or aggressed on our borders, so things aren't worse than usual that way. But our usual lines of communication are almost completely severed. You know the Fanishkorite ambassador was recalled last year, after we recalled our ambassador to them? Well, we still were in communication with their government until last week, when they accused us of spying on them and stopped talking to us entirely."

"*Were* we spying on them?"

Rokshan shrugged. "Tekentriya says not, but it's almost impossible to tell if she's lying. I know, *you* could tell, but there was no graceful way to have you eavesdrop on her thoughts. And it doesn't matter. Fanishkor believed it, and that was enough for them."

Lamprophyre considered what she knew of Crown Princess Tekentriya, heir to the throne and commander of Gonjiri's spy corps. She was suspicious, devious, and permanently angry, but she was also devoted to her country. Rokshan was right; Tekentriya could as easily have set spies to investigate Fanishkor, on the grounds that she was protecting Gonjiri, as she could have refrained from sending spies on the exact same grounds. "What happened to her?" she asked. "Her leg. You said there was an accident."

"She was riding, and the horse tripped, or was spooked—nobody knows exactly what caused it to fall. It landed on her and fractured her pelvis and hip, and by the time she was found—"

Lamprophyre turned to look at him. "What do you mean, found? She was alone?"

"She used to go on long rides alone. Said it cleared her head.

Anyway, she wasn't found immediately, and between that and the complexity of her injuries, healing couldn't do enough. I imagine she's in pain much of the time, but, well, you've met her."

"I know she hates being pitied. I don't blame her." Lamprophyre would have felt more sympathy for Tekentriya if the crown princess didn't dislike her little brother Rokshan so much. Tekentriya was never subtle about her dislike, either, and Lamprophyre couldn't forgive her for that.

"Anyway," Rokshan went on, "Fanishkor is upset, my father is annoyed with them, and I have never been so grateful to be your liaison as I have the last few weeks, because it takes me away from all of that." He yawned. "I'm going to nap, unless you want me to read to you."

"Napping sounds good." She liked it when Rokshan fell asleep beside her, how her sense of his presence intensified with physical contact. She rested her head in the crook of her arms and closed her eyes.

But sleep eluded her. Her memories of the two ecclesiasts and their absurd demand kept her from relaxing. They were fortunate they hadn't gone to Hyaloclast, because the dragon queen had a short temper when it came to dealing with humans and even less respect for their traditions than Lamprophyre had. Hyaloclast would have sent them running home. The image made Lamprophyre smile. Only a year ago, she wouldn't have dared to think of Hyaloclast so informally, and now...

Lamprophyre blew out a cloud of smoke and watched it drift up to the ceiling and then out the window holes. A year ago, she would have sworn Hyaloclast despised her. Stones, that might even have been true, and partly justified, given that Lamprophyre had felt herself an inadequate daughter for a dragon queen and behaved accordingly. Now, Lamprophyre had seen beneath Hyaloclast's stern exterior and understood better who she really was, not to mention having a better sense of her mother's love for her. They would never have a warm relationship, but Lamprophyre no longer minded.

She thought back to her last conversation with Hyaloclast, after the dragon queen had restored Lamprophyre to her dragon form. It had not been a short conversation, and Lamprophyre and Rokshan had done most of the talking. They'd told Hyaloclast everything they'd learned about the ancient entity who had been responsible for turning Lamprophyre human so it could arrange for her death—how the entity was a dragon, one of those who had been behind the Great Cataclysm that had nearly wiped out civilization and had left humans ignorant of dragons' survival. How she—at the time, they hadn't known her name, Sardonyx—had the ability to communicate mentally with others, coercing or tempting them to do her evil bidding. How she intended to return and finish the destruction she'd started.

Hyaloclast had listened to their story in the silence she was famous for. She had remained silent for several beats after they finished. Finally, she had said, "And you believe the humans' prophecies, the ones that echo our words 'the skies will burn,' refer to this dragon."

"It makes sense, doesn't it?" Lamprophyre had said. "And Dharan says he's sure those prophecies are about both Cataclysms. The one that happened, and the one this dragon wants to cause."

"I agree," Hyaloclast had said. "But it's very little to go on."

"We wondered if you knew more," Rokshan had said. "Dragons already have a better memory of what happened in the catastrophe—the Cataclysm. You chose to separate yourselves from humanity, right? We humans incorrectly believed you were all dead. It seems possible much of what else we believe about the incident is also wrong."

"We know less than you imagine," Hyaloclast had said. "This is knowledge shared only among dragon queens, passed down through the generations, but I have a feeling concealing knowledge will hurt us in the long run. And there isn't much to tell—certainly nothing secret." She had cast a stern look on Rokshan and added, "It is, however, sacred knowledge, and I expect you to treat it so. No human has ever heard this, but as you are pair-bonded to my daughter, you're not exactly an ordinary human."

Lamprophyre smiled to remember how this had made Rokshan turn red with embarrassment. "He's not," she had said, still basking in the warmth of her new pair-bond.

Hyaloclast had given her a quelling look. "The death rites are our oldest memories, dating back to the Cataclysm," she had said. "When a dragon's time on earth draws to a close, the dragon queen takes her aside and instructs her in how she is to approach Mother Stone. She is to fly as high as she can manage before the air is too thin to support her wings, then make an ice cave for herself. In the time before she falls into unconsciousness and from there into death, she sings the death-song, which the dragon queen teaches her before her journey."

"I'm sorry if this is rude, but how does that relate?" Lamprophyre had asked.

"I don't know," Hyaloclast had said, "except that it is the only thing we have that comes from the same time as our enemy. And, as I said, any knowledge may be useful."

Now Lamprophyre closed her eyes and let the words of the death song well up within her. She only needed to hear a song or poem once to memorize it, but this was a song that would have stayed with her even had she only had a human's memory:

Born of wind and fire and stone,
To breath and ash and stone return.
I am all dragons in the bone,
All dragons end here in their turn.
My body, the stone
My breath, the wind
My heart, the fire
Let stone and wind and fire combine
Bind those who end their journey here.
Fly, heart and spirit intertwined,
Lie, body, now stone, 'til end of time,
In Mother's love rest without fear.

Though the words were somber, making Lamprophyre think of endings and dragons' spirits flying into Mother Stone's eternal rest, the tune was surprisingly cheerful. She imagined her father, Aegirine, singing this song as he slipped into his final sleep, and it comforted her. They had both fallen ill with cave sickness, and she had been delirious when Aegirine realized he would not survive. So she had come to herself to learn her beloved father was already gone. She had never had the chance to say goodbye. Running through the song in her mind felt like a proper farewell.

Now, two twelvedays after that conversation, she still had no idea how knowledge of the death-song could help them. When she had learned the evil dragon's name was Sardonyx, she'd spoken to Hyaloclast, but the dragon queen hadn't recognized the name and neither had old Scoria, repository of so much dragon lore. Whoever Sardonyx was, the dragons had lost all knowledge of her in the Cataclysm.

Lamprophyre sighed and tried to make a smoke ring, but managed only a distorted puff. Coquina had tried to teach her, but Lamprophyre couldn't manage the trick. At least Sardonyx hadn't attacked again since confronting Lamprophyre in mental battle. Lamprophyre wished that was more comforting. It might only mean Sardonyx had found a way to build her forces that Lamprophyre didn't know anything about. She hoped she'd done damage to the evil dragon, but she knew it hadn't been a killing blow.

She sent up another failed smoke ring and watched the blob dissipate. There was nothing she could do about Sardonyx now. She hummed the death-song quietly to herself and remembered her father until she finally fell asleep.

CHAPTER THREE

Though the streets of Tanajital were normally crowded with humans and their sour-sweat odor, almost no one ever came to the neighborhood where the dragons of Lamprophyre's clutch lived. Wooden warehouses, tall and broad enough to fit a dragon, lined both sides of the street, their dark walls making the street seem narrower than it was. At night, lit only by lanterns lashed to poles, the street almost vanished entirely. It was an illusion, but Lamprophyre still kept her wings tightly furled whenever she visited.

The short stretch of street wasn't in the middle of the industrial district, but it wasn't isolated, either, and since the humans who owned their own warehouses in the area chose to stay out of the dragons' way, that meant some of those humans had to go a very long way out of their way to get to their property. Lamprophyre had worried about resentment building up, but Rokshan had talked to the owners, money had changed hands, and the dragons had privacy they hadn't asked for.

She sat at the end of the dragons' street and half-listened to the conversation Rokshan was having with a wagon driver. It didn't have anything to do with dragons, so she felt justified in listening to the sounds of the city instead. Today Tanajital sounded peaceful, its citizens undisturbed by anything unpleasant. Or by anything exciting, for that matter. There were no celebrations scheduled, no holy days, just people carrying on their business and their everyday lives.

"Lamprophyre?" Rokshan said. "Is that all right?"

"Is what all right?"

Rokshan gave her a meaningful look. It said she should have been paying attention. "The sum we've agreed on to purchase the warehouses outright. It seems dragons are a permanent part of Tanajital these days, and we'll save money in the long run by purchasing rather than renting." His tone of voice suggested that he knew just how long she hadn't been paying attention. Well, it wasn't as if she really understood the value of money, or whether the transaction was good business.

"Oh," she said, trying to sound wise. "Of course. We can afford it, yes?"

"Certainly." Now Rokshan's look was one of amusement, the way he looked when she said something only a dragon would come up with. He turned back to the woman—Lamprophyre was wrong, she couldn't be just a wagon driver if she owned these warehouses—and handed over a not very small purse. The woman's thoughts were all of awe at Lamprophyre's size and satisfaction at selling warehouses that weren't doing her any good as they were. Lamprophyre guessed if she'd been listening to the woman's thoughts all along, they might have gotten a better deal. She decided not to say anything to Rokshan. He'd use it to remind her of her ambassadorial duties, which she already knew about; she just didn't like some of them.

The woman returned to her wagon, which was stopped a good distance down the street. A man stood at the horses' heads, keeping them calm. The reddish-brown animals weren't downwind of Lamprophyre, so they weren't terrified, but they were restless enough Lamprophyre knew they were aware of her presence. Of course, she didn't eat horse these days, and certainly wouldn't eat horses owned by someone else, but the horses didn't know that.

Rokshan lifted a hand in farewell as the woman steered her wagon back toward the center of the industrial district. "You really ought to pay attention when we make these transactions," he said. "It's your job—"

"As ambassador, yes, I know, but Rokshan, you manage the negotiations. I just agree to them. I still have very little sense of the worth of human production."

"It's politeness. Also, it builds goodwill if humans have your attention. They feel as if they've earned your respect."

Lamprophyre shrugged. "You're right. I'll remember that. Does this mean Bromargyrite can go ahead with the new construction, if he owns the warehouse?"

Rokshan turned and strolled down the street beside her. "Yes. We can do anything we like so long as it doesn't affect someone else's property. I didn't know Bromargyrite was dissatisfied with his warehouse."

"He wants bigger windows for more of a breeze, like we have in the embassy." Lamprophyre stopped at Bromargyrite's warehouse and knocked on the wall next to the open doorway. All the dragons had removed their warehouse doors so they felt more like caves. "I'll tell him."

Dolomite poked his head out of the warehouse opposite. "Tell him what? He's not here. He went to talk to his adept friend."

"Oh." Lamprophyre sat back on her haunches and stretched her wings out. She'd kept them furled during the conversation with the warehouse owner and they felt stiff. "We bought the warehouses. So you can do whatever you like with them."

Dolomite brightened. "I want to paint the walls of mine," he said, "on the inside, you know, so I can make new drawings. I ran out of space a twelveday ago."

"It's too bad most houses are too small to fit us," Lamprophyre said. "I'm sure there are hundreds of people who would pay you to decorate the insides of their houses."

"Why not the outsides?" Dolomite asked. "Tanajital's buildings are so plain."

"Because buildings are taxed according to how colorful they are," Rokshan said.

Dolomite frowned. "What's taxed? It sounds like a bad thing."

"Depends on whether you're paying or collecting," Rokshan said wryly. "It just means money people pay the government to do certain things, like maintain the streets or fund the city guard."

"I don't understand how human money works at all, except for how I need rupyas to exchange for chalk or paint," Dolomite said. "And how I can get rupyas by giving stone to people."

"That's more or less all you need to know," Rokshan said. He looked up, shielding his eyes against the sun. "That's Bromargyrite now."

Lamprophyre moved back to allow room for her clutchmate to land. He was large for a male, almost as big as she was, and no matter how he tried, he couldn't overcome the clumsiness he was known for in the dragons' flight. "I thought you'd learned everything you need to know from that adept," she said.

Bromargyrite furled his wings and stretched his neck as if he were Rokshan popping his joints, though dragons' anatomy didn't work that way. "Kamil's not as oblivious and self-centered as I thought," he said. "He's kind of obnoxious about stone, but on every other topic he's easy to talk to, not at all smug or arrogant. He loves the dragon races, too. I've been thinking, if we can make the harness work right, it might not be bad to let him ride."

"That's a surprise," Lamprophyre said. It always struck her as odd when her clutchmates made human friendships. The feeling didn't make any sense, given her closeness to Rokshan, but flying with a human was so intimate it felt strange knowing her friends were that close to people she'd never met.

Bromargyrite shrugged. "It's a thought. We'd need more harnesses, for a start. But you did say Sardonyx hates the idea of humans and dragons working together, so it seems to me we ought to be looking for ways to make that happen."

"That's so obvious I don't know why I didn't think of it."

"So should I try to make a human friend?" Dolomite asked. "I'm not sure I want someone riding my shoulders. It looks so uncomfortable. And I'd have trouble not listening to their thoughts."

Lamprophyre regarded the dark green dragon. Dolomite was sweet, and easy to get along with, but he was also guileless and tactless without meaning to be. She had trouble picturing him befriending a human, someone to whom little white lies were a commonplace and who might not respect Dolomite's limitations. "I don't think it's useful for us to simply pick humans at random," she said. "If you make a friend, that's fine, but don't feel obligated."

Dolomite relaxed. "That's good, because suppose it was a female human? I'm not sure I could manage what you and Rokshan did, falling in love. Humans are so fragile and unattractive."

Lamprophyre clenched her teeth on a snappish retort. Trust Dolomite to find the least tactful response to any situation. And you couldn't even hate him, because he was so innocent about it. "I think Rokshan and I are unusual, Dolomite," she said, exchanging pained glances with Bromargyrite. "Bromargyrite, we came to tell you we've purchased the warehouses and you can go ahead with the alterations to yours."

"Thanks." Bromargyrite stood. "I'll need to warn everyone to stay out of the way of the workmen. I'd hate someone to be stepped on."

"I think I'll go buy that paint now, and see if they have any larger brushes," Dolomite said. "Are you staying, Lamprophyre?"

"I have to meet with builders myself," Lamprophyre said. She lowered her shoulder to let Rokshan climb up. "We're making the servants' houses nicer—more windows, better roofs, things like that. So I suppose I'll see you at the races tomorrow."

She rose into the air, waved at Bromargyrite, then Dolomite, who flew in the opposite direction. It really was a peaceful day, with nothing much to do, no petitioners to see, no events to attend as ambassador. Maybe they could go for a swim after talking to the builders.

She felt Rokshan lean to one side. "It's so interesting to see people from this perspective," he said. "More of them look up now, did you realize? They love to watch you fly."

Lamprophyre looked down at the sea of dark heads. Some weren't so dark, as people tilted their heads back to watch. She drifted lower and slowed to give them a better look. She might not have Coquina's dramatic coloring or Flint's handsome body, but Rokshan insisted her blue and copper was striking and very attractive to humans.

"I love seeing the children look at me," she said. "Sometimes I'm in a position to hear their thoughts, and they're always so innocently awestruck. It's a wonderful feeling."

"I can imagine," Rokshan said. Then he froze. "Stop!" he shouted. "Go back, go back!"

Lamprophyre, startled, flailed around and lost elevation before she pulled herself up. "What—Rokshan, are you all right?"

"I'm fine, just go back!" He waved his arms where she could barely see them. "Turn around, and set down in the street."

"I can't do that! Look at how many people there are—I'll crush someone!" She turned and flew back, looking around wildly for whatever had upset Rokshan.

"Descend slowly, and they'll get out of your way. This is Tanajital—they're used to dragons by now."

Lamprophyre wasn't sure this was true, at least as far as getting out of her way went, but concern and fear drove her to obey. People scattered, their thoughts confused and surprised but not fearful, and she found they'd left her enough space to land, after all.

The moment both her feet were on the ground, Rokshan tumbled off and pushed his way through the crowd, which parted for him nearly as readily as it had parted for her. Confused, Lamprophyre took a step or two to follow him, but came up against a mass of people that had already backed away as far as they could go against the stores lining the street. "Rokshan, what's wrong?" she exclaimed.

Rokshan stopped. He was facing someone his body entirely blocked, someone who didn't move when he accosted them.

Lamprophyre rose to her full height, trying to see over him, but whoever it was was short enough that the surrounding crowd concealed them. "Rokshan, tell me something or I'm going to panic," she shouted.

Rokshan turned to look at her. He looked devastated, his breathing heavy, his mouth curved in a frown, his pupils dilated. "I—it's—" he said, then shook his head as if words couldn't convey his meaning. "Look."

He came back toward her, followed by the person he'd towered over. It was a woman, and she was struggling against Rokshan's grip on her wrist. She was very short and very plump, with large breasts and round hips and long, straight black hair. Rokshan towed her along, ignoring her protests.

"Rokshan, let her go," Lamprophyre said, alarmed. She'd never known him to be anything but respectful of women, but he looked as if he were beats away from kidnapping this one, regardless of the crowds watching. No one had moved to stop him, but Lamprophyre heard briefly the thoughts of the watchers, and they were considering how far they were willing to let a man go in his treatment of a woman, even if he was a prince.

Rokshan came to a halt beside Lamprophyre. "It's her. You. Her." He shook his head again. "You don't recognize her?"

The woman did look familiar, but Lamprophyre didn't know from where. "No. Should I?"

"It's Lelitha," Rokshan said.

CHAPTER FOUR

Lamprophyre gasped. "But I—" In time, she remembered not to give away that she'd been temporarily given a human body. "Lelitha?"

"My name is *Viveki*," the woman shouted, yanking on Rokshan's hand. "Let me go!"

Lamprophyre bent to peer at the woman. "Rokshan, let her go," she said. "I don't understand. How is this possible?"

Rokshan released the woman, who stood rubbing her wrist but didn't flee. "How dare you handle me like that?" she shouted. "I don't care if you are a prince, you have no right—"

"But who are you?" Lamprophyre asked. She prodded the woman's shoulder. Now that she knew, she recognized traits she'd only ever seen in the mirror: the round face, the tiny brown spot at the base of her throat, the black hair that was tangled from Rokshan's rough handling of her. "How do you look like m—like Lelitha?"

"I don't know any Lelitha," Viveki said. "I demand an apology. You attack me in the street, you grab me and force me to go where I don't want to go—if this is how dragons treat humans, I think it's revolting."

Lamprophyre looked at Rokshan. He was staring at Viveki as if he'd never seen a woman before. A cold sense of dread filled her. How must Rokshan feel, looking at a body that had belonged to the woman he'd fallen in love with? She wasn't so stupid as to think this meant Rokshan was going to fall in love with this Viveki, but it had to be confusing for him.

"You're right," she said when it became clear Rokshan was past speech. "You deserve compensation. If you'll come to the dragon embassy, I'll present you with a formal apology and something to make up for your ordeal."

Viveki looked up at Lamprophyre, and some of her anger visibly ebbed. "Compensation?"

"Yes, but I would prefer to discuss it in private. Though I apologize now for my—for Prince Rokshan's behavior. He believed you were someone else, and the surprise carried him away." Lamprophyre bowed to the woman, conscious of her tail and the chance she might hit someone with it. Bowing was so difficult for dragons.

Viveki's mouth set in a straight line. "All right, I'll come," she said. "But I expect you to make proper amends."

"I promise." Lamprophyre nudged Rokshan, who was still staring at Viveki. "Rokshan. Let's go."

"She might not come to the embassy. I don't want to leave her," Rokshan murmured.

"Neither do I, but she doesn't deserve to be harassed," Lamprophyre muttered. "Climb on and stop being stupid."

Rokshan gave Viveki one last long look, then climbed up and gripped Lamprophyre's ruff so tightly it almost hurt. She imagined the colors bleeding away from the tightness of his grasp. With a leap, she left the street behind, not looking to see if she'd knocked anyone over. She didn't need to deal with any more apologies, real or undeserved.

They flew in silence back to the embassy. Lamprophyre couldn't think of anything to say. That had clearly been Lelitha, except it just as clearly wasn't. Lamprophyre knew sometimes women gave birth to identical babies at the same time, and maybe

Viveki was Lelitha's twin. No, that couldn't be, because Lelitha had been created by the adept Evart, who'd transformed Lamprophyre into that human body, and it wasn't as if he'd taken a living human body and crammed Lamprophyre's spirit or mind into it. Probably.

Lamprophyre scowled. No, she was certain it had been a true transformation, which meant...what? That Evart had coincidentally imagined a real person when he transformed her? Hyaloclast had said transforming Lamprophyre back meant being able to keep her true body in memory for the time it took the magic to work. It made sense that Evart had needed the same thing to turn her human. She simply had no idea why he'd chosen Viveki.

She descended to land in the embassy courtyard. This time, Rokshan didn't climb down immediately. "Rokshan," she said, turning vainly to look at him and seeing only her own shoulder. "Rokshan. What do we do?"

Rokshan pressed his face to the back of her neck and mumbled something. "I don't know," he said when she asked him to repeat himself. "I don't know what it means, other than that Evart probably used that woman as a model for your human body." He slid down and walked into the embassy, his head bowed and his shoulders slumped.

Lamprophyre followed him. "So she must know him."

"Maybe. Maybe she's a total stranger he was obsessed with." Rokshan leaned against the wall and slid gradually down it until he was seated on the ground. "It was such a surprise, I'm afraid I reacted badly. It felt—" He covered his face with his hands.

"It felt like seeing me as human again," Lamprophyre said. A cold ache had set up in her heart. She'd known Rokshan wouldn't go on loving her the same way once she was a dragon again, which made sense, because how odd to feel romantic love for someone not of your species? She was the odd one for still loving him. But she hadn't counted on someone who looked exactly like her human body coming into their lives. Hot jealousy countered the cold ache before she ruthlessly quashed it. Love was about more than physical bodies. Rokshan wouldn't love this Viveki woman just because he was attracted to her body.

She hoped.

Rokshan pressed his fingers to his closed eyes and let out a sigh that sounded like it had come from somewhere near his feet. "I'm not in love with her," he said.

"I know."

He lowered his hands and looked up at her. "It doesn't matter what she looks like. And from what little I've heard, she's abrasive and self-centered. She's not you. And you are the one I love."

His words didn't make her feel better. She'd never been more conscious of their differences. "I know," she repeated. "She's a stranger who looks like I used to. That's so strange I don't even know where to start, except that it has to mean something. Her appearance, I mean."

"That was smart of you to have her come here. I wonder if she will?"

Lamprophyre shrugged. "There were too many people for me to hear her thoughts, but I think you're right that she's self-centered. If she's also greedy, she'll want whatever recompense she thinks I'm willing to give."

"Recompense to keep her from complaining about the prince to his royal father," Rokshan said with a grimace. "So what do we think is going on?"

"She must have some connection to Evart," Lamprophyre said. "I realize now he couldn't have chosen her in passing, because seeing her once or twice isn't enough for the transformation magic, at least according to Hyaloclast. So they're closer than chance-met strangers."

"Which suggests she may know something of his research." Rokshan stood and paced between the wall and the door. "And if she knows about the transformation magic—"

"It might tell us what we need to transform you," Lamprophyre said. She flapped her wings a couple of times, excitement making it impossible for her to remain still.

"Don't get excited," Rokshan warned. "We know nothing about this woman. It might all still be coincidence."

"All right," Lamprophyre said, but her heart continued to leap about like fish swimming upstream, jumping in silver flashes from wave to wave. River fish were too small to be a mouthful, but they had fascinated her from her childhood, and now the image of flying specks of silver leaping in as much excitement as she felt captivated her. This had to be it. It had to be what they were looking for.

She turned and settled herself in the embassy doorway so the sun warmed her head and arms and her wings were still inside. It was a position she felt made her look smaller and less threatening, one she used when she wanted to put petitioners at their ease. Rokshan came to stand next to her, resting a hand on her shoulder. "I'm serious, sweetheart," he said. "Don't get your hopes up. We have no idea what Viveki knows."

"You can't tell me you're not hopeful, too."

Rokshan sighed. "I am, but I'm also more cynical than you. And I've gotten used to expecting the worst these last two twelvedays. I'll be thrilled if she can help us, but I'm not counting on it."

Lamprophyre leaned into his touch. "That's the sensible approach, but I think—"

She stopped. Viveki had appeared at the end of the street that opened on the courtyard. She took a few more steps, then stopped, her gaze fixed not on Lamprophyre, but on Rokshan. Lamprophyre listened to her thoughts and was dismayed to hear bitter anger at Rokshan, far more than Lamprophyre thought was justified.

It wasn't just that Viveki was angry with him for having handled her so roughly; she also resented the fact that he was a prince, and handsome, and wealthy, and even that he was confident. She hated him—actually hated him!—for having a life she envied. Lamprophyre didn't know what to do with that. Having Rokshan present for this conversation might be a mistake, but she needed his insights.

"Stay back," she murmured. Rokshan's brow furrowed in confusion, but he didn't step forward when she did.

Lamprophyre came fully into the light and stopped near the center of the courtyard. "Thank you for coming," she said, bowing. "Again, I apologize for your mistreatment."

Viveki glared at Rokshan. "Just because he's a prince doesn't give him the right to grab people off the street."

"No, it doesn't, but as I said, his highness was startled at your resemblance to a friend he thought was lost," Lamprophyre said. "You understand what it feels like to be startled, yes?"

"That's no excuse." *Idiot prince can't even apologize himself, makes the dragon do it,* Viveki thought.

Lamprophyre kept from groaning in annoyance. The woman hated Rokshan and she craved his apology. Humans were so odd. "Prince Rokshan would like to apologize as well," she said, wishing with all her heart he was already a dragon and could hear Viveki's thoughts.

Rokshan came forward and bowed. "It's true, I was surprised," he said, "but that's no excuse for my behavior. I hope you can forgive me."

Thinks he's better than me, Viveki thought, and Lamprophyre again suppressed a groan. She was starting to wonder if Viveki could know anything that would make this conversation worthwhile.

Viveki eyed Rokshan speculatively. "You think a prince can get away with acting like that?" she said, scorn dripping from every syllable.

Rokshan, Lamprophyre remembered, had been raised from birth to hold on to good manners no matter the provocation. He ignored Viveki's tone and said, "I may be a prince, but I'm also a man like any other. If I wanted to get away with treating you poorly, I certainly wouldn't have apologized, would I?"

Viveki opened her mouth to say something else that by the sound of her thoughts would be scathing. Lamprophyre said, "I hope you will accept his apology as well as mine, Viveki. And I would be delighted to repay your generosity of spirit with a small token of our regard. But—" She paused, tilting her head to give the impression that she had just thought of something. "I wonder. You do look so much like our friend Lelitha—do you happen to know an adept named Evart?"

Viveki took a step backward, her thoughts suddenly a tangle of confusion and bitterness. "Evart?" she said. "Why do you care about that old bastard?"

"Then you do know him," Lamprophyre said.

Viveki smiled. It was as bitter an expression as her thoughts. "Not much," she said. "He's my father."

CHAPTER FIVE

Lamprophyre sucked in a startled breath. "Your *father?*"

Viveki shrugged. "Not that it means anything to him. Haven't seen him in two years. So if he's done something wrong, don't go looking to me for restitution." *Bastard never cared for anything but magic, never me or nothing else,* she thought.

Rokshan looked at Lamprophyre wide-eyed in an expression she knew well. Normally she avoided listening to his thoughts, a courtesy she would give any of her close friends. Now she let herself hear him think *If she hasn't seen him in years, she doesn't know about his magic pursuits* overlaid with a deep feeling of discouragement. It really was unfortunate he couldn't hear her thoughts in return—but if he could, he'd be a dragon, and they wouldn't care about what Viveki did or didn't know.

"It's not that," Lamprophyre said, hoping Rokshan would stay quiet. If Viveki's abrasiveness could stay directed at Evart, maybe she'd be cooperative. Though Rokshan was probably right, and she didn't know anything useful. Still, Evart had used her as a model for Lamprophyre's human body, and that had to mean something.

"We encountered Evart a little over a month ago," she went on, "and, um, talked to him about what magic artifacts he was working on. He had one artifact in particular that interested us. Something he'd probably been creating for a long time."

"And you think I know anything about that?" Viveki laughed, a harsh, curt sound like the bark of a dog. "I'm no adept. Did he refuse to tell you? Sounds typical of him. He never wanted anyone to know about his work." *Not even his own blood,* she thought. The bitterness in her words and thoughts roused Lamprophyre's sympathy for the prickly woman.

"I just wondered, maybe you'd seen something, or he'd used the artifact elsewhere, as a test, maybe?" Lamprophyre asked. Viveki likely wouldn't be cooperative, but her thoughts were as open to Lamprophyre as a blooming flower.

Viveki raised one eyebrow. She did it so well Lamprophyre felt stung by how derisive the gesture was. "Why don't you ask him? You're wasting my time. Give me payment, because I've got places to be."

Lamprophyre and Rokshan exchanged glances. *Don't tell her,* Rokshan thought. It had been Lamprophyre's first instinct as well. Except if they went on deceiving Viveki, pretending Evart was still alive, what would happen when she found out the truth and that Lamprophyre and Rokshan had known it all along?

"I'm sorry, Viveki, but Evart is dead," she said. "I thought you knew."

Viveki's face went completely expressionless, but her thoughts became a whirlwind of emotion, pain and sorrow and satisfaction all mixed together with anger. "What happened?" she said.

"It was an accident with an artifact," Lamprophyre said. "It broke, and released so much energy it killed him." That was all true except for the 'accident' part, but Lamprophyre didn't want to try to explain that Evart had broken the artifact intentionally. Too many secrets were tied up with that one action.

Viveki let out a slow breath. "Figures," she said. "Mam always said his experiments would be the death of him. I don't suppose it was in his workshop? Anyone else hurt or killed?"

Lamprophyre was surprised at the question. She'd have thought

Viveki didn't give a damn about anyone but herself. "It—no. I was there, and so was Rokshan, but nobody other than Evart was close enough to be caught in the blast."

"Small mercies," Viveki said. She lowered her head and restlessly drew a line in the earth with the toe of her sandal. "Well, it's no real loss. Nobody liked him, and it's not like he used his magic to help people. Probably whatever artifact killed him was for selfish purposes." *Never a chance to say* echoed through Lamprophyre's head, and for a moment pure regret shot through Viveki's tangled emotions.

"He was still your father," Rokshan said, "and we're sorry for your loss."

Lamprophyre winced. She could tell Rokshan was trying to help, but his words just made Viveki angry.

"As if you'd know anything about it," she snarled, taking a few steps toward Rokshan with her hands clenched. "Don't go assuming you have a right to tell me how to feel."

Anger touched Rokshan's thoughts. Lamprophyre put a restraining hand on his shoulder, gently so as not to hurt him. "It sounds as if he wasn't a very good father," she said, "and we don't know anything about your relationship with him. Maybe it doesn't make you sad that he's gone. But we're both sorry you had to learn about it this way."

Viveki's anger ebbed, not much, but enough that Lamprophyre felt safe saying, "The artifact that killed him is the one we wanted to know more about. But if you haven't seen him in two years, you wouldn't know anything about it. Come with me, and let me give you something for your trouble."

Viveki didn't move. She tilted her head so she could see more of Lamprophyre. *Maybe not a waste of my time,* she thought. "I don't know," she said. "He was working on the same artifact for five years. Maybe there's something I know."

Lamprophyre didn't like the calculating tone of her thoughts. She was sure Viveki only wanted money and was likely to lie to get it. Rokshan's thoughts indicated he felt the same. "And you'll tell us in exchange for money," he said.

Viveki's scornful gaze flicked over him before she returned her attention to Lamprophyre. "And what if I do?" she said. "I don't think I should give away what I know for free."

"Or maybe you don't know anything and feel entitled to cheat us because of how Rokshan treated you," Lamprophyre shot back. "You already said Evart never talked about his work. Rokshan, give her something and she can be on her way."

Rokshan dug in his belt pouch, the one that held the embassy funds, and extracted a few silver coins. Viveki eyed the pouch. *Definitely flush,* she thought, *I bet I can get more.* "I said he never wanted people to know about his work," she said, taking a step back from Rokshan. "I didn't say I didn't know about it anyway."

To Lamprophyre's surprise, Viveki wasn't lying. "All right," she said, leaning down to put her head even with the woman's. "What do you know?"

"Lamprophyre," Rokshan said in a warning voice.

"I don't talk without you pay me first," Viveki said.

Rokshan gave her the rupyas he held. "There. With my apologies for treating you poorly. Now, we don't want to keep you from your business."

"I'm not paying any more until you convince me you know something useful," Lamprophyre said.

"*Lamprophyre*," Rokshan said again. "We're wasting our time and Viveki's. And I'm sure she doesn't want to talk about her father and bring up painful memories."

Lamprophyre suppressed a smile. Rokshan was good at getting hostile people to give away more than they intended. Sure enough, Viveki's irritation with the prince flowered into words she believed would hurt him. "Like you'd know anything about it," she said. "I don't feel anything but happiness that he's dead. So stop pretending you care about my feelings."

"All right," Rokshan said. "I don't care. You've got your money. Be on your way."

Lamprophyre had never seen her mate give a better impression of a haughty, condescending prince. It was impressive and a little scary.

Viveki's thoughts revealed Rokshan's ploy had worked; she felt she had the upper hand. "Thought you wanted to know about Evart's doings. You want to know about that artifact, I can tell you more."

"You'll have to prove it," Lamprophyre said. "I won't pay for nothing. Tell me what it looked like."

Viveki shrugged. "It wasn't finished when I saw it," she said, "so I don't know what it looked like, if he did actually finish it. But it was a green stone with black splotches on it, about six inches long and shaped like a prism."

Rokshan made a pained noise, and Lamprophyre realized she'd closed her hand too tightly on his shoulder. "That's the one," she said, removing her hand. "Do you know what it did?"

Viveki tilted her head to one side like a malicious sparrow. "That's the kind of knowledge that would be worth something," she said.

Lamprophyre glanced at Rokshan, who dipped into the pouch again. He held up two rupyas between his fingers. "What did it do?" he asked.

Viveki shrugged. "I don't know what it actually did, but I know what he wanted it to do. He meant to transform one kind of stone to another."

"So he didn't succeed?" Rokshan said.

Viveki gave him a meaningful look and held out her hand. Rokshan dropped the rupyas into it without touching her skin, as if physical contact with the woman revolted him. "He hadn't succeeded two years ago," she said, "but two years is a long time, so you'd know better than me whether he did it."

Then she laughed. It was such a cheerful sound, so at odds with what Lamprophyre knew of her personality, it sent a chill through Lamprophyre's heart. "Don't know why he bothered," she said. "He needed a model for the transformation, so if he couldn't afford an expensive stone, it wasn't like he could create it out of nothing."

"He needed a model, but he hadn't succeeded yet?" Rokshan said.

Viveki nodded. "He was certain of needing the model. And that it would only transform like to like. He'd failed to change quartz to gold, for example."

"But if he failed to change quartz to sapphire, too, how could he know if it worked at all?" Lamprophyre asked.

Wonder how much more I can get out of her, Viveki thought. "Not sure," she said. "I guess there's failure, and then there's *failure*, you know what I mean? Like, maybe a roast goes rotten, and maybe you cook it too long, and either way you can't eat it, but you know the difference."

Oddly, the example made sense. "I understand," Lamprophyre said. "That fits with what we know of the artifact."

Viveki's eyes widened. "You mean the old fool made it work?"

Surprised by Viveki's leap of logic, Lamprophyre stammered, "He did. It worked, but it was destroyed."

"And you want to make another one. What did he transform? You want to make it happen again?" Viveki sounded unexpectedly excited, and warning bells went off in Lamprophyre's head. If she'd already told the woman too much—

"What we want with the artifact is our business," Rokshan said. He withdrew a few more rupyas from the pouch and handed them over. "Thank you for your information."

It was a dismissal, but Viveki didn't move. "I can get you his notes," she said.

"His notes?" Lamprophyre said. "But there weren't any notes in his workshop."

"You didn't look hard enough. I know where he kept them." Viveki smiled, a much nastier expression than her laugh. "Or where he was likely to keep them. The old bastard thought he was so clever, but nothing gets past me. I know where to look."

"Where? His workshop?" Rokshan asked.

"As if I'd tell you." Scornfulness dripped from her words. "But I want more than a scrabbling of rupyas. Two vahas for the lot."

"Excuse me?" Rokshan said. "You want how much?"

"You're not deaf, *your highness*," Viveki said, investing *your highness* with even more derision than before. "Two vahas."

"What makes you think those notes are worth so much to us?" Lamprophyre said, pretending casual indifference.

"I think there's something you're not telling me, and I think, because of that, you're willing to pay to learn Evart's secrets." Viveki stepped forward until she was within a handspan of Lamprophyre's face. *Make my fortune with this, keep her paying,* she thought.

Lamprophyre made a lightning-fast decision. Viveki was greedy, but she wasn't stupid. She wasn't likely to cheat Lamprophyre, though she wouldn't think twice about wringing as much money out of her as she could manage, and who knew what secrets those notes might contain? "Two vahas," she agreed, "on condition the notes are what you say they are."

"Agreed," Viveki said. "I'll bring them tomorrow or day after at the latest. You have my money ready." She sneered at Rokshan and walked away without looking back.

"She's going to cheat us," Rokshan said when Viveki had disappeared down the street.

"Her thoughts say otherwise," Lamprophyre countered.

Rokshan shook his head. "She might not lie about the notes, or try to pass off a forgery, but I wouldn't be surprised if she 'found' some of the notes and then extorted more money for her to 'find' the rest."

"That's true, but we don't exactly have a choice." Lamprophyre turned and went back into the embassy. "Unless she thinks about the notes' location where I can hear her."

"She didn't, did she?"

"Unfortunately, no. Though I can't imagine they're anywhere but hidden in his workshop." Lamprophyre settled heavily on the ground and rested her head on her arms. "At least we know there actually are notes. She wasn't lying about that."

Rokshan leaned against the wall with his arms folded across his chest. "I'm not sure it will matter. We don't need to know how to create an artifact, we need to know how to make one work."

A bird flew in through one of the high windows and fluttered around, squawking its distress. Lamprophyre watched it carom off the ceiling and spin dizzily down a few handspans before regaining its balance. "I think you're forgetting something," she said. "We now know Evart's artifact worked the way ours does."

"How do we know that? You mean, because Viveki looks exactly like Lelitha?"

The bird straightened its flight and zoomed out another window. "Yes," Lamprophyre said. "Evart had to have a model, right? He used his memories of his daughter to transform me into an identical copy. And Hyaloclast used *her* memories of me as a dragon to restore me. So the secret for doing it might be in Evart's notes."

"It still doesn't change the fact that we don't have a model for me," Rokshan said. "If we use one of the dragons in the clutch, we'll end up with identical dragons, and I don't know if that's a good idea."

"It's a terrible idea. Dragons are supposed to be unique." Lamprophyre blew out a lopsided smoke puff. She still didn't know how to blow a smoke ring and didn't feel she'd gotten any closer in the past few days. "But we can figure that out later. And maybe there's something about it in the notes, too."

"Today seems to be your day for optimism." Rokshan crossed the embassy and sat beside her, not leaning against her side, but with his legs crossed and his chin propped in his hands in the Contemplative Monkey pose Lamprophyre found amusing. "I wish I understood what happened to that woman to make her so angry with me just for being who I am."

"She resented you even as she wished she could be you. Not *you*, exactly, but rich and noble and all that." Lamprophyre sighed. "I wish I could say I didn't understand, but I used to feel that way about Coquina, so I guess I do."

"I'm trying to remember she didn't have the best home life, but she's a nasty piece of work and I wish we didn't have to deal with her."

Lamprophyre craned her neck to look at Rokshan. "And she looks like me. Like Lelitha."

"If you're worried I might forget she isn't you, don't," Rokshan said with a smile. "I can't imagine anyone less like you. Though..." The smile fell away. "It is disconcerting, hearing that voice coming out of your lips."

"I can imagine."

A shadow crossed the doorway, and Lamprophyre looked up to see a man dressed in the green and yellow livery of the royal house. "My lady ambassador?" he said, bowing. "I have a message for you. From his majesty, King Ekanath."

Rokshan rose and held out his hand for the rolled paper. "Does he expect a response?"

The man bowed again. "No, your highness, but I will wait on my lady's pleasure, if she wished to respond regardless."

Rokshan handed the message to Lamprophyre. It was unusually large, which still made it small to her. She rose and carried it to her magnifying lens, unrolling it beneath the glass so she could more easily read the writing. "Huh," she said when she'd gotten past the address and salutations at the top. She read it through twice, then handed it to Rokshan. "The Fanishkorite ambassador has requested a meeting with your father, and she asks that I be present. To discuss a 'resumption of diplomatic relations between all parties.'"

Rokshan was already reading the message himself. "All parties?" he said, letting the paper roll up with a snap. "Fanishkor has never had a diplomatic relation with dragons."

"Exactly the opposite, in fact." Lamprophyre blew out another puff of smoke. "Will you tell the king we'll be there tomorrow at the appointed time?" she asked the messenger, who bowed yet again and left.

"Curious," Rokshan said, resuming his seat.

"Very curious," Lamprophyre agreed. "Fanishkor cuts off communication with Gonjiri, and then wants to negotiate a peace?"

"It might not be peace. It might just be walking back from their antagonistic stance." Rokshan let the paper roll back up and tapped it against his thigh.

"They'd have to do a lot of walking to make amends to dragons," Lamprophyre said. The memory of a golden dragon's egg in the hands of vicious strangers still burned within her. Whatever Fanishkor wanted, she didn't feel inclined to give it to them.

CHAPTER SIX

Lamprophyre hadn't been in the grand entrance hall of the palace since her transformation back into a dragon. It disconcerted her to remember seeing it from both a dragon's and a human's perspective. Her human memories saw the hall as enormous, arching well above her head, and the stairs to the upper passages that led into the palace proper tall enough to leave her breathless at the end of the climb. As a dragon, the tops of those stairs were only a few handspans above her head, and she was close enough to the light hanging from the ceiling that she could touch it if she stretched.

She looked up at the light, which was a metal contraption filled with bright specks like giant fireflies. It shed only a dim light over the hall; most of the illumination came from lanterns in ornate brass cages hanging on three of the four walls. The two staircases each ended at an arched doorway with another lamp above, shedding a warm glow on the little hallway beyond. Lamprophyre thought of the beautifully gaudy room that lay just past the right-hand hallway, and a pang of sadness surprised her. She didn't miss being in a human body, but it seemed there were things she wished she hadn't had to leave behind.

Ahead, on a dais Lamprophyre had never seen before and concluded was temporary, stood an ornate gilded chair with a fat red cushion on the seat. It was perfectly centered between the staircases and had a painted three-part screen behind it. The lighting was too dim for Lamprophyre to see clearly all the tiny details, but it was obviously a painting of Mother Stone under a night sky studded with stars much larger than actually existed. If this was the king's seat, and Lamprophyre couldn't imagine who else would dare sit there, what an impressive way to suggest how powerful he was.

She heard movement behind her and stepped to the right, out of the way of whoever wanted to enter. The Fanishkorite ambassador, probably. Beside her, Rokshan shifted and tugged the hem of the heavy, sleeveless tunic embroidered with a golden dragon that he wore over his shirt. Lamprophyre thought it was ugly, and so did Rokshan, but he'd told her, "It's important that we always make it clear that I act on your behalf and not on my royal father's, which means not wearing the colors of the royal house. Ugly doesn't matter."

A couple of young people, male and female, walked through the outer door, followed by a handful of humans dressed in red with white six-pointed stars on the fronts and backs of their tunics. The formal tunics were the same style as Rokshan's, but despite the stars, they looked much plainer. If this was Fanishkorite livery, Lamprophyre preferred the Gonjirian green and yellow that reminded her so much of her old mentor, the dragon Sapphire.

After those humans, there was a pause, and Lamprophyre heard shuffling and murmured talk. She listened for thoughts and heard only confusion and a couple of sharp mental words: *won't fit* and *stupid privileged git.* That made no sense, so she watched the door and wondered what the ambassador looked like.

Eventually, two men entered the hall. Lamprophyre saw immediately what the problem was: they carried a couple of not quite man-high poles attached to a red canopy with a peaked roof and a rigid frame. White stars like the ones on the tunics spattered the red fabric at random, making it look as if giant birds had emptied their bowels over it. The frame was wide enough that it scraped the sides of the doors with an unpleasant scratching sound. The two men didn't look concerned about the state of the canopy, and Lamprophyre couldn't make out individual thoughts to know if they were embarrassed.

Beneath the canopy, walking close together, were three humans. The canopy kept Lamprophyre from seeing whether they were men or women, and she didn't want to look foolish by bending over to look. They were followed by two men carrying the back two poles of the canopy who looked as stolid and indifferent as the first two. They bore the canopy forward until it stood directly before the chair. Then, as Lamprophyre watched with great curiosity, the four men worked complicated latches that allowed lengths of wood to slide out from where they'd been concealed in the poles. The men worked the latches a second time, then set the canopy down. The extra length kept the canopy off the heads of the three beneath it. It was so clever Lamprophyre immediately plotted how she might get such a portable canopy for herself.

She listened again for thoughts and heard the usual muddle of thoughts that happened when enough people who felt strongly about a subject were in the same room. Whatever the Fanishkorite ambassador had in mind, her retinue was as agitated about it as she was. Or...maybe not. One mental voice stood out, a thread of calm in the muddle, and though Lamprophyre couldn't hear that person's thoughts above the others, whoever it was didn't have the same worries as the rest. That might be the ambassador, or it might just be someone who didn't have much of a stake in these negotiations. Either way, it didn't help Lamprophyre now.

Her chalcedony pendant, a fist-sized chunk of shining blue stone in a silver wire frame, rubbed lightly over her breastbone. It looked decorative enough, but she wore it today because it was an artifact that allowed her to communicate with Hyaloclast. If Fanishkor did, in fact, intend to propose some kind of treaty with dragons, Lamprophyre wanted the dragon queen to be informed.

Being the ambassador was one thing; making binding promises in Hyaloclast's name was something else.

They all waited. None of the Fanishkorites approached Lamprophyre or said anything to her or Rokshan, though they did cast glances her way occasionally, and Lamprophyre caught the odd thought of *big blue monster* or *could crush us without a thought*. These mostly amused her, though she wasn't thrilled about "monster." Well, it wasn't as if Fanishkor had had dragons around to get used to them. If a Fanishkorite agent hadn't stolen a dragon egg to try to incite a war between Gonjiri and dragons, that might have changed.

The sound of a horn startled her out of her reverie. The horn blower stood at the top of the right-hand stairs as if waiting for their attention. She blew the horn again, a long, deep blast of sound like a bass-voiced duck, then descended the stairs. A line of men and women dressed in royal livery followed. All of them were as stern-faced as statues, but Lamprophyre heard enough of their thoughts before the room was too full to know most of them were very bored. So to them, this was just another diplomatic event. If Ekanath felt nervous, he hadn't communicated that fear to his attendants.

As she thought this, Ekanath himself appeared at the top of the stairs. He wore his formal multicolored robe over a white shirt and matching trousers, and a gold circlet pressed his white hair close to his head. He, too, walked as if he didn't have a care in the world. Lamprophyre wished he'd arrived before the Fanishkorites so she could hear his thoughts. She wanted very much to know what he thought about all this, because that would give her an idea of how she ought to behave.

She found she was tapping one foot and made herself stop. Nerves had temporarily gotten the better of her. Rokshan didn't look at all nervous—of course, he'd been raised to this kind of pomp, and whatever he might say about hating politics, he certainly understood it well. Lamprophyre reminded herself that she was a dragon and therefore a mystery to humans, and they would be as nervous dealing with her as she was with them.

Trailing more green and yellow-clad people in his wake, Ekanath crossed the room and seated himself in the golden chair. His retinue arranged themselves around him. Lamprophyre's eye was drawn to a woman who, unlike the others, sat on the dais near Ekanath's feet, her own feet drawn up beneath her as gracefully as a dove fluttering to a perch. She held a large white book and a pen carved from—Lamprophyre sniffed—bright green anyolite with thin streaks of pink giving it a lively look. She'd never seen a stone pen before and guessed it was an artifact, though of what kind, she didn't know.

Ekanath settled his hands on his knees. "Gonjiri gives Fanishkor respect for its desire to restore communications between our peoples," he said. "Chaaksha, I greet you. You may approach."

There was shuffling beneath the canopy, and a woman stepped forward. She wore her long black hair bundled high on her head the way Rokshan's sister Manishi always did, but tidier, and secured with ebony sticks from which faceted rubies dangled in long strings. "Your majesty is gracious in his greeting," she said in a gravelly, almost masculine voice. "Fanishkor respects Gonjiri's generous welcome."

"I admit to curiosity," Ekanath said. "When last we spoke, you gave me to understand that Fanishkor had no interest in a cordial relationship with Gonjiri. There was some unfounded accusation of spying...?"

Chaaksha bowed her head briefly. "I do not wish to antagonize your majesty, but it was hardly unfounded. We had proof."

"Proof we denied." Ekanath leaned forward. "But I choose to believe you did not request this meeting to reopen that argument. You claim we spied. We say we did not. That, to me, is an impasse."

"My apologies. You are right. That is not why Fanishkor requested this meeting." Chaaksha's head came up. "His majesty King Damen tires of the hostility between our countries. Many years ago, we were allies. He would like to see a return of those days."

"Would he, now," Ekanath said. "And yet you did not come as a supplicant."

"We recognize that both Gonjiri and Fanishkor are powerful. We offer you a hand in friendship and request you do the same." Chaaksha's voice was strong and confident. "It is why I requested the presence of the dragon ambassador. As an impartial third party, she is capable of acting as witness."

Lamprophyre thought that was something Chaaksha should have requested before the meeting started, but maybe that was a diplomatic thing Lamprophyre didn't understand. "So, you want me to impartially watch you come to an agreement?" she asked.

"And mediate any points of disagreement we cannot resolve," Chaaksha said.

"The dragon ambassador would be happy to witness," Rokshan said, a little too loudly. Lamprophyre didn't need to hear his thoughts to know he was urging her to go along with him. She nodded, conveying an air of ancient wisdom. She hoped.

"Fanishkor offers renewed favored trading status," Chaaksha said to Ekanath, "and a restored diplomatic presence here and in the Fanishkorite capital Leksital." She bowed again. "And, to prevent future misunderstandings from breaking this treaty, Damen proposes to offer his daughter Yalini's hand in marriage, to join the royal families by blood."

She gestured, and a woman walked forward to join her. She was taller than Chaaksha, not by much, and she wore her hair loose around her shoulders in a style Lamprophyre was unfamiliar with. Her face was pleasingly symmetrical, and so was her body. Confused, Lamprophyre peered at her more closely. Surely Chaaksha couldn't mean...

Rokshan made a strange noise. Ekanath shot him a glance, then returned to closely watching Chaaksha. "He proposes his daughter marries my son," he said.

CHAPTER SEVEN

Lamprophyre felt as if she'd been kicked in the stomach, waking her out of her confusion. "But—" she began, and Rokshan grabbed her knee and squeezed. It didn't hurt, was barely palpable, but it shut her up. Nobody knew about her relationship with Rokshan, and it absolutely was not something they could bring up in the king's court.

"You make an interesting proposal," Ekanath said. "And it's true a closer relationship between the royal families—"

"No," Rokshan said.

Ekanath turned his terrible gaze on his son. "What was that?"

"I said I will not marry the king of Fanishkor's daughter," Rokshan said. "You'll have to seal your arrangement a different way."

The young woman, Yalini, didn't react at all to Rokshan's vehement outburst. Her placid expression didn't change. Lamprophyre wondered if she understood what was going on. Surely she wasn't stupid?

Chaaksha regarded Rokshan closely. "You are unmarried, and it is your duty to serve Gonjiri," she said.

"Not that way." Rokshan put his hand on Lamprophyre's flank. "I refuse."

Now Chaaksha looked at Ekanath. "I'm afraid a royal marriage is a point upon which Fanishkor cannot bend," she said. "Command your son."

Ekanath raised an eyebrow. "Did you just tell me what to do?" he said.

"It was a statement of what must be. If you want peace with Fanishkor, you will insist on this match." Chaaksha smiled at Rokshan. It was an indulgent smile, the kind of smile someone used when trying to cajole a child into good behavior, and Lamprophyre wanted to burn it off her face. Chaaksha gestured at her companion. "Princess Yalini is beautiful, talented, charming—you could not dream of doing better."

"I'm not interested in being a diplomatic pawn, and my father knows it," Rokshan said. He sounded as angry as Lamprophyre felt.

"Then we are again at an impasse," Ekanath said. "Ambassador Lamprophyre, what do you say?"

Startled, Lamprophyre flexed her wings involuntarily, sending up a draft that ruffled Ekanath's robe and hair and set Chaaksha's strings of rubies flying. Everyone except Rokshan and Yalini flinched. "I can't make that decision for you, your majesty."

"You are an impartial witness," Chaaksha said. "You have no interest in the outcome of this discussion. Where does wisdom lie?"

Lamprophyre wanted to laugh. No interest, indeed. "Dragons don't have a concept of dynastic marriage," she said, hoping she remembered the correct term because she couldn't exactly say *forcing Rokshan to marry like a breeding animal.* "We mate for life, and we pair-bond with the one who holds our heart. I don't think it's right to demand two people who've never met—am I right about that, Rokshan?"

"I've never seen Princess Yalini before today, no," Rokshan said. His hand on her flank steadied her.

"I don't think the marriage of two people who don't know each other should be the basis for a diplomatic relationship between two countries. Surely Gonjiri and Fanishkor can agree to deal with each other honestly without being forced to it by being related?"

Chaaksha's face was set in a frown. "It is a long-standing tradition," she said. "They will grow to know each other over time."

"It's an *old* tradition," Ekanath said. "Chaaksha, Gonjiri is willing to forget the past and look to the future. We accept your offer of a diplomatic exchange and favored trading status. We will not, however, require our son to marry into the Fanishkorite royal house. Though, in the interests of compromise, arranging for him to converse with the princess would be acceptable. If a match were to arise—"

"Father," Rokshan said. Lamprophyre leaned on him just enough to make him emit a pained yelp and stop talking. She didn't like the idea, either, but it wasn't as if Rokshan were going to fall in love with this princess, so agreeing to talk to her was harmless.

But Chaaksha was shaking her head. "I'm sorry, your majesty," she said, "but this is a matter upon which I am not authorized to bend. If you will not agree to the marriage, I will be forced to withdraw our offer."

"That's ridiculous," Lamprophyre said without thinking. "You both want peace. You're not willing to bend even a little bit?"

"It is Gonjiri that refuses to bend, my lady ambassador," Chaaksha said. "Last chance, your majesty. It is your decision." Her expression said clearly that she thought Rokshan's opinion on the matter was irrelevant.

Ekanath glanced at Rokshan. A look of indecision crossed his face. "I don't," he began. He shook his head slightly. Rokshan tensed, his fingers on Lamprophyre's flank curling into a fist. "No," Ekanath went on. "Gonjiri left such barbarities behind centuries ago. I will not buy peace with my son's life."

Rokshan let out a deep breath. His hand relaxed. Lamprophyre realized she'd been holding her breath and let it out with a puff of smoke that was almost a ring.

Chaaksha bowed to Ekanath. "I regret that we could not come to an understanding," she said. "I cannot say I agree with your reasoning, but I respect your commitment to your values." She backed away under the canopy, prompting the bearers to return the extended poles back to their original position. Yalini turned and followed her, not once looking Rokshan's way. With a lot of shuffling, the procession made its way back through the door, once more scraping the canopy's sides, and exited the hall.

Ekanath sat on his chair, staring after them. "Father," Rokshan said, then appeared to run out of words.

"You're not attached to anyone, Rokshan," Ekanath said. "You couldn't have agreed to this one small thing?"

Rokshan recoiled. "You said you wouldn't buy peace with my life. Were you lying?"

"I wouldn't force you into a dynastic marriage," Ekanath said, sounding very tired. "But I hoped you'd consider that this was something you could do to serve your country. You can't pine after Lelitha forever, son."

He gave Rokshan a look that said clearly he'd spoken for the sake of listening ears. Ekanath knew "Lelitha" had been Lamprophyre and believed Rokshan's romantic relationship with that woman had been a sham. Lamprophyre hoped that was all he knew.

Rokshan shot a quick glance at Lamprophyre. "I don't want a loveless marriage."

"Would you have made an effort if they'd agreed to my terms?"

Lamprophyre held her breath again. Rokshan looked terribly torn. "I...yes," he said, and once again Lamprophyre felt as if she'd been kicked. "Yes, I would have gotten to know Yalini. It was a fair compromise."

Ekanath sighed. "Well, we're no worse off than we were before. My lady ambassador, thank you for speaking sense. You didn't just say it because we're allies, did you?"

She couldn't say *I did it to protect my love*. "It was just common sense, at least dragon common sense. I'm sorry it didn't work out."

"So am I, to my surprise." Ekanath rose and extended a hand to the woman with the stone pen. "I don't know that we'll need a record of that conversation, but any time I meet with a potential enemy, I like to keep a close eye on what she says."

"Is that an artifact?" Lamprophyre asked.

Ekanath nodded. "It writes by itself, recording every word spoken within its hearing." He took the book from the woman and flipped its pages, scanning the lines. Lamprophyre looked over his shoulder and admired the beautiful penmanship. Hers wasn't nearly so graceful.

"At any rate, that's over," Ekanath said, closing the book. "My lady ambassador, thank you again, and Rokshan—" He sighed once more. "When you're willing to tell me who it is you're in love with, I'm ready to listen. I don't know how unsuitable she must be for you to keep it a secret, but I promise your mother and I won't make snap judgments." He nodded politely to Lamprophyre and walked back up the steps, trailed by his retinue.

When the room was empty, Rokshan said, "He doesn't know. I don't think he's even guessed."

"Well, obviously, or he would have said something." Lamprophyre turned and trod heavily toward the door. "I had no idea a forced marriage was even a possibility."

"Neither did I." Rokshan followed her, moving as slowly as she did. "You know it wouldn't have mattered. I mean, me getting to know that princess."

"I do," Lamprophyre said. She wasn't as sure as she sounded. The longer they went without Rokshan becoming a dragon, the greater the distance between them would become, until one day a beautiful human woman would catch his eye, and then it would all be over. Except that Lamprophyre would love him for the rest of his life, however he felt about her. She'd never felt this discouraged in her life.

They flew in silence back to the embassy, where they found Abhit and Rassika chasing each other around the courtyard, with Rassika's baby sister Kavari sitting in the doorway of the embassy, laughing at their antics. Lamprophyre crouched to let Rokshan down and said, "I don't recognize this game."

"We're just running to make Kavari laugh," Abhit said. "Do you want to play hide and seek?"

"Not right now, Abhit," Lamprophyre said. She felt weary enough that the only thing she wanted was to sleep and sleep until she could wake up in the world where Rokshan was a dragon. "But you can keep running. It won't disturb me."

"They both have chores, my lady," Bhakriya said. She stood at the front of the dining pavilion and clapped her hands. "All of you, time to tidy up your rooms. Then we'll have a meal, and then Abhit promised to read aloud to all of us."

Lamprophyre scooped up Kavari, making the child scream with delight, and handed her off to Bhakriya. "I'm going to nap, but it won't be long," she said. "Rokshan, do you want to eat here?"

"I'm meeting Dharan in half an hour, and we'll eat together," Rokshan said. He ran his hand over the scales on her shoulder and patted her lightly. "I'll come back this afternoon, and we can go for a swim, yes?"

Lamprophyre nodded, though she still felt weary enough that the idea of swimming made her bones ache. She'd feel differently after a nap.

She hung the chalcedony pendant on its peg inside the embassy and brushed its smooth surface with one finger. Dragons didn't cut or polish stones, and she'd always thought of chalcedony as a boring stone until she'd seen what humans could do with it. Even their non-magical stones were beautiful.

She lay down, closed her eyes, and listened to the quiet noises of the children tidying up their little houses that lay behind the embassy. The builders had agreed to return in a few days, and probably Lamprophyre should have everyone remove their belongings so they wouldn't be damaged by the renovations, but that could wait until tomorrow. The sounds were peaceful, but Lamprophyre's heart felt made of stone, it was that heavy. She covered herself with her wings and eventually fell asleep.

"My lady. My lady!" It was Depik, shaking her shoulder. Lamprophyre stirred and swam up out of her deep sleep, where she'd been dreaming of an evil voice whispering in her ear that even Jiwanyil's presence couldn't dispel. "My lady, there are people here to see you."

"People? What people?" Lamprophyre rose on her hands and stretched out her back and tail.

"People in red with white stars," Depik said. He was whispering, though Lamprophyre still had her wings spread over both of them and that would keep speech from spreading. "They say they have business with the ambassador. Do you want me to tell them to come back later?"

"No, it's fine." It wasn't fine. Why would Fanishkor and its ambassador have come here? Surely they weren't so angry about her siding with Gonjiri that they wanted to attack her in her own embassy? "I'll meet them outside," she added, and got to her feet.

She knew there were a lot of people in the courtyard by how hard it was to hear individual thoughts, but she didn't realize until she emerged from the embassy that it was the entire retinue she'd seen at the palace, complete with white-blotched red canopy. Chaaksha stood beneath the canopy, flanked by Yalini and a man in Fanishkorite colors. Chaaksha walked forward when Lamprophyre appeared.

"My lady ambassador, greetings," she said. Her voice was as deep and gravelly as before, but it sounded somehow more pleasant. "I hope we did not disturb you."

"Not really," Lamprophyre lied. "Is there something I can do for you?"

Chaaksha bowed. "I would like to discuss a diplomatic relationship between Fanishkor and the dragons of Nirinatan," she said.

CHAPTER EIGHT

Lamprophyre twitched, and barely managed to keep it from becoming a more obvious movement. She felt stunned enough not to correct Chaaksha about Mother Stone's true name. "Dragons?" she said. "You want an alliance with dragons?"

Chaaksha looked directly at Lamprophyre for the first time, and Lamprophyre once again felt stunned, because her eyes were like Evart's: deeply-set and so dark the irises weren't distinguishable from the pupils. "We believe dragons should rejoin the wider world," she said, "and that allying only with Gonjiri does not allow them to achieve their full potential. We offer an alliance that will benefit both of us."

"You know we've agreed to support Gonjiri if Fanishkor attacks," Lamprophyre said.

Chaaksha inclined her head. "I do. But we do not intend to attack Gonjiri, so that provision of your agreement is irrelevant. Fanishkor simply wishes to gain the same benefits Gonjiri has from its relationship with dragons."

Discomfort made Lamprophyre edgy. "Dragons have not forgotten that Fanishkor ordered a dragon egg stolen," she said coldly. "That doesn't incline us to like you."

"That action was not authorized by our government," Chaaksha said. "And the rebel who attempted it is dead. We offer our apologies, though we do not admit to culpability, as a gesture of friendship. Surely dragons are not so vindictive as to pursue vengeance against someone not guilty?"

Lamprophyre wished more than ever that she could hear the woman's thoughts. She was virtually positive Harshod, who'd been behind the egg theft, had been acting on his government's behalf and Chaaksha was lying. Or maybe she'd been lied to by her government and was telling the truth as far as she knew it. In any case, Lamprophyre didn't think Hyaloclast would be willing to make an alliance with Fanishkor without a substantial gesture of goodwill from that country.

"And what would this alliance look like?" she asked. She folded her arms across her chest and loomed over Chaaksha.

To her credit, Chaaksha didn't flinch. "We would invite a dragon ambassador to join the king's court. We would open trading channels. And we would provide territory for your dragons to settle—we know you are fond of the livestock humans breed. Other possibilities would, of course, present themselves over time."

None of that struck Lamprophyre as highly desirable. Dragons already had all of that in Gonjiri; they didn't need Fanishkor to provide it. And yet, if dragons could contribute to keeping the peace between Gonjiri and Fanishkor, wasn't that a good thing? All right, Hyaloclast probably wouldn't see it that way, given that she didn't care about humans and their conflicts, but Lamprophyre cared about war not breaking out because she had too many human friends who would be hurt by it.

"You claim Fanishkor's king was not responsible for ordering the theft of a dragon egg," she said, "but you haven't offered any proof that this is true. I don't think you understand what a serious offense that was, if you can come here so casually suggesting we overlook it."

"I swear to you King Damen knew nothing of the plot," Chaaksha said. "And you're correct that we don't understand dragons as well as we would like. The ones responsible for the plot have been executed, if that will satisfy your need for vengeance. I'm not sure what more we can do to assure you of our sincerity."

Lamprophyre leaned closer to the ambassador. "Executed?"

She meant to express suspicion—if the king had executed those responsible because they'd attacked dragons, why hadn't he sent word immediately with an apology and an explanation? But Chaaksha interpreted her intent stare differently. "If that seems barbaric to you, I'm sorry. But we must send a message to those who would act in the king's name, given that the king is the one who will bear the consequences if those actions bear evil fruit."

Lamprophyre nodded. "I'm not interested in judging your people or how they exact justice. But, ambassador, you don't realize how close your country came to destruction. I had to argue with Hyaloclast—the dragon queen—to prevent dragons razing your cities in revenge."

Chaaksha's eyebrow went up in that familiar human gesture of surprise and consternation. "Why would you do that?"

"Because attacking a dragon egg—"

"No, I quite understand why dragons would be angry. I meant, why would *you* argue on behalf of humans? Humans you'd never met and believed to be your enemies?"

Lamprophyre glanced at Yalini, who remained as still and expressionless as she had in the palace. It was unsettling. "Because I didn't believe ordinary people ought to suffer for their government's mistakes," she said. "Even if Harshod was acting with the king's approval, that still means hundreds of thousands of citizens would die for one man's choice. We took our vengeance on the one directly responsible."

"You did," Chaaksha said. "Then you admit to murder?"

Lamprophyre recoiled. "He tried to kill me, and that led to his death. And I'm not sorry."

"I see." Chaaksha bit her lip in thought. It was the first nervous gesture Lamprophyre had seen her make. Admitting to complicity in Harshod's death might have been a mistake, but Lamprophyre was at peace with herself for that decision, and she didn't care what Fanishkor's representative thought of it, or her.

"Then I believe the matter should be settled," Chaaksha said abruptly. "Dragons have their vengeance on the one directly responsible for the crime, and Fanishkor apologizes for the necessity of that vengeance. I believe we should move forward instead of looking to the past. Do we have an arrangement, ambassador?"

Lamprophyre again glanced at Yalini, who showed no sign she was paying attention to this conversation. "Why is she here?" she asked impulsively.

For the first time, Chaaksha looked confused. "Why, she is a member of the royal family, and interested in the negotiations. She came because we intended to see her married to Prince Rokshan."

"Yes, but that doesn't explain why she's *here*, in my embassy." Lamprophyre stepped past Chaaksha to look more closely at the princess. "She doesn't seem to notice anything. Is she ill?" She refrained from asking if the princess was mentally deficient. That seemed impolitic.

Yalini blinked and focused her eyes on Lamprophyre. "I like to observe," she said. Her voice was beautiful, with tones that reminded Lamprophyre of the low coo of those tiny gray birds that lived in the plaza. Rokshan called them rats with wings, but Lamprophyre loved the sound of their voices. She would never eat them, not even as a snack.

"And what have you observed?" Lamprophyre asked.

Yalini shifted her weight and clasped her hands loosely in front of her. "You care for the prince," she said. "He is close to you, and his well-being matters to you. That tells me he's worth knowing. I think he will make me a good husband."

"He's not going to marry you," Lamprophyre said sharply.

The princess's light brown eyes no longer looked vacant. "We'll see," she said.

"Your highness, please don't say anything more," Chaaksha warned.

"I thought you'd rejected the idea of an alliance with Gonjiri,"

Lamprophyre said. "You wanted a marriage that will never happen." A thought occurred to her. "That's not what you wanted, though, is it? You made that demand to put King Ekanath in a position of weakness."

"Your suppositions are irrelevant," Chaaksha said, "and I must ask you not to repeat them to the king, unless you want Fanishkor to believe dragons are Gonjiri's tools."

"We're no one's tools," Lamprophyre said hotly. "And your negotiations with Gonjiri don't interest me."

"Then let's talk about our negotiations with dragons," Chaaksha shot back. "Are we in agreement?"

Lamprophyre eyed Yalini. The princess had returned to staring into space with that air of paying attention to something else, but Lamprophyre wasn't sure anymore that the princess was a decorative piece in Chaaksha's retinue. She didn't like the speculative expression the princess adopted when she talked about Rokshan. If Chaaksha hadn't actually given up on the idea of an alliance rooted in a royal marriage, Rokshan could be in trouble.

"I have to take this to Hyaloclast," she said. "At the moment, dragons consider Fanishkor their enemy, and only the dragon queen can decide whether to change that relationship." She hesitated, then added, "Personally, I think it's a good idea, but it's not something I can agree to."

"Understood," Chaaksha asked. "Shall we meet again soon? How long will it take you to return?"

"Oh, I can talk to her from here. I have a chalcedony artifact," Lamprophyre said.

Chaaksha said, "I'm afraid I don't know what that is."

A brief flash of anxiety gripped Lamprophyre. She'd thought the chalcedony artifacts that allowed for communication at a distance were, maybe not common, but at least known throughout the kingdom and beyond. If she'd just given away important secrets... well, it didn't matter now. "It allows for instantaneous communication at a distance," she said. "So I don't have to fly home every time I need to consult with Hyaloclast."

"Astonishing," Chaaksha said. "That is something we would want to trade for. I didn't realize dragons made artifacts."

"We don't. This was a gift..." Lamprophyre realized she was digging herself deeper and stopped. "If you're willing to wait here, I can discuss the matter immediately. Would you care for something to drink?"

She hurried to the dining pavilion to find Depik and Bhakriya deep in conversation. Normally, this would have thrilled her, as she hadn't given up hope that the two would eventually fall in love—or, more accurately, that Bhakriya would finally reciprocate the love Depik felt for her. Just then, it didn't seem important. "We need to serve drinks," she whispered. "Please tell me we have something nice to offer a distinguished guest."

"Of course," Depik said, rising from his seat. "Bhakriya, if you'd get the glasses, I laid in a store of wine and I think it's not too early for that."

"Thank you. I can leave it to you, then?"

Bhakriya smiled. "I was an experienced hostess once," she said, "and Depik's manners are as good as any man's. We'll be fine."

Lamprophyre decided not to cross the courtyard again, instead going through the dining pavilion to the embassy's back door. She removed the chalcedony pendant from its peg and settled it around her neck. She breathed on its shining blue surface to activate it, then considered how far sound might carry and stepped out the back door again, closing it behind her.

"Hyaloclast," she said in a low voice—whispers tended to sound like unintelligible buzzing through the artifact— "Hyaloclast, I need to discuss something with you."

She waited. The embassy was silent except for the clinking noise of glass tapping glass that was probably Depik and Bhakriya serving drinks. She still didn't understand the appeal of eating and drinking while you were carrying on important negotiations, not even now that she'd been in human form. A dragon would take it as disrespectful, though dragons didn't eat their food in tiny morsels the way humans did at diplomatic events, and those little bites weren't as distracting as tearing into huge chunks of meat would be.

She wondered where the children had gone. At this time of day, they were usually all over the embassy, playing games or chasing each other, sometimes with the neighborhood children involved as well. She didn't hear Abhit's high voice raised in reading aloud to the others, either. Maybe Depik had sent them to play at Anamika's house to give Lamprophyre some quiet for entertaining her diplomatic guests.

The mist had nearly evaporated from the surface of the pendant. Lamprophyre breathed more heavily on it and said, "Hyaloclast. Please respond." She suppressed impatience and leaned against the embassy wall, waiting. She couldn't make Hyaloclast respond more quickly for being impatient, and the dragon queen would be scathing with her if she was rude or sarcastic over having to wait.

"*Lamprophyre.*" Hyaloclast's voice, clear as if she were standing next to Lamprophyre, made her jump. "*Something diplomatic, or something personal?*"

"Diplomatic." She wondered if Hyaloclast thought Lamprophyre might have news of Rokshan's quest. Since Lamprophyre wasn't sure if Hyaloclast approved of Rokshan's quest, this was a good sign. She didn't resent her mother's disapproval, if that's what it was, because she could see the situation from Hyaloclast's point of view: the dragon queen's only child, pair-bonded by accident to a human, doomed to decades of sorrow because they were physically incompatible, and hopelessly committed to finding a way to change that. But she still hoped Hyaloclast was on her side.

"*Diplomatic. Continue.*"

Lamprophyre quickly went over Chaaksha's proposal. It was easy to leave out Yalini's presence, given that the princess had nothing to do with the proposed alliance, but it worried her that she felt so satisfied at pretending the woman didn't exist.

When she finished, Hyaloclast said, "*No. We're not interested.*"

Startled, Lamprophyre said, "Just like that? We shouldn't consider this carefully?"

"*Fanishkor has never reached out to make amends,*" Hyaloclast said. "*To me, this suggests that they don't take the egg theft seriously. And I'm not sure I believe their assertion that the theft was the action of a rebel or rebels within the government. Everything you've told me implies that Fanishkor suddenly wants something from us and hopes enough time has passed that the outrage has faded in memory.*"

"Which it hasn't, I agree," Lamprophyre said. "But I don't know if we gain anything by not accepting their apology."

"*You can't listen to this ambassador's thoughts to know the truth?*"

"There are too many people here. Besides, if I were the Fanishkorite king, I would keep the ambassador ignorant so she could negotiate in honesty. I don't know that we'll ever know the truth. But I don't think it matters."

"*The egg theft doesn't matter?*"

"No, I mean we've taken revenge on the man who planned it, and we did it in a way that warned Fanishkor not to try it again, even if it was the king who was behind it. Also, I told the ambassador we nearly burned their cities to the ground."

Hyaloclast chuckled. "*A good warning, indeed.*"

"Anyway, my point is that whoever was actually responsible, we've ensured they'll never do it again, and we've had sufficient revenge. I think we should make this alliance."

Hyaloclast was silent for a few beats. Finally, she said, "*And Fanishkor's relationship with Gonjiri?*"

"The ambassador, Chaaksha, she says they don't intend to attack Gonjiri."

"*That's not the same as the countries being at peace. What overtures did she make to Ekanath?*"

Lamprophyre suddenly found it hard to speak. "She wanted an alliance, and Ekanath rejected it. Because she insisted Rokshan marry the king of Fanishkor's daughter."

"*I assume the young prince refused? Or has Ekanath taken a moral stand?*"

"Both, actually."

"Then relations between the countries continue hostile, which means if Fanishkor attacks, we will be drawn into Gonjiri's defense. I don't want us compromised by having an alliance with Fanishkor."

"But I think it's true Fanishkor doesn't want to attack. I have a feeling..." She paused, groping her way to an understanding of something nebulous she barely saw. "I think Fanishkor is afraid of Gonjiri. Of those pyrite weapons. Something must have changed, because before this, Fanishkor broke off all communications with Gonjiri, and now they want an alliance? And I think from something the princess said that they haven't given up on that alliance, marriage or no."

"You seem unusually bent on changing my mind," Hyaloclast said drily.

Lamprophyre was glad her mother couldn't see her blush. "It's just that if we're allied with both countries, I think they'll think twice about going to war. We could do so much for the humans this way."

"You know I don't care about what humans do to each other."

"I know. But it benefits us, too. If they're at war, we can't trade for artifacts, or cows, or any of the things we've come to enjoy."

There was a long silence. *"You make good points,"* Hyaloclast finally said, *"but my instinct is that we should stay clear of Fanishkor. I'm willing to give their king the benefit of doubt about the egg theft, but that doesn't change the fact that they haven't dealt honestly with us in the past and may not be dealing honestly now. Until their conflict with Gonjiri is settled, I will not form an alliance, trading or otherwise, with Fanishkor."*

Lamprophyre's heart sank. She didn't like the answer, but it was hard to argue with Hyaloclast's logic. "All right," she said. "I'll tell them that. Does that mean if they come to an agreement with Ekanath, we'll change our minds?"

"If you're that certain we'll benefit from this agreement, yes." Hyaloclast sighed. *"I wish I could blame your interest in humans on your time in a human body, but this unusual preference you have predates that by most of a year."*

"They're interesting, and it astonishes me how much they accomplish in their short lives," Lamprophyre protested.

"*I said unusual, not aberrant,*" Hyaloclast said with a laugh. "*I see more of your father in you every day.*"

Lamprophyre's breath caught. Her mother never, ever referred to Aegirine, not in public and not to Lamprophyre in private. "You think he would have felt the same about humans?" she ventured.

"*I think he would have wanted to be ambassador in your place,*" Hyaloclast said. "*Now, go give the news to the Fanishkorite ambassador. And don't grovel and make excuses. She needs to see us as strong and committed to our position, or she'll think she can walk all over us. Understand?*"

Lamprophyre, who'd been considering how she might make the news more palatable, blushed again. "Yes. I'll let you know if anything changes."

The misty blue surface of the chalcedony pendant cleared. Lamprophyre removed it from around her neck and held it between her palms for a few beats, letting her mind clear. Then she pushed open the back door and let herself into the embassy. This was her least favorite part of being ambassador, having to turn a reasonable request down. She hoped Chaaksha was as reasonable as her request, and would see that this wasn't shutting a door, it was leaving open a window.

Chaaksha stood beneath the canopy, talking quietly to the man in Fanishkorite colors. She held a wine glass in one hand and was using it to emphasize a point, gesturing gently enough that the wine barely sloshed. Yalini stood motionless as usual, though she also held a wine glass that appeared less full than Chaaksha's. No one paid attention to Lamprophyre, sitting in shadow just within the embassy, so she watched Yalini for a while. She was pretty, Lamprophyre believed, though she still didn't fully appreciate all the varieties of human beauty, and a jolt of jealousy shot through her. Pretty, and royal, and eligible, and smarter than she let on...if she also had an interesting personality, she was the kind of woman any man would be attracted to. Even Rokshan.

She shook her head to dismiss the image of Rokshan taking

Yalini's hand in affection and stepped forward, drawing everyone's gaze. Chaaksha handed her glass to the man and came to meet Lamprophyre. "Did you speak to the dragon queen, ambassador?" she asked.

"I did," Lamprophyre said. "I'm sorry, but she rejects your request. The dragon queen is not interested in allying or trading with Fanishkor at this time."

Chaaksha stood up straighter. "You reject our apology?"

"No, it's not that. We accept your explanation and choose not to hold the egg theft against your government. But dragons have a pact of mutual military aid—" Rokshan had taught her that phrase, and another pang shot through her— "with Gonjiri, and dealing with Fanishkor could compromise us. Therefore, Hyaloclast decrees that until Fanishkor and Gonjiri are no longer at odds, we will not treat with your country."

Chaaksha's dark complexion went darker. "Then dragons don't mind being the pawns of humans," she spat.

"Please don't try to taunt me into changing my mind. It's bad manners," Lamprophyre said. "We will be happy to reconsider once Fanishkor and Gonjiri have resolved their differences."

"You realize you made that impossible when you sided with Gonjiri earlier," Chaaksha said. "If you'd backed our proposal of a dynastic marriage, all this would have been settled."

"That was never going to happen," Lamprophyre said. Despite her resolve, she was becoming angry. "And so long as we're being insulting, I think it's barbaric that you would marry your king's daughter to a total stranger and think that somehow makes your alliance stronger."

Chaaksha stiffened. "On your own head be it, then," she said, and turned her back on Lamprophyre to return to her position under the canopy. Lamprophyre recognized a deliberate insult and decided to ignore it. Chaaksha's dramatic exit was spoiled by her need to wait for the canopy's legs to be retracted, and Lamprophyre could afford to be magnanimous.

Unlike Chaaksha, Yalini continued to watch Lamprophyre while the canopy was prepared. Lamprophyre stared back, afraid to look away and not sure why. It might have been Yalini's expressionless face, still as a statue; her impassivity felt like an attack, like goading Lamprophyre into an emotional reaction Yalini would not respond to. Lamprophyre watched her until the canopy began to move, when Yalini placed her wine glass carefully on the ground and turned to walk away. It felt like being released from a golden cage, pretty to look at but still a trap.

Shortly, the embassy courtyard was empty of everything except a scattering of glasses across the dark earth, some of them lying on their sides, others upright as if their owners intended to return. Lamprophyre let out a deep breath. She wished Rokshan were here, though she was glad he hadn't been here while Yalini was. It was irrational, but she feared them having any contact.

Bhakriya and Depik emerged from the dining pavilion and began collecting glasses. "I offered them the use of the pavilion, my lady, but they refused," Bhakriya said. "It's so awkward having a glass with nowhere to put it."

"It's all right." Lamprophyre backed into the embassy and settled down to watch the two carry the glasses away to be washed. She felt even more tired than before. Between the failed negotiation in the palace and the failed negotiation just now, she felt heartsick and weary and longed for Rokshan to be with her. It was just when they were apart that she felt uncertain of him, because when they were together, she felt confident that they could manage anything. But she remembered Yalini's direct gaze, remembered the princess's words, and wondered if she was right.

CHAPTER NINE

From very high above, Tanajital looked like a slab of white marble strewn with chunks of pyrite, the whiteness of its walls contrasting with the gold and copper sheathing of its many towers and roofs. The fact that pyrite wouldn't be found together with marble only enhanced Lamprophyre's sense of the city's artificial nature. Humans had constructed a home that would never have arisen naturally.

"How do you feel?" she called over her shoulder to Rokshan.

"Comfortable enough," Rokshan shouted back over the sound of the wind in her wings. "I'm not entirely warm, but I'm not frozen. The scarf keeps slipping, though." His voice was muffled by the cloth drawn over the lower part of his face, but Lamprophyre's draconic hearing understood him perfectly.

"I'm going to go higher," Lamprophyre said. "Tell me when it's too cold. I want to get an idea of how high we can safely go." To her, the brisk winter air was refreshing, and she was sure she could endure temperatures much colder than was safe for her passenger, so Rokshan's responses were important.

Rokshan patted the side of her neck with his gloved hand in acknowledgement. She aimed for a patch of cloud floating all alone in the clear blue sky. It was too high for them to safely reach, but it made a good visual reference to keep her flying in a straight line. It could be dangerous for dragons to fly too high, too fast—she'd done it once as a child and had felt nauseated and achy for a few days afterward—and humans, so much more fragile than dragons, had to be at greater risk for becoming ill. She hoped Rokshan had taken her warning seriously when they took off on this trip.

They hadn't spoken much this morning. Lamprophyre hoped it was because talking, for Rokshan, meant inhaling frigid air and chilling him beyond what was comfortable. She had told him about Chaaksha's visit, but not about Yalini's presence or the princess's odd response to Lamprophyre's insistence that Rokshan wouldn't marry her. It was stupid, she was being stupid, but the more she thought about her, the more convinced she was that Yalini was a threat. She needed to talk to Rokshan, because he was her best friend in addition to being her mate, but she didn't know how to bring it up without sounding stupid or pathetic.

They had left Tanajital behind as they flew south, following the Green River, which at this altitude was a thread of gray-blue spooling across the plains. Lamprophyre saw a few smaller cities like geometric moss snugged against the river or sitting atop low rises that were themselves no more prominent than shadows. The land was winter-pale between settlements, where the fields were a dark contrast, their earth in the process of being tilled for the spring planting.

Ahead, the horizon was misty with distance, but Lamprophyre could still see hills, nothing as grand as her mountain home, but tall enough to stand out against the sky. The farther south one went, the higher those hills became, until they were the mountain range that marked the border between Gonjiri and Sachetan. They wouldn't go that far today, but if they could fly this high always, taking advantage of the updrafts, that trip wouldn't be so punishingly long as usual.

"That's it," Rokshan said, patting her neck again. "My feet are getting numb."

"You weren't supposed to let it get that far," Lamprophyre chided him as she wheeled around and began her descent.

"I was curious. And it's not like they're frozen. I can still move them. It's my fingers I'm more concerned with. These gloves are made for protection while riding, not to hold in heat."

"*Are* there gloves meant to keep you warm? I'd think that's not a thing Gonjirians worry about."

Rokshan's feet in the stirrups scraped lightly across her sides as he shifted his weight. The new saddle was a big improvement, he'd said. "I think someone could make them like that. Lined, maybe. I'll ask the seamstress who did the rest of this gear."

"I assume everything else is as warm as promised," Lamprophyre said. He'd looked so odd and bulky when he was dressed in the heavy coat and thick trousers he'd found some seamstress to make for him. Lamprophyre had never seen a coat like that one. All the coats she was familiar with were made to keep the torrential rains of summer off, and were thin and waxy-looking. This one was of heavy twilled cotton lined with sheepskin, Rokshan had said, and it made his arms stand out from his body slightly. Between that, the similarly thick trousers, and the white cap with the cloth to protect his neck, he'd been almost invisible.

"Very comfortable," Rokshan said. "I think I need extra layers in my boots, though. Something flexible and warm to cover my feet. Foot gloves."

Lamprophyre laughed. "I can't believe this. No one's cared about keeping a human warm at altitude in, well, at least a thousand years, if the stories are correct. And now look at us."

Rokshan hugged her neck, resting the side of his face against the sensitive spot. "Look at us," he agreed.

His proximity, the touch of his skin against her scales, made her feel embarrassed at her insecurities. "Rokshan," she said, "there's something I didn't tell you about Chaaksha's visit."

"Oh?"

"Yalini was there. And she said things that implied she hasn't given up on marrying you."

Rokshan became very still. Then he sat up. "Why didn't you say anything earlier?"

His tone of voice, verging on angry, made Lamprophyre glad she couldn't see him. "Because I was stupid. She's beautiful and smart and I was afraid..." She couldn't bring herself to say it.

Rokshan finished the thought for her. "You were afraid if I knew she wanted to marry me, I'd fall in love with her. Lamprophyre—"

"I know! I'm sorry! It's just—Rokshan, we're not the same species anymore, and that has to make a difference."

"Not to me. Not to what I remember. You aren't going to fall in love with some dragon, so what makes you think I'm going to be any less faithful?" Now he did sound angry. "Do you realize how insulting that is?"

"I'm sorry," Lamprophyre repeated, misery settling like a stone in her stomach. "I don't know what I was thinking. Of course I don't think that of you."

Rokshan was silent for a very long moment in which Lamprophyre wished she were human again, just so she could weep tears of sorrow and frustration. "No, I'm sorry," he finally said. "I shouldn't have gotten angry. Because you're not wrong that we're in a terrible situation. But you're my best friend. Even if I didn't love you, I couldn't bear to make you miserable by betraying you."

The stone lightened a little. "I suppose I feel uncomfortable because this pair-bond is so one-sided. You can't feel connected to me, and that means if you wanted to fall in love with someone else—"

"Which I don't. Particularly not that stone-faced Fanishkorite princess."

"But if you did, there's nothing stopping you. I mean, nothing physical."

Rokshan ran his hand over her scales again. "Sweetheart, every human who's ever been married has been in that position. They have nothing but their honor keeping them from straying. And yes, many humans give in to temptation and cheat on their spouses, and sometimes couples fall out of love and decide to divorce. But most of them stay true to their love once they've made vows to do so. And I consider us married. I'm not going to desert you."

Happiness made her load fly away like a bird. "I'm sorry I doubted you."

"I'm sorry I didn't make that clear earlier. Or did you think it was just idle fancy that has me so intent on making that transformation artifact work?"

Lamprophyre shook her head. "I know. We'll figure it out. We have to."

"And now we have a new possibility in Evart's notes."

"We haven't heard from Viveki yet."

"She was supposed to bring the notes today at the latest. I'm not worried. So long as she has those vahas gleaming in her eyes, she'll arrive."

Lamprophyre descended in a wide spiral over Tanajital. "Look. The green flag is flying over the Archprelate's palace."

"I see it. So Khadar is back. Should we talk to him?"

Lamprophyre thought about it for a few beats. "If Viveki comes today, I don't want her to go away because we weren't there to greet her. But I do want to talk to Khadar about the Mother Stone prophecy eventually."

"If he's willing to talk to *us*," Rokshan said. "He's not as arrogant as he used to be, but he still doesn't like either of us much. But you're right that he'll likely know more about that prophecy."

"Or the Archprelate. I have a hard time believing she encouraged those ecclesiasts to accost me so antagonistically. Even though I'm sure she believes the prophecy is true."

"There's something to it regardless," Rokshan said, "and we should investigate. I thought we were going back to the embassy," he added as Lamprophyre descended into the center of the city.

"We are. But we're going to the warehouses first. I want to return the harness to Flint so he can make a start on making more of them. Unless there was another adjustment you wanted?"

"No, I think it's as perfect as we can make it. Not nearly so tight in the saddle, and the adjustable stirrups were a good idea."

She landed neatly at the end of the street and crouched to let Rokshan off. "Where is everyone?" she said. She couldn't hear the drifting surface thoughts that signaled the presence of other dragons.

She peered inside Dolomite's warehouse. It was empty and very bright, the walls painted a gleaming white that shone even in the indirect light from the windows. Maybe Dolomite wanted his windows enlarged, too, to give him better light for his art.

She heard someone thinking *what time is it?* just before Bromargyrite emerged, yawning and stretching. "Sorry, I was asleep," he said. "Did you need something?"

"Just to give Flint the harness. Help me off with it, would you?"

Bromargyrite helped lift the saddle away and gathered up all the straps and buckles. "Flint and Coquina went to have some privacy, but I'll leave this in his warehouse. I don't know where everyone else went. Dolomite may have gone to work on his new project."

"What project is that?" Rokshan asked.

Bromargyrite shrugged. "He won't say. He wants it to be a surprise. I doubt he'll be able to keep it secret for long. You know what he's like when he's excited about something." He examined the straps. "How does it feel to wear this?"

"Odd. But no worse than human sandals, touching your skin constantly." Lamprophyre shuddered. "We have to meet Viveki now. At least, I hope she comes soon."

"The woman with Lelitha's body, right?" Bromargyrite nodded. "I hope she has good news, but you know what I always say—"

"Don't get my hopes up, yes, I know. You're the most rational person ever."

"I doubt that, but then how many people do you actually know?" Bromargyrite grinned. "I hope I'm wrong. Good luck, Lamprophyre."

CHAPTER TEN

Lamprophyre flew low over the crowds to give the humans something beautiful to look at and alighted neatly in the embassy courtyard. Rokshan leaped down and immediately took off the heavy coat. "Much too warm at ground level," he said.

Lamprophyre took it from him and hung it on a peg she'd hammered into the wall of the embassy just for that purpose. "It will be perfect for trips to the gleaning fields."

Rokshan followed her inside and stripped down to his shirt and the short, thin pants he wore to cover his male parts. "That's appealing. They're always so cold."

Lamprophyre settled herself on the floor and watched him dress in his usual clothes. "I suppose now we wait," she said. "I'm already bored."

"I'll read to you," Rokshan said. "One of those books Dharan brought."

Lamprophyre made a face. "I don't want to act ungrateful, and I promise I'm not, but how many books are we going to find that all say the same things? Human knowledge of the Cataclysm is limited, and even if we assume the stories are metaphorical, we still haven't learned anything new about Sardonyx in weeks."

"We won't know unless we try," Rokshan said. "Everything we've learned so far has been by accident, more or less—or at least in places we didn't know would be important. And I don't want to wait around for her to attack again when we're not expecting it. Somewhere in all these books must be information we can use."

"You're so optimistic," Lamprophyre said with a smile. "You're like the opposite of Bromargyrite, except he's not pessimistic so much as realistic."

"Sometimes those are the same thing," Rokshan said. He settled himself against her side and opened the book. It was small and smelled of dust and old leather, and when Rokshan changed his grip on the cover, tiny brown flakes sifted down like a dirty snowfall over his legs. "It's odd how I never really cared about the condition of books before I handled so many of them. Having a preference about how they feel in my hands, that's something Dharan would do."

"Being small enough to handle the books myself is one of the few things I miss about being human," Lamprophyre said.

"Oh? What else do you miss?"

She smiled. "Kissing. I realize that's silly, but dragons don't kiss, and human bodies are so sensitive, it's like nothing else in the world."

"I agree, and I don't think it's silly." Rokshan scooted closer to her shoulder. "I try not to dwell on the memory, because—anyway." He cleared his throat. "This book is a collection of—hmm." He riffled through the pages. More brown flakes fell. "It's tempting to call them eyewitness accounts, but that's impossible. They're more like descriptions of the catastrophe by near-contemporaries. I've read—*we've* read—some of them in other books, but this author collected them all in one place."

"We don't have to read the ones we've already read, right?"

Rokshan tilted his head to look at her. "No, but it might be useful to see those in context."

Lamprophyre sighed. "You're right. I'm just eager to find something new. Maybe reading them all together will reveal a hidden detail."

Rokshan turned back to the beginning. "This one is by someone whose name was never recorded. They think it was a woman because in the era this comes from, most of the scribes and historians were female." He cleared his throat again, and read:

"'*The storm caught them unawares, wind and fire, ash and stone raining down upon their cities. Dragons and warriors rose to meet it and were swept aside.*' It's discouraging how most of these stories suggest the defenders didn't stand a chance against Sardonyx."

"At least they tried."

"True. '*When at last all hope was gone, the mountains rose up and swallowed the storm. Humans mourned their losses, and the Lonely God wept to have no children. The gods circled round Katayan in his grief. Meyari's roots dug deep to sustain him. Vrelok's creatures howled a funeral dirge. Jiwanyil's people grieved with him. And Nirinatan guarded their rest.*'" Rokshan closed the book on his finger. "This is nothing we didn't already know. Some event stopped Sardonyx, but only after all the dragons were dead."

"Except they weren't dead. They were just in hiding. Or seclusion." Lamprophyre tried another smoke ring and watched the puff of smoke float upwards before dissipating.

"Maybe it's partly true," Rokshan said. "Maybe all the dragons who fought Sardonyx with the humans were killed. Maybe no one who challenged her survived."

"That makes sense. What I wish we understood was what it means that the mountains swallowed her up. That's consistent across nearly all the stories. But there's no evidence the mountains have moved at all, certainly not in the last thousand years."

"It might not be the dragons' mountains," Rokshan pointed out. "There's the mountains on the southern border."

"I don't think those have moved, either." Lamprophyre sighed. "It has to be magic, but what magic could destroy an army of evil dragons? Or—not destroy, since Sardonyx is still around somewhere, but bury, or trap."

"You think Sardonyx is trapped?"

"Don't you? Otherwise, she'd attack directly."

"Unless she can't. Unless that magic crippled her." Rokshan opened the book again. "'*Humans in their sorrow rebuilt, and the gods watched over their efforts. It was in this time Jiwanyil first spoke to men and women, warning them and warding them against danger.*' That's different. No one's ever said Jiwanyil didn't speak to humans before the catastrophe."

"Well, if your religion changed to include Katayan after the Cataclysm, maybe that was part of the change. I mean, I assume before the Cataclysm everyone knew about Mother Stone, if dragons and humans lived together."

"You mean, the names for the gods changed after the catastrophe?" Rokshan sat up. "Or that we didn't worship those gods before then?"

"I don't want to insult your religion, Rokshan."

Rokshan shrugged. "There's a lot we don't know. For that matter, what if dragons didn't worship Mother Stone until after the catastrophe? Suppose they learned about her after all those dragons were killed?"

Lamprophyre sat up as well. "That's blasphemy!"

"Not if it was a truth the catastrophe revealed. Maybe dragons did worship Katayan, and found out later what the truth was."

His words battered at her, fat freezing snowballs that didn't hurt so much as overwhelm. "Rokshan—"

She heard footsteps approaching and stopped speaking to look out the doorway. Viveki came toward them, striding like an unstoppable force across the courtyard and ignoring Bhakriya, who approached her, saying, "If you have an appointment with my lady—"

"It's all right, Bhakriya, we were expecting her," Lamprophyre said. Rokshan rose and set the book back on the pile, then stood with one hand on the doorway. Viveki's wordless thoughts of being paid sharpened into irritation when she saw Rokshan. *Better not use smooth words on me,* she thought.

"Don't try to sweet-talk her," Lamprophyre murmured to Rokshan. Rokshan shot her a sharp look, then nodded once. It was all the interaction they had time for before Viveki stood in front of them. She wasn't carrying anything.

"You didn't find the notes?" Lamprophyre asked, her heart sinking.

Viveki smiled, not a nice expression, and reached into her shirt. She withdrew a black leather book, messy with loose pages crammed into it and the tips of feathers sticking out at random. "Right where I expected," she said. "You people didn't look very hard if you didn't find it."

Lamprophyre declined to take the bait. "Thank you," she said, holding out a hand for the book.

Viveki didn't move. "Payment," she said.

"Not until I see it. I'm not paying for something that isn't what I'm looking for." Lamprophyre's hand didn't waver.

Viveki regarded it for a few beats, then slowly handed the book over. Lamprophyre handed it to Rokshan, who paged through it. She wasn't sure what he was looking for, what would prove this had belonged to Evart, so she kept her face impassive and hoped she looked mysterious and confident.

Rokshan stopped near the middle of the book, where a long gray and white bird's feather marked the place. "This is the first mention of the transformation artifact," he said. "He describes buying the serpentine stone. It's the right book." He flipped to the end and looked up at Viveki. "The last entry is dated a year ago. Where's the rest?"

Viveki's expression didn't change. "Are you accusing me of something?"

"Of course not. But he didn't stop taking notes. There has to be another book."

Now the woman smiled again. "Maybe. This was all there was in that hiding place. But he probably had others. Unless the book was on him when he died."

"It wasn't," Lamprophyre said. She remembered searching

Evart's body for the serpentine stone and finding only his anti-mind-listening pendant. "And you're about to tell us you know where the other book is, and will find it—for a price."

"You dragons are clever," Viveki said. "The other places I have in mind are a lot harder to get into. More dangerous. It's going to cost you more."

Rokshan said, "How much more?"

Viveki spared him a dismissive glance before returning her attention to Lamprophyre. "Another five vahas. In advance."

"*Five* vahas? Are you out of your mind?" Rokshan said.

"Five, or no book," Viveki said, her smile widening.

"Excuse us for a moment," Lamprophyre said. She nudged Rokshan to the back of the embassy, well out of earshot. "That book might be important."

"And it might tell us nothing," Rokshan said. "I don't like giving any money to that greedy little—"

"We don't have to give her anything if it turns out not to be useful. And we'll get an idea of whether that's true by studying the book she just brought." Lamprophyre glanced past Rokshan at where Viveki stood. "We're certainly not paying her in advance."

Rokshan followed her gaze. "Do you think she can tell we're desperate?"

"No. Though if we paid her five vahas in advance, she'd figure it out." Lamprophyre put a gentle hand on Rokshan's shoulder. "It's just money."

"Money we're swiftly running out of," Rokshan grumbled.

They returned to where Viveki stood. The woman seemed not at all impressed at being in the dragon embassy. "You haven't paid me for that book yet," she said, pointing at the black leather book Rokshan held.

Rokshan scowled and dug out a couple of square gold coins he slapped into Viveki's outstretched hand with some force. "But you're not getting five in advance," he said. "One, to show we appreciate the difficulty of the next task." He held up another gold coin, then didn't release it immediately when she took hold of it. They glared at each other briefly.

When Rokshan finally let go, Viveki shrugged and pocketed the coins. "I didn't think you'd fall for that, but I had to try," she said. "It will take a few days. I'll be back." She turned and strolled across the courtyard, vanishing up the street.

Lamprophyre watched her go until she was swallowed up by the crowds. "I wish I didn't feel like that was a mistake," she said.

"It's just because she's so unpleasant to deal with," Rokshan said. "Let's read this, and hope something useful will appear. Like the key to keeping the desired form in memory long enough for the transformation."

"That's worth far more than two vahas," Lamprophyre agreed.

CHAPTER ELEVEN

The stands flanking the race ground were as full of humans as they always were despite the brisk wind that blew dust into Lamprophyre's eyes, forcing her to close her nictitating membranes. It had to be worse for the humans, who she could see were shielding their eyes to look across the obstacle course.

Orthoclase was at the top of the course, zigzagging through the barriers—incautiously, it turned out, because he kept brushing against them. Every bump sent up the jangle of bells, and sounds of disappointment rose from the stands. No one would ever shout criticism at a racing dragon, and the sound reminded Lamprophyre more of shared dissatisfaction at a mistake than displeasure.

Despite the mistakes, Orthoclase made good time, and the timing artifact next to Lamprophyre showed he'd run the course in under seventy beats—a new personal best for him. Lamprophyre saw him scowling and concluded he probably didn't see it as a victory. He flapped up to where she sat, on the stand at the end of the course. "That wind is a nightmare," he said. "I hate making excuses, but it really threw me off."

"I don't think it's making excuses to be aware of environmental challenges," Lamprophyre said. "I wonder how Porphyry will feel about it. He's up next."

"Are you going to take a turn?"

She shrugged. "I don't know. I'm never sure how it looks for the ambassador's dignity to show how slow I am."

"You're not slow," Orthoclase said. "You're better at the obstacles than I am."

"I'll think about it."

Porphyry's appearance at the top of the course was greeted with wild cheering. The bright red dragon with his cheery good manners was a favorite among the humans who came often to the dragon races. He swam through the air, doing loops and twists to limber himself up. Orthoclase snorted. "Show-off."

"I think it's funny." Lamprophyre reached around to twist the knob of aquamarine set in a palm-sized frame of the same stone. The white numbers displayed across the sheet of fine-grained flint flickered and disappeared, and the round-cut topazes set into the corners of the flint flared a brief yellow light. Lamprophyre had spoken with the adept who'd created the timing artifact, and his explanations had been confusing, but she understood that the aquamarine calculated the time, citrines embedded in the flint displayed the numbers, and the topazes magnified those numbers so they were visible to the watchers. He'd also said something about other uses for topaz, but Lamprophyre had been too astonished to listen.

Not for the first time, she considered what she knew of human magic and was astonished all over again. They were so *casual* about it. In her studies of the stones they used, she'd found over and over again that humans took for granted that a particular stone would do a particular thing, no question, nothing but the skill of the lapidary-adept determining success or failure. And the people who used the artifacts saw them as no more marvelous than lighting a lamp or putting wheels on a cart. It was odd, when you thought about it.

But, on the other hand, were dragons any different? Dragons were creatures of magic, their bones made of an unbreakable substance they called stone that was nothing like, their wings carrying them effortlessly despite the plain impossibility of anything a dragon's size being able to fly, their bodies immune to the fire or acid they contained in their second stomachs. Dragons were as casual about all that as humans were about their magic. Lamprophyre felt there was a difference, but she couldn't have said what it was.

She saw Porphyry settling in front of the course and moved her hand to the button that would start the timing artifact and signal for him to go. Porphyry spread his wings, Lamprophyre mashed the button, and a bright yellow flash went off as numbers appeared on the flint. Porphyry took off, propelled by the sound of hundreds of voices screamed encouragement.

"He's definitely more agile than I am," Orthoclase murmured. Porphyry navigated the barriers neatly, brushing two of them and prompting groans from the watchers. "See? Even he's doing it. This wind is a nightmare."

A gust of wind blew dust into Lamprophyre's face at that moment. She sneezed. "We should call it a day after this. I'm ready to curl up with a good book and wait for the storm to pass. We could use the rain."

"In a dozen twelvedays I'm going to remind you you said that," Orthoclase said with a grin.

Porphyry furled his wings and let momentum carry him through the giant hoop at the center of the course, then snapped them open before he could fall. In another five beats, he sped past Lamprophyre and Orthoclase, and the numbered display on the flint surface flashed his final time. "Sixty-three beats," Lamprophyre said. "Very nice." The cheering crowds agreed.

Porphyry winged his way back to them and settled on the end of the ledge. With all three of them perched on it, one of them female, it was crowded. "That wind is a nightmare," he panted.

"That's what I said," Orthoclase said. "Let's talk to people for a bit and then go back to the warehouses. I need some stone to keep my strength up."

"Eating in the middle of the day, how decadent," Lamprophyre teased, though secretly she'd been dreaming of a slab of mica to nibble on while she read.

She lifted off the ledge and flapped leisurely across the course. They'd modeled it after the oval of the red sandstone coliseum at the center of Tanajital, though without the arched walls. Instead, long wooden stands twice the height of a dragon paralleled the long sides of the oval, their rows of benches stacked along an incline so there were no bad seats. The ledge and the timing artifact stood at the southern short end of the oval, not quite as tall as the stands, but still readily visible from every seat.

Lamprophyre headed now for the northern end of the course where the royal stand was. It was as tall as the rest of the spectator stands, but narrower, with a green and yellow canopy matching the royal family's colors shielding the chairs—no benches for royalty. The royal family wasn't in attendance that day except for Rokshan, but there were always plenty of minor nobles and courtiers allowed to use it.

A rickety-looking contraption clung to one side of the tall wooden stand. Lamprophyre shuddered when she looked at it. She'd ridden the lift exactly twice, and even now that she was in a dragon's body and couldn't fall to her death, the memory of its shaking ascent sent a shiver of fear through her. She'd never mentioned her fear to anyone, not even Rokshan. How humiliating to be a dragon afraid of heights! Which she wasn't. Not anymore.

"We're going to stop," she began as she neared the stand. Rokshan stood at the front rail, watching her approach. She opened her mouth to say more when she realized he wasn't alone. A woman, her dark hair whipped by the rising wind, stood next to him, her face turned toward him, a smile on her rosy lips.

Yalini.

Jealousy surged through Lamprophyre for half a beat before rationality took over. She trusted Rokshan not to lie to her, and she had no reason to believe Yalini's charms were so overpowering as to make him desert his mate. Besides, Rokshan's expression was the hard, blank half-smile that said he was seriously annoyed but couldn't reveal his annoyance.

Yalini, for her part, looked like she'd won a prize. Her thoughts were all focused on Rokshan: *so handsome, wonder if he's intelligent, gives a good impression of not but I think it's a ruse.* It would be interesting if Lamprophyre could steer her into thinking about why she wanted to marry Rokshan. But the look on Rokshan's face told her it would be better to get them both away from the Fanishkorite princess immediately.

"Princess Yalini, welcome," Lamprophyre said, backwinging into a hovering position. "I thought you'd left Tanajital."

"Why would I do that?" Yalini turned her smile on Lamprophyre. *Dragon's unnaturally close to the prince, not sure why*, she thought.

"Well, the negotiations didn't work out, so I thought..." Lamprophyre's words trailed off in the face of Yalini's unwavering smile. From stone statue to overly friendly woman—Lamprophyre would put that down to human oddity, but now that she'd been human herself, her instincts about what humans found normal had changed. She felt certain anything Yalini did was part of a very deep game, one Lamprophyre didn't know how to play, let alone win.

"Fanishkor isn't at war with Gonjiri," Yalini said, "and the diplomatic party chose to remain in Tanajital for a few weeks. To experience everything Gonjiri has to offer, of course. I'd never seen dragons race before, and Prince Rokshan was kind enough to invite me."

Rokshan's eyes widened. Lamprophyre listened to his thoughts and was nearly bowled over by their force and incoherence. *Tricked me stupid woman can't believe* was all Lamprophyre could make out. She would have laughed if Rokshan hadn't been so clearly furious.

"That was kind," Lamprophyre managed, but her own anger had been roused by Rokshan's distress. She already didn't like Yalini, and this short conversation hadn't done anything to change that. "We're going to stop the races because of the wind. I'm sorry you didn't get more of a show." She bared her teeth at Yalini in what she hoped looked like a smile.

Definitely too close to the prince, almost like a jealous woman, Yalini thought. "Oh, I'm sorry I didn't get to see you race," the princess said. "I'm sure it's a...spectacle."

Lamprophyre's non-smile tightened. Yalini's thoughts about her were not flattering. How dare the woman compare her to a flying cow? "It is," she said, hanging on to politeness with all twelve claws.

"Well, if it's too difficult, I suppose there's nothing for it," Yalini said with an air of complacent unconcern. *Don't know what Father was so worried about, these dragons are practically tame,* she thought.

That was enough. "Difficult isn't the issue," Lamprophyre snapped, "and if you're so interested, I don't see why I shouldn't oblige you."

"Lamprophyre," Rokshan said, his tone of voice a warning.

"I'll just make one run, Rokshan," Lamprophyre said. She flapped backward, wheeled, and crossed the field to where Porphyry hovered, talking to a handful of humans still in the stands. "Porphyry, will you work the artifact? I'm going to run the course."

"But everyone's gone," Porphyry said.

"It's just to—" Lamprophyre remembered the listening ears in time to keep from saying *show that stone-faced princess what real power looks like*. "We have a visiting dignitary, and I want to show her what dragons are capable of."

Porphyry shrugged. "All right, but only once, because I want to get back and nap."

Lamprophyre flew to the starting point, glancing over her shoulder once at Rokshan and Yalini. The princess still smiled as if this were normal entertainment. Rokshan looked ready to explode, though likely no one but she would recognize that expression, since he was good at putting on a diplomatic face. She stretched, flexed her wings, and crouched, waiting for the signal.

The lights flashed. She pushed off from the ground and was halfway across the field in a single beat. First, the spiraling tower, prone to dizzying a dragon if she wasn't careful. Lamprophyre spun around it to the top, rang the bell that hung there, and swept back to the ground to zigzag through the barriers. She didn't so much as brush up against any of them, and she couldn't help smiling in triumph at her success.

She tore out of the barriers and swung through the parallel bars, reaching from one to the next. Wings couldn't help here; it was all about arm strength, and she was more powerful than a male, with a longer reach. The bars made their own kind of zigzag course, but vertical rather than horizontal, and by the time she reached the top she was breathing heavily but not painfully. She still had plenty of stamina for what she intended next.

She kicked off backwards and let herself fall a short distance before snapping her wings open to catch herself—it would lose her some time, but the show was more important. And she intended to put on a show for Yalini. Curving sharply down, she set a course for the final obstacle.

This one had been Rokshan's idea, and his design, though it had been a clever metalsmith who'd executed it: a giant metal hoop barely big enough for a female dragon to fit through with her wings furled. It took speed and perfect timing to make it through, and Lamprophyre had both. She beat the air to speed up until she was racing along, faster than either Orthoclase or Porphyry. Another smile tugged at her lips. What came next was something no male dragon could do.

As the hoop neared at a sickening speed, she sucked in a deep breath and spat fire at the hoop. The oil coating its surface caught fire immediately, blazing hot and bright and streaming in the wind. It filled the center of the hoop, but that didn't matter; Lamprophyre furled her wings and dove through the fire, letting her momentum carry her through and over the finish line.

She heard distant cheers as she spread her wings and coasted to a stop. Breathing heavily, she turned and flew back to the royal stands, where only Rokshan and Yalini remained. Rokshan still looked as if he was containing his anger, which worried Lamprophyre. She'd thought her stunt would cheer him up at least a little.

Yalini's smile hadn't altered. "Why, that was impressive, ambassador," she said. Her thoughts were oddly cheerful, almost triumphant. *See what they can do, make use of that.* And then, with a certainty that almost made Lamprophyre fall out of the sky, *She's in love with him, don't know how, disgusting.*

"I'm glad you liked it. Rokshan?" Lamprophyre tilted her shoulder in invitation. She felt sick and dizzy and humiliated by the dismissive, horrible tenor of Yalini's thoughts. She wanted Rokshan near and she wanted him far from the princess, far away where Yalini couldn't make any more devastatingly accurate conclusions.

"I have to escort Princess Yalini to her residence," Rokshan said, his voice flat and hard. Lamprophyre listened to his thoughts long enough to know he wasn't angry with her, but with himself. She wasn't sure why, unless it was to do with feeling tricked by the princess.

"Of course," Lamprophyre said. Her thoughts were in a whirl of unanswerable questions. How could Yalini have guessed? Why would anyone believe a dragon could love a human? And, worse, what might Yalini, who Lamprophyre was now certain was her enemy, do with that information?

She turned her back on Rokshan and Yalini and flew to meet Orthoclase, high above the course. "We may have a problem," she told him quietly, though there was no way any human could hear them. "That Fanishkorite princess is plotting something."

Orthoclase peered over her shoulder at the royal stands. "Her? Why would we worry about her? She's not even a king."

A rush of wings heralded Porphyry's approach. "I smell rain in the air. Let's get undercover," he suggested.

"Lamprophyre's worried about that foreign princess," Orthoclase told him.

Porphyry looked in that direction just as Orthoclase had done. "Worried how?"

"Let's fly, and I'll tell you on the way," Lamprophyre said.

But they ended up flying in silence, thanks to the wind stealing their words away. Lamprophyre went over what she'd heard from Yalini's thoughts. The princess thought Rokshan was handsome—well, so did lots of people, because he was, but her thoughts were focused on his good qualities in regard to her intent to marry him. *That* was never going to happen, but the fact that Yalini was still convinced it was possible despite knowing Rokshan and Ekanath were both opposed to the marriage suggested either that Yalini was stupid, or that she had a plan nobody else knew about. And Lamprophyre didn't think Yalini was stupid. So that was one thing to worry about: Yalini had set her sights on Rokshan.

Following hard on that problem was how Yalini had guessed Lamprophyre was in love with Rokshan. The memory of Yalini's dismissive thoughts still made Lamprophyre feel ill, as if Yalini's disgust were something objective that could affect Lamprophyre. She didn't know if Yalini thought Rokshan returned Lamprophyre's affection, but maybe it didn't matter, since Lamprophyre had no idea what Yalini could do with that information.

True, Lamprophyre and Rokshan wanted it kept secret, mainly because it was no one's business but theirs, but even if it became public, what difference would that make? Lamprophyre decided not to dwell on the many possible negative reactions humans might have upon learning of their prince's possibly aberrant desire. There were other concerns that mattered more.

The main concern—well, secondary to her worry about Yalini's intent to marry Rokshan—was what the king of Fanishkor wanted from dragons. Yalini's thoughts revealed that King Damen was worried about dragons, probably worried that they might attack his kingdom given that she'd immediately gone on to think about how tame Lamprophyre and her clutchmates were. So then why would Damen care about making use of dragon capabilities like flying and spitting fire? He had to know dragons wouldn't work with him so long as the specter of the egg theft lay between their peoples, and dragons certainly wouldn't attack Gonjiri for him. True, there were other kingdoms, but the principle was the same.

By the time they reached the warehouses, Lamprophyre wasn't any closer to a conclusion, and she felt a delayed sickness from taking the spiral tower too fast. She descended more slowly than usual and came to a halt in the center of the street. "I need something to settle my stomachs," she said.

"Wait a few beats," Orthoclase said. He disappeared into his warehouse and emerged shortly afterward with a hunk of dusty white talc, which he handed to Lamprophyre. She bit into it, making a face at how the dust powdered her lips and chin, but a few swallows later, she felt better.

"So explain about the princess," Porphyry said. "I thought she must be friendly, since Rokshan brought her to the races."

"She tricked him into an invitation." Lamprophyre finished off the talc and wiped her face. "And she was thinking all sorts of conniving plots. Like how she wants to marry Rokshan."

Orthoclase laughed. "She's going to be a very sad princess if she's pinned her hopes on that outcome."

"What worries me is that she has a plan I don't know about. And if she could trick Rokshan into taking her to the races, who knows if she's got other tricks she might play?" Lamprophyre checked inside Flint's warehouse and, finding it empty, settled inside as the first fat drops of rain spattered the ground and the top of her head.

"Rokshan's not stupid," Porphyry said. "If you warn him it's a possibility, he can defend against it."

Lamprophyre sighed. "I trust him to be careful. But she worries me. She was also thinking about what use Fanishkor might have for dragons. *And*, worst of all—she knows I'm in love with Rokshan."

Porphyry sat up abruptly and smacked his head on the door lintel. "She couldn't. How?"

"I don't know. Apparently I behaved like a jealous woman. But it's supposed to be too absurd a possibility for anyone to guess. Maybe it doesn't really matter, because what can she do with that guess? But I feel so...exposed, maybe. As if she might guess any number of other secrets."

"It would be a scandal if humans knew," Orthoclase said. "And you'd look like a fool, which is bad for all dragons."

Lamprophyre scowled. “I hadn’t considered that. Now I’m more worried than ever.”

The rain was falling harder now, hard enough that she didn’t hear the approach of giant wings. Dolomite’s appearance startled her. She ducked reflexively as he flapped his wings hard to clear them of raindrops and then hurried into his warehouse. “Flying in rain is so uncomfortable,” he said, “but I wasn’t paying attention, and it caught me by surprise.”

“You must be preoccupied not to notice the weather,” Porphyry said. “Any clues as to your secret project?”

Dolomite shook his head. “And don’t go listening for it, because it will be a wonderful surprise,” he warned them.

Lamprophyre eyed Dolomite’s feet. The soles were paler than usual, dusted with a damp white powder that clung to the creases of his feet. He’d either been somewhere very dirty, or he’d been tromping around in stone dust. A quarry, perhaps? She kept her suppositions to herself. Dolomite was usually very bad at keeping secrets, but he’d stayed silent about this one for several days now, and that deserved some consideration.

“We need more information,” she said. “No, not about you, Dolomite.” She quickly filled him in on what she’d learned listening to Yalini’s thoughts. “Which means one or more of us will have to encounter her. And since she’s a princess of a foreign country, it should be the ambassador. At least I’ll have the best excuse to get close to her.”

“But won’t that convince her even more that she’s right about you and Rokshan?” Dolomite asked. He sat on the ground and absently rubbed dust from his feet.

“Maybe, but on the other hand, since she already believes she’s right, it’s not like I have anything to hide. And—” A new thought occurred to her, cheering her. “If I continue to act like a jealous woman, it might fool her into thinking that’s my only reason for approaching her. Wanting her to stay away from Rokshan, I mean. And who knows what else I might get out of her?”

“I hope you’re right,” Porphyry said. “I admit I’m worried about what the Fanishkorite king thinks he might get us to do. Given that you've already turned down an alliance."

Lamprophyre lay down and pillowed her head on her arms. The rain beat down less than a handspan from her nose, making a pleasant pattering sound on the hard-packed ground. "He has no power over us," she said, and suppressed the distant fear that she might be wrong.

CHAPTER TWELVE

Lamprophyre lay with her head propped on her hands and watched Rokshan pace the doorway of the embassy. The rain had passed, leaving the air smelling clean and fresh and damp. "She was just so damn *calculating* about it," Rokshan said. "Every step so very innocent, but they all added up to me being forced to take her to the races. It was infuriating."

"It makes me angry, too," Lamprophyre said. "She's so sly. Like a cat. Only cats are more honest about it."

Rokshan stopped and ran his hands through his hair in a frustrated gesture, tilting his head back to stare at the ceiling. "And I thought she was stupid and decorative. I can't believe she figured out our attachment."

"My attachment to you, you mean. I don't know if she knows you're in love with me."

"Either way. That speaks to a level of perceptiveness that makes me uncomfortable." Rokshan resumed pacing. "I'll just have to stay away from her."

"You can't. I need to listen to her thoughts again, to see if I can work out what the king wants with dragons."

"Lamprophyre, if I spend much more time with her, I'll either kill her or end up forcibly married to her. She's poison."

"Maybe that's why King Damen sent her. Or does he only have one unmarried daughter?"

"I can't remember. I think there are three. It never mattered to me before." Rokshan sat beside her cross-legged and ran his hand over her shoulder and down her side. "All right. At least now that we know she has a plan, we can arrange to meet her only in places where you'll fit. And if that's not possible, I'll see what I can do to worm information out of her."

"I don't want you alone with her if we can help it," Lamprophyre said. "Is there something a woman could do to entrap a man into marrying her?"

Rokshan gave her an ironic look. "She could lie about carrying his child," he said.

Lamprophyre blushed. She'd forgotten that had happened to Rokshan years before. "Other than that."

"I don't know. It used to be that a man being alone with a woman he wasn't related to compromised her honor, to be restored through the two of them marrying, but that's an old-fashioned notion nobody believes in anymore. There's breach of contract...if she got me to promise to marry her somehow, but I can't imagine being stupid enough to agree to anything she proposes. Or she might put herself in a situation where my promising to marry her is the only way to save her. That's complicated even for a mind like hers presumably is, though."

"So you're probably safe."

"Not so safe that I'd let myself be alone with her." Rokshan stroked her scales again. "I wish I was a dragon already. She'd have to stop pestering me then."

Lamprophyre rolled on her side, folding her wings so she wasn't lying on them. "Did you finish reading Evart's notes?"

"I did. Mostly they're about finding the right shape for the artifact, which doesn't help us. But he does refer occasionally to the need for a model. Not a human, but a stone."

"Viveki said he started out wanting to transform stone into other stone." Lamprophyre sat up. "Rokshan, what if he wrote about Sardonyx talking to him?"

Rokshan's hand went still. "Of course. At some point, Sardonyx had to have convinced him to stop what he was doing and turn his skills toward transforming you into a human. It's not in the book we have, which means—"

"That it's essential Viveki get the more recent notes," Lamprophyre concluded. Excitement surged through her. "Even if there's nothing we can use to transform you, those notes might still be valuable."

"I wish we knew where she lives," Rokshan said. "I dislike waiting on her."

"I know. We have to be patient." Lamprophyre settled back down. "I hate being patient."

They both fell silent. Lamprophyre closed her eyes and leaned into Rokshan's hand. The light touch relaxed her. Viveki would return eventually, her greed ensured that, and the other notes would be what they needed.

She heard footsteps approaching across the courtyard and sat up, hoping it was Viveki. But it was only Bhakriya, laden with baskets and roughly woven sacks. The weekly shopping trip for Lamprophyre's human household. "My lady, you're back," the woman said. "There was someone here earlier, asking for you."

"A petitioner?"

Bhakriya shook her head. "She said she had business with you, something you'd commissioned her to do. I told her you were at the races and she could come back later, but she said you should meet her at the river docks at five o'clock this evening."

Lamprophyre and Rokshan exchanged glances. "What did she look like?" Rokshan asked.

"I vaguely remember seeing her before. Young, pretty. Plump and very short. Her hair was long and she wore it loose. I admit I didn't like the look of her, for all she was attractive. She looked at me as if I weren't worth her time."

"Viveki," Lamprophyre said. "I can't believe we missed her."

"I'm more worried that she wants us to meet her," Rokshan said. "It's suspicious."

"Is everything all right, my lady?" Bhakriya asked.

"It's fine. Thank you for the message. Rokshan, what time is it?"

Rokshan fished a round bronze artifact out of his shirt. "Four o'clock. We have some time. Do you want to fly over there now and look for anything strange?"

"I think it's possible Viveki chose that location to give herself an advantage, and if she sees us approaching early, she might disappear." Lamprophyre sighed and settled back down. "We wait."

LAMPROPHYRE RARELY WENT TO THE RIVER DOCKS BECAUSE THEY were so crowded she feared crushing someone, or someone's boat. The docks were a scruff of wooden platforms jutting out into the Green River, nothing fancy or finished, just places for boats to tie up while their owners took care of business in the small shallow-roofed buildings that lined the eastern shore. More boats that were little more than collections of floating planks snugged against the shore or crossed the river to the far side. As sunset approached, those little boats were busier than usual as they took their last few fares across before darkness made the river crossing dangerous.

Lamprophyre circled low above the docks, ignoring the hum of awed or astonished thoughts from below. "I don't see her."

"We can't land close to the docks," Rokshan said. "Too crowded. Why don't you circle once more and then set down south of the docks? That gives Viveki plenty of notice that we're here, and she can come to us."

Lamprophyre nodded and began one more large spiraling pass over the river. Western Tanajital, across the river from the main city, didn't look anything like its big sister. The buildings were shorter, none taller than one story, and they looked dingier, crowded together at random instead of being laid out in the orderly way Lamprophyre now took for granted. Lights were coming on in the tiny houses, but very few of the streets were lit, unlike Tanajital proper where householders were required by law to maintain a light outside their houses. Looking at western Tanajital made Lamprophyre's skin itch as if she needed a bath. It was even less savory than Tanajital's slums.

She descended slowly, looking around in case Viveki suddenly appeared, and landed well south of the last dock. "I'd rather meet her someplace away from people, anyway," she said. "I know no one cares about Evart's research but us, but he was so secretive, I feel there's something furtive about this transaction."

"If he knew about Sardonyx, there *is* something secret," Rokshan said as he climbed down. "Since we don't want to spread that news around."

"But it's not really a secret," Lamprophyre protested. "It's not like it would hurt anyone to know."

"The news that there's an ancient evil dragon in the world intent on destroying humans and their dragon allies would cause a panic," Rokshan said. "You forget how much fear of dragons there is, despite all the work we've done. Keeping this secret while we figure out what to do about it is crucial."

"I suppose, but what if Sardonyx becomes a physical threat, and no one's ready for her?"

Rokshan shrugged. "With Gonjiri on almost a wartime footing because of Fanishkor, and Fanishkor likewise, we're already prepared to meet a threat. And we have all those pyrite weapons. I already believe there might be a day when Sardonyx attacks, and I'm in a position to influence the military to be ready. We just need to keep ahead of her, and that means learning more."

Lamprophyre scanned the shoreline. "I hate that we don't know enough."

"Me too, but we're already doing everything we can." Rokshan put a hand on her shoulder. "And these notes might be important."

Lamprophyre nodded. The motion of men and women going back and forth from ship to shore, of little boats pushing off into the current or heading downstream, kept her attention moving in all directions. A large boat, one with sails, slipped past going south. Its paint was chipped and peeling, but she could tell it would have been vibrant with color when the paint was fresh.

People crowded the side of the boat, staring and pointing at her. She waved. Some of the people waved back and shouted greetings. The boat sent waves to both sides, the water foaming in its wake. The sweet damp scent of the water and the green odor of the grass and plants crushed under her feet prompted her to breathe the smells in deeply. This time of year, the Green River ran low, and more of the banks were exposed, revealing cracked dried mud and the stems of reeds, yellow where the water usually covered them. Lamprophyre settled back on her haunches and sniffed. "Someone's cooking supper."

"I'm sure a lot of people are. Where is Viveki?" Rokshan hadn't settled down, but was pacing the river's edge in front of Lamprophyre.

Movement at right angles to that of the men and women passing from ship to shore caught Lamprophyre's attention. "There she is. Try not to act nervous."

"It might be too late for that," Rokshan said, but he stood beside Lamprophyre in a parade rest position, hands clasped loosely behind his back.

Viveki strode toward them, ignoring everyone else who crossed her path and in some cases forcing them to pull up short to avoid her. She was smiling, not a friendly smile but the smile of a predator. Lamprophyre felt uneasy. Something had changed. Viveki had been confident before, but this looked more like triumph. And since Lamprophyre couldn't think of any reason for Viveki to be triumphant over them, the woman's demeanor made her nervous.

Viveki halted about a dragonlength away. "You got my message," she said. Her wordless thoughts were filled with a satisfaction Lamprophyre found unsettling.

"Yes. I'm sorry we missed you. This must be an inconvenience," Lamprophyre said. She hoped politeness would temper whatever plot Viveki had in mind for squeezing more money out of the embassy.

"I don't mind. This is better." Viveki glanced around as if looking for listeners. "Did you bring my money?"

"Did you bring the notes?" Rokshan said, walking forward.

Viveki held up a hand and waggled it at him in a warning manner. "Not so fast. I think we should talk first."

Lamprophyre's eyes narrowed. So it was going to be extortion, after all. "If it's the right book, we agreed on a price already."

Viveki tilted her head like a bird and examined Lamprophyre closely. "It's amazing. There's no trace," she said. *No trace*, her thoughts echoed.

"No trace of what?"

Viveki's smile broadened. "Of the transformation."

Lamprophyre's mouth fell open. Beneath her surprise, her mind raced. Of course. Viveki had read the notes. They should have guessed she would. And if Evart hadn't been cautious—and why would he be, writing in his own book?—he would have written down all the details of his plan. And now Viveki knew he'd wanted to turn Lamprophyre human. But he couldn't have written that it had been successful, not if the book hadn't been on him at his death, so how could she know it had worked?

"I don't know what you're talking about," she said, as firmly as she could manage.

Viveki let out a short, barking *hah* of a laugh. "You said the artifact worked. I know what he intended it to do. You were transformed into a human." The amusement left her face. "A human who looked exactly like me. I'll never forgive him for that obscenity."

Rokshan took another couple of steps toward her. "She's clearly not human. You're delusional."

Viveki's face transformed into a terrible, vicious scowl. "You'd be wise not to antagonize me, your highness," she said. "I'm guessing this isn't information you want public. Piss me off, and I'll spread it far and wide."

"And why should we care?" Lamprophyre said. It was getting harder to hold onto her calm.

Viveki transferred her scowl to Lamprophyre. "You're not stupid. You know if it's public knowledge that a dragon can be turned into a human, there are people who will want to figure out how. There are lots of things you can do to a human that a dragon's invulnerable to. This knowledge is a danger to you, dragon, and if you know what's good for you, you'll do as I say."

"Meaning blackmail."

Viveki smiled. "I knew you weren't stupid. I don't suppose you want to tell me how you were turned back? Did the transformation not last?"

"Like we'd tell you anything," Rokshan said.

Viveki made a *tsk tsk* sound. "Remember, be polite. You don't know what might set me off."

"She's right," Lamprophyre told Rokshan, wishing he could hear her thoughts. "All right, Viveki, what do you want?"

"The rest of those five vahas, for a start," Viveki said.

"That was in exchange for the notes. Hand it over, and I'll give you your money," Rokshan said.

"I'm not stupid, either," Viveki snarled. "Like I'd give you my evidence. Now the money is to buy my silence."

Rokshan looked at Lamprophyre, his eyes wide. She heard him think *We have to get those notes away from her, wherever they are*. She agreed, but she had no idea how. She couldn't attack a human in full sight of everyone at the docks. It was unlikely she had anything she could offer in exchange. Her heart burned with fury at this petty little blackmailer, this greedy idiot who was going to ruin Rokshan's chance at transformation and might lose them valuable information about their enemy.

"Give her the money, Rokshan," she said. Rokshan's face went stony, but he handed over four square gold coins. "Now, here's our problem, Viveki," she said. "We want those notes. You want more money, I'm sure. What is it going to take to get you to hand them over?"

She's mine, Viveki thought, angering Lamprophyre so much she almost forgot to be civilized. "Oh, I don't know," she said. "Seems like you dragons are wealthy enough to afford quite a lot. At least, that's what it says here."

"There's no such thing as a dragon hoard, whatever Evart wrote," Lamprophyre said. "We're not a bottomless source of money."

"Oh, Evart was mad at the end," Viveki said. "Convinced he was in secret mental communication with some adept. Even I know that's impossible. So what if dragons don't have hoards? You mine stone, don't you? *Expensive* stone. I think you can get me as much money as I want."

Lamprophyre heard Rokshan think *let me handle this*. "You've never done this before, have you?" he said, sounding bored and dismissive. "Blackmailers are never successful in the long run. Their greed overcomes them, and they push their victims too hard. In the end, either the victim stops caring about having their secret revealed, or they turn on the blackmailer. So you're better off taking our offer. Name your price, and we'll exchange it for the notes."

"Nice try, your highness," Viveki said. "I'll take my chances. And don't think killing me will solve anything. I've left the notes, along with the details of what's in them, in a place where they'll come out if I die." *She'll believe that, can't afford to call my bluff*, she thought.

Lamprophyre couldn't take it any longer. "Interesting you mention dying," she said, advancing on Viveki. "You should be afraid of what I might do to you. Death could be a release."

Viveki looked up at her without a trace of fear. "Dragons don't kill humans," she said, "and they definitely don't kill humans where there are all...these...witnesses." She gestured behind her. Lamprophyre involuntarily followed the line of her hand. Stones, but there were a lot of people watching! She ground her teeth in frustration.

"I think you're bluffing," Rokshan said abruptly. "I don't think you've done anything more clever with those notes than putting them under your mattress."

"Shut up, your highness," Viveki snarled. *Safe where they won't find them, safe in the hole,* she thought.

That was interesting, but it wasn't enough, and Lamprophyre couldn't exactly ask 'what hole?' "No, he's right," she said. "You're just a petty blackmailer who thinks she has an advantage. You didn't hide them at all."

I'm going to enjoy destroying these two, Viveki thought, *maybe I should make copies, get ready to spread it around.* "Go ahead and taunt," she said aloud. "It will just incline me more toward ruining you."

Lamprophyre, frustrated, exchanged glances with Rokshan. This was not the time to keep pushing in the hope Viveki would think the location of the notes. "Fine," she said, pretending to be beaten. "What do you want?"

"Another five vahas." Viveki's smile was triumphant. "After that, we'll see. And don't think about following me to see where I've put the notes. It's nowhere I ever go." *See her coming from a mile off, easy to mislead,* she thought.

"We don't have five more vahas on us," Rokshan said. "You'll have to come to the embassy in three days."

"I don't like that plan," Viveki said. "I think *you* should come to *me*. At the plaza. It's nice and public, just in case you have any bright ideas about attacking me."

"Three days, then, at the plaza. In the morning," Lamprophyre said. She crouched to let Rokshan climb up. "But you're making a mistake."

"My belt pouch says otherwise," Viveki said. She waved goodbye just as if they were friends. Lamprophyre scowled and leaped into the sky.

They flew in silence for a few beats before Lamprophyre said, "I hope you're coming up with a plan. I can't see past wanting to disembowel her."

"That would be deeply satisfying," Rokshan said. "The little bitch. I can't help thinking we should have known this would happen."

"Maybe. Most people aren't as greedy and amoral as she is."

"Did she think the location of the notes?"

"No. It was worth a try, though. Good idea." Lamprophyre rose higher above the city. "I need to fly for a bit, if you don't mind. We won't go high."

"I feel the same. Let's circle the city a couple of times. Maybe that will clear our heads." Rokshan leaned forward to lie across her neck. "Then I need to return to the palace. I'm sorry I can't eat with you tonight."

Lamprophyre nodded. She was hungry, but in a distant way, her hunger pushed aside by her anger and frustration. The land slipped away beneath her, winter-pale but with the outlines of spring's tilled fields still visible. Ahead, the molten orb of the sun dipped the bottom of its curve beneath the horizon. It was an extraordinary sight that went a long way toward calming her.

There didn't seem to be anything to say. Lamprophyre reviewed that interaction in her head and wished she'd thought of something clever that would stop Viveki. The stupid girl had no idea what she had stepped into. "Maybe we should let her talk," she said.

"What? You mean Viveki?"

"Yes. Those notes could be crucial, and what are the odds anyone else will figure out a transformation artifact? Her threat could be meaningless."

"I agree," Rokshan said, "but you forget what kind of person we're dealing with. I'm more concerned that she might destroy the notes if we push her too far, just to be vindictive."

"I hadn't thought of that. Now I'm worried."

"Don't. She won't go to that extreme unless she thinks she can hurt us more by destroying her evidence than she can by blackmailing us." Rokshan ran a hand down the side of her neck. "And I think I have an idea of how to deal with her without losing the notes."

"You do? What is it?"

"I'm still figuring it out. I'll tell you when I'm prepared to act."

Lamprophyre didn't like that idea, but she knew Rokshan preferred not to discuss his plans when they were still forming. "All right," she said, "but if there's any chance, in your plan, of me scaring the Stones out of that woman, I want in."

"I promise to make it a priority," Rokshan said.

CHAPTER THIRTEEN

Lamprophyre left Rokshan outside the palace and flew back to the embassy. Her thoughts whirled so much, going from Viveki to Yalini to Evart and around again, her head had begun to ache, a rarity for a dragon. She decided on an early supper and an early bedtime, assuming the people of Tanajital complied with that wish. She didn't regret giving Depik permission to feed the hungry, but on days like this, she wished their experiment hadn't been quite so successful.

The soup kettle smelled delicious already when she arrived, well before the hour at which supper was served. "Depik?" she called out.

Depik appeared from within the kitchen. "Yes, my lady?"

"When will supper be ready? I'd like to eat as soon as possible so I can have an early night."

"Not a problem, my lady, I'll have it out to you soon."

Rather than settle in the dining pavilion, Lamprophyre went into the embassy and lay down. The idea of crossing the courtyard after her meal when it was full of humans made her even more tired. She rested her head on her arms and closed her eyes. Hopefully, this headache would go away soon.

With her eyes closed, the sounds of the embassy and the neighborhood were louder and more coherent. Children raced through the nearby streets, shouting, but at enough of a distance that the noise didn't make her head ache more. More noise, this of hundreds of people going home to their suppers, washed over her like the wake of the boat she'd waved at. She inhaled the smell of soup and the spicier scent of curried lamb. If that was what Depik had made for her supper, he'd picked the perfect time to prepare her favorite meal.

Despite her worries, tension ebbed from her back and shoulders. There was nothing she could do about any of her problems now, so why not enjoy a good meal and a night's rest? It was unfortunate Rokshan couldn't have stayed to read to her, which would have made the evening perfect, but he had military obligations that couldn't wait. Well, it was still going to be a lovely night.

"Supper, my lady," Depik said. He pushed the big cauldron on its trolley in front of her as she sat up. The smell of lamb in yellow soup filled her nostrils and made her salivate. Depik removed a large cloth he'd had draped over his shoulder and presented it to her. "And a napkin. This is a messy meal."

"I'm not a sloppy eater, Depik," Lamprophyre said with a smile. "But I appreciate your concern for my good manners."

"It's important you display the kind of manners others expect of an ambassador," Depik said with a bow.

"I know. I promise to use the napkin." Lamprophyre spread the cloth over her chest and the floor beside her, picked up the cauldron, and drank down a healthy portion of yellow soup, sweet and savory all at once. It had become her favorite human food while she was in her human body, and she'd been delighted to learn it could be adapted for dragons to digest. Some of it slopped over the side of her mouth, dripping onto the napkin, and she set the cauldron down to Depik's hearty laughter.

"You were right," she said, feeling embarrassed.

"It happens to all of us, my lady," Depik said, and with another bow left the embassy.

Lamprophyre ate the rest of her meal a little more slowly. There were no more spills, but she had to admit she was grateful for the cloth to wipe her mouth when she was finished. She tucked it into the empty cauldron and pushed the trolley outside for Depik to retrieve. The courtyard had filled up while she was eating, and the line of people waiting for soup stretched across it all the way to the street. Some nights were like that.

She waved to Darsha, who already had her soup and was standing at the far side of the courtyard, eating as tidily as she did everything else. It occurred to Lamprophyre she'd never seen Darsha wait in line for soup. She couldn't imagine the graceful prostitute standing in line for anything.

Her head still hurt, but it was bearable. She backed up deeper into the embassy hall and curled in on herself, spreading her wings to cover most of her body and snugging her tail close to her stomach. The night was comfortably cool, the voice of the city had subsided to a dull hum, the people in the courtyard were too busy eating to talk, and Lamprophyre found her earlier fears and concerns had subsided. She closed her eyes and waited for sleep to come.

She'd almost drifted off when someone cleared their throat, almost in her ear. Startled, her head shot up, and she blinked both sets of eyelids open. "What—" she began, then stopped speaking when she realized the person in front of her was a stranger. A stranger in Fanishkorite livery.

"My lady ambassador," the man said. He bowed, a complicated maneuver Lamprophyre thought looked silly. "I apologize if I interrupted your sleep, but I bring a message from my lady ambassador Chaaksha."

All Lamprophyre's peace of mind deserted her immediately. "A message?" she said. "She can't think I've changed my mind." It had been a few days, but not nearly long enough for Lamprophyre to forget what they'd discussed, even if she wasn't a dragon with an exceptional memory.

The man bowed again. "I'm not privy to my lady's thoughts," he said. "I am to give you this." He held out a small square of paper. Lamprophyre took it gingerly between two claws, conscious of how easily she could tear it. It turned out to be a larger, rectangular paper folded in half. Glancing warily at the messenger, Lamprophyre took it to her magnifying lens and examined it. The writing was small, the lighting poor, but Lamprophyre's eyes were still good enough to make it out.

"A party?" she said. "This is an invitation to a party?"

"Even so, my lady," the man said. "Tomorrow night at the estate of Acharya."

Lamprophyre had never heard of it. She listened to the man's thoughts, hoping to regain some balance, but he was one of those whose thoughts echoed his words almost completely, and the only thing she heard aside from what he'd just told her was a sense of placidity and complete nonchalance at facing a dragon. Where Chaaksha had found a Fanishkorite unafraid of dragons, Lamprophyre didn't know, but he was a curiosity.

"You're not afraid of me," she said on impulse.

The man bowed a third time. "Dragons are intelligent creatures not prone to casual violence," he said, "and I see no reason to fear you."

"That's not a common reaction for someone from your country. Dragons haven't lived in Fanishkor for humans to become accustomed to them."

The man smiled, an unexpectedly humorous expression. "I grew up hearing stories of dragons, all of which portrayed your people in a very negative light. I confess to being somewhat contrarian, and it seemed to me that it was impossible for *all* dragons to be as evil as the stories said. In fact, I felt sorry for dragons being so vilified. So when humanity regained contact with your people, I felt no fear."

"That's interesting. I wish everyone was as sensible as you. What's your name?"

"Tarakh, my lady."

"Tarakh. It's nice to meet you." Lamprophyre glanced at the invitation in her hand. She had no idea what Chaaksha had in mind, but she was certain Yalini was behind whatever it was. Which meant Lamprophyre couldn't turn down this invitation even if she wanted to, which she sort of did. "Will you convey my thanks to Ambassador Chaaksha, and tell her I'll be pleased to attend?"

"I would be happy to, my lady. Enjoy the rest of your evening." Tarakh bowed again—really, it was amazing how he managed to make each bow seem like no one had ever thought of bowing before—and walked away.

Lamprophyre tucked the invitation between the pages of a book so it wouldn't get lost and settled down again. How fortunate that attending a party no longer meant choosing an elaborate gown and wearing sandals that rubbed one's feet until it nearly drove one mad. She'd be willing to bet Rokshan had received an invitation as well. This could be the perfect opportunity to find out what Yalini's plan was. It would mean looking foolish, like a jealous woman, but Lamprophyre was willing to endure that if it meant gaining the upper hand.

AT SUNSET THE NEXT EVENING, LAMPROPHYRE DESCENDED ONTO the plains south of the city and furled her wings neatly. The estate of the wealthy landholder Acharya spanned hundreds, maybe thousands of dragonlengths, most of the land made up of fields that at this time of year lay fallow. Lamprophyre had flown over it many times without knowing it was anything more than ordinary fields. But Rokshan had told her, earlier that day when they'd made their plans, that much of the property surrounding Tanajital was owned by wealthy men and women, and those landholders alternated living on their estates and living in mansions in Tanajital.

"I don't know anything about Acharya," Rokshan had said, "other than that he's wealthy, of course, and his wife is from Fanishkor. Which is probably why he's provided Chaaksha with a place to host her party."

"So he's probably not in on her plan, whatever it is," Lamprophyre had said.

"No, that's unlikely. But we should be polite to him anyway."

Now Lamprophyre sat and surveyed the estate, or what she thought was the estate. Rokshan had been uncharacteristically vague on the topic. Sometimes he talked as if the estate were the vast fields spread out in all directions, and other times he seemed to suggest the large house was the estate. Lamprophyre hated being confused and hated even more being at a disadvantage. So she watched, and drew conclusions, and waited for the right moment to advance.

The house was much larger than any she'd seen in Tanajital, though not as big as the palace. Lights blazed at every window, making it look, if she squinted, like it was on fire. More lights, these torches attached to poles stuck into the ground, lined a path that led from beside where she sat to the house. The path was of packed earth that smelled cool and loamy from yesterday's rain. It was barely wide enough to fit her if she walked on it, which she didn't intend to do, but it would be more comfortable than the squishy ground she currently sat on.

Ahead, two litters approached the house, neither of them distinguished in any way. Lamprophyre glanced behind her and saw another litter coming toward her. She didn't feel like encountering humans yet, so she leaped into the air and flew toward the house, quickly passing the litters and landing in the semicircular courtyard centered on the house's front door.

The door opened, and a man in servant's clothes, a long-sleeved white shirt and white trousers, stepped out. He saw Lamprophyre and visibly startled. "I, um, excuse me, my lady," he said.

Lamprophyre suddenly wondered how she was going to fit into the house. Surely Chaaksha wouldn't have invited her if there wasn't room for her? "I was invited," she blurted out, and immediately felt stupid.

"We are expecting you," the man said, regaining his calm. "If you would care to, um, I suppose you could walk, or even fly, to the rear of the house?"

"Thank you," Lamprophyre said, clinging to her dignity. Conscious of how awkward she looked when she walked, she took a few steps back and leapt into the air, hoping she hadn't knocked the poor man over with the draft from her wings.

She rose over the house's roofs, dark blue slate that had come from a very long way off and was no doubt a sign of the owner's wealth, and hovered for a moment, astonished at what she saw. Bright green grass cut very short and even spread out behind the house, its dimensions marked off by more torches on poles. Vivid canopies in Fanishkorite red dotted the grass, making it look like someone had dripped blood everywhere. Humans holding wine glasses moved between the canvases or stood beneath them. There weren't many people there yet, certainly not enough to prevent Lamprophyre from hearing individual thoughts, but there was enough space that if it was entirely filled, that wouldn't last long.

Unfortunately, though the space was large, the placement of the canopies meant there weren't any places big enough for a dragon to land safely. Lamprophyre flew to one side and alit just outside the torchlit area. She heard gasps and unspoken exclamations, but no one screamed or threw things, and she was used to being a wonder.

Carefully, she walked forward with her wings furled again. "Good evening," she said. "This is a beautiful place, isn't it? I've never seen any of these estates except from far above."

Silence greeted her. She listened to their thoughts, but heard only amazement and curiosity, nothing that would guide her in what to say or do next. She didn't see Chaaksha or Yalini, and Rokshan hadn't arrived yet. Not attending together was part of the plan.

She smiled politely at the humans and continued to move forward until she'd crossed the grassy sward and had reached the far side. There was a slightly wider space between two red canopies, and she settled there to wait. Usually at diplomatic functions similar to this, people came to her. This was likely no different. In any case, it couldn't hurt for her to stay put so she didn't accidentally hit anyone with her tail.

For a hundred beats, she wondered if she'd made a mistake. No one approached her. No one paid her any attention. She might as well have been part of the décor, however much her coloring clashed with Fanishkorite red and white. Nobody had thought to provide refreshment for a dragon, which irritated her, and she was thirsty and bored and thought about leaving.

She became aware of thoughts focused on her: *really big, how can she even fly?* and *what to say to a dragon*. They were hard to hear, and Lamprophyre realized the field was more crowded than before. She dragged her attention away from the crowd and turned it on the two people approaching her. One of them was the messenger, Tarakh. She didn't know his companion, but she was dressed very finely in a gown of unfamiliar design. Lamprophyre guessed it was Fanishkorite fashion. She thanked her human experience with gowns for the knowledge.

"My lady ambassador, may I present Oresa," Tarakh said with one of his complicated bows. "Oresa is a member of the diplomatic party, attached to King Damen's court. She expressed an interest in being introduced to you." He didn't touch Oresa, but the tone of his thoughts and the sound of his voice when he said her name told Lamprophyre he had very affectionate, even loving feelings for the woman.

"It's a pleasure meeting a dragon," Oresa said. She didn't bow, but Lamprophyre could still hear snatches of her thoughts over the noise of the crowd and concluded it wasn't an insult, but rather an expression of Oresa thinking of them as equals. Whether that was true or not, Lamprophyre didn't know, but she wasn't so stuffy as to insist on people bowing to her all the time.

Lamprophyre extended a hand. She would see how committed to egalitarianism this woman actually was. "It's good to meet you, Oresa. I enjoy getting to know humans of all nationalities."

Oresa took Lamprophyre's hand with no hesitation and only the briefest thought of *swallows it up*. Lamprophyre held her hand for a beat and then released her. "What does it mean that you're attached to King Damen's court?"

"I'm a lady in waiting to the queen," Oresa said. "That means I am her companion and I assist her in dressing and in choosing her jewels. I and the other ladies join her when she attends social functions and pay calls with her."

Lamprophyre understood about half of that, but she could guess at the meaning of the other half. "So are you her representative with this diplomatic party?"

Tarakh cleared his throat. "Queen Ipsetia requested that Oresa travel with Ambassador Chaaksha to experience Gonjirian culture and describe it to her on her return."

Light dawned. "Oh, you're—" She caught herself before she blurted out the word *spy*. "You're interested in what Gonjiri is like. I find it fascinating, myself. I especially like paraveti tangal. Do you have that in Fanishkor?"

"Some of the most famous tangal performers are from Fanishkor," Oresa said. "But I hope to attend a performance here. Gonjiri must have different interpretations of certain roles."

The noise of so many thoughts had become loud enough to force Lamprophyre to stop listening to Oresa's. That was unfortunate, because a spy would definitely have interesting and potentially useful thoughts. "I always feel a little at a disadvantage in a tangal performance," she said. "So much of it depends on a shared cultural background I just don't have. But there are many that make sense even to dragons."

"I understand dragons enjoy poetry," Oresa said. "Forgive me, but that seems so odd. One thinks of poetry as a peculiarly human pursuit."

"It's not so odd if you know dragons taught humans language, centuries ago." Lamprophyre cast her gaze quickly over the assembled humans. She still didn't see Chaaksha or Yalini, and Rokshan wasn't anywhere close, though she could feel him approaching. "Poetry is older than the Cataclysm, so there's no reason dragons shouldn't enjoy it."

"I see. I meant no offense."

"I know. It's all right. Rational people don't take offense where none is intended." That was one of Hyaloclast's favorite sayings, and Lamprophyre liked it, despite thinking, after her months spent among humans, it wasn't strictly true.

She returned her attention to Oresa and Tarakh. "Dragons also love art. We draw, and we sculpt, though we'd never heard of paint before coming to Tanajital, and humans have dozens more colors of chalk than we'd ever seen."

"I would love to see dragon art. How extraordinary," Oresa said.

"Oh, I'm sure everything dragons do is extraordinary," said a new voice, one that made Lamprophyre's heart sink. She'd thought she was paying close attention to the crowd, but still Yalini had snuck up on her. And Rokshan wasn't here yet.

"Your highness, good evening," she said. "Do I have you to thank for the invitation?"

"No, that was Chaaksha's idea, but I'm glad to see you," Yalini said. "Oresa, thank you for entertaining our guest. Tarakh, perhaps you might find the ambassador something to drink?"

At the clear dismissal, Oresa and Tarakh bowed to Yalini and walked away. Lamprophyre hoped Tarakh would find her water and not wine. She didn't like the taste of alcohol any better after her time in a human body.

"Thank you, that was thoughtful," she said, hoping to buy herself time. She tried listening to Yalini's thoughts and caught a few snatches, nothing very coherent. What she needed was Rokshan to talk to Yalini while she listened in, but he wasn't there and she'd have to do her best on her own.

"It's a hostess's duty to see to the comfort of her guests," Yalini said. She held a wide-mouthed glass filled halfway with a rosy pink liquid, but didn't take a drink.

"So is this your party, then?" Lamprophyre asked. "I thought the invitation came from Chaaksha."

"It did, but the idea for the party was mine." Yalini gestured with the hand holding the glass, a circling motion meant to encompass the entire grassy area. "My father would like to demonstrate that Fanishkor means Gonjiri no harm. Much like how dragons taught Tanajital not to fear them, I'm sure."

"I know I'd prefer Fanishkor not to be an enemy," Lamprophyre said.

Yalini shrugged. "It suits me to be my father's hand in this. But really, I'm not interested in politics. My desires are more focused."

Lamprophyre's heart beat faster. She knew what Yalini would say, didn't need to hear her thoughts to know it, but she asked anyway. "And what is it you want?"

Yalini met her gaze directly for the first time since joining the conversation. "I intend to marry Prince Rokshan, of course."

CHAPTER FOURTEEN

A dozen different responses sprang to Lamprophyre's mind. In the silence that followed Yalini's statement, the sound of the party, of its many mingled conversations, seemed louder. Someone laughed, a shrill sound like the bleat of a donkey. Yalini continued to watch Lamprophyre. *See what she says*, the princess thought, one clear phrase among the vast muddle of thoughts surrounding them.

"The king turned down Fanishkor's request for a dynastic marriage," she said. A nice leading statement that should get Yalini talking.

"I don't think that should be the only reason to support a marriage between myself and the prince," Yalini said. "He's intelligent, well-spoken, charming, handsome...it makes perfect sense that *any* woman might fall in love with him."

She gave Lamprophyre a meaningful look. Lamprophyre managed not to blush, though she didn't think a blush would be visible in the flickering torchlight. Well, she'd wanted Yalini to open up. "It does make sense," she said, "and he's had many women interested in him. But, at the risk of sounding rude, why should he single you out?"

Yalini smiled and raised her glass to Lamprophyre, saluting her.

"I shouldn't elaborate. I dislike talking about myself. But I'm of his own station, I'm well-educated and well-spoken, and at the risk of sounding vain, I'm quite lovely. He could hardly expect to do better."

Time for some carefully crafted jealousy. "That may be true, but it's not as if you're the only intelligent, beautiful woman in the world. Rokshan can afford to look for more than that. Compatibility of spirit, generosity, kindness—"

"Spoken like a true friend," Yalini said, sounding not at all insulted. To Lamprophyre's dismay, she didn't hear any secret anger. "But friendship isn't enough to build a lasting relationship on."

"Of course it is," Lamprophyre replied, forgetting that her jealousy was supposed to be faked. "Friendship matters more than anything." In the background, she was aware Rokshan was approaching, and she mentally urged him to move faster.

Yalini laughed. "I'm sure you believe that," she said, laying a confiding hand on Lamprophyre's arm. "But surely you see there's no hope for you."

Her sudden frankness startled Lamprophyre. "I don't know what you mean."

"Oh, I think you do. Compatibility of body is even more important than compatibility of spirit, you know." She laughed again. "I feel sorry for you, I really do. But it's absurd, a dragon falling in love with a human. You have to know that."

Anger flowered within Lamprophyre. Yalini's patronizing tone, and the whispers of thought that said *disgusting* and *could never work, how aberrant* made her wish she could reveal the truth to the arrogant princess. "I don't know what you're talking about," she said haughtily, drawing herself up to her full height. "Rokshan is my best friend, which is why I know you don't have a chance."

"We'll see." Yalini sipped her drink. "I think he's sensible enough to see where his future lies." She nodded to Lamprophyre and turned away.

Lamprophyre drew in a deep breath and let it out slowly, refraining from trying to blow another smoke ring. She'd established herself as an unstable, soppy female pining after someone she couldn't have. Time for Rokshan to see what he could learn.

She enjoyed the sense of her pair-bond strengthening as Rokshan neared. Really, Yalini didn't know how pitiful her words were. Though of course she could have no idea that Rokshan was already Lamprophyre's mate.

She saw Tarakh headed in her direction carrying a wide-mouthed vase almost too big for him to manage. "My lady ambassador," he said when he was close enough to be heard over the crowd, "I hope this is satisfactory."

Lamprophyre took the vase from him. It was of delicate porcelain and had purple flowers with long green stems painted on it. She sniffed its contents: the sharp scent of alcohol tingled her nose. Concealing her disappointment, she said, "Thank you, Tarakh."

"I forgot to ask if dragons drink wine," Tarakh said, "so I served you according to your station. If you'd prefer something else, please let me know."

"I normally drink water, yes," Lamprophyre said, "but wine is what they serve at diplomatic events, so that's acceptable too." She sipped the wine, which was strong and fruity and burned her throat a little. It wasn't terrible. She took a larger drink. Briefly she wondered if dragons could get drunk, then decided this was not the time or place to figure that out.

"It's my pleasure," Tarakh said. "Why don't you mingle with the crowd?"

"I'm a little nervous of trampling someone." The drink was growing on her, even the taste of the alcohol.

"They know to stay out of your way, surely?"

Lamprophyre eyed Tarakh. "You seem eager to have me participate."

Tarakh bowed. "I find you interesting, and I think other people will, too. And it seems dull for you to sit in this corner all evening."

The sense of a burning brand warming her skin became intense. Lamprophyre looked in the direction of the house and saw Rokshan emerge from the door. At some point, she'd need to be with him, as part of their plan, and how much better if he didn't have to manufacture a reason to join her in her seclusion? "Tarakh, those are some excellent points," she said. "I think I will...mingle, you said?"

Tarakh smiled. "I hope you have a pleasant evening, my lady."

She waited for him to walk away before taking a few steps. He'd been right; people saw her coming and made way for her, what little she could hear of their thoughts indicating they didn't see it as an imposition. She kept her tail well elevated and her wings furled, anyway.

She deliberately didn't seek Rokshan out immediately, but she kept moving steadily in his direction. He was talking to people she didn't know, not Chaaksha or Yalini, so she slowed her progress. She wanted him to be well into conversation with Yalini when she interrupted.

Besides, the conversations she was having were as interesting as Tarakh had suggested. Humans were fascinating when you got to know them. Lamprophyre was sure many of the conversations that interested her would be considered dull by other humans, but to her, talk of land grants and farming and the endless permutations of human families were all new and intriguing.

She held up her end of the conversations by telling stories of her clutch and the other dragons. Some people wanted to talk about the races, and she explained how they'd built the race course and how the timing artifact worked, though she didn't know as much about the latter. To her amusement, some men and women wanted to know more about her clutchmates as if they were famous. Well, they probably were. It was just funny to hear Porphyry, for example, referred to as if he were some human prince whose behavior and dress were considered public property.

Finally, she looked around and saw Rokshan talking with Yalini, and a jolt of excitement ran through her. She excused herself and made her way through the crowds with greater purpose, not caring if Yalini saw her. That was the whole point.

Yalini and Rokshan fell silent when she arrived. "Rokshan," Lamprophyre said, "I didn't know you were here."

"You seemed busy with your new friends," Rokshan said. "Yalini and I were talking about duty. And honor."

Lamprophyre tried listening to Yalini's thoughts, but they were near the center of the crowd, and it was all one great cacophony. "That's heavy conversation for a party," she said.

"Not at all," Yalini said. "When two people share an interest, talking about it is never a hardship."

"You've never talked like that with me, Rokshan," Lamprophyre pouted. She hated herself a little for the pretense. Dragons were too civilized to pout.

"You aren't interested in such topics, Lamprophyre," Rokshan said. He sounded bored, and he wouldn't meet her eyes, and his body was turned toward Yalini rather than her. Lamprophyre was impressed at how well he pretended. "Your highness, I can't say I'm convinced, but you make some interesting points."

"You're too rational not to come to the right conclusion," Yalini said with a smile. "I hope we can speak again soon, but I should attend to my guests now."

"Of course," Rokshan said with a bow, one not nearly so complicated as Tarakh's. Yalini nodded to Lamprophyre, a perfunctory gesture, and walked away.

When she was out of earshot, Rokshan said quietly, "We'll talk later. It's not something I want to risk being overheard."

That roused Lamprophyre's curiosity to painful heights, but she said, "Understood." In a slightly louder voice, she said, "You were talking to that princess for a long time. What did you have to talk about that was so interesting?"

"Just things," Rokshan said, sounding bored again. "I don't know why you care. I don't pester you about your friends."

Lamprophyre let out a loud harrumph and half-turned away from Rokshan. "I don't see why you won't tell me, unless you're ashamed."

"I'd rather not have this discussion here, if you don't mind,"

Rokshan shot back. "I'm going to have another glass of wine, unless you want to criticize that, too?"

Pretending was fun. "Do what you like," Lamprophyre said, trying to convey wounded pride in that short sentence.

Rokshan walked away. Lamprophyre watched him go, hoping she looked like she was pining. She didn't know what that looked like, but it was worth trying for the sake of the ruse. Then she turned away and struck up a conversation with someone who looked surprised at being addressed so abruptly by someone tall and blue. He was boring, but Lamprophyre didn't care; all that mattered now was convincing Yalini that she and Rokshan had had a fight. And, more importantly, that Rokshan's feelings for Lamprophyre were not romantic.

She talked to a few more people before deciding she'd had enough pretending for one night. Remembering her manners, she found Chaaksha in the crowd and made a polite half-bow, all she could manage without her tail getting in the way. "Ambassador," she said, "thank you for the invitation."

"Thank you for accepting," Chaaksha said, returning the bow. "I suppose it's too much to hope that dragons have changed their mind about an alliance?"

"As I said, that's not up to me. But I have hope for the future."

Chaaksha nodded. "Not a terrible hope."

"Will you be in Tanajital much longer?"

"Another week or so." Chaaksha, Lamprophyre noticed, was the only human without a wine glass who wasn't a servant. She wished she knew if that meant something.

"Then maybe we'll see each other again. I have to leave now, but again, thank you for your hospitality." Lamprophyre bowed once more, crossed to the edge of the grassy area carefully, and spread her wings to leap into the night sky. She didn't look for Rokshan.

She flew toward Tanajital, enjoying how the night air and the darkness wrapped around her. After only a few beats, she set down beside the road and waited. In the distance, Tanajital was a fuzzy blob on the horizon, lit by lanterns and a few white magic lights.

There was no moon, and the Green River was invisible to her left. If not for the prickly dry grass, she might have felt herself deep in the midnight sky, comfortably alone in the world.

Lamprophyre tilted her head back and surveyed the sky. She knew many human constellations now, thanks to a book Dharan had loaned her, but she still had difficulty identifying them in the sky. Some of them were so strange, like the Dragon, which was a cluster of stars that made a picture with no legs or tail. Humans had the oddest ideas.

A few hundred beats later, she felt the warm sensation of a burning brand and saw a gleam of light approaching from the direction of Acharya's estate. She turned to face the person and waited in silence. Presently, the light vanished, and Rokshan became visible. He hurried to her side and climbed up into the notch. "Let's go," he said.

She leaped into the sky, beating the air with her enormous wings, and aimed at the fuzzy blob of Tanajital. Flying at night could be dangerous, not as dangerous as storm flying, but still a hazard, but they weren't going far. "What did she say?" she asked.

Rokshan was silent for a moment. "She said more than I think she intended," he finally said, "unless she's a lot more clever than I judge, and I hope by Jiwanyil that's not the case, because we could be in real trouble if it is."

Lamprophyre shuddered. "That sounds dire."

"I can't repeat the entire conversation. I don't have your memory. But the highlights were, first, that she is dead set on marrying me—"

"She said something like that to me, too. Warning me off."

"So did it work? She thinks you're pining after me?"

Lamprophyre altered her course to take them over the river, as a landmark. "She actually came out and told me she knew how I felt about you. Said I was pathetic, more or less."

Rokshan let out a hiss of irritation. "Well, you gave a good impression of a jealous lover, if you were wondering."

"And I admire how well you showed me indifference. We are very good at pretending, don't you think?"

"Maybe too good. I was so uncomfortable. I had to say things about you that weren't very complimentary. I'm sorry. Does it help to know that it worked, and she spoke more freely because she thought she was getting one up on you?"

Lamprophyre tried to twist around to look at him. "Yes. It's all right. It was in a good cause. So what else did she say?"

"It's just as well you didn't hear her marriage proposal. All very logical and completely without affection. Based on what she told me, her interest in marrying me isn't just because I'm a magnificent catch, though to do her credit, she is attracted to me for myself and not just because her father ordered it. Actually, I wasn't entirely sure whose idea it was that Yalini should be the daughter who marries me. It doesn't matter. The point is—and this is my inference, but I'm confident about it—Fanishkor wants a marriage to bind its relationship with Gonjiri so they'll be able to make certain demands."

"What demands?"

Rokshan let out a long, deep breath. "They want to wage war on dragons."

CHAPTER FIFTEEN

Lamprophyre backwinged abruptly, making Rokshan grab at her ruff to stay seated. "They want *what?*"

"Could you not knock me off, please? If dragons won't ally with them, Fanishkor wants to put Gonjiri in a position to have to side with them against dragons. They know Gonjiri has dragon-killing weapons, and they want those weapons used on their behalf."

"But—" So many objections rushed to mind Lamprophyre felt choked by them.

"I know. It's a ridiculous plan. I doubt my father would go to war against dragons even for the sake of his son's in-laws."

"I don't know what in-laws are."

"It means the family of someone's spouse. My birth family is my father and mother and siblings, and my wife's family would be my father- and mother-in-law and siblings-in-law." He let out a short laugh. "By human custom, Hyaloclast is my mother-in-law. What an unsettling thought."

"And one you shouldn't tell her."

"That's not a reminder I need." Rokshan sobered. "Anyway, my impression is that Yalini, and by extension her father, don't think of dragons as rational creatures co-equal with humans. They believe Father will obviously side with humans over dragons, just because we're the same species. So between that and a dynastic marriage, Damen believes he'll have Gonjiri's aid when he attacks dragons."

"But I don't understand. Why would he attack us at all? I thought they knew we don't hold any grudges about the egg theft."

"That, I'm not sure about. If I had to guess—and it would just be a guess—Damen is the sort of person who takes advantage of weakness, and he doesn't believe other powerful people aren't like him. I know Yalini, for all she hid it well, is afraid of dragons as a whole—"

"She's not afraid of me."

"No, but you're a pitiable creature because you're in love with someone not your own species, remember? Most dragons are an unknown factor, and to her and her father, unknown equals dangerous. So all of that together equals Fanishkor wanting to attack dragons before being attacked themselves. And they need Gonjiri's weapons to do it."

The high walls of Tanajital, shadowy except where the lanterns along their tops turned them rosy-gold, were coming up fast. Lamprophyre banked to pass over the western gate and headed for the palace. "Well, their hopes are impossible. Even if you married Yalini, Ekanath would never go to war against dragons."

"No. But there's something else he needs to know. He and Tekentriya, probably."

"What's that?"

Rokshan ran a hand down the side of her neck, idly, the way he did when he was thinking about something. "Fanishkor has a secret. Not a weapon, but some military secret Yalini alluded to."

"I can't believe Yalini could be either that indiscreet or that careless."

Rokshan laughed. "I asked the right leading questions, and she couldn't resist taking the bait. Even so, she didn't say much. What she said, more or less, is that Fanishkor isn't helpless, and if anyone were to attack, they'd get a surprise."

"That's not much to go on." Lamprophyre descended past the parkland surrounding the palace and crouched to let Rokshan off.

"It's enough that I can turn it over to the spies and have them ferret out the truth. Personally, I think it's some kind of defense, but I won't tell them that. Don't want to contaminate their search." He put his hand on her shoulder. "God's breath, but I wish...you know I love you, right? And I don't think there's anything aberrant about that?"

"Of course," Lamprophyre said, startled. "And I love you."

Rokshan puffed out his cheeks, making a comical face that Lamprophyre smiled at, and blew out a long stream of air. "I'm beginning to feel we're swimming in conspiracy. Viveki's blackmail, Yalini's connivances, and then there's the mystery of Sardonyx. Why can't things be simple? Just the two of us going for a swim or something?"

"I'd like to have just one day where we didn't have to worry about all of that, yes." Lamprophyre sat back and looked at the palace, whose golden roofs weren't more than sharp-edged shadows, gilded at the eaves where the lantern light gleamed. She liked the palace better by moonlight, when the moon turned the gold into silver and made the short grass surrounding it into a motionless sea. She'd never seen the ocean, but she imagined it like the Green River, but a field instead of a stream. And, of course, night flying was easier when the moon was full.

"Then let's do it," Rokshan said. "Swimming, and a trip to Sunital, maybe not in that order."

The suggestion cheered Lamprophyre so much it surprised her. She hadn't thought their pretending had bothered her at all, but the amount of relief she felt at being with Rokshan told her otherwise. "I'd love that."

~

Lamprophyre swept north and west, gliding low enough over the hills east of Tanajital she could see her shadow, flickering and deformed by the rise and fall of the land. Ahead, storm clouds rolled in, nearly as low to the ground as she was and sending tendrils of dark mist out to caress the afternoon sun. The sun wasn't in a position to inconvenience her by shining in her eyes, but it didn't matter, because they'd be back at Tanajital before it sank that low. Whether they'd outrace the storm was another matter.

"The clouds are moving faster than I realized," she said. "We might get wet, and not in the good way."

"If we'd brought the harness, we'd beat it for sure," Rokshan said. "It's all right. Though I'm sure the rainwater will be colder than the river."

Lamprophyre nodded. She felt relaxed enough she didn't much care if they got wet again. They'd spent the morning in Sunital, watching the foot races the city was famous for, and had a long swim in the early afternoon. That had drawn something of a crowd, which had worried Lamprophyre, because Rokshan could be sensitive about the burn scars covering his body. But he'd splashed and swam without showing any sign of self-consciousness.

Despite her physical relaxation, all her muscles feeling as if they'd been stretched and kneaded pleasantly, she couldn't shake off the feeling of sadness that had plagued her ever since perching on the wall of Sunital's coliseum. How different this trip would have been if she'd been human. Rokshan would never say it—in fact, she didn't believe he even thought it—but things had been so easy when they were both human. It didn't help her melancholy to reflect that the same would be true if they were both dragons.

She made herself focus on reality. For the moment, they were a dragon and a human in love, and that difference in species would change soon. She had to believe it, or she really would fall into despair. "Rokshan," she said, "have you thought of a way to get those notes away from Viveki?"

"I have about three-quarters of a plan," Rokshan said. "Are we agreed that we can endure it if her knowledge about your transformation gets out?"

"Yes. That's not important in the long run. Besides, if someone figures out how to make a dragon human, that suggests knowledge of the reverse will also be available."

"Then the important thing is keeping her from destroying the notes. That's where my plan falls apart."

Lamprophyre wanted to ask for details, but she knew he wouldn't give them until he was ready. "Will it be ready by tomorrow? I'd love not to have to part with five vahas."

"Yes. Tomorrow we'll have her."

Lamprophyre let out a relieved sigh. Ahead, the rosy walls of Tanajital blended with the pale gold of the wintry fields. It was such a comforting sight it made her disquiet greater. She didn't want to think of a human city as home, not when she already had a home, but she was used to Tanajital now and looked forward to returning to the embassy after some time away. She told herself to stop being foolish and sped up a little. The storm was closer now, but she cast an expert eye on the clouds and estimated they had another four thousand beats—almost three human hours—before it reached the city, and they would be well under shelter in two.

Soon, she crossed the wall, waving at the soldiers on guard. They weren't supposed to be distracted from their duties by a dragon, but she didn't think a quick wave counted as distracted. Tanajital's orderly streets and its white or tan buildings soothed her spirits. It was so beautifully alien, so unnatural, that it astonished her every time that anyone was capable of such creation. Dragons went in for more organic shapes, the curve of a cave wall or the bumpiness of a quarry ledge. And yet both humans and dragons altered their environments to suit them. The thought cheered her.

Ahead, the Archprelate's palace loomed, short and squat except for a single slim spire thrusting toward the heavens. Three flags flew above the tower, black, green, and multicolor striped. That meant the First Ecclesiast, the Fifth Ecclesiast, and the Archprelate were in residence. "Khadar's still there," Lamprophyre said.

"I saw. Now might be a good time to corner him."

Lamprophyre twisted to look back at Rokshan, though she

couldn't see more of him than his leg. "You think it's a matter of cornering him?"

"I think he won't be forthcoming unless we make it clear this is an official diplomatic inquiry." Rokshan leaned forward to lie across her neck. "And that prophecy is still important, even if it's not as urgent as everything else we've been dealing with in the past week."

Lamprophyre's curiosity roused. It was true she wanted to know why Jiwanyil had given a prophecy that dragons would be angry about. She banked, wheeled, and descended toward the Archprelate's palace.

She'd only been there once, and only just outside the front door, but she'd seen the palace and its grounds many times in her flights over the city. A high granite wall, solid and gray and topped with smooth marble slabs, extended from both sides of the palace and circled around a vast field of short-cropped grass. The field was big enough to fit fifty houses, and Lamprophyre had always wondered what the ecclesiasts needed so much space for, especially when housing in the city was at a premium, something she knew from her regulars who came for soup.

There wasn't much room for a dragon to land outside the Archprelate's palace. A wide strip of courtyard, paved not with little white bricks like most of Tanajital but with smooth gray sandstone pebbles, filled the space between the street and the palace's front door. Fortunately, it was empty, and Lamprophyre landed without incident. She furled her wings and curled her tail around herself, feeling crowded despite the relative openness of the space.

Rokshan climbed down and said, "I'll send a messenger. If that's not enough, I'll track him down myself."

Lamprophyre nodded. She watched Rokshan cross the courtyard, stone crunching and shifting under his sandals, and pass through the dark squared-off doorway. This might take a while. Lamprophyre settled in and looked around. There weren't many people in the street, since most of the buildings surrounding the Archprelate's palace were houses, and almost all their owners were at their jobs at this hour. Those who passed by all looked at her, but idly, as if she were just another person like themselves and not worthy of a second glance. Their thoughts were almost all as nonchalant as their demeanors, though a few people, mostly young adults or children, were filled with awe. Lamprophyre smiled and nodded at anyone who caught her eye. If this was what Sardonyx wanted to prevent, she'd failed.

Still, the problem was that nobody actually knew what Sardonyx wanted. Lamprophyre had a handful of ancient texts and her own experiences to go on, and even that was all inference and supposition. *Confident* inference and supposition, but it wasn't the same as knowing. And she really wished she knew what it meant that the mountains had swallowed Sardonyx up, ending her threat to humanity. An attack, a trap, a—

"Lamprophyre," Rokshan said, startling her out of her reverie. "I had someone take Khadar a message. I hope I made it sound urgent and important enough."

"If the banded desert is Sardonyx, then wouldn't mountains be other dragons?" Lamprophyre said.

Rokshan blinked. "You mean about the mountains swallowing her up? Yes, I suppose so. So maybe it means dragons overwhelmed her."

"And then died in the attack."

Rokshan leaned against her flank. "I don't know that that's the right interpretation, but it's a possibility. But it couldn't have been all dragons, because there are still dragons today."

"Still. Some dragons did something that stopped Sardonyx's attack. But they couldn't kill her—"

"Couldn't? Or didn't?"

Lamprophyre thought about that for a few beats. "Couldn't. I think if they'd been able, they'd have killed her. So instead she was trapped."

"Entombed, maybe." At Lamprophyre's surprised look, Rokshan went on, "It's what I think of when I imagine mountains swallowing something up. A tomb."

Excitement filled Lamprophyre. "But then—"

Someone cleared their throat. Lamprophyre looked up to see one of the yellow-clad attendants the ecclesiasts always traveled with, a young woman with a funny haircut like an upside-down bowl. "The Fifth Ecclesiast asks that you meet him on the field," she said, her voice high and fluting like the reed pipe hanging from her rope belt.

"Immediately?" Rokshan asked.

The girl inclined her head.

Rokshan swung himself up into his accustomed seat. "Thank you," he said. "Lamprophyre, she means behind the palace."

Lamprophyre waited for the girl to return inside the Archprelate's palace, then leaped into the sky, scattering pebbles. "That was fast," she said.

"Yes, and I'm suspicious," Rokshan replied. "I expected Khadar to put up more resistance, if only to satisfy his pride."

"Maybe he really has changed."

"Or maybe he wants something from us." Rokshan leaned forward and pointed. "Just down there."

Lamprophyre shivered with the guilty pleasure of going somewhere she shouldn't. True, she had an invitation, but the Archprelate's palace was so well shielded from the rest of the world, it felt like descending into some secret lair she might have to fight her way out of.

She'd already noticed the short grass of the field was always a vibrant green, regardless of the season. Now, up close, she saw it was cropped perfectly short and even, making it look like someone had covered the space with green fabric, smooth and perfect.

The back face of the Archprelate's palace was as smooth as the field, but white and sparkling rather than green. Lamprophyre guessed the ecclesiasts could have painted the palace as brightly as they wanted, because she couldn't imagine anyone trying to collect taxes from them, but the white surface, not much taller than Lamprophyre, had its own kind of beauty. Small round windows filled with glass that was dull in the light of the oncoming storm dotted the back wall at random, irregular intervals. The one small door in the center of the wall looked boring and unimportant. Lamprophyre still didn't know much about human architecture, but the palace impressed her.

She listened for thoughts and heard only a low hum as of dozens, maybe hundreds of people all going about their daily business. The palace was certainly large enough to hold hundreds.

Rokshan slid down to stand next to her. "I told him the dragon ambassador wanted to speak with him, so you should do most of the talking," he said.

"Good, because I have a lot of questions," Lamprophyre responded. "But most of them are accusatory, so I won't be asking those."

"You can save them for if he's recalcitrant."

The door opened. Rokshan assumed a parade rest stance, his face becoming smooth and expressionless. Lamprophyre sat up and hoped she looked intimidating. In all her previous interactions with Khadar, he'd at least never been afraid of her. So long as he respected her enough to answer her questions, she didn't care if he was afraid.

She'd expected a handful of those yellow-clad assistants, maybe several ecclesiasts, to precede Khadar. But the Fifth Ecclesiast was alone. He crossed the short patch of grass between the door and where Lamprophyre sat. He wore his usual green robe embroidered with images of the natural world and the god Meyari, represented by the willow tree. He was bare-headed, and his short black hair shifted in the rising breeze.

"I have only a few minutes," he said. "What can I do for you?"

That was more polite than Lamprophyre had expected. Well, if he could be straightforward, so could she. "There was a prophecy about a twelveday ago," she said. "Supposedly it instructed ecclesiasts to climb Mother Stone."

"It did," Khadar said. *So it's come to this,* he thought, with what to Lamprophyre sounded like resignation rather than anger.

When it became clear he wasn't going to elaborate, Lamprophyre said, "You must know that's unacceptable. Dragons venerate

Mother Stone the way humans worship Jiwanyil. We can't allow humans on her slopes—and even if we could, the trip would be fatal."

"We do not ignore Jiwanyil's prophecies," Khadar said. "What he demands, we must do. We hoped dragons would understand that. You yourself, my lady ambassador, have seen Jiwanyil's prophecies borne out. Don't you think it would be better for you to discover why Jiwanyil would instruct humans to disregard what dragons hold sacred?"

Rokshan shifted his weight. Lamprophyre remembered he'd said something of the sort, and the memory made her uncomfortable. She heard Khadar think *try to explain prophecy to a dragon, pointless,* and her discomfort flowered into anger. "I don't think it's our responsibility to bend to your prophecy."

Khadar sighed, a put-upon sound that irritated her further. "Counter to what you believe, we ecclesiasts did not simply accept that prophecy," he said. "We spent much time in prayer and study to understand its intent. We feel confident that it is in the best interests of both humans and dragons to obey its instruction."

"Oh? And why is that?"

"Our understanding is that great wisdom will arise from allowing humans to climb Nirinatan—Mother Stone. Even if the ecclesiasts do not survive, their deaths will not be in vain." Khadar's face was as expressionless as Rokshan's. *Could be there already, hear from them,* he thought.

Lamprophyre felt as if the breath had been knocked from her body. *Stones.* He couldn't possibly... In a flash, she considered her options, decided she didn't give a damn if she gave away her secret ability, and said, "You didn't. You couldn't have."

"Lamprophyre?" Rokshan asked.

"You *dared* ignore my instructions?" she snarled, ignoring Rokshan.

Khadar's thoughts became tense, but none of his growing fear showed on his face. "We told you what we had to do," he said. "Our ecclesiasts should be at the slopes of Nirinatan as we speak."

CHAPTER SIXTEEN

Lamprophyre bore down on Khadar, making him retreat. "Did those ecclesiasts tell you what would happen if you disregarded my *direct* command?"

"They did," Khadar said. He took another step back. Lamprophyre followed him. "You know that wouldn't matter to us, not when it's a question of prophecy."

Lamprophyre snarled wordlessly at him. "I'm going to speak to Hyaloclast immediately," she said. "You'd better pray she's in a forgiving mood."

"Dragons won't kill humans."

"Is that so? Humans have never threatened what we hold sacred before." Lamprophyre turned to find Rokshan had followed her. "Climb up," she said flatly. "Khadar, this isn't over."

"I make no apologies," Khadar said.

Lamprophyre closed her eyes briefly, dispelling the image of grabbing Khadar by his ankles and carrying him screaming across the city. With Rokshan firmly settled, she leaped into the air and flew as fast as she dared to the embassy.

Rokshan slid down as soon as she landed. "What can we do?"

"Tell Hyaloclast what's happened," Lamprophyre said as she headed inside. "And then—are you up for some storm flying?"

"I'll get changed," Rokshan said.

The blue chalcedony pendant warmed in her hand as she breathed on it with a little more heat than necessary. She waited. Hyaloclast didn't respond. She breathed on it again, and again, but nothing happened. Swearing, she hung the pendant around her neck and turned to look at Rokshan, who looked uncomfortably warm in his cold-weather gear. "I'm worried," she said. "Hyaloclast always eventually answers, but if they're already dealing with those damn ecclesiasts—"

"We have to hurry," Rokshan agreed. "But if you're going to outfly the storm, we'll need the harness."

"Stones," Lamprophyre swore again. "We might still have to wait it out."

Rokshan dragged the harness out of its corner. "Let's deal with that when we come to it."

Though the saddle's thinner leather made it lighter than the prototype, getting the harness settled took more time than usual without a second dragon to help. Lamprophyre and Rokshan were both swearing by the time she fastened the last buckle. When Rokshan was finally seated, the damp, prickly scent of the storm was far too close. "Hang on," Lamprophyre said, and tore into the sky.

She sped along, flashing past the wide, tilled fields and across the barren land between settlements until the forest rose up before them. It spread as far as Lamprophyre could see, tall conifers mingled with the spreading boughs of leafy trees, some bare, some clinging to their leaves like humans shielding their modesty. She'd never bothered learning the names of the trees—they were so impermanent—but at the moment, being able to put names to the trees would be a distraction.

They'd made this terrible trip once before, racing a storm. That time, they'd had to stop a war. This time, Lamprophyre wasn't sure what they intended to stop. If there were humans on Mother Stone, she wasn't sure she'd intervene to stop Hyaloclast making an example of them. But that would infuriate the ecclesiasts, who might influence King Ekanath, and that could mean she and Rokshan were trying to stop another war. Lamprophyre pushed herself faster. Humans made everything more complicated.

She still didn't have an answer to the most important question, which was why Jiwanyil had commanded humans to do something dragons would oppose. Lamprophyre knew Jiwanyil's power was real, even if she didn't worship him as a god, and she'd seen the results of his prophecies. He'd even intervened to save her life, so she knew he cared about dragons, if only in a limited way. So why did he suddenly want to set dragons against humans?

A cold prickle of raindrops struck her wings and back, and then it was more than a prickle, and Lamprophyre wiped rain from her face and flew faster. Rokshan leaned forward. "We have to take shelter," he said over the noise of the rain. "These clothes aren't waterproof."

Lamprophyre swore and dove. She knew Rokshan was as tense as she was because he didn't shout with excitement. Below, the forest loomed, and she swerved, backwinged, and descended feet-first through the trees, holding her wings high to make herself a blue arrow piercing the scant foliage.

She landed hard, plowing up earth, and crouched to let Rokshan down. The rain still fell, though the branches and what was left of the leaves kept some of it off. Lamprophyre settled on the ground, digging in to the warm, loose soil, and Rokshan sat close beside her. She arched one wing over him. "I thought the clothes were waterproof," she said.

"Water-resistant, not waterproof," Rokshan replied. "There are enough layers that my body heat won't melt snow if I for some reason end up walking through it, and it will protect me against a light sprinkle or cloud mist, but a heavy downpour—"

Lightning forked across the sky, and thunder boomed, and then the rain came down in earnest. "Like this one," Rokshan said with a grin. "They'll just get soaked. And then they'll be useless at altitude."

Lamprophyre restlessly dug her claws across the soft earth, then shook them impatiently to clean them. "We might already be too late," she said, "so I don't know why I'm worried. There's nothing we can do except—Stones, but I wish we'd tackled Khadar sooner!"

"We couldn't have known. Ecclesiasts may be single-minded, but they're not stupid." Rokshan leaned against Lamprophyre's side, making her raise her wing higher. "I thought they were investigating the prophecy. Looking for ways to cooperate with dragons. Not bull-headedly rushing off into danger."

"If Hyaloclast finds them..." Lamprophyre let her voice trail off. There was no point repeating what they both knew.

They sat in silence as the rain fell. Eventually Lamprophyre tucked her head under her wing to keep the rain pelting it from driving her mad. She rested her chin on Rokshan's leg and closed her eyes. Another few thousand beats until they reached the flight's caves, and if they were lucky, Hyaloclast had simply been away on a hunt or at a gleaning field, and Lamprophyre and Rokshan could deal with the ecclesiasts themselves.

She felt Rokshan run his hand over the top of her head. "You're nice and warm," he said. "If not for the damp under my rear end, I'd be comfortable."

She smiled. "Not too warm?"

"Maybe a little, but not enough to complain about." He stroked her head again. "I was thinking maybe I should tell my parents about us."

Lamprophyre's eyes flew open. She sat up and then tilted her wing to let rainwater roll off it, away from Rokshan. "You can't!"

"They'll have to know eventually. At the very least, when I tell them I intend to become a dragon." Rokshan laughed. "That's going to be an interesting conversation."

"Yes, but..." Lamprophyre searched for words. "But they'll be so upset! You know this relationship of ours looks so strange to outsiders. And you're a prince."

"Sweetheart, we can't keep this secret forever. It's not fair to either of us." Rokshan stood and rested his hand on the side of her face. "I'm not going to lie to them just so they won't be upset, because there's no good way to give them this information. And my father did promise to be open-minded about the person I'm in love with."

"Yes, because he thinks she's a woman who's, I don't know, a prostitute, or already married, or a hundred years older than you!"

That made him laugh harder. "Having a dragon for a daughter-in-law would be far superior to any of those options, I guarantee."

Lamprophyre drew in a breath and let it out slowly to calm herself. "I suppose I feel uncomfortable because it's like I'm taking you away from everything you were born to be."

"Which you aren't. It's my choice, Lamprophyre, and I want to be with you, whatever it takes." Rokshan cast his gaze upward. "It's slacking off."

"We have a few minutes still." Lamprophyre crouched back down. "All right. I suppose if you're going to tell your parents, it should be sooner rather than later. They might be open-minded, but you expect them to accept not only that you're in love with a dragon, but that you intend to transform yourself so you can be her mate in every sense."

"That's it exactly. I want them to have time to come to terms with it. Bend down." Rokshan tucked his gloves into his waistband and used his hands to swipe rainwater off Lamprophyre's back and out of the notch. When he finished, Lamprophyre took several steps away and shook herself to get rid of the remaining water. Flying with wet wings was uncomfortable and potentially hazardous, but they didn't have a choice.

They took to the skies again, flying faster and faster until Rokshan was hunched into the spot behind her neck and Lamprophyre felt she'd reached her limit. Storm clouds still blackened the sky, but the rain had moved south, and the air smelled fresh and clean and cool. She wished she were in a mood to appreciate it.

Ahead, the skies were clearer, and by the time they reached the foothills, the skies were blue and cloudless, and the mountains were golden in the light of the late afternoon sun. If not for the lingering chill in the air, Lamprophyre wouldn't have believed there'd been a storm at all. "What next?" she shouted to Rokshan. "Find Hyaloclast, or find the ecclesiasts?"

Rokshan leaned over so he could speak directly into her ear. "The ecclesiasts. If Hyaloclast hasn't caught them, we might still be able to resolve this without it turning to bloodshed."

Lamprophyre nodded. "Then hang on. It's going to get cold."

She surveyed the foothills, wishing she'd thought to wrest a little more information out of Khadar. Like, for example, how long ago the ecclesiasts had left, and how many of them there were. Without that knowledge, she could only guess as to how far their party had gotten. Assuming they hadn't left immediately after accosting Lamprophyre, which had to be true—even ecclesiasts on a mission from God needed time to prepare for a trip like that—they'd had less than a twelveday, maybe only eight or nine days, of travel time. It took one person with frequent remounts, Rokshan had once told her, six days to get from Tanajital to the foothills. These ecclesiasts couldn't travel that fast. Maybe they weren't even here yet.

"Maybe they haven't reached the mountains yet," she told Rokshan.

"We can't count on that," he replied. "We need to go all the way to Mother Stone, just in case. But between you and me, I'm hoping you're right."

They soon left the foothills behind, their shallow inclines yellow with winter-dead weeds, and ascended through the lower mountain slopes. There, only a mossy scruff grew on the stones, along with the occasional stunted, crooked pine with gray-green needles that in spring would smell sharp and fresh, but now gave off no aroma at all. Usually Lamprophyre enjoyed flying slowly over this ground, watching for rock hares, but today she took the slopes at speed, quickly leaving them behind for the rocky crags where only dragons and the hardiest of birds could live.

"Slow down," Rokshan said.

"Slow down? I thought we were in a hurry."

"That won't help if we fly past them too fast to see them. Or if you ascend too fast and make us both sick."

The stones beneath them were covered with fresh snow, spread by the storm that had just passed over them. It would cover any tracks made by the ecclesiasts, make it impossible to find them that way—though, on the other hand, Lamprophyre didn't think even Rokshan the expert tracker could follow someone over bare stone. "I'm not searching by sight," she said. "I'm listening for thoughts. They're the only ones who could be out here." Even so, she slowed and wheeled to fly east.

"They'd have stopped when the storm hit," Rokshan said. "Made camp somewhere. I'll look for that."

Lamprophyre nodded.

They searched for a hundred beats, two hundred beats, as more clouds, these high and thin, drifted in front of the sun and dimmed the light. Lamprophyre heard no thoughts but Rokshan's, which she did her best to ignore so they wouldn't be a distraction. Not listening to his thoughts was normally as easy as disregarding the drifting thoughts of other dragons, but when they were in close contact, she couldn't help herself. She focused on the land beneath. White-clad granite stretched out before her as far as she could see.

"I'm sure they wouldn't have tried to climb near the flight," she said, mainly to distract herself from Rokshan's thoughts of *can't see anything in this mess*. "But that doesn't tell us whether they went east or west."

"The light's fading," Rokshan replied. "That storm—"

"No sense regretting what we can't control." Lamprophyre looked northward to where Mother Stone's lowest slopes, themselves as high as the highest nearby peaks, rose dizzyingly into the sky. "We can only do our best."

They flew on for another dozen beats, and Lamprophyre was about to suggest turning around to search westward when she caught the barest whisper of a thought: *all this white stuff...no idea...so cold.* "I hear them," she exclaimed.

"Where?"

"I can't tell yet. Farther east, though."

It was hard to pay close attention to distant thoughts and fly at the same time; concentration made her effectively blind. She slowed her flight to keep from losing altitude and potentially flying into a mountain, not to mention to keep from flying past their quarry. More thoughts emerged as if from the snow beneath: *maybe camp for the night* and *so cold* and *going to get worse.* They grew louder as she flew, and with some effort she teased apart their thoughts. Five people. Not enough to give her any trouble.

"There," Rokshan said. Out of the corner of her eye, she saw him point. Blinking, she focused in that direction. At first she saw only the same blank white-covered crags. Then one of them moved, shaking off the snow covering it. It wasn't a rock, it was a swath of dun-colored canvas, and someone held it over their head, shaking snow from it. More movement showed where other humans emerged from beneath canvases made invisible by the storm.

Lamprophyre swept past overhead without stopping. "I have to find a place to land that isn't on top of them," she said when Rokshan protested. "They were thinking about camping there for the night, so they aren't going anywhere. And they certainly can't outrun us."

"They're going to have a damn cold night if that's where they're sleeping," Rokshan said. "All right. Try approaching from the north. Uphill. If you can loom over them, it's more intimidating."

Lamprophyre agreed. While her earlier anger with Khadar and the ccclesiasts had faded, it hadn't gone away so much as turned into smoldering embers. The idea of scaring these people satisfied her.

As she returned to the ecclesiasts' campsite, she heard mental cries of astonishment and dread. "They've seen us," she said. "So much for surprise."

"They're surprised, just not on our terms," Rokshan said. "Swoop low like you're going to snatch one of them up. Remember how you did that to me when we first met?"

Lamprophyre chuckled. "We have come so far from that day it's like it happened to two other people."

She dove, furling her wings for greater speed, and pulled up just before she would have plowed into the stony ground. Humans scattered, diving for any cover they could find. It *was* deeply satisfying, and she laughed as she wheeled around for another pass. This time, she scanned the area for a place to land. A gray boulder half her height that looked like it had been set down by a giant hand suited her purposes. It lay about a dragonlength from the ecclesiasts' camp and tilted toward them to form a little open cave on the downhill side.

She landed on it, gripped it firmly with both feet when the snow covering it made her slip, and spread her wings wide for balance. The gesture would also make her look large and intimidating. Excellent.

"*You were warned*," she shouted, letting her deep voice boom out over the peaks and setting the loose snow nearby trembling. "Did you think I was joking when I told you what would happen if you disregarded my instructions?"

The five humans, all of them dressed haphazardly in several layers of shirts and thick trousers not as fine as Rokshan's, stood motionless, staring at her. Their thoughts were incoherent babblings, the kind of thoughts people have when they don't know what to say. Then one of them stepped forward. Lamprophyre remembered her; her name was Ashta, and she was the ecclesiast who'd had that disastrous prophecy. "I told you we would go anyway," she said. "We don't ignore prophecy."

"Yes, but Jiwanyil doesn't expect you to be stupid about it," Rokshan said. "Following prophecy this way is going to get you killed. If Hyaloclast finds out you intend to climb Mother Stone, she will tear you apart."

"If that is the will of Jiwanyil, then we will meet our fate with honor," Ashta said. "We do not fear the wrath of dragons, only the wrath of God."

Her thoughts had become clear and coherent, and Lamprophyre

realized what she should have known the first time she'd spoken to Ashta: the woman was a zealot, a true believer who genuinely was willing to give her life in the service of her God. Lamprophyre hated zealots. In the stories, they always got other people killed.

"This can't be the only way to follow Jiwanyil's prophecy," she said, half to herself.

"Jiwanyil's path is straight, not crooked," Ashta said, "and when his prophecy is clear, the way becomes known."

"Yes, but the prophecy wanted you to reach Mother Stone alive." Lamprophyre hopped down from the boulder and walked toward the ecclesiasts, feeling Rokshan's weight shift with every awkward step. "I'll admit I was too angry when you approached me to be reasonable, but we could have come to a compromise."

"We don't compromise on prophecies." Ashta continued to stare up at Lamprophyre unflinchingly.

"And we don't compromise on Mother Stone. But I know Jiwanyil is a real god, even if he's not my god, and as Rokshan pointed out to me, I should at least want to know why he would tell humans to climb Mother Stone." Lamprophyre settled on her haunches and bent to let Rokshan down. "Please see sense. If Hyaloclast and the rest of the flight kill you, it could start a war between humans and dragons, and humans will not survive it. I don't want that to happen."

The first crack of uncertainty appeared in Ashta's inflexible mask. "Why do you care what happens to humans?"

"Because we're both rational creatures, and I have many human friends. I don't want war to turn them into enemies." Lamprophyre kept her gaze locked on Ashta, willing her to see sense.

But Ashta was shaking her head. "If you really care about stopping a war," she said, "you'd help us fulfill prophecy."

"You can't make a dragon complicit in breaking one of her people's most sacred laws," Rokshan said.

"We know climbing Nirinatan will convey blessings unlike any others," Ashta said. "You're asking us to give that up. It's unthinkable."

"That's what I said about humans on Mother Stone," Lamprophyre said. "Didn't you ecclesiasts ask for more prophecies when you received that one? You knew it would anger dragons—doesn't that mean you should have looked for clarification?"

The uncertainty spread. "But it was a clear prophecy," Ashta said.

"Khadar told us ecclesiasts had studied and prayed to understand your prophecy," Rokshan said. "It couldn't have been that clear."

Lamprophyre risked looking past Ashta at the other four ecclesiasts, if they were all ecclesiasts. The light was fading fast as the sun set, but she still recognized Ashta's companion Nirav. He looked deeply uncertain, more so than Ashta. The other three huddled together like frightened sheep. "What else did that study and prayer discover?" she asked, addressing not Ashta, but Nirav.

Nirav moistened his lips. "That the results of obedience will bless both humans and dragons," he said with a quick glance at Ashta. She didn't turn to look at him. "And that great trials will bring great rewards."

"I'm not sure I believe that, but Jiwanyil, as I've said, isn't my God," Lamprophyre said. "But the last time dragons were the answer to human prophecy, the world changed. Shouldn't you have given us the opportunity to make it change again?"

Ashta's eyes widened. Now she turned to look at Nirav, whose mouth was set in a tight, determined line that said he was ready to argue with someone, hopefully Ashta. "I...don't know," Ashta said, her voice faint. She turned to face Lamprophyre again, the light of the setting sun highlighting the planes and curves of her face. "It's prophecy," she said, almost pleadingly, as if Lamprophyre were a recalcitrant child bent on doing something destructive.

"I know," Lamprophyre said. "Please find another way of fulfilling it."

Now Ashta looked past Lamprophyre, northward to where Mother Stone loomed. Her jaw clenched. "One day," she said, "one night and one day for us to pray again. But I won't promise not to go."

"You should have faith that Jiwanyil will show you the path," Rokshan murmured.

Ashta shot him a furious look, and Lamprophyre's heart sank at the thought that Rokshan might have just ruined everything they'd accomplished. But Ashta just turned away and told her companions, "We'll camp here tonight, and spend tomorrow in prayer and contemplation. Unless that's a problem?" she asked Lamprophyre, her voice edged with sarcasm.

Lamprophyre let it go. "You're only in danger from exposure here," she said. "You don't look very warmly clad. Do you have enough food?"

"We came well supplied. We will be fine," Ashta said, in a tone of such finality Lamprophyre had to bite back a snappish retort.

She turned her back on the ecclesiasts and walked behind the boulder, followed by Rokshan. "I don't think we should leave them alone," she murmured. "I don't trust Ashta not to break her word in the name of Jiwanyil."

"I agree completely." Rokshan sighed. "Unfortunately, *we* didn't bring any food, and we have no shelter. And I doubt those ecclesiasts have any of either to spare, even if they were willing to help us."

"I'll hunt something, and I think I can keep you warm through the night. See if you can find a nook or cave or something while I'm gone." Lamprophyre spread her wings and flapped once. They were dry now, and with the emergency mostly passed, she realized she was starving.

"Good luck," Rokshan said, and waved to her as she flew away.

CHAPTER SEVENTEEN

She brought down two deer before the light faded completely. The sliver of moon was chasing the sun fast, but it still gave her enough light to disembowel and skin her prey before the slim crescent sank below the western horizon. Holding a carcass in each hand, she flew back toward the mountains and her sense of her pair-bond. By the time she was high enough that the snow-covered high peaks made it easier to see the ground, Rokshan's presence was a beacon drawing her on.

A small fire burned in the ecclesiasts' camp, giving her a visual guide. Rokshan had moved a couple of dragonlengths west of that and sat just inside a dark cave opening. It wasn't so much a cave as a place where three huge boulders leaned into each other. "You know it's dangerous going into a cave without fire," she said. "You don't know what might be living in it."

"It's only about two feet deep," Rokshan said, standing so she could see past him. "But it's enough shelter for protection if the wind picks up during the night."

"Which it usually does." Lamprophyre took her kills a short distance away and carefully roasted them, conscious of Rokshan's need for more thoroughly cooked meat than she required. When she returned, Rokshan was drinking from a waterskin he usually wore on his belt when they traveled. "Plenty of snow to fill this," he said, "but I don't know if you can drink from it."

"I'll be all right," Lamprophyre said. She tore off a chunk of meat and handed it to Rokshan. "Not very fine dining, I'm afraid."

"I'm too hungry to care."

They ate in silence until Lamprophyre felt heavy and satisfyingly full. "We can dispose of the remains tomorrow," she said. "No predators this high to disturb our rest." She took the carcasses a short distance away anyway. On her way back, she searched the snowy ground for loose stones and collected an armful of the ones about the size of a deer's head. She dropped the armload on the ground before Rokshan's cave.

"What's this for?" Rokshan asked. He was huddled in on himself and occasionally shivered.

"Well, mostly my body heat will keep you warm, but this is for an extra boost. Cold may not hurt dragons, at least not this little cold, but that doesn't mean we like it." She collected the stones into a loose heap and drew in a deep breath. Mingling the air with the burning contents of her second stomach, she breathed out fire that bathed the stones in heat. She kept exhaling until she needed air, at which point the stones were red hot and the air above them wavered with heat distortion.

Rokshan scooted over and held out his gloved hands over the hot stones. "This is wonderful," he said. "How long will it last?"

"A few hours, and then I'll do it again." Lamprophyre arranged the stones nearer to Rokshan's cave and then curled up with her tail and hindquarters near the sheltered nook. "Lean up against me."

Rokshan sat in the curve of her body and leaned back. "You're as warm as the stone. Is this how dragons live during the winter?"

"Usually we share caves with our clutchmates or our families. But yes, the females heat rocks that we put in our caves, and between that and body heat it's usually very pleasant. Though the ground...actually, that might be a problem. You're going to lose heat through the ground. Here, move out of the way." She waited for him to move, then blew a lighter, more diffuse fire at the ground where he'd been sitting. It didn't glow red, but when Rokshan knelt on it, he let out a hiss of surprise.

"Very warm," he said. This time, he lay on the ground curled into the curve of her chest. "*Now* it's perfect."

Lamprophyre laughed. "I know you'd prefer a bed."

"Surprisingly, I'd rather spend the night with you, even if we're different species and unable to share intimacy." Rokshan propped his head on his wrist and tilted it to look up at her. "Being close to you fills me with joy."

"That's how I feel." Lamprophyre moved a couple of hot stones closer and pillowed her head on her arm. "Someday, you'll feel the pair-bond, and it will be even better."

"I know."

They fell silent. Lamprophyre listened to the nearby thoughts, just in case the ecclesiasts were plotting something stupid. They were mostly thinking about how cold they were. That little fire couldn't do much more than keep them alive. How idiotic of them to climb all this way without proper clothing! Just one more reason Ashta's approach was foolish. If she couldn't even wait a few days...

Lamprophyre sighed. It didn't matter. She'd bought herself and Rokshan a day in which to figure out a solution. She let out a puff of smoke that wasn't quite a ring. One single day. It didn't feel like much.

"You breathed two kinds of fire just now," Rokshan said.

"Yes. I have a great deal of control over how hot it burns, and how concentrated. Though the maximum range for a female dragon's fire is always the same."

"You said that when you helped Sajan test the pyrite weapons. That if their range was better than yours, they could assume it would be better than any dragon's."

"That felt strange, helping him. Almost disloyal to my people." Lamprophyre remembered demonstrating her fiery breath to General Sajan, commander of the entire armed forces of Gonjiri, and watching the pyrite-studded cylinders swivel and blast distant targets. The weapons produced a bright pulse of force almost like a lightning strike, powerful enough to incapacitate a dragon, or so she guessed from seeing them in action. She wasn't stupid enough to allow them to test the weapons on her.

"Gonjiri won't use them against dragons," Rokshan said. "But doesn't it comfort you to know if Sardonyx does attack, humans can defend against her?"

"I suppose." Lamprophyre tilted her head to look at the sky. She didn't recognize constellations in any of the scattered specks of light. She looked farther back to where Mother Stone was a pale gray blotch against the starry background. Under a full moon, her eternal snows would be brilliant white. "Mother Stone guards our rest," she murmured.

"What was that?" Rokshan said. He sounded drowsy.

"I was just thinking of that story, the one in the book with the collection of writings about the Cataclysm. How Katayan grieved, and all the other gods helped him. And Mother Stone guarded his rest." She blinked. "No. It said *their* rest. All the other gods helped Katayan, but..."

"It's too late in the day for thinking," Rokshan murmured. "Go to sleep."

"Rokshan, I think this is important. Don't you remember the story?"

"Let's stipulate that I will never remember things as well as you do, and let me rest."

Lamprophyre nudged him. "It was one of the ones that said the mountains swallowed up Sardonyx and her dragons. The one that said all the dragons who fought her were killed, which is why Katayan mourned. But it said—wake up, Rokshan!"

Rokshan groaned. "All right. What did it say?"

Lamprophyre cleared her throat. "It said *the gods circled round Katayan in his grief. Meyari's roots dug deep to sustain him. Vrelok's creatures howled a funeral dirge. Jiwanyil's people grieved with him. And Nirinatan guarded their rest.* Don't you see the difference?" She felt as if her mind was humming with knowledge, like a stream in full spate of spring. "The gods didn't do anything that might be considered 'at rest.' I think that last sentence applies to something else. I think it's talking about Sardonyx and her people."

Rokshan rolled over so he could look at her. "Why would you assume that? The story doesn't support that idea."

"Doesn't it? Rokshan, you said it yourself, that it sounded as if Sardonyx had been entombed. Trapped by the efforts of dragons and humans who were killed in the process. Well, if there's anywhere in the world that could be a tomb for dragons—" She pointed at Mother Stone's vast bulk— "wouldn't that be it?"

Rokshan lay silent for a few beats. "It still doesn't make sense," he finally said. "How could an evil ancient dragon and who knows how many of her followers be trapped on dragons' holiest mountain? Wouldn't your people have known about it? And it doesn't explain how the mountains could have swallowed Sardonyx up."

"I don't know why we don't know about it, but I'm increasingly inclined to believe the thing about the mountains is a metaphor for whatever magic those dragons and humans worked on Sardonyx. If she is entombed there, it would take powerful magic to keep her contained all these centuries. Magic no one's ever heard of. And suppose..." Ideas sleeted through her brain faster than a dragon's flight. "Suppose nobody *wanted* it to be heard of? What if the metaphor is so no one knows what the magic was, and can't unravel it?"

"You are making far too many leaps of logic," Rokshan said. "I'm willing to accept your explanation about the metaphor, because so much of the rest of this story is metaphor. But if Sardonyx can talk to people, the magic must already be—" His voice cut off abruptly. "God's breath," he said. "The magic is unraveling."

"We guessed that already."

"I know, but think about it. That means unless someone does something, Sardonyx will free herself." Rokshan sat up. "And we still don't know enough."

Lamprophyre looked at Mother Stone again. "We could find her," she said.

"Find who? Sardonyx? That's insane, Lamprophyre. What would be the point?"

It felt as if the mountain beckoned to her, calling her. "The point would be finding out what exactly has her trapped. If we know that, we can get adepts to work out a way to put her back in her tomb and seal it permanently. Or maybe we find her, and bring the flight here to destroy her."

Rokshan was looking at her like she'd lost her mind. "If all those dragons couldn't kill her during the catastrophe, why would modern dragons succeed?"

"She's weak now. That has to make a difference." Impatiently, Lamprophyre rose. "It doesn't matter if we kill her or stop her. What matters is doing *something*. You've heard her speak, Rokshan. She's terrible and evil and she has no qualms about destroying anything or anyone that gets in her way. If we can keep her from hurting anyone else..."

Rokshan turned to look at Mother Stone. "It fills the sky," he murmured. "All right. You've convinced me. But there's a problem."

"Just one?"

Rokshan smiled. "I mean, sweetheart, humans aren't allowed on Mother Stone. And I'm human."

"Only nominally. You're a dragon in every other way that counts."

"You think the other dragons won't mind just because we're pair-bonded? I'm not sure they'd agree. Chrysoprase, for one, would want me drawn and quartered for my effrontery."

"Chrysoprase has a stick up her posterior and everyone knows it. Most of the dragons will see sense. Unless you want me to go alone."

"No. Not on your life. If there's an ancient evil dragon lurking on Mother Stone, you are not facing her alone." Rokshan sighed. "I guess what they don't know won't hurt anyone."

"That's a better way to look at it." Lamprophyre settled down again. "I wish we could go now."

"That would be suicide. Sardonyx has waited a thousand years. She can wait a while longer."

Rokshan settled back into the curve of her body, and Lamprophyre rested her head on her arms. She was too excited to sleep. She made herself think like Bromargyrite the pessimist. She could be wrong, and there was nothing on Mother Stone but the bones of dead dragons. She could be right, but discover there was nothing she and Rokshan could do to keep Sardonyx from escaping. She recounted dozens of possibilities to herself until she fell asleep.

~

THE FIRST LIGHT OF DAWN ROUSED LAMPROPHYRE, BUT SLOWLY, bringing her out of dreams that shredded and faded as she became conscious. She'd woken at late evening to heat the stones, then again in the dreaming hours, but despite the frequent wakings and the fact that she'd slept in the harness, she felt refreshed. The cold morning air invigorated her, sending her blood racing. It smelled of snow and, distantly, of the ecclesiasts' fire, a sour, bitter aroma that matched her mood when she thought about them.

Rokshan slept beside her, one arm flung over his face as if the pale light of dawn were a brilliant beacon. She stood carefully so as not to wake him and heated the stones a final time. They snapped and cracked in the cold, one or two of them breaking in half, but she settled them closer around Rokshan and took off for the lowlands, and breakfast.

This time, she surprised a sounder of wild boar sows and carried off two of them while the rest scattered. It was more meat than she and Rokshan needed, but she felt in need of extra sustenance that day if they were going to tackle Mother Stone.

The thought made her tremble with nervous excitement. No living dragon—none who wanted to stay living—had ever gone to Mother Stone. Even the ones who helped the very old and very ill dragons unable to make the full flight themselves went only as far as her base. Deep down, it felt wrong, blasphemous, and she shoved those feelings deeper and flew faster. This was important. It mattered more than ancient superstitions. She and Rokshan weren't doing this for fun, or to break some kind of record; they were doing it for the sake of everyone, humans and dragons alike.

When she finished skinning and roasting the boars, Rokshan was awake and sitting with his hands held over the stones. "That smells better than anything I've ever eaten," he said. "What is it about cooking outdoors that makes everything taste amazing?"

"The adventure of being away from civilization, maybe?" Lamprophyre offered him a hunk of meat, dripping with juice, that he took with his bare hands. She tore off a mouthful for herself and looked down the slope to the ecclesiasts' camp. Only a couple of them were awake, but she could hear echoes of dreams and counted five minds. They couldn't have gone anywhere in the night, but the sounds relieved her mind.

"I think we should warn the ecclesiasts that we're leaving temporarily, so they don't get any bright ideas about breaking their word," Rokshan said.

"I agree." Lamprophyre took another bite. Rokshan was right; the meat was delicious. "And this might take a while. I don't know how high we'll have to go."

"It can't be that high," Rokshan pointed out. "Even ancient dragons have limitations. And there's no reason to believe they're more capable of surviving at high altitudes than modern dragons are."

"Even so, we have to go slowly." Lamprophyre looked over her shoulder at Mother Stone, who looked innocently enormous. The sun hadn't yet touched all her slopes, and she was deep blue in the creases and crevices of her western flanks. "I wonder what it looks like. The death grounds, I mean."

"Dragons aren't afraid of cemeteries, are they? Places where the dead are buried," Rokshan clarified when Lamprophyre looked puzzled.

"No. The dead are gone, their spirits collected to Mother

Stone's rest, and their bodies can't hurt anyone. It just makes me curious."

"Well, give it a few hours and your curiosity will be satisfied," Rokshan said. He accepted another hunk of meat.

When their meal was finished, Lamprophyre collected the remains and what was left of the previous night's meal and very awkwardly flew down the mountain to leave everything where scavengers could pick the bones clean. On her return, she found Rokshan talking to Nirav. "We'll be back tonight," he was saying, "and we'll talk further then."

"Nothing's going to change," Nirav said. He looked nervous at Lamprophyre's appearance. Lamprophyre quickly did another count—still five ecclesiasts. Nirav's agitation looked guilty, but at least it wasn't the guilt of concealing the absence of one of his companions.

"We'll see," Rokshan said. "I have faith Jiwanyil will give you a solution."

Nirav thought *wish I had that kind of faith*, but said nothing, just gave Rokshan a timid salute like bidding farewell. Rokshan climbed into the saddle and fastened the straps, and Lamprophyre leaped toward the distant mountain.

"He doesn't believe," she told Rokshan when they were out of earshot of the ecclesiasts.

"I can tell. But Ashta does, for all her other flaws, and I hope she wants a solution badly enough to pray sincerely for it." Rokshan patted her neck with his gloved hand. "Let's not worry about that now. We have plenty of other worries to plague us. Like how we're doing something no one's done in more than a millennium."

That excited tingle shot through Lamprophyre again. "Are you warm enough?"

"For now. Can you fly faster?"

Lamprophyre flexed her wings. "Hold on," she said, and sped toward the mountain filling the northern sky.

CHAPTER EIGHTEEN

In less than a hundred beats, they were surrounded by the mountains that guarded the ascent to Mother Stone. Her Handmaidens, the dragons called them, every one of them tall and proud and as merciless as their mother. Lamprophyre swept between two peaks and rose slightly to fly over a low-lying cloud bank. The rocky slopes were heavy with snow, and Lamprophyre wondered how much of it melted during the summer, and whether there were snow layers that had been there since before she was born.

It was easy to imagine this place unchanged for millennia. No winds blew this morning, and the slow, steady *thwap* of Lamprophyre's wings beating the air was all that broke the stillness. She hadn't yet ascended above the lowest peaks, but she rose steadily, hoping it would be slowly enough. When she'd gotten sick from the high altitude as a child, it was because she'd flown nearly straight up on a dare from Orthoclase. Dragons in general could handle the great heights if they made smoother, more gradual ascents, but she wasn't sure about Rokshan.

"You tell me if you start to feel sick, all right?" she said. "Nausea, headache, things like that."

"I feel fine now, but I won't be stupid," Rokshan replied. "This place is extraordinary."

Lamprophyre flew past the last of the Handmaidens and continued her ascent. Ahead, a gash of exposed gray granite marked where an avalanche had bared a section of Mother Stone's lowest slope—and something else. "Look at that," Lamprophyre said, and banked to veer closer.

"What is it?" Rokshan said.

Lamprophyre slowed to hover at the top of the bare stone. A deep crack had been shaped into a hollow in the side of the mountain, and a pale shape curled within. "It's a dragon," she said. "I think it's Gabbro."

"Who is Gabbro?"

Lamprophyre leaned closer to peer into the hollow. "He went mad, slowly, over several years, and at the end he couldn't care for himself and forgot to eat. He had to have help to get here, but this is far too low."

"If he was mad, how would he know what to do when he got here?" Rokshan leaned out to get a better look. "And why is he so pale?"

Lamprophyre put out a hand to grip the edge of the cliff and dragged herself closer. "I don't know. Maybe dragons lose their color after they die. I've never seen a dead dragon before, but I know if we're injured—like, if someone accidentally gets clawed—the scar tissue is clear, like the color drains away with our blood." This didn't make sense. Even if whoever had brought Gabbro here had built his death-cave for him, they should have done it higher up, where it could be of ice.

"I wish I knew who'd accompanied Gabbro on his death journey," she mused. "And I'm sure he couldn't have sung the song."

"Does that mean anything?"

"I don't know." She flapped away from the hollow backwards, her eyes on Gabbro's body. "It's just strange. It's not at all what I was taught."

"I'm sure they had to make accommodations. Doesn't it matter more that he made it here, wherever on the mountain he ended up?"

"I suppose you're right." She wheeled and flew on with one final backward glance at the dead dragon.

The obvious approach to Mother Stone was to fly up her slopes, but that ascent was definitely too steep. Lamprophyre instead spiraled around the mountain, gradually slanting upward. "This is better anyway," she said. "We should be looking for caves, or deep crevasses."

"The glare off the snow makes it hard to see," Rokshan said. "But so far I haven't seen anything that might lead further in. I assume what we're looking for is inside."

"That was my thought, yes."

Occasional clouds blocked the sun, which was well above the horizon, but Rokshan was right; the snow caught its brightness and reflected it back a dozenfold. Lamprophyre closed her nictitating membranes and surveyed the depths beneath, just in case she was wrong and what they were looking for was below Mother Stone instead of high within her.

The wall of stone took a sudden turn, folding inward to make a deep crease in the mountain's side. Lamprophyre followed it. Within its shelter, the snow was packed deep, and the air smelled damp and stony and cold. Lamprophyre flew as close to the wall as she could without running into it and hovered, sniffing. "It smells different here," she said. "Almost bitter."

"I can't smell anything in this cold," Rokshan said.

Lamprophyre brushed snow away, nearly a handspan deep, before reaching the stone—and something else. "It's another dragon," she said. "I don't recognize this one, but I think she's very old."

"You don't mean she's alive?" Rokshan said, sounding alarmed.

"No, I mean she's been here a lot longer than Gabbro. This is more like what I envisioned." She brushed away more snow. The dead dragon lay partially encased in ice, with her head curled into her body. She was as pale as Gabbro had been. Lamprophyre sniffed. "She's the source of the bitter smell, but I don't know why. I think there must be dozens of dragons here for it to smell so strongly."

"Let's not stop to unearth each one, please," Rokshan said. "We don't have a lot of time to spare, especially if we're going to make a slow ascent."

"Right." Lamprophyre winged away from the dragon. She hadn't known what she would feel, confronted with reminders of dragon mortality, and the rush of peaceful satisfaction, the knowledge that someday she would share in this experience, filled her with hope. It was the idea that one was still a dragon after death that made it such heartening knowledge. Not that she was in any hurry to join them, not with so much of her life ahead of her, but she understood better now why this place mattered so much to dragons. It didn't feel sacred, exactly, or holy, and she had expected to sense something unusual, something divine, but there was nothing frightening about Mother Stone.

She continued her spiral, circling the mountain, as the sun rose higher. The eastern face of the mountain was sheer and patchy where the sun had melted the snow enough to cause more slides. They saw no caves, nothing that might lead to the mountain's interior.

"We're not going all the way to the top, are we?" Rokshan said. "I'm feeling a little short of breath."

Lamprophyre's chest ached too, and she'd been drawing increasingly deep breaths for the past thousand beats. "I don't think there's enough air at the top to support my wings," she said. "I'm going to assume if dragons can't reach that high, they couldn't have imprisoned anyone there. We'll make one more circle, and if we haven't seen anything by then, we search again going back down."

"Good idea." Rokshan's voice was muffled by his scarf, and Lamprophyre hoped he was still all right. She was starting to feel discouraged as the peaceful feeling the dead dragon had instilled in her dissipated. She'd been so sure her guess was right, but there wasn't anything here except snow and rock and dragon remains.

She swept onward, around the southern face. She had no idea

how far up they'd come, but the air was bitterly cold and her skin felt dry and itchy, signs that she was much higher than any sane dragon wanted to go. The insides of her nostrils and the corners of her eyes felt dry, too, and her hands and feet, while not exactly numb, felt too swollen to close properly. Just another thousand beats, and they would have to turn back.

In the glare from the sunlight, the slopes beneath them made an eyewatering pattern of black and white, black where granite protrusions extended from the white packed snow. Some of the black patches were large, and the snow glitter made them seem at once sharply protuberant and deeply carved into the surface—

She gasped. "There's a cave."

"I see it," Rokshan said. "I'm too snow-blinded to tell how big it is. It looks too small for us."

"Then let's find out," Lamprophyre said, and banked in a long, sweeping curve toward the mountain.

They'd been flying more than six dragonlengths from the surface of the mountain, and as they approached, Lamprophyre watched the cave grow larger until there was no question it was much, much bigger than they were. It had a jutting lip that extended nearly a dragonlength from the cave mouth, giving Lamprophyre an easy perch. The mouth of the cave was twice as tall as the lip and black as night, deeper than the sunlight could reach. It was impossible to tell how deep it went.

Lamprophyre crouched to let Rokshan down, and they both stared into the darkness. "I didn't think about the possibility we wouldn't be able to see," Lamprophyre said. Her chest still ached from the lack of air and she felt slightly dizzy, but so long as she wasn't nauseated, she could convince herself she was fine.

"Neither did I, but apparently I came prepared," Rokshan said. He reached inside his coat and withdrew a fat cylinder half the length of his forearm. "I borrowed this from military stores about a week ago. It's a prototype I was curious about." He held the cylinder in both hands and gave it a half-twist. A faint gleam shone from one end. "It's much brighter in darkness, obviously."

"How did you know we'd need that?" Lamprophyre exclaimed.

"I didn't. It's just too valuable to leave lying around. It's got a thumbnail-sized diamond in its core. I took it so I could walk after dark to that party Yalini hosted and then forgot to give it back." He waved the cylinder at the cave, lighting it bright as day. The cave extended deeper into the mountain, well past the range of the magic light. "What was that you said about not exploring unknown caves?"

"I doubt there's anything dangerous to you up here, and dragons have no natural predators." Lamprophyre still hesitated. It was one thing to speculate about evil dragons trapped somewhere on Mother Stone, and another to find out it might actually be true. But this was why they'd come, and there was no point being cowardly now. "Let's go."

She let Rokshan lead the way. His light artifact made a large, bright circle he swept across the path before them, illuminating the black granite walls. Lamprophyre stopped to examine them. "This was hollowed out by dragons," she said. "I think we're on the right path."

"The floor is uneven," Rokshan said. "As if they didn't care about having regular footing."

"Well, this passage is big enough for me to fly through. It would be a tight fit, though." Lamprophyre experimentally spread her wings and flinched when the tips brushed the chilly stone. "Very tight fit."

They walked on, rarely speaking, as the path gently sloped downward. Their footsteps echoed off the walls, but faintly, as if the walls swallowed sound. It was warmer now, far from the freezing winds that blew around Mother Stone day and night, and Lamprophyre saw Rokshan remove his gloves and tuck them into his waistband. The thin air was slightly damp and had that bitter smell she now associated with dead dragons, though it wasn't overpowering. Still, if this cave only led to more death-caves, it would be so disappointing.

The passage was widening now, with the floor becoming even

more irregular until they were in a perfectly circular tunnel. "I wonder if dragons just enlarged a tunnel they found," Lamprophyre said. "It would take forever to hollow this out from nothing." She picked her way over the rough floor, following Rokshan, who had his arms spread wide to keep his balance. The light danced randomly over the walls as he moved.

Lamprophyre looked past him and grabbed his hand. "Turn off the light," she whispered.

Rokshan obeyed. "Why are we whispering?"

Lamprophyre shook her head. "I don't know. It's just—there's a light up ahead."

It wasn't so much a light as a patch of gray lighter than the black granite. "We're going to need the light if we don't want to trip over this floor," Rokshan said. "Besides, I think that's sunlight. I think this place opens up to the outdoors." He turned the light back on, and they walked on, moving as fast as they dared.

The gray glow intensified and grew paler as they approached, until Rokshan was able to turn off his light. The glow seemed to be coming from above. Lamprophyre's foot slipped, and she dug in her blunt toe claws to keep her footing. Rokshan flailed briefly and then came to a stop. "It's ice," he said. "Look at the walls. They're coated with it."

Even in the dim light, it was clear Rokshan was right: patches of ice clung to the wall and the floor. Lamprophyre tapped the wall with one claw. "It's very thick," she said. "Why is there ice in the middle of the mountain?"

"If this passage is open to the outside—but where would the water come from?" Rokshan shook his head. "Let's move on."

The ice thickened and spread as they walked. Eventually Rokshan had to put on his gloves and use his hands to keep his balance on the slick surface, while Lamprophyre resorted to crawling with claws extended. The tunnel continued to widen as they neared the source of the glow, which appeared to be a hole in the ceiling. Then the tunnel came to an abrupt end, and they stopped, too stunned to move.

The tunnel let out into a vast bowl-shaped chamber completely lined with blue-white ice, its surface pitted and cracked with age. The walls curved and kept curving until they met the opening in the center of the roof and became a chimney about three dragonlengths across and impossibly tall. A speck of blue at the top might have been the sky. It smelled bitter, but the scent was still faint. Lamprophyre saw no evidence of dragon bodies aside from the smell. The chamber was as empty as the sky above Mother Stone.

Lamprophyre and Rokshan exchanged looks. Lamprophyre couldn't think of anything to say. The place inspired reverence even if you didn't know dragons were buried here. She took a step forward and paused when her foot slipped a little. "Climb up," she said. "Let's fly rather than stumble through here. It feels right."

Rokshan climbed into his seat, and Lamprophyre flapped slowly until she was midway between the floor and the roof. The ice looked thinner overhead, darker as if the granite were closer to the surface. Lamprophyre did a sweep of the chamber. There were shadows beyond the ice, indistinct shapes she told herself were dragon bodies. "This is amazing."

"What's that?" Rokshan said. She turned her head to see where he was pointing and saw a patch of ice that glowed greenish-white instead of blue. Whatever it was was embedded in the floor. She glided to land beside it, skidding slightly, and crouched so Rokshan could get off. He knelt and swept away fine, loose particles of ice crystals that clung to the leather of his gloves. "It looks like green fire, or like molten green ore," he said. "I don't know what it is."

Then he stiffened and bowed his head, his whole body rigid. The green fire pulsed once. "Rokshan?" Lamprophyre said, alarmed. "Are you all right?"

Rokshan's head came up. His eyes blazed green, solidly leaf-green from edge to edge. *"It is done,"* Jiwanyil's voice said. *"A human presence unlocks the door, as demanded in the old contract. She is free."*

Lamprophyre grabbed Rokshan by the shoulders. "What do you mean? Jiwanyil—you can't mean—"

Rokshan stared back at her, unblinking. "*Their death is in the wind and the fire, and she will not be stopped*," he said in that same terrible voice. "*Let dragon and human together fight the banded desert. The end draws near.*"

"It can't be," Lamprophyre exclaimed. "You said—the stories all said Mother Stone would prevent it. That she swallowed them up. She won't let it happen."

Rokshan felt like a stone in her hands, heavy and unresponsive. Only his lips moved. "*No god,*" he said, "*no stone, no life, no heart. You reach for what was never there. The prison doors gape open, and the fire and the wind break free. The skies will burn.*"

As Rokshan spoke those final words, the green light faded away to nothing. A tremendous groan as of a thousand dragons giving voice at once surged through the chamber. It was followed immediately by a sharp crack like thunder that made Lamprophyre let go of Rokshan and cover her ears. Rokshan fell and didn't try to catch himself. Lamprophyre cried out and picked him up, cradling him gently in her arms. "Rokshan. Rokshan, are you all right?"

Rokshan didn't respond. She carefully thumbed his eyelid up and felt only scant relief at seeing his eyes were their normal brown. She laid her cheek against his mouth and felt warm air sighing in and out, which was more of a relief. "Rokshan, wake up," she murmured in his ear. "I need you to wake up."

He still didn't move. Desperate, Lamprophyre hoisted him in her arms and turned around. The icy walls of the cavern glowed with a dozen colors, blues and reds and yellows and purples, and movement was visible beyond the ice. Lamprophyre's heart beat faster. She cast an eye on the ice chimney and saw the same colors playing over the walls. Her instincts told her escape by that route was impossible. That left the tunnel, narrow and cramped, but still a way out.

Another crack shattered the stillness of the air, along with the thunderous noise of boulders falling, cascading across the ice sheet of the floor. Lamprophyre couldn't help herself; she turned to see what had made the noise.

An enormous red shape, bigger than Lamprophyre, bigger than Hyaloclast, emerged from a hollow in the wall that had been concealed by the ice sheet. Her wings were a mass of spines and thickly ribbed with red phalanges so the gold membranes were almost invisible. Gold dusted her chest and belly scales, which were paler than the rest of her. The dragon shook free of the last of the ice shards and turned a baleful golden eye on Lamprophyre.

"How perfectly delightful," she said in a lovely voice that chilled Lamprophyre to her core. "And here I thought you were my enemy. Why did you bring a human here to free me?"

"I...I didn't...we..." Lamprophyre stammered.

"Oh, you most certainly did," the dragon said with a smile. "And now I can finish what I began...oh, it doesn't matter how long ago it was. The point is the eradication of the human pestilence, isn't it?"

Lamprophyre reflexively clutched Rokshan closer. She barely noticed that he had started to move. "No," she whispered. "I won't let you have him."

"Won't you?" The smile widened into a cruel twist of dragon lips. "Then," Sardonyx said, "I suggest you *run*."

Lamprophyre turned and fled.

CHAPTER NINETEEN

She held Rokshan tightly as she swept through the tunnel, beating her wings as hard as she could. Distantly, she heard more sharp cracks as the ice shattered, but no sounds of pursuit. She flew faster anyway, desperation making her heart pound like thunder in her ears. Sardonyx freed. Her fault. Mother Stone—she shied away from that line of thought. Jiwanyil was lying. He was a foul, horrible creature who'd lured them in so he could see Sardonyx freed.

The blackness was nearly complete within the tunnel, and Lamprophyre thanked whoever had dug it for how straight it was, because even with that, she kept blundering into walls. She didn't have an extra hand to work Rokshan's light artifact and hoped there weren't any unexpected turns—

With that, she ran face-first into a wall, dizzying herself. She collapsed on the floor, breathing heavily, unable to continue.

Rokshan stirred. "Lamprophyre, where..." he said in a faint voice.

"Can't explain," she said. "Can you ride?"

"Don't...know..." He shifted again in her grip. "Put me down?"

She gently laid him on the ground, hoping its roughness

wouldn't hurt him more. She'd seen ecclesiasts possessed of prophecies, and it always left them weak for a time. They didn't *have* time. At any moment, Sardonyx and her dragons would come pouring through the tunnel, and then it would all be over. "I *really* need you to be able to ride," she said, trying to control her impatience and fear.

"With...the harness...sure," Rokshan said.

She crouched as low as she could to give him a leg up. He moved so slowly it nearly drove her mad, but she held still and waited for him to fit his feet into the stirrups and fasten the hip straps. "Light, please," she said, and Rokshan turned on the light, revealing the turn in the tunnel that had surprised Lamprophyre. She positioned herself correctly and flew.

Rokshan's grip on her ruff was firm, and he didn't wobble or tilt, but the narrowing passage meant she started bumping into walls and had to slow, her heart screaming at her to fly faster. Finally, she burst from the tunnel's mouth and coasted in a long, smooth glide toward the valley floor. Still she heard no sound of pursuit. Maybe Sardonyx was weak from her long imprisonment. Maybe it would take time to mobilize all her dragons—Stones, how many dragons were there? All those lights, and if each light represented a dragon...

Lamprophyre made herself think rationally. The flight outnumbered Sardonyx's dragons, if that was the case, and they were powerful fighters. And the humans weren't helpless.

She flew as fast as she dared through the Handmaidens, hoping Rokshan wouldn't start asking questions. She was tired and confused and frightened and the idea of explaining everything to Rokshan made her feel even more so. Especially since she wasn't entirely sure herself what had happened.

A loud, high-pitched cry rang out across the peaks. Lamprophyre wheeled and hovered, afraid to stop and even more afraid not to see what that had been. A speck of red hovered over the slopes of Mother Stone. For one mad moment, Lamprophyre thought Sardonyx was alone, that those lights hadn't meant anything. Then a rush as of a thousand wings filled the air, and dragons began pouring out of the mountain, filling the sky. Lamprophyre closed her teeth on a frightened shriek, turned, and fled.

She flew until her tortured lungs and wings couldn't bear more abuse, then came to a stumbling halt amid the crags and sagged to hands and knees, sucking in air as if she were drowning. She barely felt Rokshan hop down and put his hands on the sides of her face. "Lamprophyre, what happened?" he said. His voice sounded breathy past the blood rushing through her ears.

She shook her head. "Just don't ask yet," she whispered. "Give me a few beats."

She focused on breathing until she felt less shaky, then settled back on her haunches. "What do you remember?"

"Kneeling to look at that green light," Rokshan said, "and then you were holding me, and I couldn't move, and it sounded like the mountain was coming down around us."

Lamprophyre closed her eyes, which made her sway as if her vision were the only thing keeping her upright. "Oh, Rokshan," she said, "we have been so stupid. And we were used."

She told him every detail. The words he'd spoken when he was possessed of Jiwanyil's prophecy. What Sardonyx had said. And her devastating conclusions about what it all meant. "He said Mother Stone is a lie," she said, hearing her voice shake. "She's not a god. The mountain was never anything but a prison, and we dragons were stupid enough—"

"It can't be true," Rokshan said. "Lamprophyre. You're not going to take the word of...I don't even know what it was that spoke through me, but I don't see how it can be a god."

"It was Jiwanyil," Lamprophyre said. "I mean, the voice was the one that speaks whenever someone is possessed of a prophecy. Which means—" She wished she were capable of tears. "It means there are no gods, because I cannot believe a god would let himself be trapped in an ice cave with a flight of evil dragons, let alone give prophecies that would allow them to be freed. And if there's no Jiwanyil, why would any of the other human gods be real? Rokshan, what are we going to do?"

"We have to warn Hyaloclast, and then my father," Rokshan said. "There's no time to have a religious crisis. Sardonyx is coming, and she wants humans dead. We have to stop her."

Lamprophyre nodded and crouched to let Rokshan up. "I'm so tired."

"Just a little farther. Hyaloclast will know what to do."

Lamprophyre rose into the air and headed south. After the frigid ice cave, she found herself craving the warmth of the lowlands. She would fly a little ways south, then head west for the flight's caves.

Off to her left, she saw movement on the rocky slopes. Her heart, which had settled into its usual rhythm, sped up again. "Rokshan, the ecclesiasts," she said. "Sardonyx is going to pass right over them."

"We have to warn them," Rokshan said.

A rush of wind blew past, and something darkened the sun. Lamprophyre looked up. Dragons filled the sky, their wings black and backlit by the sun. They flew in a tight formation Lamprophyre had never seen in anything else but human military movements. For a moment, all she could do was gape. Then she flapped into motion. "We can't draw attention to the ecclesiasts," she said. "Maybe she won't see them."

As she spoke, the formation wheeled as one and dove. Lamprophyre screamed, "No!" and followed them, pushing herself as hard as she could.

It wasn't enough.

She was still twenty dragonlengths from the ecclesiasts' camp when half the dragons above split away from the rest and soared above where the humans stood. The ecclesiasts all stared up at the dragons in wonder. Lamprophyre screamed again.

In eerie silence, the dragons opened their mouths, and fire shot from them to engulf the ecclesiasts' camp. The humans didn't even have time to scream.

"Lamprophyre, we have to go!" Rokshan was shouting. Lamprophyre's fury blinded her, and for a few beats she shot toward the dragons, with no idea what she intended to do if she caught up to them. It took Rokshan beating his fists against the side of her head to bring her to herself.

She saw Sardonyx, who alone among the female dragons hadn't taken part in the incineration. Sardonyx was looking at her, her expression indistinct at that distance, but Lamprophyre was suddenly horribly aware of how exposed Rokshan was, sitting behind her shoulders. And yet the ancient dragon's gaze pinned her, made it impossible to turn away. Suddenly Lamprophyre's terror turned into fury again. This evil creature had ordered the deaths of five rational beings just because they were humans, and she would do the same for any human she encountered. She had to be stopped.

Lamprophyre made a rude gesture she'd learned from Manishi and wheeled, not waiting to see if it was a gesture that meant anything to Sardonyx. Within beats, they'd left the ancient dragon flight behind and were well on the way to Lamprophyre's home.

Her fury bled away from her as she flew, leaving her once again feeling cold and sick. All her thoughts narrowed down to the one bleak fact that she and Rokshan were responsible for this disaster. A human presence to unlock the door. If that was why the prohibition against humans on Mother Stone existed, why hadn't the dragons who'd passed the knowledge of that ban down revealed any of the rest?

She gritted her teeth and made herself focus on the present. Sardonyx was awake and free, and never mind how it had happened. Someone needed to stop her. Hyaloclast would know what to do.

She was so absorbed in her horrible thoughts she almost overshot the caves and had to wheel round when Rokshan called out a warning. Snow blanketed the crags, everywhere but where the female dragons had melted spots for dragons to sun themselves. Dragonets too young to fly romped through the piles of snow, watched over by their parents. It was all so normal Lamprophyre felt even sicker, as if her stupidity had doomed not only humanity, but all these blissfully ignorant dragons.

She came to a running halt outside Hyaloclast's cave and nearly dumped Rokshan on his rear helping him down. The curious thoughts of the nearest dragons sharpened at the sight of a human, but no one was angry or disgusted at his presence. It would have heartened her if she hadn't been so miserable. "Wait here," she told him, and hurried into Hyaloclast's cave.

She'd lived here for the first thirty years of her life, and it was as familiar to her as her own fingers, the curving, narrow path that led to the cave big enough to fit five adult females, the traceries of phosphorescence casting a purple glow over the interior. Hyaloclast sat next to a pile of radiantly hot stones, talking to Leucite. The bronze male half-turned to look at Lamprophyre when she stumbled to a halt just inside the entrance. Hyaloclast's eyes narrowed in irritation. The irritation cleared when she recognized Lamprophyre. "Something's wrong," she said.

Lamprophyre, still a little out of breath, only nodded. Hyaloclast nodded at Leucite. "Please excuse us," she said.

Lamprophyre moved to let Leucite pass. He gave her a curious look, but said nothing. That was typical of Leucite, whose calmness and certainty of manner were normally reassuring. Now Lamprophyre felt as if no amount of calmness would make a difference.

When she heard him exit the cave mouth, she walked toward Hyaloclast and drew in a deep breath. If Hyaloclast was going to metaphorically eviscerate her, better to get it over with. "Sardonyx is free," she said. "Rokshan and I accidentally let her out of her prison."

Hyaloclast's eyes widened, but aside from that and a convulsive twitch of her wings, she didn't react. "You let her out."

"It was an accident," Lamprophyre repeated. "We realized she had to be on Mother Stone—"

Now Hyaloclast shot to her feet. "What?"

How grateful Lamprophyre was that she understood her mother better now, because she managed not to quail before the enormous dragon. "It was in the prophecies and the histories," she said, meeting the blood-red gaze fearlessly. "The dragons and humans opposed to Sardonyx a millennium ago worked some kind of magic referred to later as the mountains swallowing her up. I guessed that meant she was trapped on Mother Stone."

"That's quite a guess," Hyaloclast said. "You took a human to Mother Stone?"

"I took *Rokshan*," Lamprophyre protested. "I thought, he has a pair-bond, he's almost a dragon, I didn't think it would be blasphemous." She drew in another deep breath. "It turns out it didn't matter. It was the presence of a human that did it. Jiwanyil said so."

Hyaloclast blinked in confusion. "Jiwanyil? What does a human god have to do with any of this?"

"I don't know. But I know the voice—I don't think he's a god. He was trapped there too. And he said 'a human presence unlocks the door, as demanded in the old contract' like that's what was necessary to free Sardonyx. He's been guiding people toward this for years. He wanted Sardonyx freed."

Hyaloclast's lips thinned in a grimace. "Where is she now?"

"I don't know. She flew away. She and her flight of dragons."

"Her *what?*" Hyaloclast roared. She stood to her full height and snapped her wings open. *Now* Lamprophyre cringed. "How many?"

"A little less than two hundred," Lamprophyre said. "I didn't count. But we outnumber them, so—"

"This is a disaster," Hyaloclast said. "Where were they going?"

"She wants to wipe out the human pestilence, she said." Lamprophyre wished she dared curl up in a ball like a frightened dragonet and wake to find this all a bad dream. "I don't know where she went first."

Hyaloclast furled her wings. "We'll have to stop her," she said. "You'll show us where you saw her last. We can discuss how stupid you were later."

"I'm sorry. I don't know how to make things right."

Hyaloclast shook her head. Suddenly she looked very tired, her head sagging, her wings limp. "We have laws for a reason. If you hadn't disregarded them, this wouldn't have happened."

"Then maybe someone should have explained those laws

better!" Lamprophyre shouted. "Do you think I wanted her freed? I thought, if we could find her, the magic on her prison could be renewed. She was getting free anyway, Hyaloclast! And no, I'm not making excuses. I'm just saying I would never have done what I did if I'd known the truth, so I hope this wasn't a secret you felt you needed to keep!"

"I know," Hyaloclast said. "And no, this is not knowledge dragon queens have been sitting on for a millennium. You were foolish, but I don't believe there's any point in blaming you for more than that. What matters now is stopping Sardonyx and her flight. You and the young prince will return to the human city and warn his father. Tell him to prepare for war."

"But you and the flight will stop her."

Hyaloclast shook her head again. "I'm honored by your faith in me, but we are not warriors, and we have no idea what kind of foe we're up against. If Sardonyx's dragons waged war all those centuries ago against dragons who were powerless to stop them, I have very little confidence that this will be a fight between equals. Now—no more talking. The longer we wait, the farther away Sardonyx gets, and tracking her down will be even more difficult."

Lamprophyre stood aside to let Hyaloclast past. She felt even smaller and more ashamed than ever. If she hadn't broken the law, if she hadn't been so casually certain the law didn't apply to her...the fact that Hyaloclast hadn't torn into her only made things worse. She would have welcomed a good castigation.

When she emerged, Rokshan was waiting for her beside the cave entrance. He had his attention on Hyaloclast, who had sent up the fiery signal for the dragons to congregate. "She didn't tear you apart," he murmured. "She didn't even look at me. Did you not tell her it was our fault?"

"I did. I think she's saving up her anger for when the crisis is past." Lamprophyre sat beside him. "She wants us to show her where we saw Sardonyx last, and then fly to tell your father. Rokshan, what if it's already too late? What if Tanajital is where they were going?"

"The dragons are essential to our defense," Rokshan said. "The pyrite weapons are deployed along the Fanishkorite border. There's only a few in the capital. If Hyaloclast and the flight can catch up to Sardonyx, maybe that will be the end of it. We outnumber her."

Lamprophyre was only half-listening to the dragon queen telling everyone what had happened. Hyaloclast didn't say anything about how Sardonyx had been freed, which made Lamprophyre feel even more guilty, as if her mother had compromised her honor for Lamprophyre's sake. "We do, but Sardonyx's dragons are fighters," she said, "and if they're all as big and powerful as she is—I mean, who knows what those ancient dragons are capable of?"

A roar went up from the assembled dragons, startling both Lamprophyre and Rokshan. Hyaloclast turned to face them. "We go now," she said. "Lead the way."

Rokshan scrambled into his seat. Lamprophyre heard a couple of thoughts about how ridiculous Lamprophyre looked wearing the harness, but she was too miserable to have room to be bothered by that minor cruelty. She took off, followed by the sound of hundreds of wings beating the air.

It was easy to find the spot Lamprophyre had last seen Sardonyx. The smell of incinerated flesh still filled the air. The memory of those five faces turned toward the sky in wonder made Lamprophyre want to scream. She made herself stay calm and said, "They were headed southeast. I don't know what human cities are in that direction. It wasn't toward Tanajital."

"If Sardonyx continued in a straight line that way," Rokshan said, "she'd eventually come upon Ghiridi and Hammadi. And I'm sure there are any number of smaller villages. The desert is beyond that, and then you come to the sea."

"We will catch her," Hyaloclast said. "Warn your father that I will meet with him after we have encountered our enemy and assessed their strengths. Now, fly swiftly, and let us all hope it's not too late."

Lamprophyre nodded, wheeled in midair, and arrowed toward Tanajital.

CHAPTER TWENTY

They flew to Tanajital in silence. Lamprophyre's weariness, and the aftermath of the terror of fleeing Sardonyx, meant she flew more slowly than she wanted. She would push herself to her limit for a few hundred beats, then slowly decelerate until she realized she was almost ambling and sped up again. Her mind was too tired to torment her with memories. Instead, she ran over in her head what she would tell King Ekanath. At least he knew about Sardonyx, and she wouldn't have to convince him of the threat the ancient dragon posed. She hoped.

It felt like hours before the great pink-gold walls of Tanajital became more than a fuzzy blotch on the horizon. Lamprophyre had never felt so grateful for the Green River's guidance to her destination. Then she realized if Sardonyx knew humans settled along the rivers, the Green River would be the death not only of Tanajital, but of dozens of other human cities. She pushed herself faster.

She wished she dared find her clutch first, tell them and hope for their support, but protecting the city was more important. So she sailed past the warehouses, past the red sandstone of the coliseum, and landed neatly on the training grounds outside the palace. Rokshan was down almost before she settled. "I'll be back," he said.

Lamprophyre lay on the hard earth, not caring who saw her giving in to despair, and covered her face with her wings. It was a position that stretched her wings uncomfortably, but she liked the illusion of security that hiding behind the tough membranes gave. Maybe she should take the time Rokshan was gone to alert the clutch. Maybe he'd tell his father everything, and she would be spared having to explain, again, how she and Rokshan had been unspeakably stupid.

No. That was the coward's way out. She had made a mistake, not done intentional evil, and she could admit to that and do her best to fix things.

She put back her wings and sighed. And then there was the issue of Jiwanyil to deal with. Whatever he was, he'd deliberately led humans to learn about Sardonyx and then had given prophecies that had resulted in Sardonyx being freed. He might be a god, or he might not, but he was definitely not on the side of good.

The side door to the palace, guarded by two soldiers bearing deadly-looking pikes, opened, and Rokshan emerged. To her surprise, Ekanath followed him. She hadn't expected the king to come to her. As she sat up, she felt the chalcedony pendant shift over her chest, and she touched it to still it. She didn't remember if Hyaloclast had been wearing its twin when she followed Sardonyx, and she wasn't sure she should distract the dragon queen from her pursuit, but the pendant might be useful.

"Ambassador," the king said when he neared her. "Rokshan tells me our enemy intends to destroy humanity. What can we do?"

Lamprophyre's heart sank. "I was, um, actually hoping you would know the answer to that," she said. "We don't know where Sardonyx went, and we don't know how successful Hyaloclast will be in fighting her. I think we need to find ways to protect as many cities as we can."

"That means moving the pyrite weapons from the border," Rokshan said.

"That will leave us vulnerable to Fanishkor," Ekanath protested.

"Your majesty, Fanishkor is much less of a threat than two

hundred dragons bent on destruction," Lamprophyre said. "Also, Chaaksha did say Fanishkor didn't intend to attack Gonjiri, and I think we should take them at their word. It's a risk worth taking."

Ekanath looked conflicted, but he nodded. "But it will take days to reposition the weapons," he said. "We may not have days."

"Leave that to us," Rokshan said. "I'm going to consult with Sajan, and we'll figure out a defensive strategy. But the people should be warned. They may need to evacuate their homes, especially those in the smaller towns."

"With the advance warnings from prophecy, that should be easier," Ekanath said.

Lamprophyre blinked. "What advance warnings?"

Ekanath frowned up at her. "Notices have been coming in since a little after nine o'clock this morning. Ecclesiasts all over the city have been possessed of prophecies, more at one time than anyone has ever seen. All of them were warnings of destruction coming to cities throughout Gonjiri—nothing specific, just declarations that those places were in danger. Now that we know of Sardonyx's threat, those warnings seem more urgent and immediate than we believed."

"But—" Lamprophyre looked at Rokshan.

"You're the one who heard Jiwanyil speak," Rokshan said.

"Yes, but he—" Lamprophyre suddenly realized something that had been niggling at her since the ice cavern. "How could Jiwanyil speak through you? You're not an ecclesiast."

"What are you talking about?" Ekanath said.

Lamprophyre felt horribly conflicted. Tell him the truth, or go on pretending Jiwanyil cared about humanity? "We heard Jiwanyil's voice," she said, deciding on a partial truth as the one that would cause the least confusion. "He told us—told me, through Rokshan—that freeing Sardonyx was something he wanted. Something he had been working toward."

Ekanath's confusion deepened. "I don't understand. Why would Jiwanyil want Sardonyx freed?"

"I don't know." Lamprophyre looked at Rokshan again. "But I

think we shouldn't listen to his prophecies. Whatever he wants, it's not to help humanity."

"But then why would he warn us against disaster?" Ekanath said. "You must be mistaken. Jiwanyil's word always saves us, even when we don't at first understand his mind."

"They can't afford to ignore those prophecies, Lamprophyre," Rokshan said. "If Sardonyx intends to destroy those cities, those people could be killed. And we can't protect all of them."

"But—" Lamprophyre saw Ekanath's face and gave up. She and Rokshan were the only ones who knew Jiwanyil, whatever he really was, was a threat, and there was no time to convince Ekanath of that. "Fine. It's true we need every advantage we can get. Rokshan, I'm going to tell my clutch what's happened, and we'll meet you back here in a few hundred beats, all right?"

Rokshan looked startled at her abruptness, but he nodded. Lamprophyre bowed to the king. "Hyaloclast and the dragon flight are strong. This might already be over." She leaped into the air without looking back.

She arrived at the warehouses out of breath and dropped to all fours to recover. Around her, she heard the sounds of dragons emerging from their warehouses. "Lamprophyre? You look done in," Orthoclase said. "Something wrong?"

She nodded, still gasping for air. When she looked up, all six of her clutchmates were looking at her in some dismay. "It's bad," she finally said when she could speak again. "I'm so glad you're all here, because I don't think I could bear to tell this story one more time."

She gave her clutch more detail even than she had Hyaloclast, leaving nothing out. When she finished, she waited for the barrage of questions, but they were silent. Finally, unable to bear it any longer, she said, "You're not going to yell at me, are you? Because I feel horrible as it is."

Dolomite said, "Mother Stone isn't a god?"

Lamprophyre looked at him. If he'd been human, she would have said he was on the verge of tears, he looked so distressed. She'd told them that without thinking of how it would affect them.

"I don't know," she said. "Jiwanyil, whoever he really is, said she isn't. Maybe he was lying, or wrong. He didn't have thoughts for me to listen to. But I don't think so. I never felt any sense of a god's presence about the mountain, and don't you think I should have, if she was really divine?"

Now she looked at the rest of them. All looked as stunned and afraid as Dolomite. Lamprophyre's guilt redoubled. Freed Sardonyx, and broke her friends' religious faith. She squared her shoulders like a human. "It doesn't matter," she declared. "We're still dragons, and we can still stop Sardonyx. If that's what you want to do."

Coquina shuddered as if she were coming out of a trance. "Of course it is," she said irritably. "You think we wouldn't do everything in our power to keep her from destroying our friends?"

"We can worry about the rest later," Bromargyrite said. "I'm more concerned that Jiwanyil started giving out prophecies right when you freed Sardonyx. Why would he do that?"

Lamprophyre hadn't put together the timing. "You're right," she said. "And I don't know why. I wasn't able to stay around and interrogate him. But unless I can convince the Archprelate that he's not a god, which I really believe he isn't, there's nothing we can do about that either."

"Then we should join Rokshan and see what the military wants from us," Flint said. "I hope it's something extraordinary. I feel the need to act."

They returned to the training grounds to find them alive with activity. Soldiers forming up in ranks making squares and rectangles marched away westward, toward the city center. Other soldiers ran from building to building, or from the buildings to the palace. They moved with such energetic purpose Lamprophyre felt invigorated just looking at them. Her despair faded a little. These humans seemed so certain their actions mattered it was hard not to feel the same.

Rokshan stood at the door to the largest building, talking to General Sajan. The gray-bearded man wore his yellow uniform covered with insignia as casually as if it were any other clothing, but

Lamprophyre knew now what some of the marks meant, and she felt reassured, again, at the knowledge that Sajan had power to command all the military forces. This meant only having to convince him of the need for action and not a thousand lesser men.

Rokshan looked up as the dragons descended, scattering soldiers. “Lamprophyre, Sajan has a request for the clutch,” he said.

“I was wondering,” Sajan said, “if the pyrite weapons are too heavy for a dragon to carry.”

Lamprophyre thought back to watching them swivel and blast distant objects. “I don’t think so,” she said. “They’d slow us down, though. Am I right that you want us to move them?”

“Exactly.” Sajan looked her up and down. “We want to position the weapons where they can defend our larger cities. Between those and the warning prophecies, I believe we have a good chance of protecting ourselves while we figure out an offensive strategy.”

“Hyaloclast and the flight are chasing Sardonyx right now,” Lamprophyre said. “They can attack Sardonyx’s dragons directly.”

“Which might be more than enough.” Sajan turned to Rokshan. “You don’t need to fly with them, right? Because I need you here, commanding our forces.”

Rokshan glanced at Lamprophyre. “I...no, I don’t need to,” he said. Lamprophyre didn’t need to hear his thoughts to know how much he wished he could turn down Sajan’s request. She wished he’d lied to Sajan. Then she felt bad about her wish. Rokshan was an exceptional military commander, and her desire to keep her mate close was a selfish one that might get people killed.

“If you’ll wait a moment, I’ll show you on the map where each weapon needs to go,” Sajan said. “And...thank you. I know this isn’t your fight. It’s humans this Sardonyx monster wants dead.”

“It’s our fight because we care about humans,” Coquina said. “And Sardonyx isn’t going to be gentle with dragons who defend humans just because we’re the same species as she is. Just give us direction, and let us help you.”

Sajan saluted Coquina, sending a ripple of mirth through the flight. He collared one of the young men running here and there and sent him off for the map. "How do dragons fight dragons?" he asked. "I thought you were immune to fire and acid."

Lamprophyre held out a hand and extended her claws. "These are sharp enough to tear through dragon hide. We've never fought other dragons, of course, but we learn fast."

"I wouldn't want to face those claws," Sajan said.

"Lamprophyre, let's take off that harness before you leave," Rokshan said. "You slept in it, and it must be so uncomfortable by now."

She'd been wearing the thing for almost a full day, and when Rokshan mentioned it, she suddenly became aware of how the saddle and straps wore on her. She went for the buckles and in a few beats had stripped the harness off and dropped it on the ground. "I'll take it to the embassy before we leave," she said.

The young man came back with a roll of paper almost as long as he was. Sajan helped him unroll it to reveal a map, tiny and perfect, though of course it was enormous by human standards. "Can you all see this well enough?" he asked. When they nodded, he went on, "We have a dozen pyrite weapons currently deployed on the western border. It will take at least two weapons each to adequately defend Tanajital and our other large cities. There are three weapons here already, and we would like you dragons to carry the other weapons to those cities and position them under the direction of the commanders located in each city."

He tapped the map with a long, smooth stick. "We've got more weapons being built, but we can't wait for them, which means some of our cities are going to be defenseless. I'm hoping to discuss more options with your queen." Lamprophyre heard him think *nothing else we can do, if I stop moving I'll give up entirely* and concluded he was hanging on to his brave front with both hands. It made her sad for him even as she admired his courage.

"We're going to put weapons in Kolmira, Suwedhi, Manjaret, Sunital, Nishta, Prabat, and of course Tanajital," Sajan went on. "Rokshan tells me our enemy went east, so it's important we protect Manjaret and Sunital first. They're unfortunately the farthest from the western border, so faster would be better."

Flint moved forward to look at the map more closely. "And the weapons are currently along this line?" he asked, pointing.

"That's correct."

"I know this spot," Flint said. "I've gone this way with Lokun a few times. I can take us there, and then we can separate to take weapons to the cities. You want each city fully defended, right? Not one weapon per city and then go back for the second?"

"Exactly." Sajan tapped the map again. "I can leave this to you?"

"Of course." Flint looked up. "We'll decide who's going where when we get to the border. Everyone ready to leave now?"

Lamprophyre glanced at Rokshan. She could hardly give him an affectionate farewell in front of Sajan and all these soldiers. She listened for his thoughts and heard, barely audible over the rest of the mental noise, *take care love you*. She smiled at him and winked, which made him smile too.

She collected the harness and wadded it into a small mass. "We'll return here when we're done," she said, and leapt into the sky.

She stopped at the embassy and put the harness inside the hall. When she emerged, Bhakriya was waiting for her. "My lady, that young woman was here again," she said. "The unpleasant one. She was very rude. She said to tell you you'd regret ignoring her."

Viveki. Lamprophyre had entirely forgotten they'd been supposed to meet her that morning at the plaza. She swore one of the human curse words she'd learned from Darsha, then apologized when Bhakriya blushed. "If she comes back, tell her we'll contact her," she said. "We have more important business to attend to."

"What's that, my lady?" Bhakriya asked.

So many possible responses occurred to Lamprophyre she fell momentarily silent. "Stopping a war," she finally said. "You—" She couldn't think where to tell Bhakriya to go for safety. Nowhere might be safe. "Keep everyone in the embassy—I mean actually inside—as much as possible, and if you see a lot of dragons in the sky, bar the door and don't leave." It might be enough. But she wasn't going to leave Bhakriya ignorant.

"There's an evil dragon and her followers intent on killing all humans," she said, and went on, overriding Bhakriya's startled outburst. "We're going to do what we can to stop her, but if she comes here, you need to be prepared. Tell Depik, and keep the children safe."

"But, my lady—why? What dragon?"

"I can't explain, and I really have to leave now," Lamprophyre said. With one last glance around the courtyard, she flapped her wings, rose off the ground a handspan or two, then said, "Wait. Bhakriya?"

Bhakriya, who'd turned to enter the dining pavilion, said, "Yes, my lady?"

It was worth trying. "When things are bad, you don't want to waste time not saying things you wish you'd said. Or not telling people how you feel. I think you and Depik need to have a talk."

Bhakriya blushed again, and Lamprophyre heard her thinking *just not sure* and *what if he* and wished once again she could have beaten Bhakriya's abusive former husband. "Don't be afraid," she said, "and don't waste any more time." She flapped harder, rose into the sky, and joined her clutch, who'd been hovering patiently.

"Ready to go?" Flint asked.

"Past ready," Lamprophyre said, and with Flint in the lead, they flew westward.

CHAPTER TWENTY-ONE

The sun hung low in the sky when Lamprophyre wearily flew into Tanajital. Her bones ached with tiredness and so did her eyes. With the nictitating membranes shut so the setting sun wouldn't blind her, she swooped low over the street leading to the embassy, not looking down to greet her neighbors as she usually did. In that state, the world was slightly out of focus, as if she were looking at it underwater. Or maybe it was her exhaustion that created that illusion. Either way, she needed sleep.

She was surprised to find the courtyard as full of beggars as ever. Confused, she landed on the roof, slipped and skidded a little until she caught her toe claws on a side beam, and carefully climbed down the back of the embassy. She found Depik in the kitchen, along with the delicious aroma of roasting cow. "What's going on?" she said. "Why is everyone here?"

Depik looked up from his work. "Why shouldn't they be?"

She'd spent so much time that day in a state of tense fear and guilt the question was meaningless. "Doesn't anyone know what's happened?"

"Bhakriya told me what you said. A war, my lady? Really?"

"Yes, really." She listened, and heard only the steady hum of a lot of people thinking about supper and Depik's concern and growing confusion. "What about the ecclesiasts' warnings? I thought the king had told everyone what they meant."

"I don't understand. Why would the king understand prophecy?" Depik laid down his knife and wiped his hands on the cloth tucked into his waistband. "No one but you's said anything about war, though we have seen more soldiers about today."

It didn't make sense. Surely the people needed to know the danger they were in? "I don't know what's happened," Lamprophyre said. "Just that there are a lot of evil dragons who want humans dead. I hope Hyaloclast took care of them. I hope my trip to Manjaret was completely wasted. But that's unlikely."

Depik's eyes widened. "My lady," he said, then appeared to run out of words.

Lamprophyre's fuddled mind sharpened briefly. The king hadn't wanted a full-blown panic when there was nowhere to flee. He would keep this a secret until he had more information about Sardonyx and what her plan was. "I suppose you shouldn't mention this," she said, hoping she hadn't ruined the king's plan, though with the way her day had gone, one more colossal mistake was to be expected. "There's nothing you can do about it. But it's like I told Bhakriya—stay close to the embassy. It's mostly fireproof. And don't be afraid. All of us—the dragons and the Army—are doing everything we can to fight back."

She looked past the kitchen out the front of the dining pavilion. Bhakriya and Rassika stood by the soup cauldron as usual, serving men and women soup in wooden bowls. Beyond that, she saw Bhakriya's son Abhit playing with Rassika's little sister Kavari. Kavari was getting tall now that she had proper, regular meals. She wasn't really a baby anymore. And Sardonyx wanted them all dead. A flash of burning fury flicked through her. Sardonyx *dared* to attack innocents? Lamprophyre intended to see her defeated just for that.

"What were you doing in Manjaret, my lady?" Depik asked. His voice sounded shaky, but he'd clearly decided to face the news head-on. "The food's almost ready, if you want to sit."

Lamprophyre trod wearily into the dining pavilion and settled down nearly full-length on the floor. "I took a dragon-killing weapon there. Orthoclase and I each had one. There aren't many, but General Sajan is going to do what he can."

The pyrite weapons weren't as heavy as Lamprophyre had guessed, but they were still bulky and awkward, and they did weigh about as much as a cow despite being made of fire-hardened ceramic rather than iron. They were also uncomfortable armfuls, with the blocky, angular pyrite chunks emerging from their glossy sides to dig into arms or chests. But under Flint's direction, the seven dragons had each collected a weapon and flown off to their designated cities. Lamprophyre had never been so grateful for Flint's bossiness and how decisive he was. She didn't feel decisive at all. She felt bone-weary and muddled.

She'd apparently looked weary and muddled, too, because when she and Orthoclase had reached Manjaret and turned the pyrite weapons over to the commander of the military garrison there, Orthoclase had said, "I think you should go back to Tanajital and sleep. You've already flown far today, and there are more than enough of us to deal with the remaining weapons. Get some rest, and we'll see you tomorrow." Lamprophyre hadn't felt like protesting.

The smell of the cow grew stronger, and to her surprise Lamprophyre discovered she was hungry. She hadn't had much appetite all day. She tore into the delicious, juicy cow and revived slightly. "Thank you, Depik, I needed this," she said between mouthfuls.

"It's my pleasure, my lady," Depik replied. He walked past her to look into the soup cauldron and exchange a few words with Bhakriya. Lamprophyre shamelessly eavesdropped on their thoughts and heard nothing more than the low hum of people paying attention to someone else's words. So Bhakriya hadn't done as Lamprophyre had suggested. This depressed Lamprophyre further. If only...but it was none of her business, even though she was sure now that Bhakriya's feelings for Depik had changed, and it was only fear keeping her from telling him so.

The chalcedony pendant around her neck warmed, and its glossy surface misted over. "*Lamprophyre*," Hyaloclast said.

Lamprophyre jerked and sat up, clutching the pendant, which remained misty despite her touch. "Just a moment," she spoke into it, then hurried to the back of the embassy and hauled the door open. Safely inside and away from listening ears, she lifted it to her lips again and said, "What happened?"

"*It was a rout,*" Hyaloclast said. The chalcedony pendant roughened voices so it was hard to hear emotion through it, but Hyaloclast sounded more exhausted, and defeated, than Lamprophyre had ever heard her. "*We came upon Sardonyx as she and her flight were destroying a town. That distraction allowed us to make a successful first attack, but the enemy did not stay distracted for long.*"

Hyaloclast paused as if catching her breath, and Lamprophyre wondered if she was in the air, if she was still fleeing Sardonyx—but it was unlikely she would want to talk to Lamprophyre in those circumstances. "*They tore us apart,*" Hyaloclast finally said. "*I don't think there's a single uninjured dragon left in our flight, though most of the injuries are minor. At least seventeen are dead. We had to retreat.*"

Lamprophyre's throat ached with grief and heartsickness. "Seventeen? Who?"

"*We will mourn our dead later, Lamprophyre. What concerns me more is that Sardonyx did not order a pursuit. She let us go. That's how little she thinks of our resistance. We hurt her people, but killed none of them. She believes we are no threat to her.*" Hyaloclast paused again. "*We are returning to the city. Tanajital. Tell the king to expect us. We will need a different strategy.*"

Lamprophyre suppressed a groan. She was so tired. Sleep would be a blessing. But Hyaloclast was right; they needed to plan a different attack. Since they had been counting on the dragons to take the fight to Sardonyx, Lamprophyre didn't know what different attack was even possible. But Rokshan and General Sajan would figure something out.

"Come to the training grounds," she said. "That wide field outside the palace. I'll meet you there, and I'll tell the humans to expect you."

"*We will arrive in a little over a thousand beats, I estimate.*" The chalcedony pendant abruptly cleared. Lamprophyre tried not to feel a rebuke in Hyaloclast's abruptness.

She returned to the dining pavilion and took a few more mouthfuls of cow, thinking she needed to keep her strength up if she wasn't going to sleep soon, but the taste had turned to ashes in her mouth. "Do something with the rest of this, please?" she asked Depik when he returned. "I have to go to the palace."

"Of course, my lady," Depik said. He still had that stunned look, and Lamprophyre wished she hadn't told him about Sardonyx—but it was better he know and be prepared for whatever came next.

She once more climbed to the embassy roof, silently cursing the beggars for taking up so much space, and flapped heavily, feeling as if she were dragging herself through the air to gain altitude. The sun was halfway below the horizon and red as a cherry, its dim evening light burnishing the copper and gold roofs of Tanajital to a warm, dull bronze. Normally, the sight relaxed her, but now all she could think about was those roofs on fire, scarred by black acid and dripping in molten lumps to the streets below.

The training grounds weren't as busy as they had been earlier that day, but the soldiers still moved with that intent alacrity that said they had urgent business elsewhere. Lamprophyre stopped one of them, ruthlessly suppressing her feeling that she might be disrupting something important. "I need to speak to Prince Rokshan," she said. "Where is he?"

The soldier looked extremely surprised to be addressed by a dragon. "He—I'm not sure, my lady," he said. "You could ask at headquarters." He indicated the largest of the red-roofed buildings, a long, low edifice with many windows, most of them warmly lit. Lamprophyre had been inside once when she'd had a human body and knew it was full of desks. She didn't know what General Sajan needed all the desks for, but she guessed they indicated the importance of military business.

"Thank you," she said, and let the soldier go. She walked to the headquarters building and examined the door. She was nearly as tall as the building when she stood at her full height, and crouching low enough to make her head level with the door was uncomfortable. She did it anyway. With one finger, she tapped lightly on the door, but "lightly" still meant the door shook and the noise carried to the rest of the buildings.

Eventually, someone opened it, saying, "It's not locked, just come—oh." The soldier, who was dressed in a yellow uniform similar to General Sajan's but with fewer markings, stared up at her. "Commander," he called over his shoulder without taking his eyes off Lamprophyre, "there's a dragon here to see you."

Lamprophyre heard scrambling movement, and soon Rokshan joined the soldier at the door. "Thank you, captain," he said. The captain took that for a dismissal, and fled. Rokshan came outside and shut the door behind him. "You look exhausted," he said, laying a hand on her arm. "You should get some sleep."

"So should you," Lamprophyre said. Rokshan looked as haggard as she'd ever seen him, his jaw dark with the faintest shadow of stubble, dark rings under his eyes, the corners of his mouth dragged down. "But that's not why I'm here. Hyaloclast is coming back. The news isn't good." The ache sprang up in her throat and her shoulders again. "Sardonyx's flight destroyed a village and killed seventeen of our dragons. Rokshan, she wouldn't tell me who died, and—"

Rokshan's grip on her arm tightened. "Don't," he said. "You can't think like that."

"You don't know what I'm thinking."

"You're thinking it's your fault they're dead. Lamprophyre, we made a mistake. But all this evil is to Sardonyx's blame." Rokshan took a step closer. "She was getting free on her own, remember? If you're going to play the 'what if' game, think of what might have happened if those ecclesiasts had managed to reach that cave first. Sardonyx would have gotten free without anyone knowing about it. Suppose she'd come after the flight first? Think of all those helpless dragonets. And stop blaming yourself."

Lamprophyre drew in a deep breath and let it out slowly. "You're right," she said. "I'm just so tired I can't think straight. But I promised Hyaloclast I'd meet her here. She wants to discuss strategy."

"When will she be here?"

"About a thousand—less than an hour."

"Come with me," Rokshan said.

He led her away from the training grounds to a secluded corner where two ells of the palace met. "Sleep. I'll come for you when Hyaloclast arrives."

"I can't—"

"Lamprophyre. You're barely able to stand. You flew one and a half times across all of Gonjiri today, not to mention flying from the mountains to the capital. You're going to tear yourself apart. Now, *sleep*."

She didn't want to argue with him, not with as tired as she was. "Promise me," she said.

"I promise. I wish I could stay with you, but I still have responsibilities only I can handle, apparently." He made a rueful face. "It's a pity there's no artifact that will transport someone instantaneously across the country. I'd wear it out." He patted her arm. "I'll be back soon."

Lamprophyre heard his last words in a daze. She was asleep before he walked away.

She dreamed of flying, not the pleasant kind of flying dream where she never had to come down, but a horrible sepia-colored dream where the world was on fire, and she couldn't land because it would burn her. Then she found herself descending against her will, and she was hopping from island to tiny island in a lake of orange-yellow lava toward a shore that never got any closer.

She heard a voice, its words unintelligible, and she'd just realized it was Jiwanyil when she saw the green light that was its source. At first, it was the green glow in the ice she and Rokshan had seen, but then it was a twisted figure hovering in the air, and it kept changing from human to dragon and back again. Rage filled her, the kind of white-hot sensation only possible in dreams, and she breathed fire to engulf the creature. It didn't react, and that infuriated her further.

Then there was a hand on her shoulder, and she jerked awake to find Rokshan beside her. "Hyaloclast is here," he murmured. "You were dreaming, and saying something I couldn't understand. Just 'Jiwanyil' and then a lot of mumbling."

"It was a terrible dream," Lamprophyre said. She was still shaking from the aftereffects of rage. "I'm glad it's over."

She rolled to her feet. Full dark had fallen, but the training grounds were lit as brightly as day by enormous white magic lights that hovered high above. The sharp white lights cast knife-edged shadows, making everyone present appear to have a dark double lying flat on the earth beside them. Lamprophyre saw two dragons facing a handful of humans led by General Sajan. One of the dragons was Hyaloclast. The other was Leucite. But Chrysoprase was all but Hyaloclast's heir, she should have—

Horrible dread rose up within Lamprophyre. Chrysoprase should have been there. She closed her eyes and reflexively prayed that Chrysoprase was only injured, or that she was with the rest of the flight. Then she remembered her god didn't exist, and the dull ache of misery replaced dread.

She crossed the training grounds to Hyaloclast's side. The dragon queen didn't acknowledge her, keeping her attention on Sajan, but Leucite glanced her way and nodded briefly. She hoped it meant Leucite didn't hate her.

"We are larger in number," Hyaloclast was saying, "and we can harry Sardonyx's forces so long as we don't engage with them."

"If you can lure them in the direction we want, it won't matter if you engage or not," General Sajan said. "Both Manjaret and Sunital have weapons in place. We want the enemy to attack on ground of our choosing."

"It is a good plan," Hyaloclast said. "It's too dark for anyone to fly tonight, what with the moon just past new. We will rest and tend to our wounds, and in the morning we will find Sardonyx again and make her chase us. I will need that map."

"Have you eaten?" Lamprophyre said, and managed not to flinch as Hyaloclast turned a baleful eye on her. She knew from Hyaloclast's surface thoughts that she wasn't angry, just exhausted, but it was hard to remember that in the face of her mother's fierce gaze.

"We have not, and I understood the herds around the city to belong to private individuals," Hyaloclast said.

"I can arrange for food," Lamprophyre said, "if you'll tell me where everyone went."

"Leucite will show you," Hyaloclast said. "Now, the map."

Leucite took off without a backward glance, and Lamprophyre, startled at his abruptness, awkwardly followed him. They flew in silence past the embassy, over the city wall, and some distance north until Lamprophyre saw many, many humped shapes lying across the untilled fields. She couldn't count accurately in the darkness, but it didn't look as if they were missing seventeen—but then, the flight was large, and strictly by the numbers, seventeen wasn't so many. It was when you realized that each number was a person that the enormity of the loss struck home.

Leucite landed several dragonlengths away from the rest of the flight. "Lamprophyre," he said in his low, even voice. "Did Hyaloclast tell you of our losses?"

Lamprophyre swallowed. "She wouldn't say who died. I was afraid to press her. Is Chrysoprase...?"

Leucite shook his head. "She went after a dragon who disemboweled Hexaferrum, and she was torn apart. Three of them." He fell silent. "It's a tremendous loss. I know Hyaloclast wanted her for her successor."

In Lamprophyre's memory, Chrysoprase sped past the finish line at the racing track, a full dragonlength ahead of Coquina.

Weeping would be such a release. "It's not real yet," she whispered. "And now I feel bad about making fun of how strict she was."

"What's killing me is that we left them all behind," Leucite said. "As if they were so much refuse. They'll never reach Mother Stone."

The memory of Gabbro, of that nameless female dragon, curled up in their caves around the great mountain made Lamprophyre sick. "I don't," she began, and went silent. Now was not the time to reveal that their God was dead—had never existed. "We'll retrieve them eventually, and carry them to Mother Stone ourselves," she said.

"I hope we survive for that to happen," Leucite said. "Do you need help fetching food? I hope it's not awful for me to say I'd really like half a cow right now."

Figuring out how many cows it would take to feed the flight, even the part of the flight that hadn't stayed behind to watch the dragonets, took a couple hundred beats, and eventually Lamprophyre and several other dragons flew westward, toward one of the great farms where the owner raised cows. It surprised Lamprophyre to learn it wasn't as late as she'd thought, and the farm owner was still awake and more than happy to deal with dragons.

Lamprophyre arranged a price and a time she would deliver the coin, and she and her friends waited at a distance for the farm owner to drive their cows into a pen far from the rest of his herd. While the others slaughtered the animals, Lamprophyre positioned herself where she could scare off the rest of the cows if they came close. It seemed cruel to kill their companions where they could see.

Laden down with cows, they flew slowly back to the fields, where they discovered Hyaloclast had arrived. Lamprophyre left the cows to the female dragons for cooking and joined her mother on the edge of the territory the flight had claimed. "It should be enough food," she said.

Hyaloclast nodded. "We have a plan, and I have learned their map," she said. "A map is such a clever thing. I never realized how differently humans see the world, and how intriguingly."

"Maybe you could learn to read," Lamprophyre said. "That will open up all sorts of new human ideas."

"I think I'll leave that for later," Hyaloclast said. "Did Leucite tell you about Chrysoprase?"

"He did."

"Such a tremendous loss. All of them are. Most of them leave dragonets behind, though I think I managed it that only one member of a pair-bond came with us, if they have offspring. I don't know if that's more cruel, or not."

Lamprophyre didn't know what to say to that. "Leucite was worried about the...the bodies."

"So am I. Though if you're right about Mother Stone, I don't know that it matters what we do with them." Hyaloclast closed her eyes and threw back her head with a deep sigh. "What is there left for us, Lamprophyre? What are we, if not children of our God?"

"We're still dragons," Lamprophyre said, "and beyond that, I don't know. Something made us who we are, made us magical beings, and maybe it doesn't matter if we know who that something was, so long as we live with honor."

Hyaloclast's lips curved in a wry half-smile. "Wisely said." She opened her eyes and added, "Your mate wants you to stay with him, to carry him into battle. I told him I thought it was a bad idea."

"It's a terrible idea. I can't protect him from fire or acid. Maybe he'll settle for me taking him to the cities under siege."

"He has a fire burning in him to see justice done. Have you made progress on his transformation?"

Lamprophyre sighed. "No. We were supposed to meet someone who has information today, but other things interfered. And I'm not sure we can get the information out of her. She's blackmailing us with the threat of revealing I was transformed into a human."

A hiss escaped Hyaloclast's lips, but she didn't act embarrassed at her lapse into barbarity. "Blackmail. How horribly human. Sometimes I'm surprised at how noble they can be, when you consider the awful things some of them do to each other."

"I know. But the good really does outweigh the bad. Most of

them are kind and decent, at least to the people they care about." That made her think of Bhakriya and her former husband, and how terribly he'd treated her. If only she would talk to Depik! Now that Lamprophyre knew how love felt, she couldn't not wish it for all her friends.

Hyaloclast gripped Lamprophyre's hand briefly. "Get some rest," she said. "I'm not sure whether you'll be joining us in the morning. General Sajan said he had plans for your clutch, since you all know this area better than the rest of the flight, but he needs more information before he can implement those plans. It will be another long day for all of us regardless."

Lamprophyre nodded. "Thank you," she said.

"For what?"

"For not reminding me of my stupidity."

Hyaloclast sighed again. "From what the young prince said, you simply accelerated a process that was already well underway. Criticizing you would be self-indulgent, and I don't believe in making myself feel better at someone else's expense. Now, get."

Lamprophyre went.

CHAPTER TWENTY-TWO

When Lamprophyre arrived at the training grounds the following morning, well-rested and feeling more sanguine than she had the night before, she found her clutch there as well. "You should be sleeping!" she exclaimed. "You couldn't have arrived back before midnight."

"It was nearly the dreaming hours, and *I* wanted to ignore the messenger," Orthoclase said. "Bromargyrite threatened to sit on my face if I didn't get up."

"A dire threat indeed," Flint said. Coquina chuckled.

"It's not my fault I like mornings," Bromargyrite said. The giant orange dragon coiled his tail more closely around himself.

"I'm still mostly asleep," Dolomite complained. He yawned, and the scent of acid wafted through the air. "And I didn't—oh, but I can't talk about that."

"You're still not going to reveal the big secret?" Porphyry teased. "I don't recall you ever staying silent about a project for this long."

"You'll see why," Dolomite said. "Oh. What's wrong with that human?"

Lamprophyre followed the direction of his gaze. A handful of people had just appeared around the front of the palace. In addition to General Sajan, Rokshan, and the king himself, Tekentriya lurched in their direction. "Oh, Dolomite," she said, feeling alarmed, "that's the king's heir, and she doesn't—"

"Good morning," King Ekanath said. "I appreciate your willingness to rise so early after your late night. Thank you again for transporting the artifacts."

"It was our pleasure, your majesty," Flint said with a shallow bow.

"If you're willing, there's something else I'd like you to do," General Sajan said. "Communication with our cities has just become vital. Not all the commanders of the military forces have the chalcedony artifacts that allow me to speak to them at a distance, and almost none of the cities' rulers have them. I was hoping we could enlist you as couriers to take artifacts to cities throughout Gonjiri."

More flying. Lamprophyre managed not to make a face. She saw the rest of her clutch maintained their good manners as well. "Of course we will," she said.

"Not you, ambassador," Sajan said. "I need Rokshan in Sunital this morning, overseeing the disposition of troops. The city was struck by an outbreak of dysentery that has afflicted the Army's commanding officer and many of his subordinates. As if we needed more problems."

"Understood," Lamprophyre said, then wished she'd chosen a different word, because that one had sounded as if she were one of Sajan's soldiers. But Sajan didn't seem to notice.

She listened briefly to their thoughts. Sajan was focused on a long list of tasks he had to do. The king was thinking about how to protect the citizens of Tanajital from a dragon attack. He didn't sound as if he had much faith in the pyrite weapons. Tekentriya was in her usual bad mood, but for once it wasn't focused on Rokshan's faults. Lamprophyre brushed past Rokshan's thoughts as she always did, though she did hear briefly *can't wait* and hoped he meant he was looking forward to spending the day with her.

"What's wrong with your leg?" Dolomite said.

Everyone went very still. Tekentriya slowly turned to stare at Dolomite. "Excuse me?" she said, her voice dangerously quiet.

"Your leg," Dolomite said. "It hurts you, I can tell."

"Dolomite," Lamprophyre murmured, "she doesn't want to talk about it."

"I don't see that it's any of your business, dragon," Tekentriya said. Her voice was still quiet, but the tension in it hummed through the air.

"My name is Dolomite," Dolomite said. "I don't know if it's my business or not, but I hate to see anyone in pain. Can't the healers help you?"

Tekentriya took one lurching step toward Dolomite. To Lamprophyre's surprise, the princess's thoughts were curious rather than angry. "You can tell, huh? And how is that?"

Lamprophyre sucked in an incautious breath. She did not want anyone to know dragons could hear thoughts, certainly not Tekentriya, who wasn't evil like Manishi but would definitely find a way to use that knowledge against them. But Dolomite said, "You hold yourself as if you're searching for a position that doesn't hurt, and you never stop frowning. It must be a terrible way to live."

Tekentriya's eyes narrowed in thought. "You're not wrong," she said. "And I choose not to talk about it."

"Oh? Why not?" Dolomite leaned closer. Lamprophyre closed her eyes, waiting for the explosion.

It never came. Instead, Tekentriya said, "Pity is for the weak. I'm not weak."

"Of course not," Dolomite said. "I don't imagine anyone who knows you would think that."

Tekentriya's shoulders jerked. She worked her mouth briefly as if tasting and discarding words. "I don't know," she said. Then she turned and walked back toward the palace, her leg jerking more rapidly than usual.

Ekanath cleared his throat. "Well," he said. "Well. I imagine General Sajan would like everyone to travel as soon as possible."

"I'll have someone bring the map," Sajan said. "And I'll explain how you'll know which artifacts to give to which person."

Rokshan came to Lamprophyre's side. "I'll be in Sunital by noon," he told Sajan, patting his chest where a couple of chalcedony pendants lay. "And I'll communicate with you as soon as everything's settled."

"By noon?" Lamprophyre said. "But we can be in Sunital in a couple of hours."

Rokshan climbed up. "We have something else to take care of first," he said.

THE GREAT PLAZA IN FRONT OF THE CITY GUARDS' HEADQUARTERS was as full of people as ever, mostly street musicians and the people who stopped to listen to them, but also men and women crossing purposefully between the headquarters and the court building across from it and the occasional guardsman strolling along, truncheon in hand.

Rokshan had explained what courts were for, that humans accused of crimes went there to speak to a human with authority to decide if they were guilty or not and what the punishment should be. It seemed a rather fragile way to pursue justice, all based on one person's interpretation of the law, but Rokshan had assured her everyone involved took their responsibilities very seriously.

"Do you really think she'll come?" Lamprophyre asked again.

"I was careful not to send a message to her home, so she believes we don't know where she lives," Rokshan said, "and I'm counting on her greed and her arrogance to bring her here. If I'm right, she's more interested in taunting us with our helplessness than she is about being sensible."

"And if you're wrong?"

Rokshan shrugged. "Then she'll suspect a trap, destroy the notes, and we'll never see her again. In which case we'll be no worse off than we are now, given that we don't have the notes yet."

"I hope you're right," Lamprophyre said. She had faith in Rokshan's abilities, but she wasn't nearly as calm about the prospect of losing those notes as he seemed to be. Evart's notebook was no longer only important to their quest to transform Rokshan; it might contain information about Sardonyx, too.

Everyone in the plaza walked wide of the big blue dragon and her human companion, but there were musicians close enough that Lamprophyre could enjoy their music. Or, rather, could have enjoyed their music if her draconic hearing weren't good enough to pick up all three and weave them into a discordant tune that set her nerves even more on edge than they were. She shifted her weight and scanned the plaza again for Viveki. Surely Rokshan was right, and the woman would come.

Rokshan had his belt knife out and was fiddling with something small that glinted of gold. "What are you doing?" Lamprophyre asked.

"Part of the plan," Rokshan said. He sheathed his belt knife and dropped the square gold coin into a pouch. "And there she is, right on time."

Viveki walked toward them with her usual ground-eating stride, ignoring anyone who might cross her path. She wasn't smiling this time. She stopped half a dragonlength away and said, "You were supposed to be here yesterday."

"We were detained elsewhere," Rokshan said. Part of the plan was that he would do the talking. Lamprophyre had agreed to this because she had no idea what to say to make the plan work.

Viveki sneered. "You were detained elsewhere," she said in a falsely sweet, sarcastic voice. "You expect me to believe that?"

"Believe what you want," Rokshan said with a shrug. "You know you have us in your power. You think we would risk losing those notes for anything that wasn't urgent?"

Lamprophyre, listening to Viveki's thoughts, heard *should have destroyed them and gone on lying, don't know why I didn't.* "I won't be generous a second time," Viveki said. "Where's my five vahas?"

Rokshan didn't move. "We want some guarantee that the notes exist," he said, "or we're not paying anything."

"Now, see, that's the sort of demand that will inspire me to destroy them," Viveki said.

"It's reasonable," Rokshan said, staying calmer than Lamprophyre could have managed. "Prove you still have them, and I'll give you five vahas. Nothing could be simpler."

Viveki's expression didn't change, but her thoughts went wild, going over so many possibilities it dizzied Lamprophyre. "All right," she said. "I thought you might expect that." She reached inside her shirt and pulled out a sheet of paper. It wasn't very large, but Lamprophyre could see it was covered with writing, front and back. Lamprophyre relaxed slightly. There had always been the possibility Viveki wouldn't have any of the notes on her.

"Don't try to take it," Viveki warned Rokshan, who'd advanced to look at it. "You still don't know where the rest of it is."

Rokshan ostentatiously put his hands behind his back, prompting another sneer from Viveki. "It's Evart's handwriting," he told Lamprophyre. "What do you think?"

That was her cue. "Give her the money," she said.

Rokshan put his hand into his belt pouch, but hesitated. "When do we get the notes?" he said.

Viveki smiled. "I haven't decided yet. Five vahas now, and five more next week. Then we'll negotiate."

Rokshan scowled, but handed Viveki five square gold coins. "Next week, or nothing more," he said.

"That's up to me, don't you think?" Viveki said.

Rokshan nodded. Then he took half a step back and shouted, *"Thief!"*

Viveki looked confused. She glanced behind her as if she thought Rokshan was addressing someone else.

"Thief!" Rokshan shouted again. "Grab her, Lamprophyre!"

This, too, Lamprophyre was ready for. She took Viveki's plump arm in her large hand and held her fast.

Viveki came to herself and tried to pull away, but she was no match for a dragon. "Help!" she screamed. "I'm being assaulted!"

Rokshan shouted, "Guard! I've been robbed! I demand you take this woman in charge!"

"What?" Viveki said. "No, they're assaulting me!"

"What's going on?" A couple of men in the sky-blue tunics of the Tanajital city guard jogged toward them.

"Thank Jiwanyil," Rokshan exclaimed. "This woman just stole from me. I want her taken in charge."

The taller of the two men glanced at Rokshan, then looked at him more closely. "Your highness," he said. "Robbed, you say?"

"He's lying," Viveki said. "He told this monster to grab me. Make it let me go."

"The ambassador is not a monster," the shorter guard said. "Prince Rokshan, what proof do you have?"

Lamprophyre had sort of hoped the guards would take Viveki in charge with nothing more than Rokshan's accusation to go on, but this was even better. "She stole some of his coin," she said.

"I had five vahas in my belt pouch, and she took them," Rokshan said.

"*Liar*," Viveki said.

Rokshan ignored her. "One of them was deeply scratched along the Katayan face. Search her—you'll find them."

"Would you empty your pouch, miss?" the taller guard said. Viveki glared at him. He shrugged and reached for the pouch, but stopped when Viveki slapped his hand. He gave Viveki a look that made her cringe, as if she knew she'd gone too far.

"Striking a guard is a serious offense," he said. "Your pouch, miss. Now."

Viveki's thoughts were a roiling mass of fury. She detached the pouch from around her waist and handed it over. The guard shook out a scattering of silver and copper coins—and five bright square gold ones. On one of them, Katayan's stylized figure had a deep scratch nearly cutting it in two.

"That's it," Rokshan said. "Those are mine."

"I'm afraid we need these as evidence for now, your highness," the tall guard said. "But we'll make sure they're returned to you."

"Miss, do you have anything to say in your defense?" The short guard stood with his hand on his truncheon like he hoped she might try to run. As if she could get free of Lamprophyre to go anywhere.

"You did this *on purpose*," Viveki snarled, ignoring the guards. "They planned this! Let me go!"

"Why would Prince Rokshan and the dragon ambassador set you up to be taken in charge?" the tall guard asked. He looked as if the whole situation amused him.

"Because—" Viveki's mouth snapped shut. Her mind finished the thought, and Lamprophyre grinned. Perfect. Just what they needed. Though it would be wonderful if Viveki also confessed to blackmailing them, because that had to be a worse crime than theft of five vahas.

But Viveki wasn't stupid. She said nothing more as the guards marched her off in the direction of the guard headquarters, a giant stepped pyramid of granite blocks Lamprophyre was sure hadn't always been just the headquarters.

Rokshan said, "I'm going to make sure they hold her for at least twenty-four hours, and see if I can't get that page off her. Then...did you get it?"

"You were right. She couldn't help herself," Lamprophyre said.

"I'll be right back, and we can go," Rokshan said.

Lamprophyre followed the four slowly. She wouldn't fit into the headquarters, and Rokshan knew what to do, anyway. What mattered was that Viveki's furious thoughts had given Lamprophyre what she needed—the location of the hidden notes. She smiled again. Luck had been on their side that morning, and if it continued to be their friend, those notes would tell them not only how to transform Rokshan, but something they might use against Sardonyx as well.

CHAPTER TWENTY-THREE

Lamprophyre squatted in the street outside The Hole and tried once again to peer through the window. Bending that low made her neck ache, and the window was so grimy she couldn't see more than blurred movement in the dimly-lit room beyond. She listened for thoughts again. It was just before mid-morning, and the tavern was unusually full for that early hour. But it was on the edge of Tanajital's slums, and Lamprophyre knew enough about humans to know there was a certain class of men and women who had nothing better to do with their day than drink it away. It seemed several of them had found their way to The Hole that morning.

She counted fifteen people's thoughts, just enough that the noise deafened her but not so many as to prevent her picking individual thoughts out if she focused. Most of them were filled with wary curiosity and the low hum of people listening to someone else intently enough that they weren't thinking of anything else. A few were afraid, though she couldn't tell if their fear was of Rokshan, who'd gone inside a hundred beats ago, or of the dragon sitting outside the door. And one was furiously calculating the odds of making a profit off the prince: *bet he'd pay for them, that woman insulted me, don't know as I owe her anything.*

Lamprophyre leaned closer to the door, which stood half-open, and listened with her ears.

"I just want what she stole," Rokshan said. "Give it to me, and we'll be on our way."

"Don't know as she stole it from you," a woman said. Her thoughts said *don't much care either way*, and Lamprophyre identified her as the calculating one. "Just got your word for that."

"The word of a prince and a commander of the Army," Rokshan said. "Did you want to challenge my honor?"

Since Rokshan was lying about Viveki stealing the notes, Lamprophyre wasn't sure he should lean so heavily on his honor. On the other hand, they'd paid for the notes and hadn't gotten them, so in a sense, Viveki had stolen them. Lamprophyre didn't actually care about the technicalities.

The woman's thoughts became tinged with fear. "No, your highness, of course not," she said. "It's just, people trust me. I've got a reputation. Don't want to give over something I was paid to watch just on someone's say-so, even if he is a prince. I got to be careful."

"Then you'd rather have a reputation for aiding criminal activity?" Rokshan said coldly. Lamprophyre mentally applauded.

"No," the woman said, drawing out the syllable in an uncertain way.

"This should clear things up," Rokshan said. Lamprophyre heard paper rustle. "You can match this to the book Viveki left with you. It proves I have a right to that property."

Footsteps faded into the distance, and a door creaked open and then shut. All the thoughts except Rokshan's were now vivid with curiosity. Rokshan was thinking *Lamprophyre, I think I have her, but be ready*. Lamprophyre settled herself and coaxed her inner fires hotter.

The door opened again, and the footsteps returned. "All this proves is you took a page," the woman said. She sounded defiant, but her thoughts were wary. Lamprophyre wished for the thousandth time Rokshan could hear thoughts.

"I see," Rokshan said. "Well. If that's how you want to play this, I hope you don't have your life savings tied up in this tavern."

"Why is that?" The wariness redoubled.

"Because you have only two options. Either you give me my property, or my friend burns your tavern to the ground."

That was the signal for Lamprophyre to let out a fire-scented burp and a cloud of dark smoke that drifted through the half-open door. Several people shouted, and then the room was a riot of noise as every patron stampeded for the door. The first man through came up short at the sight of Lamprophyre sitting there. She smiled pleasantly. "It's just smoke," she said.

A clot of people formed at the door, half desperately trying to get out, the others backing away from Lamprophyre. "Oh, don't be ridiculous," Lamprophyre said. "I would never burn a building that had people inside. If you want to leave, I won't stop you." She edged to one side, never taking her eyes off the door.

The man at the front of the crowd sidled away, then ran. The rest fought and clawed to fit through the door while staying as far from Lamprophyre as they could, their thoughts terrified. Lamprophyre regretted involving them. She'd worked too hard at establishing a reputation for being non-threatening to feel comfortable frightening humans. But those notes were more important than the feelings of a handful of humans.

Soon the only two left in the tavern were Rokshan and the woman Lamprophyre concluded was the owner. Rokshan said, "You've just lost all your patrons. That means those notes have cost you custom already. How far are you willing to push this?"

Lamprophyre heard the moment the woman's thoughts went from defiant to resigned. "Take them," she said. "I don't want nothing to do with them. Let the little bitch curse. Probably weren't hers anyway."

"No, they're mine, as I said," Rokshan said. "Here's something for your trouble. And I suggest you think carefully about what property you agree to protect in future."

The outer door swung open, and Rokshan appeared. He was

tucking a couple of small books into his shirt. "Let's go, before someone thinks to call the guards and report a fire," he said, hauling himself up.

Lamprophyre took to the skies immediately. "I can't believe that worked so easily," she said.

"Neither can I, honestly. There was a small chance those patrons felt strongly enough about the sanctity of their drinking establishment they might have assaulted me."

Lamprophyre gasped. "Rokshan!"

"A *small* chance. Vanishingly small. Nothing to worry about." He let out a deep breath. "Let's get back to the embassy. We have a couple of hours before we have to leave for Sunital."

At the embassy, Lamprophyre settled herself inside the hall and peered curiously at the two books. One was bound in black leather and looked as messy as the first book Viveki had found, with loose pages stuffed inside and feathers poking out on all sides. "Bookmarks," Rokshan said. "We won't disturb those, in case they're important."

The other one was a blank book like the ones Dharan always carried. The pages were bound to a stiff board, and it had no top cover. The top page, at least, was full of writing. Rokshan flipped a few pages of this one. "Wonderful," he said in disgust. "It's in some kind of code."

"I don't know what that means," Lamprophyre said. "What's a code?"

Rokshan riffled the pages. "It's a way of disguising words so no one can read them who doesn't know the secret. We used to use a simple code at the academy, some of us students, that was a basic substitution code, numbers for letters. But it was so basic anyone could read it."

"Then what was the point?"

"We were ten, Lamprophyre. The point was feeling we had secrets from our lectors. This—" He tapped the top page— "is far more complicated. Fortunately, we know someone who breaks codes for fun."

"Dharan."

"Exactly. I'll take this to him before we leave." He put the book inside his shirt. "This one's more promising. It obviously picks up where the other book left off, and the good news is, it's only about two-thirds full. That means it almost certainly ends when Evart died, and there aren't any more books of his notes hidden somewhere."

Lamprophyre sighed with relief. "Let's see how much of it we can read before we have to go."

"And hope it contains what we need," Rokshan said.

~

KNOWING THAT SARDONYX AND HER DRAGONS ROAMED somewhere in the east had Lamprophyre expecting Sunital to be a smoking ruin. But the city lay peaceful and still in the midday light. It wasn't until they were nearly upon it that the bustle and hum of a thriving city were audible. Lamprophyre relaxed. Sunital had the weapons Flint and Coquina had delivered, its Army and maybe its people were prepared for an attack, and everything was going to be fine.

Though Sunital had a small palace that was the home of its ruling prince, it had no great parkland surrounding the palace and no Army training grounds. So Lamprophyre landed in the coliseum where she and Rokshan had watched the races only days before. It was full of soldiers rather than foot racers, and as they made way for her, Lamprophyre saw an orderly group of marching men leave the coliseum at a trot. It didn't look like a place devastated by illness.

Rokshan slid down and walked to meet a man in a yellow uniform with only one insignia on its left breast. "Lieutenant, bring me up to speed," he said.

The lieutenant saluted. "Commander, a quarter of our forces are down with dysentery," he said, "along with Commander Vriski and Captains Lotin and Calvit. The healers are doing their best, but they tell us even after treatment, the only cure is rest and plenty of clean water. So it will be most of a week before everyone's well. What if we're attacked during that time?"

"Let's not think that way, lieutenant," Rokshan said. He was speaking in the slightly deeper, musical way he did when he was being a commander. "If that's the case, there's nothing we can do except plan a new defensive strategy. With the communication artifacts, we'll have warning before we're attacked, and we have the pyrite weapons. I'm confident we'll have success."

That was such a blatantly optimistic statement Lamprophyre listened to his thoughts. She heard *have to keep morale up, these poor idiots have no idea how bad the situation is.* That, perversely, made her feel better. *She* knew how bad it was, even with the pyrite weapons for defense, and it made more sense to her to face that head-on.

She settled on her haunches and prepared to be bored. Rokshan hadn't said how long they might have to be in Sunital, and as long as she was sitting still, she had nothing but time to fret about what Sardonyx might be doing. She hoped Hyaloclast had found her and was goading her into position to attack one of the fortified cities. They would only get one surprise attack, and Lamprophyre wanted it to be a good one. If they could manage to kill Sardonyx, even better.

She made herself think about Evart's notes instead. They'd read about half the book before leaving for Sunital, at which point Rokshan had put the book away, saying the consequences of accidentally dropping the book from altitude were too great to justify continuing to read. But what they'd read had been important, and chilling. Because about fifteen pages into the new book, Evart had mentioned his first odd dream of a voice speaking to him in darkness. Knowing it was Sardonyx had given his ignorant, even innocent reaction a horrible twist.

It is as if my own mind were speaking to me, but of things my waking mind doesn't understand, he'd written. And then, several pages later: *These dreams can't possibly be the product of anything I know. As impossible as it seems, I think some adept is speaking to me in the night.*

He'd believed Sardonyx was an adept, not a dragon—there was

no way he could have drawn that conclusion—and he'd thought she was male, but aside from that, he'd been remarkably astute in assessing her character. The book revealed him to be even more paranoid and suspicious than Lamprophyre had guessed. Once he realized Sardonyx was another individual, he'd gone canny, refusing to reveal anything about himself while squeezing information out of her drop by drop. Lamprophyre didn't believe he'd been as successfully secretive as he claimed, given her knowledge of Sardonyx, but she did think the evil dragon had given away more than she realized.

He's trapped somehow, Evart had written, *though I don't know how anyone as knowledgeable as he is could be a slave. But I think he wants me to free him. He doesn't come out and say it, because that would reveal his weakness, but he hints at it. His enemy taunts him.*

The references to the enemy intrigued Lamprophyre. At first, she'd thought Sardonyx was talking about her; words like *the enemy stands in opposition* and *wants to thwart his plans* seemed an obvious reference to how Lamprophyre and Rokshan had foiled Sardonyx at every turn. But then Evart would write *this enemy is the one that has him trapped,* or he would speculate on what kind of power an enemy adept might use to trap someone, and Lamprophyre was sure he meant someone else. She certainly wasn't an adept and hadn't done anything to keep Sardonyx in her prison. Just the opposite.

Lamprophyre avoided following that trail of thought and sighed. Maybe Dharan would have better luck with the coded blank book. Evart had mentioned the transformation magic many times, but only in a general way. He hadn't yet, as far as they'd read, reached the point where Sardonyx had convinced him to change his direction of research. Right now, she and Rokshan had more questions than answers.

She'd stopped listening to Rokshan's conversation, so it startled her when he addressed her. "Yes?"

"This is going to take the rest of the day, and there's no point you sitting around," Rokshan said. "I think you should go back to Tanajital and see if there's anything else you can do. I'll communicate with you when I'm finished here." He fingered the second pendant he wore, a greenish lump of chalcedony that matched Lamprophyre's larger one. He'd given her that one to string beside Hyaloclast's blue pendant.

"All right," she said. "I hope something happens soon. I'm so tense, waiting for Sardonyx to strike again."

"I can't wish for Commander Vriski to be ill, but this gives me something to think about that isn't worrying about all those little towns out east." Rokshan gripped her hand briefly. "Take care. I'll see you soon."

Lamprophyre nodded and took to the skies, looking back once at Rokshan, who had his head tipped back to watch her go. Would anyone make anything of that exchange, she wondered? His affection for her, and hers for him, was so obvious to her it felt impossible no one else could see it.

She decided to follow the river Sunital straddled north for a few hundred beats before turning northwest to return to Tanajital. The Sonti River was broader than the Green River at this point in its course, though Rokshan had told her it grew narrower as it passed southward through the hills to its ultimate end at Lake Sonti. The river was also deeper, and its reflection gleamed like a dancer's silver-blue ribbon. Its beauty entranced Lamprophyre and made her think of long, cool swims and being swept away by the current.

She was about to wheel away from the river when she saw a moving dark cloud in the distance. Her first glance said it was a flock of birds. Almost immediately, she realized those would have to be impossibly large birds for her to see them at a distance. A hot jolt of fear shot through her. Sardonyx's flight.

She stilled her first instinct, which was to flee, and counted the winged creatures. She could bring the information to General Sajan, and maybe he could do something with it. But there were far more than two hundred dragons, and they were flying eastward, not very fast. Relieved, she shot toward them. Hyaloclast would know something about the current strategy.

After a few hundred beats of flight, she was near enough to see they'd slowed to meet her, though they hadn't stopped. She aimed for the big black dragon at the head of the loose formation. "Where are you going?" she asked, out of breath from the speed of her flight.

"We are circling the human city of Manjaret," Hyaloclast said, "and waiting for our scouts to return. We know Sardonyx's people are somewhere east of here, and our intent is to flush them out and convince them to chase us to the city, where they will be vulnerable to those weapons."

"I don't understand how two hundred dragons could just vanish."

"There is a lot of empty land between here and the desert, and between the desert and the ocean," Hyaloclast said. "And the way our enemy moves suggests she knows this territory well, which might be why she came this way in the first place."

Lamprophyre nodded. "I don't know why she hasn't just swept through this place and burned everything she sees."

"She's still just a dragon, Lamprophyre." Hyaloclast gestured at the dragons flying nearest them. "With the same physical limitations we all have. In fact, based on what we've seen of them, they can't stay in the air as long as we can, and they aren't as fast or agile. They're big brutes, and they use that to their advantage in personal combat, but they can't simply fly forever."

That made Lamprophyre feel better. "So we might have a chance."

"We *do* have a chance. And those weapons will help." Hyaloclast abruptly backwinged and signaled to the others to hover. "That's Corundum now. He's an advance scout. Let us see what he's learned."

Lamprophyre knew Corundum well; he was part of the clutch just three years older than hers. His brown scales and black wing membranes made him the dullest-looking dragon in the flight, but that dullness made him one of the best hunters the dragons had ever known, able to hide even without concealing himself magically. He also had better eyesight and hearing than most. It didn't surprise Lamprophyre that Hyaloclast had sent him ahead to scout.

"I found them," he said. He was breathing easily, but his eye ridges flared with excitement. "They're all settled about six hundred beats' flight east of here, eating. I made sure they saw me—made it look like they surprised me—but they didn't follow. Not yet, anyway."

"Good work," Hyaloclast said. "Everyone split up as we discussed, and move to your designated spots. We'll see if we can't herd these creatures like cows."

A ripple of amusement spread through the flight. Hyaloclast turned to Lamprophyre. "Will you join us, or do you have other duties?"

This would keep her from going mad waiting for something to happen, or for Rokshan to summon her back. "I'd rather stay with all of you," she said. "What is the plan?"

"Follow," Hyaloclast said. She continued flying eastward as the flight separated like one of those fluffy small white flowers that broke apart if a human breathed on them. Lamprophyre had tried it herself once, and the flower had simply wilted under her hot breath. The dragons scattered in loose groups, heading north and south and west, while a few dragons continued on with Hyaloclast and Lamprophyre.

"It's simple in the execution," Hyaloclast said. "We will goad Sardonyx's people into following what they believe are a handful of our dragons, and therefore are an easy target. Those few will pretend to flee westward, to Manjaret, where the pyrite weapons will wreak havoc on them. It's unlikely they'll kill all the enemy, but they should do enough damage to make Sardonyx reconsider attacking human cities."

"You said 'simple in the execution,'" Lamprophyre said.

Hyaloclast grimaced. "I am no human soldier, but General Sajan said that battle plans rarely survive contact with the enemy, and that is something I understand. We have no guarantee that Sardonyx will take our bait—another phrase the general used—and no guarantee she will not be suspicious at our seeming to lead her straight to humans. But we have to act. The alternative is allowing Sardonyx to continue razing cities without being challenged."

"I understand." From what she'd read of Evart's notes and her own encounters with Sardonyx, Lamprophyre felt the evil dragon's pride and arrogance made this plan extremely plausible. But she could see Hyaloclast's point: people were complicated, and reacted in complicated ways.

They flew eastward for nearly a thousand beats, following Corundum, until the brown dragon returned and said, "They're a hundred dragon lengths away and to the north. I think we should try to look as if they surprised us. Like we're scouting them."

"Follow me," Hyaloclast said. "We'll fly past, then circle back around and attack. The goal is to make them chase us without looking like that is our intent."

The twenty or so dragons surrounding her nodded. Lamprophyre caught Corundum's eye. He grinned at her, his familiar wicked good humor sparking an answering grin from her. She probably shouldn't think of this as fun, but...it was fun.

Hyaloclast banked and curved away northward. Lamprophyre followed on her mother's heels, watching the ground ahead. Soon, she saw it: a dark shadow lying across the dry yellow grasses covering the low hills, under a cloudless sky. Her heart beat more rapidly with excitement. She flew on, pretending she hadn't noticed the dragons.

Suddenly Hyaloclast came to a halt and hovered, forcing everyone else to scramble not to overshoot her. Lamprophyre flailed a little in midair, wondering what had startled her mother, fearing some flaw in the plan had made her realize it was a failure. Then Hyaloclast shouted, "Attack them! Dive, dive!" and put her own words into action.

Breathless, Lamprophyre followed, furling her wings and plummeting to make herself an arrow speeding toward the heart of Sardonyx's flight. The dragons sunning themselves on the ground below, surrounded by the scattered half-eaten carcasses of wild deer, lifted their heads like so many inquisitive rodents popping out of holes in the fields. Hyaloclast spat fire, and Lamprophyre did the same barely a beat behind her. The dry grasses went up in huge fiery bursts. Clouds of smoke filled the air, and as Lamprophyre pulled out of her dive she heard coughing and choking. It filled her heart with a fierce joy.

"Again!" Hyaloclast shouted, and Lamprophyre beat the air to gain altitude for another dive. As she turned, she saw, through the dissipating smoke, the enormous red-gold form of Sardonyx, raising herself to her feet. She looked perfectly calm—well, it wasn't as if fire could hurt dragons. Lamprophyre's elation faded. If Sardonyx knew this was a ploy—

Then Sardonyx shouted, "*After them!*" and a host of great wings, thickly ribbed with phalanges like no modern dragon had, sent the rest of the smoke flying as they shredded the air. As one, Sardonyx's dragons roared a challenge, and charged.

CHAPTER TWENTY-FOUR

Lamprophyre aborted her dive and wheeled around. In her last glimpse of Sardonyx's dragons before she sped westward, she realized not all of them were following. She didn't have time to count, but it was surely twice as many as in their own little band of twenty. Surrounded by her friends, she flew away, hoping the evil dragons would continue to follow. Only forty or fifty...maybe it wouldn't matter that it wasn't all of them, so long as they destroyed those forty or fifty.

She cast a glance over her shoulder. Hyaloclast was toward the rear, shouting something at Corundum. Corundum nodded and rose higher, then flew faster than Lamprophyre had ever seen him in the direction of distant Manjaret. Lamprophyre hung back to meet Hyaloclast. The enemy dragons were gaining on them, but Lamprophyre saw the truth of her mother's statements about their physiology. Those dragons practically lumbered in midair, like flying cows.

"Don't slow too much," Hyaloclast shouted as Lamprophyre neared. "I don't know how bright they are, and we don't want them guessing what we have in mind."

"Where did Corundum go?"

"To warn the rest to stay out of sight. If these enemy dragons see too many of us, they'll likely turn around. We need to look like easy prey. And with not all of them following, we could easily outnumber them if we're not careful."

That made sense. Lamprophyre cast another glance at their pursuers. They weren't close enough to make out expressions, but they weren't deviating in their course, and the steady, ponderous way they flew was actually frightening if she let herself dwell on it. She turned her back on them and flew on.

She'd never been to Manjaret and hoped her friends knew the way—well, they had to, to have come up with this plan. She remembered the city only because one of Sardonyx's early victims was the daughter of its ruling prince and princess. Zefira had fallen prey to Sardonyx's evil whisperings, and Sardonyx had shredded her mind when Zefira became a liability. Lamprophyre knew Zefira had been taken home when it was clear she wouldn't recover quickly, and as far as Lamprophyre knew, she had only recently regained consciousness. The knowledge that the woman, whom she hadn't liked but hadn't wanted hurt, might be lying helpless somewhere in Manjaret made Lamprophyre more determined to see the city defended.

A thousand beats. Two thousand beats. Lamprophyre was growing tired of maintaining a pace the slower enemy dragons could keep up with. Every moment had her believing this was the moment when Sardonyx's dragons would decide they'd had enough of the chase and turn around. She started lagging intentionally, glancing behind her occasionally at the terrible oncoming juggernauts.

Then Hyaloclast was beside her, shouting, "What are you doing?"

"Taunting them so they don't get bored and leave," Lamprophyre panted. The effort of going slower than was comfortable was draining.

Hyaloclast looked behind her. "Good idea," she said. "In another three hundred beats, we're going to turn and make a stand that we will abandon a hundred beats later."

"But why? We're winning!"

"Because Manjaret is just ahead now." Hyaloclast jerked her head westward. "Time to turn their tactics back on them."

Lamprophyre nodded. She sped up briefly, then pretended to lag as if she were tired. In her imagination, the hot breath of her pursuers warmed her heels, though of course they weren't that close. Just a few more beats...

Then Hyaloclast and Corundum and Zircon and Alunogen surrounded her, turning in midair to confront Sardonyx's dragons, and Lamprophyre dropped a dragonlength to get out of their way. A yellow dragon female, heavy and about half a dragonlength longer than she was, bore down on her. Lamprophyre snarled and dove to meet her.

She immediately knew it was a mistake. The female swiped at Lamprophyre's belly with savage claws, and Lamprophyre dodged, barely avoiding the blow. The female followed it up by grabbing Lamprophyre's arm and pulling her close so their wings snarled together and they fell, a sickening sensation that roused Lamprophyre's fears of falling in a wingless, helpless human form. She lashed out frantically to free herself and got in a lucky blow on the female's left wing, kicked with both feet at her belly, and disentangled herself only five dragonlengths from the ground.

She backwinged, caught herself, and darted away from her attacker, who swept ponderously toward her once again. This plan was madness. She couldn't hold the female off for a dozen beats, let alone a hundred. The best she could do was keep out of the enormous dragon's reach and watch for Hyaloclast's signal to retreat.

She slipped past the female and scored five long slits in the dragon's wing membrane. It was thicker than her own, but her claws cut it as readily. She let out a cry of triumph that turned to a cry of pain as the dragon once more grabbed her, this time by the ankle, and dug in her claws. Lamprophyre kicked her in the face with her free foot, jabbing her with her hard, dull toe claws. Too bad they weren't sharp, because she was sure she could have taken an eye out. She kicked again, and the dragon let go, snarling.

Lamprophyre's breathing was heavy, and her wings ached from the unexpected maneuvering. She and the female dragon circled each other, watching for weakness. Fear shot through Lamprophyre again. She was completely outclassed by this warrior, and the only reason she wasn't dead was that she was faster and more agile. If this were a real fight, she *would* be dead, because Rokshan always said fighting a defensive battle in the short-term was a losing strategy. She'd never understood that until now.

Then dragons rushed past her, scrambling to get away, and Lamprophyre realized the female dragon was between her and Manjaret. She folded her wings and dropped like a stone, surprising the female enough that when Lamprophyre snapped her wings open and shot westward, she left the dragon in her dust.

Now that she wasn't engaged in combat—she'd fought a dragon and survived!—she could see Manjaret in the distance, a reddish blotch against the ribbon of the Sonti River. She pushed herself faster, though she knew the city was no safe haven, even for her own flight. It sprawled, looking more like Kolmira than vertical Tanajital, and its walls and many of its buildings were of local red sandstone, giving it its distinctive color. Even though she'd placed one of the pyrite weapons herself, she couldn't see it at this distance. She aimed at that side of the city anyway. Maybe she could lure some of Sardonyx's dragons into its metaphorical lap.

She risked a glance over her shoulder. The enemy dragons were still following, faster than before. It looked as if Hyaloclast's plan had worked. They clearly believed the flight was desperate to defend the human city, and just as clearly believed the flight was no match for them. Lamprophyre stopped watching them and continued toward the city. It was almost over. She wanted so badly to see those dragons torn apart.

Manjaret was distinct now as a collection of red and cream-colored buildings inside a great red wall, not as tall as Tanajital's, but still imposing. And there was the shining sparkle of the pyrite weapon she'd positioned according to the captain's instructions.

She dove for it, shot past, and dropped as fast as she dared to be below its range.

Gasping for air, she turned to watch the weapon swivel and take aim at one of the enemy dragons. She'd worried that the presence of the flight might make it hard for the weapons to target the enemy, but all her friends had taken their instruction to heart, and had come to earth, leaving the sky full of nothing but ancient dragons.

A deep hum filled the air, the sound of the pyrite weapon coming to full power. In a single beat, the hum stopped, and the pyrite weapons shivered as with heat haze. A bright flash shot from the ceramic cylinder like tame lightning, and a *thump* shook the ground near Lamprophyre. The flash caught one of Sardonyx's dragons square in the chest, making her jerk. Her wings stiffened, and she fell, landing on Manjaret's defensive wall and sliding down it to lie in an inert heap at its base.

Lamprophyre screamed with excitement. The pyrite weapon swiveled, tracking the motion of another dragon. Another flash, another thump, and the blast missed the dragon, who swept past and opened his mouth to spray acid at the weapon and its operators.

Lamprophyre shoved off the ground and flung herself between the soldiers and the acid spray. Most of it hit her, rattling her wing membranes like stinging hail and coursing harmlessly down her back. Some of it landed on the weapon, which sizzled. And some of it struck two soldiers standing nearby who hadn't ducked fast enough.

Their agonized screams prompted an answering cry from Lamprophyre. The acid ate through their clothes into their skin as they thrashed helplessly, trying to get it off. There was nothing she could do but watch their comrades pull them into the shelter of the base of the weapon—and it was only shelter because she stood there, warding them.

"Out of the way!" one of the operators shouted. Lamprophyre dropped, and the weapon shot again, missing again. She kept her eyes on the dragons circling the weapon. They were so clumsy, not agile at all, and yet they were still faster than the weapon could aim.

A couple of enemy females descended from opposite directions. Lamprophyre realized what they had in mind in time to scream, "Get beneath me!" and mantle her wings to cover as many soldiers as she could manage. Fire struck her, heating the air uncomfortably, and the soldiers screamed, with fear rather than pain, she hoped.

"Keep down!" she told them when the fire was past, and leaped into the sky.

It seemed the second weapon hadn't been any more successful; there was one fallen dragon in the streets, one of Sardonyx's females, and to her horror she saw two slimmer dragons lying slashed and bloody a few streets away. One was Zircon, and the other was too bloody for her to identify. The sky was full of dragons swirling, darting, slashing and flying away. Lamprophyre's strategy of staying out of reach wasn't unique to her. It looked as though none of her flight wanted to get close to the enemy, and with their greater size and strength, Lamprophyre couldn't blame her friends.

She rose into the air above the pyrite weapon and shot fire at the nearest enemy dragon. It couldn't burn him, but it might keep him at bay so he couldn't spray the soldiers again. She realized Corundum was next to her, darting and weaving to keep the enemy dragons distracted. "Why aren't the weapons working?" he exclaimed.

"They are. They did," Lamprophyre said. "But they don't move fast enough. The strategy isn't working!"

"We have to protect the city," Corundum said. "I—"

Swift movement silenced him with a grunt as one of the dragons rushed him, taking him around the waist and bearing him to the ground beside the weapon. Lamprophyre screamed in surprise and fear and followed the two, slashing at the enemy dragon's thick wing membranes. The dragon ignored her, all his attention on Corundum. Corundum's wings were folded painfully beneath his back, and he gripped the dragon's hands, both of them clawing each other's hands bloody as they wrestled for dominance in eerie silence.

Slowly, despite Lamprophyre's desperate efforts, the dragon's teeth came ever closer to Corundum's throat. Terrified, Lamprophyre gave up slashing the dragon's wings to tatters and wrapped her arm around his neck, pulling the male's head back. He was as abnormally large as all the ancient dragons were, but he was still just a male, and she outweighed him. Their fierce three-way wrestling match paused as Lamprophyre and Corundum held the male in a terrible equilibrium.

Suddenly, the male stopped fighting to reach Corundum and threw himself backward, toppling Lamprophyre. He twisted and snapped his teeth at Lamprophyre's throat. Lamprophyre got her powerful legs beneath him and shoved, hard, launching him a dragonlength into the air. Before he could recover, Corundum was on his back, his arms wrapped around the dragon's chest. His weight pinned the male's wings in place, forcing him to the ground.

Lamprophyre saw how Corundum's arms shook. He couldn't hold the male for long. Without thinking, she swiped her claws across the male dragon's thick throat.

Red blood spurted from the wounds, making a hot splash across her face and chest. The dragon gurgled, thrashed, and sagged in Corundum's arms. Corundum let him fall. "You killed him," he said, breathing heavily. He sounded as if she'd done something miraculous. Given the kind of havoc Sardonyx's people had wreaked on the flight, maybe she had.

"*We* killed him," she corrected him. "It took both of us. Either of us alone..."

Corundum nodded. Orange light grew and bathed them in fire. They shielded their eyes, and when the fire was past, looked up at the dragon who'd just blasted them. "I don't think I can do that again," Lamprophyre said, "but we have to try."

"I think they're leaving," Corundum said. He pointed. "Look!"

The sky was still full of dragons, but most of them were winging their way eastward. Some of them wove through the sky erratically, as if they couldn't keep a straight course. Lamprophyre blinked exhaustion out of her eyes and said, "I can't believe we won."

Corundum grabbed her hand. "I'm not sure we did."

Lamprophyre followed his gaze. Manjaret was in flames. Dark, lifeless dragon bodies lay here and there throughout the streets. Dozens of human bodies lay beside them, most of them scorched beyond recognition or disfigured with deep acid burns. The smell of ash and bitter acid filled the air, making Lamprophyre feel sicker than she already did.

She turned to speak to the soldiers manning the pyrite weapon and choked back a cry. Some dragon had gotten in a lucky shot while she and Corundum were wrestling with the male dragon. There was nothing left of them but charred bones. Beside their bodies, the pyrite weapon glistened in the afternoon sun, as pristine and untouched as it had been five hundred beats ago. Of course fire and acid couldn't hurt it. And it had failed those men completely.

The swoop of wings told Lamprophyre Corundum had left. She looked at the dead dragon again and wiped his blood off her face. They hadn't won. The weapons were almost useless. And they'd brought death to Manjaret instead of salvation. Lamprophyre didn't care that dragons couldn't cry. Weeping couldn't make this right. Nothing could.

~

SHE SPENT WHAT WAS LEFT OF THE AFTERNOON HELPING TO PUT out fires. The only thing that had gone right that day was having the Sonti River right there, with its endless supply of water. She carried canopy after canopy filled with water across the city, her mind numb, her hands focused on her task so she wouldn't have to think about anything else. Every time she flew over a dead dragon, she averted her eyes. She'd know soon enough who the flight had lost.

It turned out Manjaret hadn't been thoroughly destroyed. Sardonyx's dragons had either been incompetent or lazy or arrogant or all three, because they hadn't delivered the kind of focused destruction that would have eradicated the city. That had been another piece of luck, that Sardonyx hadn't been there to direct her dragons. Lamprophyre was sure she wouldn't have let a single human survive.

When the last fires were out, Lamprophyre returned to the pyrite weapon. The bodies of the soldiers had been removed, which was a burden lifted. Lamprophyre couldn't help feeling as if the weapon's failure had been her fault. She'd been so eager about the pyrite weapons, so certain they could kill dragons. And they did. So long as the dragon in question held still long enough to be targeted, they did kill dragons. It was almost worse than if they'd been useless.

She wondered idly what they'd done with the dragon the weapon had killed, the one that had fallen outside the walls. She still didn't know how many of her friends were dead and didn't think she was ready for that knowledge. Sinking down onto her haunches, she regarded the walls, her mind feeling numb and unresponsive. Rokshan might contact her soon. She craved his nearness even as she feared having to tell him what had happened. He'd feel even worse about the weapons' failure than she did.

A dark shadow passed over her. "Lamprophyre," Hyaloclast said as she landed nearby. "Come with me."

"What's wrong now?" she asked, too late realizing her weariness had come out as petulance.

But Hyaloclast didn't respond with irritation. "I need you to come," she said. "We've taken an enemy dragon alive."

CHAPTER TWENTY-FIVE

"Alive?" Lamprophyre's fuzzy mind didn't understand why that was significant. She shook her head vigorously, hoping to clear it. "Why?"

"A shot from one of the weapons grazed him and brought him down. I ordered him subdued." Hyaloclast sounded grim. "I intend to force him to reveal as much of Sardonyx's plan as possible. But I need your assistance."

"Mine?" Lamprophyre realized she sounded witless, with all her inane questions. "I mean, of course I'll help. But you have others—"

"You've told me Sardonyx is capable of listening through the minds of others. You're the only one of us who knows how to identify her presence. I don't want her learning our secrets through this male." Hyaloclast, Lamprophyre now realized, had a long, bloody gash along her left shoulder and held that arm stiffly. She looked weary, but her eyes were fierce and her jaw tight with suppressed fury.

"All right," Lamprophyre said. "I'll listen for Sardonyx's thoughts, but I have an idea that might help. We need to find an adept."

"An adept? What can an adept do for us?"

Lamprophyre cast a glance into the distance, to where one of the pyrite weapons glittered in the light of the setting sun. She could understand Hyaloclast's disdain, given how human adepts had failed them all. "Something only a human would think of," she said.

~

THE CHAIN HOLDING THE CHLORITE ARTIFACT TO LAMPROPHYRE'S wrist itched, and it was too tight for comfort, but it was the biggest chain they'd been able to find at short notice. Hyaloclast, flying beside her, occasionally rubbed her wrist as if hers bothered her, too. It felt so odd to hear none of the dragon queen's thoughts, just the dull background hum that gave nothing away. It might not matter. The enemy dragon had already been exposed to the thoughts of those who'd captured it. And maybe she was wrong, and all the ancient dragons had Sardonyx's ability to communicate mind to mind. But they couldn't afford to take chances.

Ahead, about ten dragonlengths from the city wall, the dull green shape of the captured dragon stood out against the pale, desiccated grass of the plains. He lay on his back with his wings spread wide and high, a position that forced his chest upward and arched his back painfully. Huge, heavy red stones that looked like they were left over from building the city wall pinned his wings to the ground, out of reach of his hands. He might have been able to break free, but at the cost of ripping his wings from their sockets.

Hyaloclast alit a dragonlength away, and Lamprophyre landed beside her. "Dragon," Hyaloclast said, walking toward him. "Tell me your name."

The dragon, who was breathing heavily as if he'd exerted himself, sneered and said nothing. He was doing his best to conceal his fear, but it was audible to Lamprophyre beneath his bravado.

"I don't actually care what your name is," Hyaloclast went on. Her voice was even, unemotional, and with her thoughts dimmed by the artifact, Lamprophyre might have imagined her an obsidian statue come to life. "I thought it might grant you some shred of dignity, given that we've taken all the rest of it away. You look like a butterfly impaled on a thorn."

"An ugly butterfly," Lamprophyre said. Hyaloclast shot her a glare, but Lamprophyre saw her lips tremble as if suppressing a smile.

The enemy dragon's sneer faded. "I am Shurtak," he said. His voice was higher than Lamprophyre had imagined given his build. His thoughts were still angry, but now they were tinged with uncertainty as well as fear.

"Shurtak," Hyaloclast said. "I am Hyaloclast, dragon queen."

Shurtak jerked. The stones pinning his wings didn't shift. "There is only one dragon queen," he snarled. "You are an upstart pretender."

"What is Sardonyx's strategy for attacking the human cities?" Hyaloclast asked, as calmly as if he hadn't spoken.

Shurtak's gaze flicked from Hyaloclast to Lamprophyre and back. "What are you?" he breathed. "You have no thoughts. What kind of monster has this new world bred?"

Lamprophyre listened closely to his thoughts and heard, above his growing fear, *can't hear must know monsters* and *hope Sardonyx listen*. She blocked his thoughts abruptly, fearing Sardonyx's presence, and then told herself she was stupid. That was why she was there. Sardonyx couldn't hurt her.

She'd been paying close enough attention to Shurtak's thoughts that she'd missed Hyaloclast's next question, but whatever it was, it made Shurtak calmer. "I will tell you nothing," he said. "We will slaughter you all, and then we will burn the human cities to the ground. You cannot defeat us."

"Interesting," Hyaloclast said. "I thought you were braver than that."

"What?" Shurtak said. *Braver than her, she is mad,* his drifting thoughts said.

"Obviously you believe we would thwart you if we knew your plans," Hyaloclast said. "You lack the courage of your convictions."

Shurtak jerked against the stones again. Lamprophyre looked

nervously at them, but they still didn't shift. "It doesn't matter what you know," he said. "We will defeat you."

"Through secrecy and subterfuge," Hyaloclast said. She looked away from Shurtak toward the city, as if he bored her. "Those things ought to be beneath you. No true dragon attacks from the shadow."

This infuriated Shurtak. He tried to sit up, his arms flailing to reach the stones, and this time Lamprophyre thought they might have shifted the tiniest bit. She tensed, ready to fling herself on him if he got free. His thoughts fluttered madly through rage and fear and indignation. "*We do not*," he shouted. "We strike the most important cities first. Wipe out the human leaders. Soon they will all be dead!"

"Important cities," Hyaloclast scoffed. "Villages. Is that really all you're capable of? Destroying those tiny towns to make yourselves feel bigger?"

A tiny spark of confusion appeared within his furious thoughts. "Hamadri was small," he said. "It was the greatest of human cities and we found it much reduced. This world is different." Now he sounded petulant, a human child denied a treat.

"Hamadri was destroyed by you dragons centuries ago," Lamprophyre said. "You made a mistake."

"No mistake," Shurtak said, baring his teeth at her. "It was there. But it was small."

Lamprophyre tried to remember what cities the dragons had gone for first. Ghiridi, and Hammadi...Hammadi. Hamadri. "I see," she said. "You're going after the cities you remember."

"Not anymore," the dragon said. He smiled, a nasty, secretive expression. "We will learn this new world, and we will make it burn."

"You only found this city because we led you here," Hyaloclast said. She gave Lamprophyre a warning look that didn't need thoughts for Lamprophyre to understand it: *keep quiet*. "Forgive me if I don't quiver in terror at your so-called plan."

Shurtak must be one of Sardonyx's stupider followers not to see how Hyaloclast was leading him, Lamprophyre thought. But this time, his thoughts were less angry and more calculating: *tell her lies, if I can't hear her thoughts she can't hear mine.* "Sardonyx sees far," he said. "She has the power to see through our eyes."

"No, she can't," Lamprophyre said, listening to his thoughts. "She can talk to you, one at a time, but she only knows what you tell her."

Shurtak's eyes widened. He clumsily tried to conceal his thoughts behind meaningless poetry, but Lamprophyre was excellent at teasing out deeper thoughts if she chose. "And she's abandoned you, hasn't she," she went on. "If she knows what happened here, she doesn't know you're still alive to speak to, because all your friends left you for dead." That last was a guess, but she felt confident about it.

"That's enough, Lamprophyre, leave the male some fragment of hope," Hyaloclast said.

Shurtak jerked again. "*You*," he said. "Lamprophyre. You freed us." He began laughing, a breathy, choked sound because of how his chest was stretched. "Sardonyx will see you killed last, slowly."

It would have been more frightening if Shurtak hadn't been helpless. "Strong words," Hyaloclast said. "Where will Sardonyx strike next?"

South and west, Shurtak thought. "I refuse to tell you anything," he said, struggling against the stones again.

"Randomly hoping to come across a helpless village?" Hyaloclast said, her voice taunting him.

"We see everything," Shurtak said. *Scouts*, he thought. *Quartering the land.*

Lamprophyre wondered how much of Shurtak's thoughts Hyaloclast heard, as she was intent on her interrogation. It was too bad she couldn't communicate with the dragon queen, give her direction. If Sardonyx had scouts looking for new targets, that might be something Hyaloclast could use. Lamprophyre and Corundum had proved the flight could take down a solitary ancient dragon.

"And what have you seen?" Hyaloclast asked.

Shurtak seemed to have given up on keeping secrets. "Many towns," he said, "many cities not where they were before. We will drive the humans before us and we will watch them burn." *Find the capital,* he thought.

Then an oily, nasty sensation filled Shurtak's mind. ***You're alive***, Sardonyx whispered.

They know! Shurtak thought.

Lamprophyre gasped. "She's here," she said, gripping Hyaloclast's hand.

Hyaloclast bent low, pressing her hand against Shurtak's chest. "Tell me where you're going next," she shouted.

Sardonyx's attention focused on Lamprophyre. ***You'll pay for this, my dear,*** she snarled. She withdrew so rapidly it felt like being sliced by icy claws. Shurtak convulsed, once, twice, and after the third time he went frighteningly limp.

Gone, he thought, and then his thoughts vanished.

Lamprophyre realized she was crushing her mother's hand in hers and let go. Hyaloclast stood up. "She killed her own kind rather than allow him to give her away," she murmured. "If we didn't already know what kind of a person she is, that would be revelatory."

"How much of his thoughts did you hear?"

"Almost none. All my attention was on keeping him off-balance so he would think the right things." Hyaloclast absently touched the gash in her shoulder. "I hope we learned something."

Lamprophyre nodded. "They have scouts searching the area for cities. And they're flying south and west next. Obviously he doesn't know the city names—" She gasped. "Sunital is south and west of where they were. Rokshan is there." She fumbled with the green chalcedony pendant.

"Be calm," Hyaloclast said. "For once, we have an advantage."

Lamprophyre paused with the pendant halfway to her mouth. "We do?"

"Two advantages, one more dubious than the other." Hyaloclast took a few steps away from the dead dragon. "For one, I'm told the human adepts in Tanajital and other large cities have artifacts that allow them to see things at a farther distance than the eye can manage, even the dragon eye. They're engaged in searching out Sardonyx's flight so they can follow them as they move. They may already have spotted her."

"That's...actually, I hadn't remembered that. I've seen some of those artifacts work. What's the other advantage?"

Hyaloclast stopped and looked up at the sky. The sun was setting, and in the east, the stars were out, barely dimmed by the crescent of the new moon. "The human god Jiwanyil has given dozens of prophecies indicating which cities are in danger. So far, every one of those prophecies has proved correct. In several cases, the news of the prophecy came in time for the town to evacuate."

"Stones take Jiwanyil and his damn prophecies," Lamprophyre exclaimed. "He's a fraud, Hyaloclast! He gave those ecclesiasts a prophecy that would have put *them* on Mother Stone instead of Rokshan and me. He wanted Sardonyx freed, and now he's protecting humans from the consequences? I don't understand it at all!"

"Neither do I, but we are severely outmatched by Sardonyx," Hyaloclast said grimly, "and I will take any advantage we're given." Her mouth went thin and straight in a frustrated grimace. "What else did the male think?"

"The scouts. They're looking for the capital—maybe more capitals than just Tanajital. You heard him say they thought they were wiping out important cities, cities they remembered, but some of them are gone and others are much smaller. I guess it makes sense that Hamadri was never rebuilt to its former size."

"I take it you're familiar with that city."

"It was one of the clues that led to discovering the truth about the Great Cataclysm." Lamprophyre looked past Hyaloclast at Shurtak's body. "What do we do with him?"

"Bury him far from the city," Hyaloclast said with a grimace. "Then I suppose we bury our own dead as well. Only seven this time. It infuriates me that I can be grateful over any number of dragon deaths, so long as it's fewer than before."

"I suppose carrying them to Mother Stone is pointless."

Hyaloclast nodded. "I left it to the flight to decide. They were all in agreement that it would be a betrayal of our dead's spirits to put their bodies there, now that we know it was never anything but a prison. But we cannot simply leave them to rot beneath the sky."

"That's how I feel." Lamprophyre realized she still held the pendant. "I need to talk to Rokshan. He'll probably have to go back to Tanajital. Do you mind if I don't stay?"

Hyaloclast waved a weary hand at her. "Go. Stay safe. Tell us if anything changes."

Lamprophyre wasn't sure what Hyaloclast meant, but she nodded and flew off southward, following the Sonti River. She would talk to Rokshan on the way, and take comfort in his strength. It was far better than dwelling on death.

~

ROKSHAN WAS WAITING FOR HER IN THE COLISEUM WHEN SHE arrived, feeling bone-weary and ready for something to eat. She smelled cooked cow as she descended and found her mate sitting on the edge of a wagon, eating steak, next to a butchered, cooked cow that steamed in the cool darkness. "Ohhh," she breathed. "I have never loved you more than I do right now."

Rokshan laughed. "I thought you probably wouldn't have eaten. We have some time for food."

Lamprophyre tore into the cow and licked up warm juices running down her chin. She'd have sworn she didn't have an appetite before smelling the cow. "Are you finished here, then?"

"I still have work to do. They need direction and a temporary reassigning of duties. I'm afraid Commander Vriski is one of those extremely competent leaders who's bad at delegating." Rokshan took another bite of steak. "Are you all right?"

She'd told him the basics of what had happened at Manjaret

that afternoon. "Right now I'm miserable over the failure of the pyrite weapons. It really is almost worse to know they *can* kill a dragon, but they just aren't mobile enough."

"It's something the Army can work on. Don't fall into despair, sweetheart. You learned important things today." Rokshan leaned against her flank. "Will you be all right to fly in the morning?"

"Are you sure we can't leave tonight? I don't want to stay here overnight. Sunital isn't built to accommodate dragons, and I miss the embassy."

"I'm sorry, but by the time I'm finished, it could be after midnight, and the moon sets early. I don't want to risk it." Rokshan set his plate aside and stretched. "And we left the harness in the capital."

"You make sense," Lamprophyre said with a scowl. "All right. I suppose I have to sleep in the coliseum?"

"There's really nowhere else, unless you want to go outside the city." Rokshan put a hand on her arm. "We can leave at first light, if that helps."

Lamprophyre took another bite rather than respond, not wanting her bad mood to overwhelm her or spill over onto Rokshan. A handful of soldiers entered the coliseum then, and she watched him talk to them in idle curiosity. What a strange way to live, being in such danger of conflict you needed a whole subset of society dedicated to attacking others and defending against attacks in turn. And yet it was something Rokshan was naturally good at. Fortunately, he was good at many things, because how sad if you had a talent for something that didn't exist in your society?

Finally full, she pushed the carcass away and stood. Almost everyone had left the coliseum, taking the lights with them, and she found a quiet corner and settled in to sleep. A flutter of wings swept past her, startling her, but it was only an owl out hunting. She hadn't realized owls hunted in the city. She yawned, tucked her head into her chest, and fell asleep.

CHAPTER TWENTY-SIX

She woke at first light, a little later than she'd hoped because the walls of the coliseum made dawn come later. Rokshan wasn't there. The coliseum was empty and smelled of dust and dead earth rather than cooked meat. Once more she suppressed irritation. She shouldn't expect Sunital's military to know she was awake and immediately provide food.

She got up and prowled to the entrance, which was too low for a dragon to fit through. Outside, the streets already bustled with wagons and handcarts hauling produce and meats to the Sunital city markets. The smell of freshly butchered meat roused her hunger. She retreated a few paces and breathed on the green chalcedony pendant. "Rokshan, where are you?" she said.

Rokshan didn't immediately respond. She was about to speak again when he said, "*Lamprophyre. I'm sorry, I overslept.*"

"It's all right. I'm just hungry and that instinct is at war with my desire to get back to Tanajital. What should I do?"

Rokshan laughed. "*I'll be there in a few minutes.*"

It was more than a few minutes before Rokshan arrived behind another wagon carrying a couple of cooked sheep. He had bread that smelled of sharp, creamy cheese wrapped in a napkin and was biting into the folded-over bread as he walked. "Eat up," he said. "We'll leave when you're finished."

Lamprophyre had never eaten so fast. She wondered in passing why she was so eager to get back to the capital. It wasn't as if it was home, though she was certainly fonder of it than she was of any other human city. And it wasn't as if she was afraid of Sardonyx's dragons attacking Sunital, because she knew now she could defend herself against them. No, it was just that she felt more confident there, surrounded by her clutch. Surely they hadn't gone into battle? There were stories of clutchmates knowing instinctively when bad things happened to each other, but Lamprophyre didn't believe those were anything but fantasy. So if something did happen —if one of them were hurt or killed—she was too far away to be told about it. She wanted to be safely with them again.

With Rokshan seated behind her shoulders, she soon left Sunital behind, soaring northwestward. The great plains between the two cities lay smooth and yellow-gold in the wintry sunlight. South were the hills that grew into the mountainous border with Sachetan; north was the enormous forest through which the Green River rolled. The river was invisible at this distance, but would eventually come into sight as a gray ribbon unreeling from its source deep within the dragons' mountains.

She remembered the first time she'd seen the river with Rokshan, how she'd wondered why it was called Green when it was gray-blue like every other river. Now she thought about the Sonti River and the lake where it terminated. "Who is Sonti?" she asked.

"Who?"

"The river. Was it named for someone named Sonti?"

"Oh. I suppose so. That name is older than the catastrophe, so who knows who it really was?" Rokshan leaned forward. "It's so quiet up here. No other dragons, no birds, even. We might as well be the only two people in the world."

Lamprophyre agreed. "It's so peaceful."

Rokshan laughed. "That would be the perfect time for something to attack us."

Lamprophyre's head swung around, searching the sky. She relaxed. "There's no one around."

"I know. It was just a thought." He patted her neck. "Today, will you come with me to talk to my parents? I intend to tell them about us."

"Now?" Lamprophyre said, alarmed. "Is this really the time, with a war going on?"

"There's never going to be a perfect time. And I want to get it over with."

Lamprophyre's heart beat faster. "I…suppose."

"I could tell them by myself, if you're afraid."

"Afraid? I'm not afraid! I might feel some minor trepidation." It wasn't fear. It was guilt. She knew this was Rokshan's decision, but he'd made it for her sake as well as his own, and she didn't want to see the look in his mother's eye when she realized her youngest son was in love with a dragon and wanted to change his species.

"You still feel guilty, don't you," Rokshan said.

Rokshan was too damn perceptive. "Suppose I do. I know it's not rational."

"Sweetheart, it will be all right. My parents are not going to blame you. They might blame me for not having the decency to fall in love with a human woman, but they know how many of my relationships with women have ended badly. They might even be relieved."

That was a possibility Lamprophyre hadn't entertained. "At least I haven't tricked you into marrying me."

"Exactly. Don't worry about it. Think instead of how nice it will be not to have to keep this secret from people I care about."

Below, the gray streak of the Green River appeared in the distance. Lamprophyre banked to follow it north. "You're right," she said. "That, I can look forward to."

They flew in silence the rest of the way, until the walls of Tanajital loomed before them. "The palace?" Lamprophyre asked.

"The training grounds," Rokshan replied. "I have to report to Sajan."

Lamprophyre dutifully swept low over the streets in the direction of the training grounds. She flew over the warehouses, but saw none of her clutch there. Disappointed, she focused on her destination. They were probably all running errands for Sajan, and maybe some of them were with him now.

She coursed over the palace and coasted to a running stop on the training grounds. She'd been right: Flint and Dolomite were there, as were Sajan, Tekentriya, and a couple of soldiers in captain's insignia. Flint and Dolomite's thoughts were concerned, and Flint also sounded a little embarrassed, the kind of embarrassment that results from listening to other people argue in public. Curious, she crouched to let Rokshan down, then walked forward to join her clutchmates.

"My people are not soldiers," Tekentriya was saying, "and I refuse to allow you to co-opt them as if they were cattle."

"I didn't say that, your highness," Sajan said, his voice taut with tension. "But your spies—"

"My *agents.* Spying is for amateurs."

"Your agents, then. They're admirably suited for the task I have in mind, more so than any soldier."

"And what task is that?"

Sajan glanced at Rokshan, nodded briefly to acknowledge his presence, and returned his attention to Tekentriya. "The military's adepts haven't yet successfully managed to locate Sardonyx's forces using scrying artifacts. Thanks to the many ecclesiasts possessed of prophecies, we have some warning as to which cities will be struck, but not when. I need eyes in the field to track down those enemy dragons and send word when they spot them."

Tekentriya shook her head. "You have soldiers for that."

Sajan glared at her. "We have limited reconnaissance capabilities because *you*, your highness, convinced his majesty that there was no point in the military duplicating your efforts. You've guaranteed we need to depend on you. I'm asking you to fulfill your end of the bargain."

Lamprophyre listened to Tekentriya's thoughts, which were as angry as ever, but also tinged with embarrassment. *Did tell him that,* Tekentriya thought. No evidence of her inner turmoil showed on her face. "Very well," she said. "I'll send a message to the man who coordinates our internal information gathering network. It will take a few days—"

"We don't have a few days!" one of the captains said. "We're all on edge waiting for those dragons to appear on the horizon—we need to know where they are!"

Tekentriya ignored his outburst. "Two or three days," she said. "He moves between locations, and it will take time for a messenger to reach him."

"But you do know where he is," Sajan said.

"I know where all my people are." Tekentriya made it sound like this was so obvious he should be the one embarrassed.

"Then why don't you take the message yourself?" Sajan asked. He was trying and failing to sound reasonable.

Tekentriya gave him a look that should have fried the hair from his scalp. "I don't ride," she said.

"Why not?" Dolomite asked.

Everyone jumped, including Lamprophyre, who'd almost forgotten her clutchmates were there, they'd been so still. "Dolomite," Lamprophyre said.

"Oh. It's your leg," Dolomite went on, ignoring Lamprophyre. "If that's what worries you, a dragon might be able to carry you. We're shaped much differently than horses."

Tekentriya turned her baleful glare on Dolomite. "I'm afraid it's impossible," she said.

"I don't think so. I've been watching how you walk, and I think you might fit—I don't know how comfortable it would be, but it wouldn't have to be a long flight." Dolomite flexed his wings, creating a downdraft that ruffled the humans' hair.

The glare was fading from Tekentriya's face, which was turning red. "I...can't," she said, sounding as if the words were being wrung out of her. "My hip doesn't move properly."

"Oh, but that's what makes me certain it will work," Dolomite said. "Your hip is already at the right angle." He knelt low before her. "Climb up and see."

Flint sucked in a breath. Lamprophyre couldn't stop staring at Tekentriya, who at any minute was going to blast Dolomite for his impudence, and then Dolomite's feelings would be hurt, and Lamprophyre wasn't sure she could stop herself shouting at Tekentriya for being a cast-iron bitch, or whatever it was Rokshan always called her.

Tekentriya, for her part, stared at Dolomite. The redness in her cheeks faded. "Climb," she said. She took a few awkward steps to his side. Dolomite leaned over so his ruff was easy to grab. She put her hand on his side, then used both hands to grab his ruff and haul herself up, her bad leg dangling. With some effort, she slung her good leg across his neck and settled herself into the notch, then used her hands to shift her bad leg forward.

Then she sat perfectly still. Lamprophyre, still listening to her thoughts, heard nothing but a distant sense of wonder—not at being perched on a dragon's shoulders, not at having managed to climb up, but at how in that position, with her hips wide and her legs crooked naturally, she felt, for the first time in over five years, no pain.

"You see? It's not awful," Dolomite said.

"No," Tekentriya said in a quiet voice Lamprophyre couldn't believe belonged to the abrasive princess. "No, it's not."

"Then we can go? I'd be happy to take you, because I think you'll enjoy flying," Dolomite said.

Tekentriya lowered her head and put her hand on her damaged hip, then gripped Dolomite's ruff. "Do you know where Umrit is? We'll start there."

"I do. Let's hurry, shall we? It sounds as if General Sajan wants us to be quick. Goodbye, Lamprophyre." Dolomite rose with a great flapping of wings and soared off southward.

"Stones," Flint said. "Did that just happen?"

"And did you—" In time, Lamprophyre remembered not to give

away the dragons' ability to hear thoughts. "She didn't tear him apart."

"Better him than me," one of the captains murmured.

"Show some respect," Sajan said. "Rokshan, I want to know what happened in Sunital. Ambassador, thank you for your assistance. I hear you fought in Manjaret. Thank you for that, too."

"I...yes, General Sajan." She couldn't bring herself to say *it was my pleasure*. That was definitely not true.

"Lamprophyre, why don't you go back to the embassy, and I'll join you later," Rokshan said.

"All right. What are you doing here?" she asked Flint.

"I have been taking those chalcedony artifacts all over Gonjiri," Flint said, "and was just reporting in. Dolomite, too." He yawned. "I'm ready for a rest."

Lamprophyre felt fresh and ready to fly some more, but without Rokshan, that seemed pointless. "I have to tell you what happened in Manjaret, but it can wait until afternoon. Go get some sleep. I'll join you later."

She flew lazily back to the embassy, which was empty for once, all except for Depik's horrible hollow despairing thoughts as he lay in his house, wakeful and miserable. Lamprophyre never knew what to do when his illness took him, and she was too big to fit in his house anyway, so she blocked his thoughts out, feeling it was a courtesy she owed him. She settled inside the hall, hung the chalcedony pendants on their pegs, and idly picked over her books. Nothing appealed to her. Maybe napping was the only option left. That felt so self-indulgent when there were dragons out there intent on destruction.

She was drawing a map of Gonjiri from memory on one of her slates, trying to see a pattern in Sardonyx's attacks, when she heard someone coming across the courtyard. It was Dharan. A jolt of excitement went through her. "Did you read Evart's notes?" she asked before he was halfway to her. "Rokshan said he sent them to you."

"Good morning to you, too," Dharan said. "I did. But don't get too excited. I'm not sure how helpful they are."

Lamprophyre settled back on her haunches. "You have to have learned *something*."

"I did, but I'm not an adept. Some of what he wrote was meaningless even decoded." Dharan sat beside her and took the scribbled-on blank book out of his shirt. "Meaningless to me, anyway. The clear part is that for a human to use it, the transformation artifact has to work in conjunction with a memory enhancing artifact. Evart tried dozens of those. All of them failed."

"It couldn't have been all of them, or he couldn't have transformed me."

"That's true. All right, all but one of them failed. The problem is that he didn't keep detailed notes about his experiments." Dharan flipped through the book's pages. "For example, he writes here that he used a blue sapphire—I don't know why he had to specify the color—"

"Sapphire comes in more colors than just blue."

"Oh. Anyway, he used a blue sapphire to enhance his memory, and then he simply writes that it didn't work. No details about what exactly he did with the sapphire." Dharan closed the book with a snap. "So there's two things. One, we have a list of a lot of stones that didn't work."

"That's progress."

Dharan shook his head and held up a second finger. "Two, we have no idea if it was his experiment rather than the stone that failed. It's possible, from what little I know of magic, that one of those stones might have worked if he'd used it properly."

"And now I'm discouraged again."

"Don't be. I only say that because it's a possibility we should keep in mind. What we *do* have is the final stone he used. The one that worked."

Lamprophyre sat up indignantly. "You could have started with that!"

"Sorry. Again, I'm not sure how helpful that is. He says only that he used sodalite wrapped in gold wire, and that's the end of the book. There are more pages left, so that tells me it's probably the artifact that worked."

"I know gold enhances the magic of a stone." Lamprophyre couldn't sit still any longer. She rose and paced a few steps, keeping her tail well away from Dharan. "But sodalite doesn't enhance memory, it makes you more observant. At least, that's what my research says. I still don't know as much about the powers of stones as an adept."

"Maybe noticing tiny details is enough," Dharan said. "Maybe it's not about holding a shape in memory."

"But Hyaloclast was very certain that's how it worked. Even the adept she got our serpentine artifact from did it that way."

"I didn't know that," Dharan said. "I thought the problem was a human doesn't have a good enough memory to use the artifact."

Lamprophyre shook her head. "Not good enough to transform something as complicated as a dragon, or a human. The adept who showed her how the artifact worked transformed a bird into another kind of bird. Much simpler."

"Oh. I was excited there for a minute." Dharan restlessly tapped the second book against his palm. "Well, I'm convinced Evart used this sodalite and gold artifact in conjunction with the serpentine stone to transform you, with the memory of his daughter as the model. We just need to figure out how."

"And find a model for Rokshan." Lamprophyre blew out a blob of smoke. It drifted up and out through one of the windows. "It's progress. And his notes tell us more about Sardonyx, too."

"Did you read all of it?" Dharan asked.

"About half of it. Evart was obscure on purpose. I think he was afraid Sardonyx could see through his eyes and read what he was writing. You know he believed she was a male adept, right?"

"Yes."

"Well, he knew she was trapped, or bound, and that she had an enemy who was even more powerful. Though some of the time, what he said about that enemy seemed to refer to me. And maybe the rest of the book has more detail about the real 'enemy.' If we could find out who that was, maybe he or she would be on our side."

"That's interesting," Dharan said. "I don't suppose you have that book now?"

"No, Rokshan still has it." Lamprophyre blew out an impatient blob of smoke and watch it drift away and out through one of the windows. "That could be so important!"

"I take it the war isn't going well."

"I'm not sure it's really a war if it's just Sardonyx occasionally attacking a city that we're almost entirely incapable of defending. We can't do damage to her dragons unless we get lucky." She remembered slashing the throat of the dragon in Manjaret and was disturbed to find the memory didn't bother her. She'd saved Corundum's life as well as her own, but even so, she'd have thought taking a dragon's life would affect her more. Maybe the aftereffects were waiting for a quiet moment to leap on her.

Dharan stood to look at the map she'd drawn. "This is her progress?"

"As much as I know, yes." Lamprophyre pointed at Manjaret. "After they attacked here, they were going to move south and west. We know they started by attacking the cities they remembered, like Hamadri, but they also have scouts flying around looking for new and better targets." She sighed, and another smoke puff escaped her lips. "I don't know what we can do."

"I can't believe I'm saying this," Dharan said, "but Jiwanyil's prophecies have made a difference. I've heard people in at least five towns escaped before Sardonyx attacked."

"Don't defend him," Lamprophyre said bitterly. "You were right. He's not a god."

Dharan raised an eyebrow. "I know I'm more or less a heathen, but I don't know that I've ever said he wasn't a god."

"Then let me tell you what Rokshan and I found on Mother Stone," Lamprophyre said.

She told him all the details, everything her draconic memory wouldn't let her forget, and watched his face grow still and expressionless. She finished with, "I don't understand why he would do all of that. Maybe he's mad. Maybe his prophecies now are part of a plan to see humanity destroyed. It just doesn't make sense."

Dharan's eyes were unfocused, as if he were looking at some distant horizon. "I'm not sure," he said. "Maybe you're looking at it in reverse."

"I don't understand."

He focused on her. "Maybe freeing Sardonyx was part of saving humanity."

"That's insane," Lamprophyre blurted out. "I'm sorry, Dharan, but Sardonyx has already killed hundreds of people in those smaller towns where no one knew to flee. Imprisoning her kept humanity safe for a thousand years. And all the dragons she's killed—how can this be a good thing?"

"I don't know," Dharan said, his voice sounding distant the way it did when he was thinking hard. "I need that book Rokshan has."

"Take it. Maybe you'll see something we haven't."

"*Lamprophyre.*" Rokshan's voice came from the wall.

Lamprophyre realized the green chalcedony pendant had misted over. She picked it up. "Rokshan?"

"*Where are you?*"

"I'm at the embassy with Dharan. He wants to read Evart's book."

"*Fine. That's fine.*" Rokshan sounded distracted. "*Wait there for me, and put the harness on. We have to leave immediately.*"

"Leave? For where?" Yet another messenger run.

"*For Fanishkor. The Archprelate was possessed of a prophecy.*" Now Rokshan sounded breathless, like he was running. "*Sardonyx is on her way to their capital right now.*"

CHAPTER TWENTY-SEVEN

Fifty beats later, Rokshan ran into the courtyard and came to a stop outside the embassy, breathing hard. "Here," he said, thrusting the book at Dharan. "Take care of it. Lamprophyre, we have to go *now*."

"But what can we do?" Lamprophyre said even as she bent to let Rokshan climb up into the saddle. "Hyaloclast said the flight is already on the way."

"Go, go!" Rokshan shouted, and Lamprophyre, startled, leaped into the air and ascended almost vertically until she rose above the highest towers. She knew nothing of Leksital, the Fanishkorite capital, except that it was west and a little south of Tanajital, so she flew westward, burning with questions.

"Why are we doing this?" she demanded when they'd left Tanajital behind. "Even if we beat Sardonyx there, there's nothing the two of us can do against her dragons except bleed and die."

"This isn't about fighting," Rokshan said. "Leksital has no pyrite weapons. No dragons have ever set foot in the city. They're completely defenseless. And we have no idea if Jiwanyil, whatever he is, has bothered to warn them Sardonyx is coming. We have to get them to evacuate the city, and since they still aren't in communication with Gonjiri, you and I are the fastest way to make that happen. We're closer than Hyaloclast and you're faster than any of Sardonyx's people."

"I should have known you'd care about the fate of strangers," Lamprophyre said.

Rokshan laughed and patted her neck. "It's probably a fool's errand, but I couldn't live with myself if we didn't at least try. Head a little more south. It's maybe three thousand beats' journey? Something close to that, anyway."

"If I could go faster—but you said it makes you feel like your eyeballs are trying to escape your head."

She felt Rokshan shift in the saddle. "I have a solution," he said. "Glass eyepieces. You—no, you can't see me from there. Don't worry about it. Go as fast as you can."

Lamprophyre tried to look over her shoulder anyway. She couldn't imagine what he was talking about. Well, if he knew what he was doing... She increased her speed, pushing herself until they were skimming along nearly at her maximum speed. For the first time in days, she felt powerful, ready to take on the world. Sardonyx would not destroy the people of Leksital, not if Lamprophyre and Rokshan could stop her. And stop her they would.

Speaking at that speed was impossible. Lamprophyre occupied the time by thinking over what Dharan had said and what little Rokshan had read to her of the book. Somehow, Evart had used a sodalite artifact to control the serpentine stone and transform her. Lamprophyre knew, thanks to Hyaloclast transforming her back, that it didn't take an adept to use the serpentine artifact. But maybe it took an adept to understand how it worked in the first place. She felt so muddled. It was time to take the problem to an adept. And the only adept who could help was, unfortunately, Manishi.

Lamprophyre didn't want to ask for Manishi's help again. They were already in debt to her more than Lamprophyre felt comfortable with, including the promise of a dragon eggshell. And the last time Manishi had helped them, she'd lost her hand. But Manishi already knew half the secret—that Lamprophyre had been temporarily human—and that put her halfway to understanding the rest, unlike every other adept in Tanajital.

But was this really the time to worry about transforming Rokshan? He was needed as a commander, and while he could go on being a commander as a dragon, Lamprophyre couldn't help thinking of how hard it would be to explain the situation to everyone, particularly those he had authority over. Maybe they needed to stop focusing on that problem until Sardonyx was dealt with. Lamprophyre refused to consider that they might lose. That was defeatist, and she'd learned from Rokshan that giving up when you hadn't been beaten guaranteed you would lose the war.

She thought about Sardonyx instead. Someone had kept her and her dragons imprisoned all those years. There was no evidence that that person wanted her freed. So why had there been a release clause, so to speak, built into that trap? Because Jiwanyil had been clear that humans on Mother Stone was something he'd anticipated. Something that was part of an 'old contract.' It made no sense. But it did give Lamprophyre hope that maybe, somewhere in the world, was a power greater than Sardonyx that might be willing to work with humans to defeat her. Of course, she had no idea who or where that power was, but the possibility made her feel better about the chance that she was now racing toward her doom.

The plains west of Gonjiri turned into rolling hills, and those grew steeper until they reminded Lamprophyre of the foothills near her rocky home. They swept over villages nestled into the valleys and larger towns sprawling across the hills. Most of the hills bore the marks of regular tilling, which intrigued Lamprophyre. She didn't know how crops could grow on a hillside, and she wished she could ask Rokshan about it.

Ahead, a dark blotch backed up against one of the steeper, taller hills resolved into a walled city, not as large as Tanajital and less towering. It still looked intimidating, probably because its walls were of forbidding black basalt thicker than Tanajital's rosy-gold granite. Its position against its hill made Lamprophyre think of a dragon father crouched in his cave, guarding his dragonet—though nothing preyed on dragons but other dragons, so the image was more frightening than she'd first realized.

She slowed in her approach and called out over the wind, "What now? Will they shoot at us?"

"I don't think so," Rokshan shouted back. "But let's swing wide around the city and see if there's an obvious place to land. If we do that without attacking, that should tell them we're harmless."

"All right."

She swung lower and prepared to circle above the city. Now that she was close, she could see movement outside the walls and around the gap to the south that was an enormous gate, at the moment wide open. Curious, she dropped down for a better look. A road of round-topped stones pressed deep into the earth led to the gate, and people thronged it, all headed for the city.

It took Lamprophyre a few beats to identify what felt wrong about the scene, and then she realized there were no wagons. Tanajital's southeastern gate, which accepted trade from Sunital and Prabat and Manjaret and all the other eastern cities, was always packed with wagons bringing things to sell at Tanajital's markets. There also weren't any large animals, though maybe Leksital didn't allow animals to be brought in by the main gate. Lamprophyre looked. There was another gate to the west, but it was closed, and there were men in uniform guarding it. Odd.

"What are all those people doing?" she asked.

Rokshan was leaning over her right side. "I don't know. But if they were warned somehow, and they think they'll be safe inside the city, this is going to be harder than I thought."

None of the men and women pressing forward to the gate did more than glance in their direction. The soldiers on the western gate watched them, but didn't shoot. That relieved Lamprophyre's mind. She banked to avoid the protective hill and shot around to the southern gate again, dropping lower. "I see the king's palace," she said. "I think it's the king's palace. It's got gold roofs like the one in Tanajital."

"There's a field north of that I think we can land in," Rokshan said. "It's close to the palace, but not so close they'll feel like we're attacking them."

Lamprophyre nodded and turned north. Leksital didn't have the towering, gold- or copper-topped spires of Tanajital; its buildings were all low to the ground and roofed in colored slate, gray or deep blue or mossy green. There were trees everywhere, which confused Lamprophyre. Trees all in one place to make a parkland, she understood, but trees growing beside the streets or behind the larger houses made no sense.

The field Rokshan had pointed out had a row of trees defining its northern edge and was surrounded by streets on the other three sides. Lamprophyre couldn't make out what it was used for. It was completely empty and so, as she landed, were the streets. People screamed and ran at her appearance, and while it saddened her—she hadn't unintentionally frightened a human in months—it also reassured her that she wasn't invisible. The non-reactions of the people at the gate had worried her.

She crouched for Rokshan to leap down and looked around. The golden roofs of the palace rose above a handful of shorter buildings that lay just the other side of the street on the field's southern border. "Well?" she asked. "We need to speak to the king. I don't want—"

The blue chalcedony pendant misted over. "*Lamprophyre, where are you?*" Hyaloclast said.

"I'll go to the palace," Rokshan said. He pressed something cold and flexible into her hand and ran off without waiting for her assent.

Lamprophyre took the pendant in her other hand and said, "Rokshan and I just reached Leksital. Where are you?"

"*About a thousand beats away. We can see Sardonyx's flight in the distance. We are faster than they, but they have enough of a lead that we won't reach them before they attack the city. You intend to evacuate? These hills will be the perfect hiding place for humans.*"

"That was my thought, too. Though if they don't leave soon,

nothing will help." Lamprophyre gazed off after Rokshan, who'd crossed the street and disappeared between the buildings. "Rokshan's gone to talk to the king. I wonder what he's like." She remembered Rokshan's analysis of King Damen after Chaaksha's party. Rokshan was very good with people, and he understood how they thought. If Damen really was afraid of dragons, he might not be willing to listen to her. She hoped he wouldn't renew his insistence that Rokshan marry Yalini.

"*We are moving fast, and I have nearly the entire flight with me. The city may not need to hold out for more than a few hundred beats.*"

Lamprophyre didn't point out that despite outnumbering Sardonyx's people, the flight was still made up of a lot of dragons who knew nothing about fighting. "Does it feel strange to be defending a country that tried to steal an egg?"

She heard Hyaloclast sigh. "*I find I can't stand by and let Sardonyx slaughter defenseless humans, even humans who are still technically our enemy. I must be going soft.*"

"No, just honorable," Lamprophyre said. "Maybe we'll get that alliance I wanted, after all."

"*Let us see first if Sardonyx leaves us anything alive to ally with,*" Hyaloclast said, and the pendant cleared. Lamprophyre released it to swing against her chest and settled on her haunches to wait.

She looked at the thing Rokshan had given her. It was two glass circles set into flexible leather cups, joined by a very short strap and with a couple of longer straps dangling off the sides of the cups. Lamprophyre sniffed it; it smelled of leather and Rokshan's familiar musky scent and human sweat. She held it up and looked through one of the glass circles, which were as clear as human ingenuity could make glass. If she held them right, she could picture the cups fitting over each of Rokshan's eyes, with the long straps holding them close to his head. This would definitely protect his eyes from the wind. Lamprophyre couldn't wait to see him wearing them.

It wasn't long before Rokshan returned, walking this time beside a very tall, very fat man who reminded Lamprophyre of the Second Ecclesiast, the representative of Katayan. Unlike that ecclesiast, who moved ponderously and always gave the impression of a lumbering ox, this man moved as swiftly as Rokshan despite his size. He wore a loose white shirt with a deep V-neck and loose trousers with legs wide enough Lamprophyre at first thought they were a skirt, and his black hair, while still short, was long enough that the breezes disordered it.

"Lamprophyre," Rokshan said when they neared her, "this is Akuti, King Damen's high chancellor. Akuti, Lamprophyre is the daughter of the dragon queen, Hyaloclast, and her representative to Gonjiri."

Akuti bowed. "It's an honor," he said, bowing low enough Lamprophyre felt sure he meant what he said. His voice was deep and rich and made Lamprophyre think of molten ore.

"Thank you for your welcome," Lamprophyre said, bowing in return. "Did Rokshan explain why we came?"

Akuti's thoughts, which had been as smooth as his voice, sharpened, and he thought *think they're our saviors, damn them*. Lamprophyre managed not to let her astonishment show. It was not at all what she'd expected.

"The prince was good enough to inform us, yes," Akuti said. Now his voice sounded chilly as well as rich. "But, as I told him, there's no need. We will not evacuate the city."

Lamprophyre sat up in alarm. "High chancellor, maybe you don't understand," she said, hoping she sounded reasonable and not shrill. "There are two hundred dragons headed this way, intent on destroying your city. They wield fire and acid, and they're almost indestructible. There is no way humans can defend against them. Your only hope is to flee into the hills and hide."

"Your concern is touching," Akuti said. "And misplaced. I thought dragons weren't interested in the fate of Fanishkor. Or am I wrong, and you've decided to ally with us?"

"We don't have to be your allies to care about what happens to you," Lamprophyre said, irritation flowering within her. "Hyaloclast is following Sardonyx—the leader of those enemy dragons—and she and the flight will do their best to distract them while you go. But you really do have to go now."

"We will not." Akuti delivered this statement with the certainty of a king. Lamprophyre briefly wondered how much power this man had. "Jiwanyil has told us what we must do in the face of this attack. We are to shelter within Leksital's walls and wait."

"High chancellor, that will be fatal," Rokshan began.

Akuti turned on him. "We're not interested in Gonjirian opinions," he said. "You rejected our overtures of peace. I question why you're so intent on seeing us disregard Jiwanyil's prophecy. Do you want us dead so badly?"

Rokshan's hand clenched. "That's a vile accusation," he said.

"Then I apologize. We appreciate that you made such an effort to reach us." Akuti bowed again. "But we know what we must do."

Lamprophyre turned away, infuriated. A small black cloud caught her eye in passing. A black cloud in a clear blue sky. She swung around and pointed. "They're almost here," she said. "It's too late."

"You're welcome to stay," Akuti said, "and partake of Jiwanyil's protection." Lamprophyre heard him think *might as well learn the truth now, can't hide it anymore*. She recalled what Yalini had said to Rokshan about Fanishkor's secret—something about any attacker getting a surprise? Akuti knew something he wasn't telling.

"We'll stay," she said, "and if we have to defend the city, we'll do that too."

Another of those sharp, irritated thoughts crossed Akuti's mind, this one wordless. He smiled, and bowed. "I'm afraid we have nowhere in the palace to fit you, my lady. And I imagine the prince would prefer to stay with you. But my place is at his majesty's side, so if you'll excuse me?" He turned and walked away before Rokshan could reply.

Rokshan said his favorite curse word, the one he wouldn't tell her the meaning of. "I know what that one means now," Lamprophyre said. "It means when a man and a woman—"

"I'll never use that word again," Rokshan said. He turned to look at Sardonyx's oncoming flight. "What are we going to do?"

"He was thinking about something Fanishkor has kept secret," Lamprophyre said. "Isn't that what Yalini said, too?"

"Something that can fight off a hundred evil dragons?" Rokshan said. "We need to get out of here. We can fly wide around them and join Hyaloclast."

"There is no way I'm taking you into combat," Lamprophyre said. "None. If we leave, we're going back to Tanajital, and I can't bear doing that while all my friends are here, fighting and maybe dying. I think we should stay here and see what has Akuti so confident. He didn't strike me as particularly devout."

Rokshan climbed up into the saddle. "All right. But be ready to leave when the city goes up in flames, all right?"

They sat and watched as the cloud grew and became a mass of bird-sized specks. Then it was a mass of tiny dragons that grew and grew until individuals were clearly obvious. Sardonyx flew at the head of the flight, her bright red scales dusted with gold catching the midafternoon light. Lamprophyre's nerves were taut, twisted nearly to breaking. Having Rokshan perched on her shoulders made her even more afraid. She couldn't help picturing herself the target of a stream of fire or a spray of acid that enveloped her helpless mate. It made her even more determined to see him transformed and invulnerable.

The dragons flew on, unswerving, until the entire flight swept over Leksital and curved to follow the contours of its wall. Lamprophyre held her breath, waiting for the moment when they would dive, spitting out acid or breathing out fire. Ten more beats. Five beats.

They dove.

The precision of their timing, the sweep of their great wings, was beautiful and terrifying. Lamprophyre couldn't bear watching and she couldn't bring herself to look away. Twenty dragons split off from the main host, soaring toward the palace. Of course they would attack it first, with its gleaming golden roofs and the way it lay spread out, surrounded by trees, as if offering itself for immolation.

In perfect silence, those twenty females snapped their wings open to glide over the palace. Twenty mouths gaped open. Fire shot from twenty dragons.

A shining orange-yellow dome sprang up two handspans from the highest roof. It spread in an instant to cover the city from wall to black basalt wall. The fire struck the dome, splashed like water against stone—and vanished.

CHAPTER TWENTY-EIGHT

The dragons above floundered, apparently as surprised as Lamprophyre. They backwinged, struggled away from each other, and flapped wildly in all directions. One or two of them spat fire at the dome again. This time, Lamprophyre saw the orange-yellow glow brighten as the fire struck it and was dissipated just as before.

"*Stones*," she breathed. "How did they manage that?"

"Even I don't believe Jiwanyil is responsible for that," Rokshan said. "It must be an artifact."

Another group of dragons, these male, swooped down in nearly as perfect a formation as the females'. Their acid sprays were ragged, not as well timed as the first blast of fire, but it didn't matter: the dome deflected the acid as easily as it had the fire. Now Sardonyx's perfect formations were completely disordered. Lamprophyre couldn't hear their voices at this distance, but she could see Sardonyx shouting at the others, chivvying them back into ranks, she thought.

"I wonder what happens if a dragon tries to go through that thing," Rokshan said.

"I'm not interested in trying," Lamprophyre replied.

"Of course not. I was hoping one of them might."

It seemed none of Sardonyx's dragons wanted to try the experiment either. They tested the limits of the dome, attacking the walls, attacking the place where the dome met the walls, but nothing they did penetrated. Lamprophyre watched them fly about, looking increasingly frustrated, until some unseen signal gathered them together and sent them flying westward, with Sardonyx again in the lead.

"Hyaloclast will be here in a few beats," she told Rokshan. "I think we need to find out if we can safely leave. I'll warn her."

"I'll ask," Rokshan said. "And behave with suitable humility. Though we couldn't have known they were safe."

Lamprophyre nodded and picked up the pendant. It took only a handful of beats for Hyaloclast to respond. "*We saw them leave,*" she said. "*What happened?*"

"Fanishkor has some kind of shield that deflects fire and acid," Lamprophyre told her. "We don't know what it does to a physical body."

"*We will land outside the city,*" Hyaloclast said. "*Come to us when you can. This changes everything.*"

When Rokshan returned, he was alone. "They say it doesn't stop anything more solid than a heavy mist," he said. "Let's hope Sardonyx doesn't get the idea of dropping big rocks through it."

"Did they explain why the Stones they didn't tell anyone about it?" Lamprophyre demanded. "All our cities—"

"I asked to speak to Damen, but he wouldn't see me. Akuti said they are in the process of putting up shields like that one over all their major cities. He did not come right out and tell me they wouldn't give us the secret, just made a lot of noise about how their resources are stretched thin and of course their own people take precedence. Damn him."

"But he could tell us how it works! We have adepts who could build them for Gonjirian cities."

"He doesn't know how it works. Lamprophyre, this is politics at its worst. They'll wait until we're desperate, then offer the knowledge to us in exchange for crippling concessions. Damn, but I hate politics."

"Don't they care that people are dying?"

Rokshan climbed into the saddle and settled himself. "I doubt Damen cares if his *own* people are dying." He sighed. "No. That's unfair. But I told you I think Damen is paranoid and doesn't believe other people aren't like him. And he hasn't seen the devastation those dragons leave behind. This is the first Fanishkorite city they've attacked. Maybe once they've destroyed a couple of his own villages, he'll change his mind."

The orange-yellow dome had faded to almost nothing, but Lamprophyre still cringed when she passed through it. It felt like nothing, not even traces of fire or acid. She flew high above Leksital anyway, searching the sky for signs of Sardonyx, and saw nothing. Breathing out in relief, she descended to join Hyaloclast and her flight, all of whom were spread out over the slopes east of the city.

"I feel no urgency to pursue Sardonyx deeper into Fanishkor," Hyaloclast said when Lamprophyre and Rokshan finished explaining what had happened. "Particularly not if the king intends to behave so dishonorably. Let him keep his shields. We will return to Gonjiri and plan a different kind of defense."

"What kind?" Lamprophyre asked.

Hyaloclast sighed. "I have no idea," she said. "I'm very tired from having crossed most of Gonjiri and half of Fanishkor, and grateful that we didn't have to fight a battle here. We will rest, and then we will sleep, and in the morning maybe something will have occurred to me."

"That's a very good plan," Rokshan said. "I'll tell the Army's adepts what we observed of the shield. Maybe it will be enough to get them thinking in the right direction."

"Your constant optimism is an inspiration," Hyaloclast said. "In the morning, then."

"Did Hyaloclast just give me a compliment?" Rokshan said as they flew away.

"I think she's getting used to you," Lamprophyre said. "If you were a dragon, she'd welcome you to the family with open arms."

"I'm relieved. She's terrifying." Rokshan leaned forward and hugged Lamprophyre's neck. "Mother-in-law. How disturbing."

"I did say never to call her that to her face, right? I doubt her tolerance of you extends that far."

"I'm not insane. And I like my head where it is, thanks."

They returned to Tanajital a couple of thousand beats before nightfall. Lamprophyre decided to stop at the warehouses before going to the embassy for supper. Now that the terror of Sardonyx's attack was over, she found herself curious about what had happened with Dolomite and Tekentriya. She hoped Dolomite wasn't too miserable. There was no way his accord with the bitter princess could have lasted the length of a flight to Umrit, let alone much farther than that.

To her surprise and delight, all her clutchmates were present. She let Rokshan climb down and then hugged Orthoclase, who was nearest. "I've been so worried the last few days," she said. "All of us scattered across the country, and Sardonyx the Stones know where...is there any way we can stay together for a while?"

"I can try," Dolomite said, "but Tekentriya has a lot of places she wants to go. But not until morning."

"Dolomite, you know you don't have to do as she says," Rokshan said. "And don't put up with her rudeness."

Dolomite tilted his head in a curious way. "She's not rude," he said. "She's angry all the time because her body hurts and it doesn't move the way she wants it to. But I was right that flying is different. I'm not sure why she cried, if it stopped hurting. I don't understand humans sometimes. But I don't mind if she makes up reasons to go places."

The rest of them went silent. "Dolomite," Lamprophyre said, then couldn't think of anything else to say.

Porphyry cleared his throat. "You may be the nicest person I know," he said, clapping his clutchmate on the shoulder.

"Am I?" Dolomite sounded puzzled. "Maybe. But there's—"

"Excuse me," someone said from behind Lamprophyre.

She turned, carefully lifting her tail because the speaker was human. He looked perfectly ordinary, though his clothes were rather fine, and Lamprophyre's understanding of human body language told her he was not at all afraid of the seven of them all looming over him.

Rokshan's head came up in surprise. "Zekran," he said. "What brings you here?"

"Hello, Rokshan," the man said. Lamprophyre recognized him now. Zekran was Tekentriya's nonentity husband. She'd seen him a few times before her transformation and once or twice while she had a human body, but had never spoken to him. His thoughts were surprisingly calm and straightforward for someone so bland; she'd always assumed they would be as boring as he was.

Her second surprise was the core of pain he carried deep within himself. She hadn't seen anything like it in anyone but Depik, who despite his growing confidence still felt fundamentally broken. Where it came from, she had no idea, but it changed the way she looked at him.

"Is something wrong?" Rokshan asked. "Or do you have a message?" He sounded as if he was reaching for an explanation of why Zekran would have come all the way to the dragon warehouses when he'd never shown any interest in dragons before.

Zekran shook his head. He walked forward to face Dolomite. "I would like to know," he said, still in that calm way, "what you did to my wife."

"Is your wife Tekentriya?" Dolomite shrugged. "I didn't do anything. We flew to a few cities and she talked to people, and then we flew back. I left her at the palace—did you think she was missing? Because we *were* gone longer than I expected. I'm sorry if you were worried."

Zekran shook his head again. "You must have done something," he said. "She was smiling. I can't remember the last time she smiled, certainly not the last time she smiled at me. She..." He glanced around, looked briefly at Rokshan, then returned his attention to Dolomite.

"I love her, you know," he said, as placidly as if he and Dolomite were the best of friends and the only ones present. "I have only ever wanted her happiness. But after the accident, she changed. There was nothing I could do, and we both knew it. Today I saw the first hope I've had in five years that she might still be herself, deep inside. So, whatever you did—I beg you, go on doing it. I feel I finally have Tekentriya back."

Dolomite lowered his head to look Zekran in the eye. "I don't think she knows how to tell you what she needs," he said. "Which means you have to tell her. I don't think mates should be frightened of each other."

Zekran's eyes narrowed. "You think I'm afraid of her?"

"Everyone is afraid of her," Dolomite said. "She wants them afraid so they won't come near her. But I don't think she meant to include you."

Zekran nodded, slowly. "I think I've made a mistake," he said. "A five-year-long mistake. Thank you. I don't know your name."

"It's Dolomite."

"Dolomite. Thank you." He met each dragon's eye, nodded at Rokshan without saying anything, and turned and left the way he'd come.

Once more, everyone was silent. Lamprophyre felt as if one more surprise would flatten her. The idea of Tekentriya having a loving relationship—of Zekran the nonentity being actually capable of such profound feeling—made her wonder what else she'd been wrong about. Maybe Manishi...no, Manishi was almost evil. Lamprophyre was sure about that.

Orthoclase shifted his weight. "I think I could eat," he said, "unless that's too anticlimactic."

"No, not yet," Dolomite said. "I have something else to tell you. Show you, anyway."

"Are you secretly the first dragon king? Because I would believe it," Bromargyrite said.

Dolomite blushed and shook his head. "You are all behaving like you've never seen me before."

"You continually surprise us, Dolomite," Lamprophyre said.

"I hope so. For this surprise, anyway." Dolomite grinned, a cheeky, cheerful look. "My secret project is finished."

Amid gasps and exclamations, Coquina said, "I can't believe you kept it a secret! Tell us immediately. I've been dying to know—all right, I confess I figured out it's some kind of art project. I hope that doesn't ruin it."

"No, because there's no way you could guess what else it is," Dolomite said. "Let's go, before we lose the light."

He led the way south along the river, not flying very fast despite his words. Lamprophyre, bringing up the rear with Rokshan, considered where along this route a secret art project might be stashed. What kind of art project it might be, for that matter. She remembered the pale dust on Dolomite's feet a while back. A sculpture, maybe? But why wouldn't he sculpt it in his warehouse, then? Unless the light in there wasn't sufficient as she'd suspected. It was a true mystery.

After a while, Dolomite turned right, away from the river toward the Kresetni Hills. Lamprophyre had been there with Rokshan once and knew there were several mining operations going on. Maybe Dolomite had mined gems and created something dazzling. There had been talk of making the harnesses—Flint had at least three more finished—more brilliant, and Dolomite had been the one to say it looked like wearing jewelry.

She followed the others in their descent into a quarry, its high, white walls scored deeply from where enormous blocks had been removed. A marble quarry. They were closing down work for the night, and very few humans still moved around the base of the walls. The dragons had no trouble finding places to land despite the irregularities of the ground. Marble dust filled the air, its smell almost overpowering. She hadn't realized how hungry she was.

Dolomite led them past the main, active part of the quarry to where the geometric, angular shapes gave way to untouched hills, some of which still had scrub grass growing on them. Part of the hill was covered with an enormous cloth—no, Lamprophyre looked closer and discovered it was actually many cloths stitched together to make a sheet big enough to wrap a dragon in. Whatever was beneath the sheet was oddly shaped, sharp-edged and rounded by turns, and she couldn't identify it by its outline.

"Orthoclase, no snacking," Dolomite said sternly. "Are you ready?"

"I will personally pin your wings back if you don't tell us *now*," Porphyry said.

Dolomite took hold of the cloth. "It's amazing," he said, and swept the cloth away.

Lamprophyre took a step back. The shape beneath the cloth was a dragon, but it was no one she knew. In another beat, she realized he wasn't moving. "It's a sculpture," she breathed, stepping forward to look more closely.

Dolomite had outdone himself. The male dragon stood poised with wings half-raised, ready to take flight. His shapely torso and the firm line of his jaw were so beautiful Lamprophyre couldn't stop staring. All the carving was exquisite. And it was fully painted, which accounted for Lamprophyre's mistaking the sculpture for a real dragon: emerald green shading deeper in the curves of his body, gold membranes and eyes catching the last light of the sun. He was the most perfect, most attractive dragon Lamprophyre had ever seen.

"Green and yellow was more obvious," Dolomite was telling Coquina, "but that would look too much like Sapphire, and I thought that could be a problem. But the gold is even nicer."

"More obvious, how?" Coquina said.

Dolomite's eye ridges came together in a frown. "Well, the royal colors, of course."

Lamprophyre turned away from the sculpture. "Did you mean to give this to the king?"

The frown deepened. "Of course not. This is for Rokshan." When they all stared at him, he gestured at the sculpture. "It's Rokshan's dragon body."

CHAPTER TWENTY-NINE

Lamprophyre whipped around to stare at the sculpture again. "Rokshan's..." she breathed. She took a step backward and bumped into Bromargyrite, whose thoughts were as stunned as her own. "Dolomite. That's *brilliant*."

"Isn't it, though?" Dolomite sounded so excited she thought he might be bouncing. She couldn't take her eyes off the sculpture to see if her guess was right. "We need a model, and this isn't like anyone else in the flight. It's completely original. No, that's not true. I borrowed my memories of other dragons for some of the shape. But no one dragon looks anything like this."

"But will it work, if it's not a living dragon?" Porphyry said. "When Lamprophyre was transformed, it was into a shape that was a living person. Suppose this turns Rokshan into a statue?"

"Oh," Dolomite said. "I hadn't thought of that."

"It won't," Rokshan said. "I'm certain of it." He walked forward and put a hand on the half-spread left wing, lightly touching it. "Evart might have known his daughter's physical form well, but he wasn't an expert on internal anatomy. He only had to keep the outer shape in mind, and the inner organs followed naturally."

"How do you know that?" Lamprophyre asked.

"It's the only thing that makes sense." Rokshan ran his fingers over the wing's edge again. "If someone had to have a perfect knowledge of living systems to successfully transform a creature, it could never happen. Nobody knows bodies that well. Part of the magic must include making sure the transformed creature is viable."

"That still sounds like a guess, Rokshan. You're risking your life on that guess."

He turned to face her. "I'm confident it's true. And this—" He pointed behind him— "this is the ideal way to accomplish the transformation."

"But we still don't know how to make it work," Flint pointed out. "Unless you've deciphered that book."

"Oh!" Lamprophyre exclaimed. "I forgot. Dharan decoded the mystery book. He said the other artifact we need is sodalite wrapped in gold."

Exclamations went up all around. "Then we just need an adept to build one for us," Flint said.

That silenced them. Rokshan sighed. "I don't want to approach Manishi—"

"We don't have to," Bromargyrite said. "I can ask Kamil."

"Kamil?" Lamprophyre involuntarily looked at Rokshan. "I don't mean to be rude, but we don't know him. Is he trustworthy?"

Bromargyrite didn't look insulted. "I trusted him enough to tell him I could hear his thoughts," he said. "He's kept that secret. I don't know if he's as skilled as Manishi, but he's more than competent. I'm sure if he has access to Evart's notes, he can create the artifact we need."

Rokshan looked back at Lamprophyre. "I would really like not to owe Manishi for anything more than we already do."

"I agree." Lamprophyre nodded at Bromargyrite. "Will you talk to him? Explain the situation? I'll get the decoded notes from Dharan for him."

"I wish we could do this now," Dolomite said, "because I've been so impatient to tell you all the secret. But I suppose I can wait a few more days."

"We should get back to the city before it's too dark," Rokshan said. He patted the model once more, then climbed into the saddle.

The clutch flew in silence through the gathering dark. Lamprophyre felt unexpectedly let down. It made no sense, because they were closer than ever to fulfilling Rokshan's dream—her dream of being united with her mate. Probably it was the necessary delay that did it. Dolomite's solution was so perfect, it seemed wrong that it couldn't be implemented immediately. She thought of cheerful things instead. Of Rokshan coming to live in the embassy. Flying together as dragons. Sex—Hyaloclast had insisted on teaching her about sex after she was pair-bonded, even though she and Rokshan weren't physically compatible. Sex would be wonderful.

"Take me to the palace, please," Rokshan said abruptly, waking her out of the trance she'd been flying in. She'd followed her clutchmates to the warehouses without thinking, and now she waved goodbye and veered off eastward. Rokshan had to report in to General Sajan, probably. The reality of the war was so distant despite the attack on Leksital. She couldn't stop seeing that beautiful male dragon and trying to picture it a living creature. Her mate.

But Rokshan directed her to land not by the headquarters, but at the palace side door. "Wait for me," he said as he climbed down. "I'll be back shortly."

Lamprophyre smiled pleasantly at the guards flanking the door. They didn't smile back. They weren't allowed. She settled down and prepared to wait. Lying on the comfortably soft earth made her realize how tired she was, how much she'd exerted herself that day. She extended her claws just enough to prick her skin and keep herself awake. She should have asked Rokshan what he had in mind. As it was, she found she didn't care so long as it meant she could sleep soon. She was tired enough she didn't even feel hungry anymore.

She was nodding off when Rokshan returned and climbed back into the saddle. "Up and across the roofs," he said.

Lamprophyre yawned. "Why?"

"We're going to speak to my parents."

That hit her like icy water to the face, waking her fully. "What—right now? Tonight?"

"We can't put it off any longer, not now that we have a model and knowledge about the artifact. I'm certainly not going to tell them after the fact."

"But it's so late. They don't want to be disturbed at this hour."

"It's barely seven-thirty. They'll have finished supper and be in their sitting room. It's the perfect time. There, that's the royal garden. Descend there."

"I'm going to be shot at!"

"I told everyone you were coming and not to shoot. Stop complaining. I know this will be uncomfortable, but it's the right thing to do."

Lamprophyre felt ashamed of herself. Whatever discomfort she endured, it had to be a thousand times worse for Rokshan. "I'm sorry. You're right. I hope they're as understanding as you believe."

"So do I," Rokshan said.

She'd seen the royal garden several times in flying over the palace, and once from inside the palace when she'd had a human body, but she'd never walked through it. Now she descended through the fragrant cedars with their thick needles, looking for a place to land. Lights from the room overlooking the garden, the sitting room open to the air a story above the ground, gave scant illumination to the grassy space at the bottom. It felt like floating down a well, with the palace walls forming a rough oval surrounding the garden. Only the king's sitting room looked out on it, making it the most private place she'd seen in Tanajital.

The sound of running water alerted her moments before she would have landed with her foot in a marble fountain. The spray brushed her scales, dampening her skin until she stepped away. There were two of these fountains, burbling merrily as water shot from the metal nozzles at their tops. A couple of iron benches that looked like lacework stood near enough to the fountains that mist would brush anyone sitting there. How comfortable they would be in the heart of summer.

Lamprophyre walked closer to the open balcony of the sitting room. From her position, she saw what had been hidden from her the last time she'd been here: a stone staircase, its top shrouded on the inside by one of the red and gold curtains, curved down from the balcony to the garden, guarded by a slim iron rail. It was the only access to the garden aside from the way she'd come in.

Lamprophyre's first thought was how sad it was that only the king and his family or guests ever saw this place. Then she thought of the king's difficult job, how he was on display all the time, and decided it was fair he should have a place to go that was private. She'd never imagined she would have sympathy for the king in any way. She remembered by human custom, she was his daughter-in-law, and a nervous shiver went through her. Related to a human king. She understood now why Rokshan said thinking of Hyaloclast as his mother-in-law was unnerving.

She crouched for Rokshan to climb down and examined the balcony. It was taller than she was by six or seven handspans, which was unfortunate because she'd rather liked the room and wished to see it again. Rokshan made for the stairs. "Wait here," he said.

As if she could go anywhere. She nodded, afraid nerves might make her voice shake if she spoke. She settled back on her haunches and furled her wings. The dimness, and the smell of the water and the cedars and the grass she crushed underfoot, would have made the perfect accompaniment to sleep, but that was out of the question.

Somewhere nearby, she heard the deep *hoo* of an owl's hunting cry, and the shrill scream of some small creature cut off before it was more than a squeak. The owl's wings beat the air, and then it was gone. What would it be like, being able to hunt the darkness? She half-turned to look for the owl, though she knew she wouldn't see it. The farthest reaches of the garden were completely dark, and except for the bulk of the palace wall, a solid mass of black that loomed over the garden, she could have imagined herself in the forest north of Tanajital. Another shudder ran through her. Flying through darkness was one thing; being surrounded by Stones knew what was something else.

She heard a door open, and voices approaching. "...being so mysterious," Queen Satiya was saying.

"Not mysterious," Rokshan replied. "It's just that this is something Lamprophyre needs to be present for."

"I see," the king said. To her dismay, Lamprophyre heard him thinking *impossible, can't be what I think, please God let it just be a prostitute.* She opened her mouth to warn Rokshan that his father had already guessed, realized that was a terrible way to break the news to Satiya, and stayed silent.

Rokshan and the king and queen came to stand at the balcony rail, looking down at Lamprophyre. "Good evening, Lamprophyre," Satiya said. "I hope you are well. I understand you fought at Manjaret. Such terrible losses, but they would have been worse without you dragons."

"Thank you, your—Satiya," Lamprophyre said, trying not to sound shaky. She'd called the queen by her name when she was human, and by Satiya's thoughts the queen expected her to go on doing so.

"Mother. Father." Rokshan's voice was much calmer than Lamprophyre had managed. "You already know my resistance to marrying the Fanishkorite princess is more than just a distaste for a loveless marriage. There's someone else."

Ekanath's thoughts sharpened, became incoherent the way thoughts usually did when someone was listening to another person speak. Satiya thought only *finally*.

Rokshan rested his hand on the balcony rail. Lamprophyre was sure only she could see it tremble. "It's not going to be easy for you to understand, because—she's not an ordinary person. I hope you'll hear me out before you start yelling."

Now Satiya's thoughts were concerned. Ekanath thought *guessed right damn it*, and said, "Just tell us."

Rokshan's back was to Lamprophyre as he faced his parents, but she chose not to listen to his thoughts to give her an idea of how he felt. She already knew. "When Lamprophyre was human," Rokshan said, speaking more rapidly now, "she and I fell in love. And that feeling hasn't altered now that she's a dragon again. I still love her, and she loves me. And that's not going to change."

Lamprophyre watched the king and queen closely, listening to their thoughts. Satiya's were incoherent with surprise. She stared at Lamprophyre, her eyes wide. Lamprophyre returned her gaze without flinching, though inside she was a mass of churning emotion, guilt and fear and embarrassment at having her dearest secret exposed. "You can't," Satiya said, speaking to Rokshan though she hadn't taken her eyes off Lamprophyre. "She's not human."

"Not anymore, no, but that's not going to matter soon," Rokshan said. He, in turn, was staring at his silent father. Ekanath's expressions were usually harder for Lamprophyre to read because of his beard, but hearing his thoughts helped her decipher his feelings, and his discouragement and disgust made her wish she could flee.

"What do you mean?" Ekanath asked.

Rokshan took a deep breath. "We still have the artifact that transformed Lamprophyre into a dragon again. I intend to use it to become a dragon myself."

Satiya gasped. Ekanath swore explosively and turned away for a moment, his thoughts a muddle of fury and despair. "*You will not*," he said, turning again to face Rokshan. "I forbid it. It's impossible."

"Not impossible," Rokshan said, more calmly than Lamprophyre was sure he felt. She was so glad he couldn't hear his father's thoughts. "And I'm of age. You're in no position to forbid me anything."

"Rokshan," Satiya said, taking his hand, "why? Why do you want to take such a drastic step?"

"Because I can't bear the thought of living without her, and this is the only way we can be together. Surely you can see that." Rokshan put his other hand atop their clasped ones. "I'll still be your son, whatever shape I take."

"It's disgusting," Ekanath said. "You're human. You were born human and you will die human. What am I supposed to tell the kingdom—that my son's aberrant emotions—"

"Stop," Rokshan said, raising his voice. "I told you, it's not as if I fell in love with a dragon. We were both human when it happened. It's not aberrant for me to continue to love her, any more than if she were disfigured, or crippled, or anything else that changed her body."

"Rokshan, don't talk about me as if I weren't here," Lamprophyre blurted out. Her fear subsided in the face of her desire to not let him walk this path alone. "Your majesties, Rokshan is my best friend. It was natural that when we were both the same species, that friendship would turn into something more profound. Can't you be happy for him?"

"Happy that he wants to become a creature like you?" Ekanath exclaimed.

"Don't insult her, Father," Rokshan said angrily. "This is my choice, not hers."

"I don't understand," Satiya said, almost pleading. "If you are in love, why didn't Lamprophyre stay human? Surely that would solve your problem."

"I was in danger as a human," Lamprophyre said. "I had to regain my dragon body to save my life. But there was a time when we thought I couldn't be transformed back, and I intended to marry Rokshan as a human woman. That he wants to change so he can be my mate...you don't understand how much that means to me."

"So you entrapped him," Ekanath said.

"No. It was his idea." Lamprophyre pushed off from the ground and flew upward, hovering so she could meet Ekanath at his eye level. "But, if it would be easier, I would be willing—"

"You're not turning back into a human," Rokshan said.

"Shouldn't that be my decision?"

"Not if it's a decision based on making my parents happy." Rokshan gripped his mother's hand more tightly. "Lamprophyre, you're still in danger in a human body, and what's more, you are more suited to being a dragon than I am to being human. And there's even less chance of the transformation working on you, because Evart is dead and no one else knows a human body well enough."

"It doesn't matter. I forbid you to do this, Rokshan." Ekanath's thoughts, though, were growing tired and resigned. Lamprophyre couldn't understand where the difference between his thoughts and words came from.

"And I told you, you can't forbid it. I wanted you to know my intentions because I didn't think it was fair to you to find out after I transformed." Rokshan sounded suddenly tired himself.

Ekanath sighed. "You're right. I can't forbid you as your father. I *can* forbid you as your king. You can't go on commanding the military as a dragon, and as we are currently fighting a war, I require you to give up this ridiculous notion."

Rokshan went very still. "I can go on—"

"The soldiers won't take orders from you if you're a figure of ridicule. You would cripple our Army to satisfy your selfish needs?"

Rokshan didn't say anything. Lamprophyre dared listen to his thoughts. They were a muddle of defiance and frustration and resignation, and overlaying all that was such a terrible sadness at losing Lamprophyre's companionship her throat ached with shared misery. "Rokshan," she said, "that's something I've worried about, too. The Army needs you."

"You need me," Rokshan said. "How is that less important? It's not like I can't still fight."

"We've waited all this time. We can wait a while longer."

"This war could go on for years."

"You know it won't." As she spoke, a terrible resigned fear shot through her. It was true, the war wouldn't go on forever, if only because they had no way to fight Sardonyx directly. And suppose Gonjiri figured out the shield the Fanishkorites had? That would delay the inevitable only slightly.

"You'll stay human until this is over," Ekanath said. "After that, I don't give a damn what you do. If you aren't human, you're not my son."

"He's still your son regardless of his species," Lamprophyre insisted. "Are you really so angry about this? We're both rational creatures, you know. It's not like he wants to become some mindless thing."

"You stay out of this," Ekanath said. "I wish you'd never come to Gonjiri."

"Ekanath, please," Satiya said. "She's right. This isn't so terrible." But Satiya still felt confused and sad, and it hurt Lamprophyre to hear it.

"I thought you'd finally realized your duty to this family. To this kingdom." Ekanath's voice shook with anger. "I see now you're just as self-centered and selfish as ever. I don't know how we managed to raise a child who would think this proposal was normal." He turned and strode away, and shortly the door opened and slammed shut.

Rokshan watched the place where his father had gone. His thoughts were so angry Lamprophyre blocked them out again, feeling he should have privacy for his pain.

"It will be all right," Satiya said. "He wasn't expecting this."

"I think maybe he guessed," Lamprophyre said, remembering in time that Satiya didn't know she could hear thoughts. "And hoped he was wrong."

"Well, *I* didn't guess. You both must feel terrible about having to keep the secret." Satiya released Rokshan and moved forward to face Lamprophyre. "I don't know how you are still in love when you're not the same species, but I can guess how hard it would be."

"I'm sorry," Lamprophyre said. "We didn't want to cause anyone pain, but Rokshan said it was important we tell you sooner rather than later. So you can get used to the idea."

"I don't know that I'll ever get used to having a dragon for a daughter-in-law," Satiya said with a rueful smile. "Does Hyaloclast know?"

"The dragons all do," Rokshan said. "They've accepted me." He put the slightest emphasis on "they've" that made Satiya's smile falter. Lamprophyre wished she could kick her mate for his insensitivity, but he was probably still angry and hurt and not caring about who he lashed out at.

"Thank you for not being angry," she said quickly. "And the king is right. Rokshan can't abandon his duties now."

"You've always been reasonable, whatever your father thinks," Satiya told Rokshan. "It will be hard—"

"You have no idea," Rokshan said curtly.

"It will be hard," Satiya repeated, not offended by his interruption, "but I assure you, if you truly love each other, the wait will make your eventual union sweeter. I know I feel that way about your father. He and I went for years not saying the right things, wishing we knew how to tell each other how we felt." She smiled at Lamprophyre. "I don't believe either of you planned this, but I'm the last one who'd tell you to give up just because it's hard."

"Thank you, Satiya," Lamprophyre said.

Satiya patted Lamprophyre's hand. "I'll talk to Ekanath," she said. "I hope he will come around. I'm afraid he can't see past the idea of his youngest son despising his species enough to want to change it."

"That's not it at all, Mother," Rokshan protested.

"I know. It's just how he thinks. Give it time." Satiya hugged Rokshan, who didn't hug her back, smiled once more at Lamprophyre, and disappeared into the dimness of the sitting room. Once more the door opened and shut, quietly this time. Lamprophyre gradually descended until she was resting on the grassy garden floor.

"That actually went better than I feared," she said.

Rokshan sighed heavily. He came down the steps without a word and climbed back into the saddle. "I want to stay at the embassy tonight, if you don't mind," he said. "Being called a deviant wastrel makes me crave your nearness, as a reminder that I'm not actually broken."

"You are *not* a deviant wastrel." Lamprophyre leapt into the air. "There's nothing wrong with you."

"I keep seeing that beautiful sculpture, and thinking about what it will be like to take that shape, and my father's words make it such a tawdry desire. I hate that."

"I understand. But you know he's just one person, right? Even if he is your father."

"I didn't tell him about the Fanishkorite shield. I'd meant to, as a reassurance, but when he started talking about how aberrant we both were, I became angry. He can find out about it later. Let him have one more sleepless night worrying about how to protect his people." Rokshan sounded so bitter Lamprophyre wished more than ever to have her human body back, to give him comfort.

"Let's get something to eat," she said. "And then we can sleep, and worry about everything else later."

"I'm not hungry."

"Neither am I, but experience tells me I will be hungry at midnight, and it's a lot harder to find food at that hour."

"You're so sensible." Rokshan leaned forward to rest the side of his face against the back of her head, sending a pleasant tingle through her. "I was just so eager..."

"There's still so much to do. It's not as if we could have transformed you tomorrow. This is a reasonable wait."

She felt Rokshan nod against her scales. "And I do have a lot to do. Discuss the possibility of that shield, and I had an idea about the pyrite weapons. Making them more effective."

"Which you will not tell me because it's a work in progress. Rokshan, sometimes I think you do things just to wind my curiosity to the breaking point."

Rokshan laughed. "If Dolomite can keep a secret that well, imagine what I'm capable of," he said.

CHAPTER THIRTY

Lamprophyre took Rokshan to the military headquarters the next morning before flying off to join her clutchmates at the warehouse. When she left him there, she'd said, "Won't you please tell me what you have in mind for the weapons? It would be such a reassurance."

"If it doesn't work, you'll have gotten your hopes up for nothing," Rokshan said. "And I feel enough of a failure lately not to want to see you look at me in disappointment."

"I would never do that! And you're not a failure. You've done so much to fight Sardonyx."

Rokshan had rested his hand along her cheek with a smile. "I'm used to being a physical threat to Gonjiri's enemies, Lamprophyre. All I can do to Sardonyx or her dragons is be a momentary distraction. You know that, or you wouldn't refuse to carry me into battle. Let me have this secret. I promise you'll know soon enough."

Lamprophyre had nodded, though her heart still ached to know Rokshan was so discouraged. It was his father's rash words that did it. Rokshan and Ekanath had come so far from the day Lamprophyre had arrived in Tanajital, when Ekanath had disdained his son for failing to do his duty by his country and Rokshan had believed his father would never respect him. And now Rokshan's desire to become a dragon seemed to have ruined all that progress. Well, that was Ekanath's fault, not Rokshan's. Lamprophyre wished she could shake sense into the king, but only time would see if he would come around.

She arrived at the warehouses to find only Orthoclase and Porphyry there. "Dolomite left at first light to travel with Tekentriya," Porphyry said, "and General Sajan asked Flint and Coquina to take messages to a couple of towns about a possible attack. More of Jiwanyil's prophecies. I keep waiting for something to go wrong with those. Like, a discovery that Jiwanyil is telling these towns to evacuate so they'll go somewhere that something worse can happen."

"Me too, but it doesn't look like it," Lamprophyre said. "I wish I understood better who this creature is and what its plan is."

"It does make me wonder about who God really is," Orthoclase said. "I agree with you, Lamprophyre, that it's unlikely a god would let himself be trapped like Jiwanyil was, and of course now we know Mother Stone isn't a god, but does that mean God doesn't exist at all? *Something* made dragons, after all."

"I don't know, and I don't think I care," Lamprophyre said. "Whoever God is, he hasn't done anything to help us against Sardonyx. So either he doesn't exist, he's not powerful, or he supports Sardonyx. None of those things inspire me to worship him."

"But if we don't know the nature of God, we can't say whether any of those things should be proof of his existence," Orthoclase persisted. "We always believed Mother Stone didn't interfere in dragon lives because she expected us to act for ourselves and not depend on her for everything. What if that's still true, except our God is someone we don't know yet?"

"You're making me dizzy," Porphyry said. "Does it matter? Whether God exists and wants us to fend for ourselves, or there's no God, we're still back to fending for ourselves. It's the human

God that's the issue now. If Jiwanyil really is their God, he's playing a very deep and confusing game."

"Yes, and so long as his prophecies are accurate, the humans can't afford to question his nature," Orthoclase said. "Which I think is unfortunate. It's not a good idea to go on worshipping someone just because he's powerful. A god ought to be more worthy of worship than that."

"You're turning into an ecclesiast, what with all that speculating on the nature of God," Lamprophyre teased.

Orthoclase shrugged. "It interests me. Humans are so casual about God, what with taking for granted that those prophecies are true. And now that dragons have no God, well, this gives me something to think about that isn't Sardonyx killing our friends."

Lamprophyre nodded. "I hope Rokshan's plan works out. He has something he's doing with the pyrite weapons he hopes will make them more effective. He won't tell me what it is until it's successful."

"Can he still do that after he's transformed?" Porphyry asked.

"I don't know if that can happen soon. We spoke with his parents last night—"

Orthoclase whistled, a long, drawn-out sound. "By your thoughts, I can tell that didn't go well."

"Not even a little bit." Lamprophyre dragged her tiny sixth claw through the grooves between the small white bricks that paved the street, tracing their outlines. "The one thing Ekanath said that I mostly agree with is that Rokshan can't be as effective a military commander if he's a dragon. So maybe we should put off the transformation until this war is over, or at least until he has a replacement."

"But he's too good for them to be able to replace him," Orthoclase said.

Lamprophyre nodded again. "So it could be a long time."

"That's awful," Porphyry said. "We're so close. Bromargyrite should be back with Kamil any time now."

"I forgot about that. Evart's book is back at the embassy.

Dharan left it last night." Lamprophyre made as if to launch herself into the air. "I can go get it now."

"Wait," Porphyry said, putting a hand on her arm. "I think we should meet this Kamil before we commit to anything. It's not that I don't trust Bromargyrite's instincts, it's that Kamil might not be the best choice. Though I really hope he is."

"That's sensible," Lamprophyre said, settling back. "I think I want to meet him, too."

"They're coming," Orthoclase said, pointing southward. A bright orange speck in the distance swooped toward them, flying rather erratically. "Though I don't know what he's doing. He looks like he's avoiding invisible airborne obstacles."

Lamprophyre closed her nictitating membranes to block the morning sun. "I think he's making the ride more exciting for Kamil. I do that sometimes with Rokshan. They must be good friends if he's entertaining Kamil that way."

"And he's wearing a harness," Orthoclase said. "I mean no offense, Lamprophyre, but the idea of putting on a harness makes me uncomfortable."

"It's different when it's for the sake of someone you care about," Lamprophyre said. "I think it would be wrong to do it for a stranger who just wanted a ride somewhere, or maybe for us to take cargo to another city. But when it's about keeping your friend safe, it's not the same."

Orthoclase nodded. His attention was still on Bromargyrite. "That makes sense. I suppose I don't know any human that well yet."

"I've had people ask if they could ride," Porphyry said. "Because I'm a popular racer, that is. I've never met anyone I'd want to single out, though."

"I've just pictured you diving through the hoop with a rider who didn't duck. We don't need human fatalities on the course." Lamprophyre stepped back with the others to give Bromargyrite room to land.

"Of course not," Porphyry said. "Imagine the uproar."

"What uproar?" Bromargyrite said. He crouched and twisted to one side for his passenger to climb down. "You're not planning something dramatic and dangerous, are you?"

"No, just talking about how some humans thrive on danger," Lamprophyre said. "Is this Kamil?"

"He is," Bromargyrite said. "Kamil, this is Porphyry, Orthoclase, and of course you know Lamprophyre."

"Everyone knows the dragon ambassador," Kamil said. Lamprophyre was better at guessing human ages after all these months in Tanajital, and it surprised her to see how young Kamil was. If he was an adult, he was only barely so, which meant he was sixteen or maybe seventeen. He was thin, with knobby elbows and enormous hands that were mostly knuckle, and he wasn't very tall. Lamprophyre suspected he still had some growing to do, if the size of his hands was any indication.

But his size didn't matter. He was so *young*. Lamprophyre's heart sank. There was no way this young man knew enough to figure out how to create the sodalite artifact they needed. Still, she could be polite. "It's nice to meet you, Kamil," she said.

"I didn't realize how Bromargyrite compared in size until now," Kamil said. His voice was pleasantly low for a human, and he looked at Lamprophyre without a trace of fear—well, if he was friends with Bromargyrite, who was nearly Lamprophyre's size, he was used to being towered over. "So dragon males are smaller than females? Why is Bromargyrite so much bigger?"

"We're no different from humans in that respect," Orthoclase said. "There's average sizes, but that's why they're averages—we have dragons who are bigger and smaller than that. Hyaloclast, our queen, is enormous even by female standards, and Lamprophyre is likely to be that big when she achieves her full size."

"Amazing," Kamil breathed. "And here you are walking around Tanajital just as if you're not the stuff of legends." His thoughts were as amazed as his words, and Lamprophyre caught a snatch of *just like the stories, but bigger*.

"Bad legends, apparently," Lamprophyre said. "When I first arrived, everyone I met seemed to think I wanted to eat them."

"Dragons do feature as monsters in most of our stories," Kamil said, "but that's no excuse for being stupid. I'm glad things have changed."

Bromargyrite caught Lamprophyre's eye. She heard him think *haven't told him why he's here, should we?*

Lamprophyre thought about that for a few beats. This short conversation wasn't enough to tell her much about Kamil, but her instincts said he wasn't dangerous, and she felt suddenly certain he wouldn't spread her secret around. She nodded at Bromargyrite, the smallest bob of her head. Bromargyrite nodded back. *Your story*, he thought.

"Kamil," Lamprophyre said, "we have need of an adept, and Bromargyrite vouches for you. But what I'm about to tell you must stay secret, understand? Don't make Bromargyrite a liar."

Kamil's eyes widened fractionally. "Why would a dragon need an adept? I thought you were magical creatures. At least, I know you can hear thoughts—and I haven't told anyone about that, in case that helps."

"It does. Let me tell you a story."

Lamprophyre quickly told him the general details of what Evart had done and what they'd learned after Lamprophyre was transformed back into a dragon. Kamil listened with rapt attention, his thoughts a blur punctuated by sharp moments of insight Lamprophyre couldn't discern.

When she finished, she said, "So you see our problem. We need someone to build the artifact that will allow us to work the serpentine stone to transform Rokshan. And it has to be someone trustworthy."

"I'm trustworthy," Kamil said. "And I'm as skilled an adept as you're going to find."

Lamprophyre shifted uncomfortably. "Not to be rude," she said, "but you're barely an adult. How experienced can you possibly be?"

"If you doubt my abilities, why did you tell me all that?" Kamil shot back. His thoughts didn't sound insulted, just confident—maybe too confident. Lamprophyre remembered what Bromargyrite had said about Kamil being obnoxious about stone, and wondered if her instincts were mistaken.

"You know this wouldn't be the first time someone's underestimated your abilities," Bromargyrite said in his comforting rumble. "Tell her the rest."

Kamil crossed his arms over his narrow chest. "I've been studying stone since I was nine," he said. "My parents are wealthy, and they could afford to indulge my hobby. Except I really was talented. I started designing my own artifacts just a few years later, and by the time I was thirteen I was selling my lapidary skills to adepts more than twice my age. I've come close to perfecting the mind-reading artifact, close enough that the military approached me to help in its development. I'm the only civilian working on that project except Manishi, and she doesn't count." He made a face when he said Manishi's name. "I know the theory behind the use of every stone known to adepts. I'm young, true, but if anyone can do what you ask, it's me."

"Huh," said Porphyry. "Bromargyrite was right. You really are, um, interested in stone."

"The word I used was 'obnoxious,'" Bromargyrite said.

Kamil grinned. "I prefer to think of myself as confident in my knowledge," he said. "And I want to help. This transformation artifact could be useful. You know they use serpentine in small transformations for healing, yes?"

"We do," Lamprophyre said. "I'm surprised you do. I understood that to be a new procedure."

"I told you I know everything about stone. I make it my business to know when someone comes up with a new use." Kamil's brow furrowed in thought. "Imagine being able to repair much older damage. Prince Rokshan's burn scars, for example. Though if we succeed at giving him a dragon body, those scars won't matter."

Lamprophyre looked at Bromargyrite. He was smiling. "I told you," he said.

"You were right," she replied. "Kamil, I have the notes of the man who transformed me. I can give you everything we have."

Kamil nodded. His thoughts were intent on the problem already. Lamprophyre listened closely, but heard no evidence that he intended to betray them. That might just mean he was waiting for his moment, but she had a feeling, again, that that wasn't the case.

"Bromargyrite, bring Kamil, and we'll go to the embassy," she said. "After that, I think we should all go to the training grounds. Sardonyx may still be in Fanishkor, but if she's headed back, General Sajan may need us to fly messages."

"I hope not," Porphyry said. "That is, we've taken those chalcedony artifacts all over Gonjiri, and those are faster than we are. And you've got your own chalcedony artifacts, so Hyaloclast or Rokshan will tell you if anything bad has happened."

"Nevertheless." The truth was that she hated feeling helpless. She needed to be doing something, anything, that would stop Sardonyx killing any more people.

She led the way to the embassy, where she and Bromargyrite nearly filled the courtyard. One more dragon would make things very tight. "Wait here," she said, and ducked inside the embassy hall. Abhit was reading to Rassika and Kavari. Rassika could read now, but Abhit loved reading aloud. Maybe it was time to send him to the academy. She could certainly afford it, but she might have to argue with Bhakriya about letting her pay Abhit's way.

Rassika looked up when she entered, and Abhit stopped reading. "Is everything all right?" Rassika asked.

"Fine, Rassika. Has anyone been here looking for me?"

Rassika made a face. "Ecclesiast in the green litter. The one who's got a stick up his ass about dragons."

Khadar. "You shouldn't be rude about any ecclesiast, Rassika. And Khadar isn't as self-righteous as he used to be."

"'S what Rokshan said about him, and it's his own brother, so he'd know, right?"

"Stick up his ass!" Kavari shouted. Abhit shushed her, but his eyes were gleaming with amusement.

"Yes, but Rokshan..." She'd have to have a word with him about the things he said where impressionable young people could hear. Though Rassika was looking more like a young woman than a girl every day. Humans grew so fast. "Anyway, what did Khadar want? Was he here alone?"

"No, had them yellow ones with the ugly haircuts, and the pipers, and the reverends." Rassika sounded impressed despite herself. "Said as he had been possessed of a prophecy for you. Didn't sound like he thought it was urgent."

"A prophecy for me?" That made Lamprophyre nervous. She didn't want to hear anything Jiwanyil might have to say, and she didn't intend to act on whatever it was. On the other hand, if it gave her insight into Jiwanyil's nature, that might be useful. Just not the way Jiwanyil intended.

"Did Khadar say if he was coming back?" she asked.

"He asked us to ask you to go to the Archprelate's palace," Abhit said. "He said 'at your earliest convenience,' but I think he wanted to say 'immediately.'"

"And where was Bhakriya in all of this?"

"She and Depik have been out back for hours," Rassika said. "Talking about stuff."

Lamprophyre listened for Bhakriya and Depik's thoughts. Maybe...but she didn't hear anything from either of them that suggested romance was in the air. They were talking about Abhit and the academy, to Lamprophyre's surprise. Maybe Lamprophyre's suggestion wouldn't be unwelcome.

"Thank you," she said. "I don't know when I'll be able to meet Khadar, but he's roused my curiosity." She picked up Evart's decoded book and returned to the courtyard.

Kamil had climbed down and was looking at the dining pavilion. "I heard you serve soup to beggars," he said. "Why is that?"

"It was my cook's idea. He wanted to help people, and we thought it would make them less afraid of me." Lamprophyre held out the book to Kamil. "The man who decoded this said there were still incomprehensible parts, but we hoped that meant an adept would understand it."

"There's not much I can't figure out," Kamil said without a trace of modesty. He flipped through the pages too rapidly to be reading them, even if he'd been Lamprophyre. "Give me a few days, and I'll have something for you."

"That soon? You mean you can build the sodalite artifact by then?"

"I'm not *that* good," Kamil said with a smile. "I mean I'll know what kind of artifact it is and how to build it. Creating it will take more time. But I'm confident I'll succeed."

"You succeed, and you can be as obnoxious as you like," Lamprophyre said.

CHAPTER THIRTY-ONE

"I can't believe Jiwanyil would deliver a prophecy for you," Rokshan said. They were flying across the city from the training grounds, where there had been no news of attacks by Sardonyx and her dragons. Rokshan had looked grim, but he wouldn't say anything about his plan for the pyrite weapons, not even that it had failed. Hyaloclast's pendant had been inert on Lamprophyre's chest all day. It was a measure of how frustrated Lamprophyre felt that she saw talking to Khadar as desirable.

"You mean because he has to know I won't listen?" Lamprophyre banked right and began the long, curving descent toward the Archprelate's palace. "Maybe he doesn't know that. He did seem aware of my presence in the cave, but it's not like I challenged him then. He might be oblivious to how I feel."

"Or he's evil, and he wants to confuse you," Rokshan said.

"That's a very cynical thing for you to say," Lamprophyre replied, a little taken aback.

Rokshan sighed. "I don't really believe that. I want to believe that whoever Jiwanyil is, he doesn't hate humanity. But having seen what Sardonyx has done to some of our cities, and knowing he wanted her freed, I can't feel certain of that belief."

"I agree. Which is why I'm curious."

She set down in the field behind the Archprelate's palace and crouched to let Rokshan down. It was as peaceful as ever, with even the background noise of the city dulled to a quiet, monotone hum. The smell of the grass crushed under her feet made her think of lazy afternoons by the riverside, with the green scent of the mossy growth along its banks filling the warm, damp air. Flowers also grew in the vast field, scatterings of white and blue Lamprophyre didn't think were intentional. Their sweet scent almost disappeared behind the smell of the grass.

Rokshan crossed to the door and tried the latch. "Locked," he said. "I guess we wait. Khadar did say to meet him here, didn't he?"

"It was the messenger's instructions," Lamprophyre said. She listened to the drone of bees passing from flower to flower. They were small enough as to be nothing more than their buzz, an invisible moving sound that rose and fell as it came close and then flew away. Somewhere nearby came the snap of a cloth being shaken out. She wondered what it would be like, living next door to all those ecclesiasts. She was sure they didn't worry about crime in this neighborhood.

The door opened, and Rokshan took an involuntary step back. Khadar emerged. For once, he wasn't wearing his green Fifth Ecclesiast's robe, and his hair didn't look as tidy as it usually did. "I suppose I should have expected to see you, Rokshan," he said, sounding irritated. "I thought I specified the ambassador only."

"You didn't, and I would have brought Rokshan even if you had," Lamprophyre said. "I'll just tell him whatever you say, you know. Why waste time?"

Khadar shrugged. "I suppose it doesn't matter." He walked past Rokshan to within arm's reach of Lamprophyre and looked up at her. He looked exhausted, his eyes dark-circled, his lips drawn down in a frown. "I'm surprised you came."

"Why wouldn't I come?"

His lips twitched. "We're not friends, ambassador. You know how I feel about dragons not worshipping Katayan, and I know how you feel about my attitude toward you. And you're loyal to my brother, so I'm sure you'd take his side against me."

Lamprophyre felt uncomfortable at his candor. "You're right, we're not friends," she said, "but I know you are genuinely possessed of prophecies, and I respect that."

"Even if you believe Jiwanyil is not God?"

Lamprophyre hadn't realized the Archprelate had spread that news around, even if it was probably only as far as the High Ecclesiasts. "He exists, whoever he is, and I want to know what he says."

"I was of the opinion that you shouldn't be told about this prophecy, because you are antagonistic to our faith," Khadar went on, "but the Archprelate insisted, and I do not question her authority. I would caution you to respect Jiwanyil's word, but I know you'd ignore that caution."

"Stop being a jackass, Khadar," Rokshan said. "If you were possessed of a prophecy for Lamprophyre, you ought to be respectful of that yourself and not use it as an opportunity to browbeat her."

Khadar ignored him. "I don't, of course, remember what I said," he told Lamprophyre, "but there were many witnesses, and from their memories we have reconstructed Jiwanyil's words." He cleared his throat, and in a resonant, sing-song voice, said, "This is the prophecy: '*The binding speaks too late. Fly far, fly fast, she arrives before you. The stone speaks true, the wind carries the witness, the fire burns the skies. Return, and be made one.*'"

Lamprophyre blinked. "That makes no sense."

"You would think that, wouldn't you," Khadar said. "I don't know why Jiwanyil would waste words trying to convince you of anything."

"He spoke to Lamprophyre on Mother Stone," Rokshan said. "You ought to be less arrogant about what your God does and does not think is a waste of words."

Khadar's eyes narrowed. "How could Jiwanyil speak to you?"

"Maybe that's what I ought to ask you," Lamprophyre said. "He spoke through Rokshan, just as if Rokshan was an ecclesiast. Leaf-green eyes and all."

"That's impossible," Khadar said. "Jiwanyil can't speak through anyone who isn't born to hear his voice. And you're far too old to be possessed of a first prophecy."

"Well, he did," Lamprophyre said, "and what's more, I spoke to him and he replied."

That made Khadar go completely still. "Impossible," he repeated, his voice faint. "Jiwanyil does not respond to our speech. That never happens."

"You see why I'm convinced Jiwanyil isn't what you think he is." Lamprophyre felt the tiniest bit of guilt at pushing Khadar, but she remembered the twelvedays of torment the ecclesiasts had inflicted on her and her clutchmates and the guilt disappeared. "At the very least, you don't know your God all that well."

Khadar shuddered. "You will take me to him," he said.

"What? I will not!"

"You're out of your mind," Rokshan said. "Lamprophyre won't agree to carry you as far as the palace, let alone to Mother Stone."

"I must speak to Jiwanyil," Khadar said, ignoring Rokshan. "If he was willing to speak to an apostate, imagine what he might say to me."

"No," Lamprophyre said. "Mother Stone might not be sacred to dragons anymore, but don't think I've forgotten that your stupidity in sending ecclesiasts there might have freed Sardonyx with no advance warning if Rokshan and I hadn't intervened. And all that aside, it's still a dangerous journey and I refuse to be responsible for your well-being."

Khadar grabbed Lamprophyre's wrist. "You *must* take me," he said. "If there is the slightest chance of communication with God, would you doom Gonjiri, doom all humankind, for the sake of your pride? I can talk to Jiwanyil and ask him directly how we can stop this evil."

"Whose pride are we talking about?" Rokshan said. "Jiwanyil has given dozens, maybe hundreds of prophecies about Sardonyx by now. If he's God, he no doubt believes that's enough. Thinking you need to talk to him to gain greater insight is the height of hubris."

Khadar's face became stony with anger. "Then you refuse."

"I refused more than once," Lamprophyre said, "though it doesn't surprise me you weren't listening."

"Then leave," Khadar said. "Take your prophecy, and much good may it do you." He sounded as if he'd rather damn their names instead. He turned and strode back into the palace, slamming the door behind him.

Lamprophyre and Rokshan looked at each other. "I might have guessed that would happen if we told him what happened on Mother Stone," Rokshan said. "Still, I think you should stay away from the Archprelate for a while."

"The Archprelate? Why?"

Rokshan seated himself in the saddle. "Because Khadar is going to tell her about Jiwanyil speaking to you," he said as Lamprophyre pushed off and flapped to gain altitude, "and if you think Khadar is eager for a face-to-face conversation with his God, imagine how the Archprelate will feel."

"I'd feel worse about turning her down. I like her. But I'm not taking anyone to that cave."

"Of course not. And obviously Jiwanyil can talk to people at a distance, so it's not like it's necessary."

Lamprophyre thought back over the words of the prophecy. "Of course not," she echoed, but she was afraid she might be wrong.

LAMPROPHYRE OFFERED TO RETURN ROKSHAN TO THE MILITARY headquarters, but he said, "There's nothing I can do there at the moment, and Sajan will contact me if there's news of more attacks. I need a rest. I've been so on edge waiting for disaster to strike I might be useless if it does. Let's go for a swim."

"That feels so frivolous," Lamprophyre said. "I don't know if we should enjoy ourselves when people are dying."

"We're responsible for saving those people, as far as we're able," Rokshan said, "and we're no good to them if we're too exhausted from being keyed up all the time." He shifted his weight, and the metal stirrups scraped across her side. "I'm more worried at how relieved I am that Sardonyx seems to have disappeared into Fanishkor. Let them deal with her for a change."

"I understand. I don't want people hurt, but it is easier knowing Gonjiri isn't in immediate danger."

She passed over the wall and descended to land in a secluded bend of the Green River. The dragons had more or less claimed it as their own swimming place, scooping out the steep banks to make a shallow slope where they could step gradually into the water. Willow trees grew thickly at that point, their drooping branches providing shade during the worst of the summer heat. The river ran slow and sluggish this time of year, not shallow, but not as deep as usual. It still smelled wonderfully of green growing things and silty water, and despite her worries Lamprophyre relaxed.

Rokshan removed his shirt and trousers and waded into the current. "Oh, cold," he said with a shiver.

Lamprophyre dipped her hand in the water and flicked him with a handful of droplets. "You don't know what cold is," she said. "At its source, this river is freezing. This time of year, there are chunks of ice floating on its surface."

"So it's warmer here. It's still colder than I like." Rokshan submerged and popped up a few handspans farther downstream. "Though I'm getting used to it. Come on in."

Lamprophyre waded into the river, carefully keeping her wings out of the water. Swimming was nice, but wet wings were a misery. She watched as a dozen or more tiny white birds burst from the reeds on the far side of the river and flew away southward. The rustle of their wings scared a frog, who leaped into the water with a loud *plop*.

She swam toward Rokshan, who was floating on his back staring up at the sky. High, thin clouds obscured the sun, making the day almost cool. Lamprophyre stretched out her tail and floated on her stomach with her face turned away from the water. With her wings furled, the current carried her gently downstream. The sound of the water grew louder, and she lifted her head to see a large boat being poled along in the opposite direction, close to the far shore. It wasn't making much progress against the current, and it didn't help that most of the crew were standing along the rail, staring at her and pointing.

She closed her eyes and ignored them. Their thoughts were full of wonder and amazement, so she didn't have to worry about having things thrown at her. Let them stare.

"Who's that?" Rokshan said. He was farther away than she'd thought. She opened her eyes to see him pointing at the sky. Lamprophyre sat up, splashing her wing membranes, and followed the line of his arm. A dragon crossed the sky, high above, a rust-orange blotch against the pale grayish-white of the clouds.

"It's not any of the clutch," she said. "I don't recognize her."

"I wonder why Hyaloclast sent a messenger," Rokshan said, though it was clear the dragon didn't intend to land in Tanajital.

"She wouldn't," Lamprophyre said.

Then it struck her. That wasn't any dragon she knew.

Lamprophyre thrashed her way to shore, swamping Rokshan. "Run and get the clutch," she panted. "We have to stop her."

"The clutch? Lamprophyre, why—"

"That's Sardonyx's scout," Lamprophyre said. She scrambled to the top of the bank and shook her wings vigorously, shaking away the water clinging to the membranes. "We can't let her get back to Sardonyx. She knows where Tanajital is."

"Take me with you," Rokshan said. "Or at least go to the warehouses. Don't chase that dragon alone."

"There's no *time*," Lamprophyre said. "I'll slow her down. Just get everyone moving!" With a tremendous leap, she was in the air, streaking toward the distant dragon.

She couldn't tell if the scout was flying slowly because she didn't feel threatened, or because she couldn't fly fast, but the dragon certainly ambled as if she had all the time in the world. Even so, Lamprophyre pushed herself to her limit, hating the dampness of her wings that slowed her down. Her thoughts circled round and round what she would do when she caught the scout, who was bigger and more heavily muscled than she. Coming to blows would not end well for Lamprophyre, but she couldn't think how else to stop the dragon.

The scout noticed she was coming when Lamprophyre was within a dozen dragonlengths. Lamprophyre saw her glance behind her and then speed up, not by very much. Lamprophyre curved upward, getting above the scout. The scout glanced back again. She backwinged, slowing herself so Lamprophyre shot over and past her. Lamprophyre turned her climb into a curving dive and swept back toward the scout.

The female spread her wings wide and beat the air, slowly gaining momentum until she was flying directly for Lamprophyre. Lamprophyre swallowed. The female was *enormous*. With all her claws extended and the thick phalanges of her wings bristling and the sharp rust-colored spikes on her back gleaming in the sunlight, she looked less like a dragon and more like an implacable force of nature, something shaped from the earth specifically to kill dragons.

Lamprophyre's jaw tightened. This might be the end for her, but she wasn't going to give up just because it was impossible. She just had to hold out until the clutch arrived.

She reversed in midair, driving toward the scout feet-first with her wings furled to make herself a projectile. The female had time to realize Lamprophyre wasn't going to stop before Lamprophyre rammed into her, taking her in the chest. The blow drove the air from the scout's lungs, and she choked and fell a few dragonlengths before catching herself. "You won't do that again," she snarled. Her voice sounded dark and horrible, a raspy sound that ground across Lamprophyre's nerves and made her wish she could flee.

Lamprophyre didn't waste breath responding. Talk wouldn't win this battle. She curved around and beat hard to gain altitude. Attacking from above was a tremendous advantage, if she could go on doing it.

The female saw what she intended and followed her, not attacking, but trying to get above Lamprophyre. Lamprophyre realized immediately she was at more of a disadvantage than she thought. The scout was slow over long distances, but her greater wingspan helped her in the short term. Gradually, she inched ahead of Lamprophyre, rising higher. Lamprophyre heard the ghost of a thought: *kill this foolish female.* She couldn't let the scout get above her if she wanted to survive this fight. Unless...

Lamprophyre furled her wings and dropped like a stone, startling the scout, who immediately followed. Lamprophyre fell as the scout gained on her, the female's ungainly body gaining momentum with every beat. When the scout was close enough to grab Lamprophyre, Lamprophyre snapped her wings open and let the scout shoot past, then dove after her. She grabbed the scout around the shoulders, tangling her wings, and swiped at the scout's face with her deadly sharp claws.

The scout turned in midair, far too fast for someone her size, and made a grab for Lamprophyre. Instantly Lamprophyre realized her mistake. She struggled to get free, snarling like an animal in her desperation. The scout's claws raked Lamprophyre's lower wing membranes, making her wobble. A flash of memory struck, something Rokshan had mentioned, and Lamprophyre threw her head back and then smashed her forehead against the female's skull.

It didn't work as well as Rokshan had said, but then her face and her nose were shaped differently than a human's. Mostly it seemed to startle the scout, but her grip loosened, and Lamprophyre tore free, gouging the scout's belly with her powerful feet and toe claws. Once more the scout let out a sharp *pah* of breath and fell a few handspans. Lamprophyre hovered above her, breathing heavily. She didn't know what else to do. The dragon outweighed her, and Lamprophyre's fighting skills were mostly exhausted.

The scout recovered and hung, hovering, in midair. Her dark, fathomless eyes, almost solid black from edge to edge, gazed at Lamprophyre maliciously. "You've already lost," the female said. Then she turned and flew away westward, trailing thoughts of Sardonyx and the rest of Sardonyx's flight.

Lamprophyre shot after her. At least Sardonyx hadn't yet been in mental communication with the scout. But that was small comfort. She absolutely could not let this female escape to tell Sardonyx the location of Tanajital. All those helpless humans...

She caught up to the scout and, not knowing what else to do, grabbed the female's tail and pulled, digging her claws into flesh and dragging her downward. The scout shrieked, an unexpectedly shrill sound, and turned, grabbing for Lamprophyre. Lamprophyre kept pulling on her tail, doing her best to stay out of reach. Pain flared in her right shoulder as the scout scored a lucky hit. Lamprophyre twisted out of her grip and kept flying toward the ground. Maybe the scout would be ungainly enough on the ground that Lamprophyre would have an advantage.

Then the scout twisted impossibly, got her hands on Lamprophyre's side, and dug in with her claws, pulling Lamprophyre into a terrible embrace. Lamprophyre screamed as the scout bit her arm and stabbed her again in the side with her claws. The scout pinned Lamprophyre's arms to her sides so all she could do was beat helplessly at her captor with her wings. Lamprophyre fought to free herself, scratching the scout's body but unable to put any power behind the attack. The scout's teeth ground down harder, and dark red blood ran freely down Lamprophyre's arm and side.

Then something hit them both, loosening the scout's grip and dazing Lamprophyre. She tore free instinctively and flapped hard to put distance between herself and the scout. Her vision was blurry from pain and the impact, and she blinked to clear it. A green and rose-colored blur battered at the rust-orange scout, and farther away someone dark blue shot around the two, looking for his moment. Coquina and Flint. But they'd been away—Lamprophyre shook her head hard to dispel the fuzziness. She didn't care that their presence was impossible. She was too grateful not to be dead.

The scout screamed in pain, and Lamprophyre saw blood trickling down the female's side. Coquina had gotten in a lucky hit. "Lamprophyre!" she shouted. "Drive her down!"

Lamprophyre nodded, drew in a deep breath, and surged toward the two locked in combat. Coquina detached herself from the scout to allow Lamprophyre to slam into the female, knocking her farther away and down. Flint soared in, looking terrifyingly small next to the scout, and raked her belly with his claws. More blood flowed.

"We can't close with her!" she shouted. Coquina nodded. Lamprophyre distantly heard her think *drive her to ground* and felt relieved that Coquina had had the same idea she had. Lamprophyre shot higher and then plummeted, once again reversing to strike the scout in the middle of the back, right between where her wings emerged. The blow shook Lamprophyre to her core, but the scout dropped, not trying to slow her fall.

Lamprophyre and her clutchmates followed. If the scout didn't regain consciousness, the landing from this height would kill her, turn her organs to jelly and shake her brain inside that thick dragon skull past recovery. It was a horrible thought she didn't regret at all.

But the scout stirred, then spread her wings to catch herself. She rolled on her back and spat fire at the three following her, forcing them to close their eyes. When Lamprophyre could see again, the dragon was gone, once more heading westward. Lamprophyre shot after her.

Now the scout was running scared, speeding along faster than before. Unfortunately for her, Lamprophyre and Coquina were faster. They caught her and each grabbed a wing, staying far from the scout's deadly claws as she struggled to free herself. Lamprophyre slashed the tough membranes, which were almost invisible among the thick ribbing of the phalanges. Across from her, Coquina did the same. The dragon's struggles grew more frantic.

Finally, when the scout's wings were shredded, Lamprophyre let go, and Coquina followed a beat later. The scout fell, her wings thrashing futilely. Lamprophyre dove after her. The scout was doomed, but Lamprophyre didn't want to take chances.

The ground was coming up fast. Lamprophyre slowed, letting the scout fall past her. They were some distance from Tanajital, over the rolling untilled plains that were yellow and gray this time of year. For a moment, everything was still. Then the rust-orange shape of the scout hit the ground, driving deep into the earth and sending up a cloud of soil particles. The dull thump startled a flock of birds, black with blue bands across their wings. They shot into the air, crying out with voices that sounded like dragonets crying for their fathers.

Lamprophyre descended to look at the body. The scout lay twisted in a shallow pit of earth dug by her impact. She was motionless, apparently dead, but Lamprophyre approached cautiously anyway. Behind her, Coquina and Flint landed and came forward to join her. "She's dead?" Coquina said.

Lamprophyre nodded. "I don't feel sorry even though that was a frightening way to die."

"She was a scout for Sardonyx, wasn't she?" Flint asked

Lamprophyre nodded again. She remembered her fear of falling and suppressed a shudder. They shouldn't have done it—but that was stupid, because if they hadn't killed the scout any way they knew how, thousands of humans would have died.

She looked away from the dead dragon. The Green River, far to the east, ambled along in its course exactly as if she and Coquina hadn't killed someone. Beyond that, specks of color flew toward them. "The others are coming," she said. "We'll need to bury the body. And warn General Sajan that Sardonyx is still searching."

"She's building a new map for herself," Coquina said. "I'm sure of it. And once the map is complete, she'll turn the world to ash."

"Skies will burn," Lamprophyre said. "We have to stop her."

They all looked down at the body. Lamprophyre blocked her clutchmates' thoughts. They were the same as her own, anyway: it had taken three of them to kill just one dragon, and they hadn't escaped unscathed. Lamprophyre's side and arm were in agony, her lower wing was tattered, and blood continued to spill from her wounds. She wasn't sure she could fly back to the city, but walking would be so much worse.

"Skies will burn," she repeated, almost to herself. And dragons would burn with them.

CHAPTER THIRTY-TWO

The next day, and the next, passed so quietly Lamprophyre had the illusion that the death of that scout had stopped Sardonyx's plans. But really it was that Sardonyx was still in Fanishkor, and with no communication between that country and Gonjiri, no one knew what kind of damage she was doing. Hyaloclast and the flight were flying the border between the two, watching for Sardonyx's return. "*We would fight for them, but Fanishkor has refused our aid,*" Hyaloclast told Lamprophyre the evening of the second day. "*And I refuse to humiliate myself by begging. They will live or die on their own terms. I respect that.*"

"It's the dying I don't like," Lamprophyre said. "The ones doing the dying are not the ones making that decision. I hate that."

"*So do I.*" Hyaloclast went silent, and Lamprophyre thought about the shield over Leksital and whether it protected any other Fanishkorite cities.

"*And you're healed,*" Hyaloclast finally said. "*Proving that human healing magic works on dragons.*"

"I was sure it would." She'd been mostly sure, given that all other artifacts worked as well on dragons as they did on humans. It was just that if any artifact were to fail, the healing jades and moonstones would be the most devastating of failures. She stretched her arm and looked at the spot where the scout had bitten her. Not a trace of the mark remained, not even a discoloration of her scales. Remarkable.

"Rokshan spoke to General Sajan about making sure there are plenty of healing supplies near the towns and cities named in Jiwanyil's prophecies," she went on. "But he knows there's not much point. There's only so much healing can do, and when we don't know how soon those prophecies will be fulfilled..." She let her words trail into silence. Hyaloclast knew all this, probably better than Lamprophyre did.

"*We watch the skies. Sardonyx won't slip past without our noticing.*" Hyaloclast sounded grim, and Lamprophyre didn't need to hear her thoughts to know how uncertain the dragon queen was of this assertion. There was a lot of border to watch, and not enough dragons. Lamprophyre looked at the slate leaning against the wall. She'd written the names of every dragon who'd been killed by Sardonyx's people, and even in her smallest handwriting it was nearly full.

She heard Rokshan crossing the courtyard and said, "I have to go. Good luck." She couldn't quite bring herself to say *I hope Sardonyx doesn't come back,* given what that would mean to the people of Fanishkor.

"*Good luck to you,*" Hyaloclast said, and the stone cleared.

She hung the pendant on its peg and said, "Still no news."

"Nothing from Fanishkor's government, either," Rokshan said. "We're going to wear ourselves out with watching. Staying alert all the time means eventually losing our edge."

"But there's nothing else we can do."

Rokshan sighed. He sat on the floor and took off his boots. They were too warm for the weather, but he wore them always, and kept his cold-weather clothes handy, in case they needed to fly high and fast. "I want to visit the flight tomorrow. There are things they can do to stay alert but keep themselves from wearing out."

"That's a good idea." Lamprophyre looked out the door and saw

Bhakriya beckon to her from the soup kettle. "Supper is ready. Are you hungry? I think it's pig."

They ate in silence, listening to the quiet talk going on in the courtyard. It was busy enough that Lamprophyre couldn't eavesdrop on thoughts, but that felt like too much work, anyway. The juicy pig, salty and rich, calmed her nerves. It was hard to stay anxious when you were eating delicious food.

So many of her regulars were here tonight it calmed her further. Sumaan, the one-legged man, stood propped against the wall with his crutch leaning next to him. He had a job now, but he still came for supper occasionally at her invitation. There was a trio of men, one blind, the others deaf, who helped each other like long-time friends, and an old woman who'd struck up a friendship with Bhakriya.

And there was Darsha, resplendent in a green silk gown the color of new grass, drinking down the last drops of soup as if it weren't bad manners. She was graceful enough everything she did looked natural. Lamprophyre nodded at her and tore off another mouthful of pig, chewing until all the juice was gone and swallowing the meat. Having so many people here under her watchful eye made her feel better about not knowing where Sardonyx was.

Darsha returned her bowl to the box of dirty dishes beside the cauldron and continued into the dining pavilion. "Good evening, Lamprophyre," she said. "Your highness."

"Don't bother to bow," Rokshan said drily.

Darsha smiled. "I show my respect in other ways, as I'm sure you know. Tonight, for example."

Lamprophyre laid down the pig leg she was chewing on. "What do you mean?"

The smile disappeared. "I've been hearing things I thought you should know. Odd, frightened, angry comments about dragons. There are those in Tanajital who believe our dragons are a danger to the city. As in, you draw the attention of the dragons bent on destroying it."

"That's ridiculous," Lamprophyre said. "Sardonyx wants humans dead. If anything, she'll strike at cities where there aren't any dragons to give her a fight."

"Humans aren't known for rationality, Lamprophyre. Some of my clients have made noises about ridding the city of dragons once and for all. They're upper-class citizens, some of them with the king's ear. It's unlikely they can hurt you, but they might make life uncomfortable."

"I doubt my father will listen to them," Rokshan said, "but you're right that we don't need any more sources of conflict."

"There's another thing," Darsha went on. "Some of my sisters asked me about your treasure. Your dragon hoard."

Lamprophyre blinked in surprise. "I don't have a hoard."

"Which is what I told them, but they'd heard from *their* clients that dragons are flush with gold and gems, all stolen from the good people of Tanajital. Someone's spreading rumors aimed at stirring up the citizenry against dragons."

Rokshan dropped his knife on his plate with a clatter. "Someone. I bet I know who."

"Who—you mean Viveki? I thought she was locked up."

Rokshan had a very sour expression. "Only for twenty-four hours. I told the guards since I got my money back, I didn't want to pursue the matter further. I thought, since we have the notes, she was harmless. I should have known better."

"If all she's done is spread easily-disproven rumors, she is harmless," Lamprophyre said. "But I'll have Rassika run to the warehouses and warn the others. Just in case someone decides to attack."

Having sent Rassika on her way, she returned to sit beside the table where Darsha now sat opposite Rokshan. "You can't let your parents dictate your life," Darsha was saying. "It's true you owe them thanks and maybe even respect for bringing you up, but trying to please them is a fool's errand, with no bottom to that hole."

"I said I wasn't going to live according to their wishes," Rokshan said, sounding more sour than before. "But it's not as simple as that.

I'm part of the ruling family, and what I do has repercussions beyond my own life. My father is right that I can't afford to abandon the Army during this crisis."

Lamprophyre listened to this with a growing feeling of dread. "Rokshan," she said, "what are you talking about?"

Darsha cast a wise, knowing eye on her. "You might not believe it, given my profession, but I'm very good at identifying when two people are in love. Even when that love seems impossible."

"But...we're not..."

"She wormed it out of me, Lamprophyre," Rokshan said. "Though I think maybe I wanted to tell someone. I hate feeling like there's something unnatural about how we feel."

"I'm certainly in no position to judge," Darsha said. "And your proposed solution is so romantic. Turning yourself into a dragon to be with the one you love. I think, if you did spread this news around, you'd find a lot of people on your side for that alone."

"That's reassuring," Rokshan said, though he didn't sound very reassured.

"At any rate," Darsha said, "I can tell you want your father's approval in general, but you're never going to get it so long as all you ever do is bend to his will."

"And you know this, how?"

Darsha shrugged. "Years of experience listening to men talk about their sons. They all say their boys should listen to them, learn from their actions, but the only times they're really proud of them is when those boys show they can make their own decisions, even when they're counter to their fathers' expectations. Fathers want their sons to be men. A king is no different from a poor tinker in that respect."

Rokshan's irritated expression had gradually given way to thoughtfulness as Darsha spoke. "I think I see," he said. "It's not easy."

"It's not," Darsha agreed. "But nothing worthwhile is." She looked up at Lamprophyre. "As I'm sure you already know." She rose from the table. "Good luck to you both. Anything you want me to pass on to Tekentriya? Something secret? Other than the obvious."

"Have you spoken to her lately?"

Darsha nodded. "This morning. She was preparing to head out with some dragon. I swear she was actually pleasant. Any idea what happened?"

"She made the right friend," Rokshan said.

When Darsha was gone, Lamprophyre said, "You wouldn't tell people our secret, would you? I don't think I'm ready."

"I wouldn't. But we can't keep it hidden forever, sweetheart." Rokshan laid a hand on her forearm. "Is it all right if I stay the night again?"

"Of course. I wish you'd stay here all the time, but I'm sure it's not comfortable. And it probably looks strange."

"I don't care how it looks." Rokshan sighed. "I wish...it's not important."

Lamprophyre shamelessly listened to his thoughts, easier now that the crowd had mostly gone. "You wish we'd had sex when we had the chance. So do I."

"I don't know if that would make it better, or worse, remembering something we can't have yet." Rokshan pushed his chair back. "I'm going to help with the dishes, and then maybe we can read for a while."

"I'd like that more than anything." Lamprophyre rose and ambled to the embassy hall. Sometimes she remembered kissing, and the memories stirred her body in unexpected ways. Then she wished more than ever that Rokshan was transformed. They could live in Tanajital, or in her comfortable cave in the mountains, and never have to be separated again.

She picked over the piles of books. On the other hand, if Rokshan wasn't human anymore, they'd have to give up these comfortable reading times. Reading, or sex. No question which one she'd choose.

They met the flight the next morning north and west of Tanajital, covering the long stretch of empty land that was the Fanishkorite border. Though there were so few dragons one could hardly call them a full flight. Hyaloclast winged to meet them, a great black shadow that even the morning sun couldn't make anything but ominous.

"We fly patterns, covering the ground to well south of here," she said without preamble. "Tiresome, but effective."

"It's the tiresome part that concerns me," Rokshan said. "If you're fully alert all the time, eventually that alertness will wear off, and soon you'll be too exhausted to be effective."

"Is this human military tactics, young prince?"

"It is, but it applies to any sentry force," Rokshan said. "May I suggest a change?"

Hyaloclast nodded. Lamprophyre could hear her thinking *more confident than I believed, pity he's not a dragon already*.

"You see farther when you're in the sky, but you can't fly forever," Rokshan said. "Cut the time each dragon spends on patrol in half. Send them out in pairs—one to watch, the other to rest. How are you in communication with the others?"

"Each dragon is within hearing distance of another." Hyaloclast made a motion with her finger near her head. "Thought hearing, that is. When a dragon sees an enemy, she alerts those nearest her, who pass the message along until all are aware. Though we haven't seen any enemies, so this is all theoretical."

"It should work, though. That's how our sentry lines are designed, though with sound in mind rather than thoughts." Rokshan shifted his weight as if he were looking southward. "You're positioned well."

"Thank you," Hyaloclast said. Her sardonic tone clashed with her amused thoughts.

Rokshan either didn't notice her reaction or chose not to respond. "Some adepts with seeing artifacts have located Sardonyx herself. She's in southern Fanishkor. But after what Lamprophyre encountered, I'm sure we're in danger of her scouts being Jiwanyil knows where. So this line of defense is essential. I hope you know how much Gonjiri appreciates your efforts. This is only peripherally your battle."

"I choose not to subjugate myself and my flight to that monster," Hyaloclast said. "And I find myself more in sympathy with humans the longer this fight goes on. When this is over, I will have to have a talk with your father. Our alliance benefits dragons more than I'd believed possible, and I would like to see that expand."

"I hope he'll be willing to listen," Rokshan said, sounding bitter. "He's not happy about my proposed transformation."

"No more than I was to see my daughter take human form. It's a natural reaction." Hyaloclast smiled. "Parents want the best for their children, but it takes us time to understand what 'best' means. It's easier to define that word as 'what I think matters.' But I wonder if he's considered how having a dragon for a son will strengthen our alliance."

"You mean, like a dynastic marriage?" Lamprophyre said.

"He would have married you to the Fanishkorite princess to solidify that alliance, yes?" Hyaloclast flapped her wings to bring her closer to Lamprophyre and Rokshan. "I don't think it's occurred to him that you're effectively marrying a dragon princess, at least as humans understand things. I will bring this up with him as well."

"Thank you," Rokshan said. "I know I'm not the mate you might have wished for Lamprophyre."

"You are not," Hyaloclast said, "but as I said, my definition of what is best for my child has to give way to what she actually wants. What she needs. And I admit you're remarkable for a human." She wheeled and flew away before Lamprophyre, feeling stunned, could make a response.

"God's breath," Rokshan said. "A dragon princess. I hadn't thought of that, either."

"Because I'm not really a dragon princess," Lamprophyre said.

"No, but in dynastic terms...my father might actually care about that." Rokshan patted her neck. "Let's fly down the border before we go home. I want to be able to tell Sajan how far south the dragon line extends."

Lamprophyre agreed cheerfully. It would give her a chance to say hello to everyone and reassure herself that the flight was still one, despite its many losses. It still hurt not to see Chrysoprase at Hyaloclast's side. Leucite was a good friend, but he couldn't take Chrysoprase's place, because he was male—

She gasped. "Rokshan. I just had a strange thought. What if Leucite is courting Hyaloclast?"

"Leucite?" Rokshan leaned forward to hear her more clearly over the wind. "But Hyaloclast...that can't be right. I can't imagine her in a romantic relationship at all."

"She loved my father, and that wasn't strange. But he's been dead for nearly thirty years, and she's been alone all that time, *and* Leucite is with her constantly." Lamprophyre shook her head. "That can't be right. I've never seen her act in any romantic way toward him."

"Would that make him your stepfather? Or whatever the dragon term is."

"No. He'd just be my mother's mate, and father to my siblings if Hyaloclast had any children. But it has to be my imagination." The thought of Leucite and Hyaloclast together wasn't awful, because she liked Leucite even if he was a bit strange about turquoise, but it was the oddest notion.

She shook her head again and flew faster. If they hurried, they might be in time to share supper with the clutch, and maybe Kamil would be there with the information they needed. Even if Rokshan had promised not to transform until the war was over—not that he'd done that, in any definite sense—she wanted the comfort of knowing it was possible the moment he decided he was ready.

Flying the length of the border was tiring, but greeting her friends cheered Lamprophyre as much as she'd anticipated. She returned to Tanajital that afternoon in a better mood than she'd been in since freeing Sardonyx. "Let's go straight to the warehouses, and then buy some cows and cook them outside the city," she said over her shoulder.

"That's an excellent plan. I hope Dolomite is there. I confess to wanting to hear more gossip about Tekentriya. It's just so odd thinking that she's made friends with anyone, let alone a dragon."

Lamprophyre banked into the long curving descent into the city. "But don't you think it makes sense that Dolomite would be the one? He's as straightforward as they come and really hard to insult, because he takes everyone at face value."

"That's true. Well, I'm happy for her. I remember what she was like when I was a child—she was interesting and exciting to be around, and she actually liked me back then. It would be nice to see her return to her old self. But I'm not holding my breath."

Lamprophyre made a running stop and crouched to let Rokshan down in front of Coquina's warehouse just as Coquina stuck her head out. "Oh, good, it's you," she said. "A runner came from the palace a few hundred beats ago, looking for you. Apparently she went to the embassy first, so whatever they want, it's been a while."

Lamprophyre sat up. "Did the runner say what the message was?"

"Just for you and Rokshan to return to the palace immediately. Official business." Coquina yawned. "Sorry. I've been up since before dawn, flying errands. I don't suppose you saw Flint? He left when I did."

"No, we were at the border." Lamprophyre crouched again. "I guess we should see what the king wants."

Once in the air, Rokshan said, "I'm worried."

"About what?"

"Sending a messenger to the embassy and leaving the message there is normal. Running around the city trying to find us is something else. I'm afraid something's gone wrong and we're in trouble."

"Like what? We haven't done anything wrong."

"Not by our standards. But if my father is still upset, he might turn something innocent into a chastisement."

Lamprophyre coasted along until the palace roofs loomed

before her. "But we don't know what it is, so I think we shouldn't worry until it turns out there's something to worry about."

She alit in front of the massive front doors. They stood open, though they were too big and heavy to be welcoming. The guards with their pikes eyed Lamprophyre, but made no move to stop her entering behind Rokshan.

Inside, the great entrance hall was empty. It must not be an audience day, or maybe it was just late enough that everyone had gone home. Rokshan said, "I'll let them know we're here," and bounded up the right-hand steps. Lamprophyre settled in to wait.

She examined the doors, which looked solid and unmoving. She'd nearly broken them down once, trying to reach Rokshan, and then the Army had broken them further, trying to reach her. They showed no sign of damage—it *had* been a while ago. She delved within herself, looking for a feeling of guilt at having attacked the palace, and found nothing. Well, it had been their fault for not letting her inside in the first place.

She cocked her head to look at the light hanging from the ceiling. It was an oddly-shaped mass of iron, like a long, thick strand of metal tangled into a very loose knot, and tiny flecks of bright light clustered throughout like fireflies caught in a net. It was pretty, but was too high to shed much light. She stood, stretching to her full height, and could barely brush her fingers against it. Someday she really needed to ask someone what the point of it was.

Approaching footsteps, a lot of footsteps, prompted her to leave the thing alone and settle back onto the floor. Soon Rokshan appeared, followed by Ekanath and nearly a dozen men and women of the court. Lamprophyre didn't recognize any of them except Mekel, the king's chamberlain, but there were so many of them living in the palace she wasn't surprised.

The crowd descended the stairs, the courtiers staying a respectful distance from the king. Ekanath moved more rapidly than Lamprophyre had ever seen, almost outpacing Rokshan. "What did you do?" he demanded when he was within a few handspans of her.

"What did *I* do?" Lamprophyre looked at Rokshan, who opened his mouth to speak and was overridden by his father.

"The Fanishkorite ambassador, Chaaksha, demands an audience," Ekanath said. "Demands. 'The king of Gonjiri and his dragon allies.' She won't say more than that. You must have done something to anger Fanishkor, damn you—"

"Don't talk to Lamprophyre that way," Rokshan said, putting himself between them. "There's no reason to think this is her fault. Did you agree to the meeting?"

Ekanath's gaze shot to Rokshan. "Not yet. Not until I find out what this dragon has done. Fanishkor had no interest in a diplomatic meeting until we had dragons lined up on the border. If this is in response to our aggression, I swear I'll repudiate you. We do not need a war with Fanishkor on top of dragons razing our cities."

"Those dragons are there to protect Gonjiri, to warn us if Sardonyx comes back," Lamprophyre said. "They're not aggressing on anyone."

"And I'll wager Fanishkor knows it," Rokshan said. "This is their way of putting us on the defensive. And it's working. Father. You never used to be so hasty."

Ekanath closed his eyes. He looked like he was praying for patience. "You're right," he said, startling Lamprophyre with how quickly his demeanor changed. "This is ridiculous. Whatever Fanishkor wants from us, they must feel they're in a weaker position to behave so aggressively."

"Right," Rokshan said. "Which means we can either pretend we didn't notice, or go on the offensive."

"We can't afford to fight back," Ekanath said. "If there's any chance of us getting the secret of the shield artifacts out of them, we have to be...damn it, we have to be humble. Much as I'd like to throw them out on their asses."

"So send a reply allowing them to set the time of the meeting, at a place of our choosing. One that will accommodate a dragon." Rokshan turned to face Lamprophyre. "If they really want to meet with our dragon allies, that will limit their power. They're the ones proposing the meeting, however they want to dress it up. They're the petitioners."

"And we should remember that." Ekanath surprised Lamprophyre again by putting his hand on Rokshan's shoulder. "Son, you understand the situation so well. Can't you see what you have to offer this country? How can you think to turn your back on your destiny?"

Rokshan cast a glance over the assembled courtiers, all of whom were pretending not to listen. "It's not that straightforward," he said, "and I don't want to discuss it here. But can't *you* see that my destiny isn't what you expected—and that's not a betrayal of anything?"

Ekanath's hand fell away. "I don't know," he said. He looked like he wanted to say something more, but only turned away to ascend the stairs once more, followed by his retinue.

When the hall was empty, Lamprophyre laid a gentle hand on Rokshan's shoulder. "He was so torn," she said. "Thinking how you were taking a path he couldn't understand. Maybe he's not a villain."

"He's not," Rokshan said. "And he's not stupid. I just don't know if he'll ever let himself come around." He patted Lamprophyre's hand. "Let's get out of here. They'll send word when the meeting is scheduled. I hope Fanishkor doesn't ask anything in exchange for those shields we can't afford to give."

"So do I," Lamprophyre said.

CHAPTER THIRTY-THREE

Word came the next morning, when Lamprophyre and Rokshan were having breakfast. Rokshan read the paper and let it roll up into a loose cylinder. "Tell my father we'll be there," he told the message runner, who took off after one last stunned look at Lamprophyre. "This afternoon," he said. "Fanishkor is more anxious about this meeting than they want us to believe."

"Surely they know how this decision looks?" Lamprophyre said. "Chaaksha isn't stupid, and if she were, Yalini is smart and wouldn't let her do anything that would lose Fanishkor power. I can't believe they're ignorant of how desperate this sounds."

"That's what worries me. They must feel secure in their power to let themselves look weak in this small way." Rokshan rose and paced the length of the dining pavilion, tapping the rolled-up paper against his palm in a slow, measured way at odds with his anxious movements. "I don't see what we can do about it, except be prepared."

Lamprophyre nodded. She'd woken that morning with the remnants of a bad dream echoing in her mind. It had been the kind of dream where she was searching for something, all the while feeling dread grow as time passed and she failed to find whatever it was. The feeling of dread hadn't left her after she woke, and the message only made it worse. She had a terrible feeling that this meeting would end in catastrophe.

She didn't say anything about it to Rokshan. She'd never been given to moments of insight about the future, and when she thought about it logically, she had no reason to believe this wasn't just leftover dream figments. There was no sense in dragging him into her bad mood, not when he might already feel the same. She tore another mouthful of cow from the carcass. It tasted dry and unappealing, no doubt thanks to her bad mood. Stupid Fanishkorites ruining her meal.

"There's still no word from Hyaloclast, so Sardonyx is still in Fanishkor," she said. "Unless she crossed the border farther south than the dragon line extends."

"Let's try to stay optimistic," Rokshan said. "Word from Sachetan is that they haven't seen any dragons anywhere. Sardonyx's people aren't many, in the absolute sense, and she can't be everywhere at once. We have time to learn how to build those shields, and make the pyrite weapons more effective."

"You're still not going to tell me what you have in mind, are you."

"No."

"Rokshan, it would really improve my peace of mind."

Rokshan shook his head. "I don't know how it's progressing myself. I left it to the Army adepts and weapons designers. So I couldn't tell you even if I wanted to, which I don't. I don't want you pinning your hopes on something that might not be effective."

Lamprophyre scowled and took another bite. She pushed the rest of the carcass away. "I don't have much of an appetite."

"Then let's go flying for a while. Clear our heads. And hope that pendant stays clear." Rokshan took his plate to the kitchen. Lamprophyre left the pavilion and paced restlessly around the courtyard. She smiled half-heartedly at Bhakriya, who was at the water barrel supervising the children's washing up. Bhakriya never distinguished between her own son and the girls she had essentially adopted, a word Lamprophyre had learned from Rokshan. Dragons had the concept of taking in a dragonet who'd lost her parents, but no word for it because it happened so rarely.

She suddenly felt frustrated. Bhakriya and Depik acted as parents to these children, so why couldn't Bhakriya tell Depik how her feelings had changed? "Bhakriya," she said sharply.

"Yes, my lady?" Bhakriya sounded startled, which made sense considering how Lamprophyre hadn't really tried to conceal her anger.

"Bhakriya, why don't you—"

Depik came out of the pavilion and went to the water barrel. "You didn't eat much, my lady," he said. "Was anything wrong with the meal?"

She couldn't confront Bhakriya with Depik right there. How humiliating for both of them. And she liked them enough not to want them humiliated, however angry she was. "I don't have much of an appetite this morning," she said. "We have an important meeting this afternoon, and I suppose I'm too nervous to eat."

"We'll make something special for supper, then, to give you something to look forward to," Depik said. He washed and dried his hands and tousled Abhit's hair, making the boy grin. "And there was something we wanted to discuss with you, Bhakriya and I, but it can wait until later."

He was thinking about Abhit and the academy. Irritation flared once more. They were behaving like the boy's parents, so why...? "Of course. After supper, then."

Rokshan emerged from the pavilion and came to Lamprophyre's side. "Let's go to Kolmira," he suggested. "I need to talk to the commander there, anyway."

Lamprophyre nodded. A long flight was just what she needed. She retrieved Hyaloclast's pendant from the peg and crouched to give Rokshan a leg up. Maybe her sense of dread would diminish once she was in the air.

NOT ONLY DIDN'T HER DREAD DIMINISH, IT GREW MORE INTENSE as the hours wore on. She'd forgotten how depressing Kolmira was compared to Tanajital, how dour and dark its roofs were, how close together its buildings. She didn't understand why Dharan liked it so much. Granted, he'd been born there, but surely that would make him more likely to see its many flaws?

She grumped her way through Rokshan's meeting with the military commander and grumped her way through examining the pyrite weapons. That made her even more anxious with dread, remembering the weapons' failure at Manjaret. By the time they left for Tanajital, she felt sick to both her stomachs in anticipation of meeting the Fanishkorites and wished it could be over already. Maybe Depik's "something special" was her favorite curried lamb. That cheered her slightly, but not enough.

Ekanath had set the meeting for the training grounds, which Lamprophyre thought was a mistake. Better to do this in the entrance hall, with its greater privacy and reminder of who was really in charge. But Rokshan had said, "This is part of us looking like we believe they have power over us. Having the meeting inside the palace would put Fanishkor at a disadvantage, which would give them incentive to demand more and greater concessions to offset that. But we couldn't let them choose the place, because the king coming to them is the act of a conquered nation. So this is the best option."

Now Lamprophyre waited on the training grounds for Rokshan to return from changing into his official dragon-liaison clothes. Someone had erected a canopy tall enough that Lamprophyre could see beneath it without having to lower herself all the way to the ground. Peculiar backless chairs that folded for storage were set beneath the canopy, with more folded chairs in a stack nearby. Only three had been set up, and Lamprophyre thought about that: chairs for the king, Chaaksha, and presumably Yalini, but not for Rokshan. That could be because Lamprophyre, not Rokshan, was part of the negotiations, and of course there was no folding chair big enough to fit her.

The sick feeling, which had faded somewhat on the flight back, redoubled. She was more confident in dealing with humans diplomatically than she had been when she first arrived in Tanajital, but up until now, all the humans she'd had diplomatic interactions with had been friendly or even subservient. They'd wanted to deal with dragons as equals, and it was to their benefit to be polite. This was the first time she'd face an antagonistic foreign power. She'd never been so grateful for her ability to hear thoughts. So long as Chaaksha didn't bring a huge retinue, she would have a secret advantage.

She heard Rokshan approaching and scowled at the tunic he wore over his shirt. "Did you really have to wear that?"

Rokshan straightened the gaudy, gold-embroidered tunic with the picture of a dragon on it. "You're in a foul mood," he observed. "You know why I have to wear this. Are you going to be all right?"

Lamprophyre sighed, releasing a puff of smoke she didn't even try to turn into a ring. "I'm sorry. I just want this to be over."

Rokshan squeezed her hand. "Soon enough. Don't worry. The worst they can do is refuse to help. And since they've already done that, we'd be no worse off than we already are."

"Even so—"

The dying-duck sound of the horn announcing King Ekanath's arrival cut her words off. She straightened to watch the procession coming toward them, and her heart sank. There were at least a dozen courtiers accompanying the king, and if Chaaksha brought that many, it would be impossible for Lamprophyre to hear anyone's thoughts. "Is there any graceful way to ask the king to send those people back inside?" she murmured.

"They show he has power," Rokshan said. "Why—oh. Too much noise."

Lamprophyre nodded. "I really wanted to eavesdrop on Chaaksha."

"It might still be possible," Rokshan said, but he didn't sound hopeful.

Ekanath greeted them politely before taking a seat on the

nearest folding stool. "And now we wait," he said. "We may wait a while, depending on whether Chaaksha feels the need to hammer home the point that we're the petitioners."

"It doesn't matter," Rokshan said. "If they're willing to give up those shields, they can ask anything they like."

"Then there's been no progress on the weapons."

"We were in Kolmira this morning. They haven't improved the firing rate. And as to the other thing, I haven't heard any news."

Lamprophyre felt annoyed that the king clearly knew more about Rokshan's secret weapons project than she did. "I don't see why," she began, and Rokshan put a hand over hers to still her.

"They're here," he said.

The big red and white-splotched canopy was approaching across the field. This time, only Yalini and Chaaksha walked beneath it. Behind the canopy trailed a double handful of men and women in Fanishkorite red. So much for Lamprophyre's secret edge.

She kept her face impassive as the Fanishkorites approached, though it was unlikely any of them were capable of interpreting draconic expressions. The canopy bearers brought their burden to where its front edge brushed the king's canopy and extended its legs, and Chaaksha and Yalini paused there for a few beats before walking forward. The two women didn't bow, just sat gracefully on the backless chairs. Chaaksha wore a plain red robe over her white shirt and trousers; Yalini's gown was a dark orange that reminded Lamprophyre unpleasantly of the dragon scout she and Coquina had killed. She sat as still as the statue she'd appeared to be on their first meeting.

No one spoke at first. Lamprophyre didn't know what speaking first would mean in terms of the power struggle this was only the opening moves of. Finally, Ekanath said, "We are pleased to meet with you, ambassador, your highness. You are gracious to extend the offer."

"As you are gracious to accept, your majesty," Chaaksha said in her deep voice. "We hope you have considered the outcome of our last meeting and are prepared to make different choices."

"We are surprised at your willingness to return, given that we rejected your first proposal." Ekanath sat as straight as if his chair had a back. "Tell me, how have matters changed?"

Chaaksha smiled. Lamprophyre really wished she could hear the woman's thoughts, because she was certain Chaaksha was about to lie. "Fanishkor has seen the results of dragon depredations on human settlements," she said. "While we have the means to protect ourselves, we understand Gonjiri cannot say the same. King Damen's heart goes out to the victims of these attacks, though they are not his subjects. He wishes to offer Gonjiri assistance."

Ekanath leaned forward slightly. "That's extremely generous of him. I take it you speak of the shield artifacts?"

"Indeed." Chaaksha inclined her head in the barest of nods. "They are effective. I understand the dragon ambassador has seen this for herself?"

"I have," Lamprophyre said. She didn't relax. The hammer, as Rokshan put it, hadn't fallen yet. Chaaksha wasn't here out of the goodness of her heart; she wanted something in exchange. "So all Fanishkor's cities are protected?"

Chaaksha's pleasant smile faded slightly. "We are in the process of shielding all our larger cities."

"Not the towns. Not the villages," Lamprophyre persisted. "Fanishkor's citizens are still in danger from Sardonyx."

"Sardonyx," Chaaksha said. There was a speculative tone in her voice Lamprophyre didn't like. "Of course. We believe Sardonyx isn't interested in those smaller towns when she can make a big show of intimidation attacking our cities."

"That's not true," Lamprophyre said. "She wants humans dead. All humans. I've seen her set dozens of dragons to kill only five humans. You're exposing helpless people to her attacks."

"We wouldn't dream of contradicting you, given that Gonjiri was the first target of these ancient dragons," Chaaksha said. "Though we are concerned at to what degree you expect us to take your word for what these dragons intend."

"You question our honor?" Ekanath said. He didn't sound angry, but Lamprophyre didn't need to hear his thoughts to know he wasn't happy with Chaaksha's words.

"Not at all," Chaaksha said. "But you must admit it's quite a coincidence. Ancient dragons from a time before the catastrophe suddenly appear. They supposedly raze Gonjirian cities to the ground before attacking Fanishkor. Why shouldn't we believe these are actually your dragon allies, intent on making our king believe he must prostrate himself before you and give up our defensive secrets?"

"That's ridiculous," Lamprophyre said, ignoring Rokshan's warning hand on her arm. "You're just trying to put us on the defensive. Why don't you say what you came here to say, and stop making up stories?"

Chaaksha's smile widened. "I meant only to illustrate how the situation looks to King Damen," she said. "Of course we believe your story. It's unlikely dragons would attack Leksital with one of their own inside. And we have independently confirmed the reports of destroyed Gonjirian villages."

"Then I feel I should echo the dragon ambassador's question," Ekanath said. "We are aware that Fanishkor is far better protected against dragon attacks than Gonjiri. We have asked for the secret of the defensive shield and been rejected. We appear once more to be at an impasse. So—what is the point of this meeting, if not for Fanishkor to lord it over this country in its time of crisis?"

Lamprophyre had never been more impressed with the king. He'd delivered that statement in firm, confident tones that said he didn't care what Fanishkor had in mind, and their attitude of superiority meant nothing to him. But Rokshan's hand tightened on hers before releasing her, and she wondered what she'd missed.

"As I said, King Damen wishes to offer Gonjiri assistance," Chaaksha said, just as if Ekanath's bold words hadn't offended her. "We are prepared to give you the secret of the shield artifacts, as well as enough of them to protect Tanajital."

Ekanath didn't react. "And in return," he said, "King Damen wants..."

Chaaksha shot a quick glance at Yalini. "King Damen acknowledges that the shields are no permanent solution, particularly if the dragons figure out that they are no barrier to physical entry," she said. "He asks that the dragons of Nirinatan fight the ancient dragons when they attack Fanishkorite cities."

Lamprophyre opened her mouth to protest, but Rokshan overrode her. "Since we're being honest with each other, we should inform you that modern dragons aren't a match for ancient dragon warriors. We're willing to do as King Damen asks, but he should know they aren't the solution he's looking for."

"My father wants his people to see that he takes their safety seriously," Yalini said, losing the stone statue demeanor she'd worn until then. "The sight of dragons fighting in defense of our cities would boost morale."

"Dragons are not a battle standard," Rokshan said, once more overriding Lamprophyre's outraged retort. "But I take your meaning. Ambassador, will Hyaloclast consent to entering Fanishkor to defend its cities?" He gave her a fierce look that said *don't let anger get the best of you* as clearly as if she'd heard his thoughts.

Lamprophyre calmed herself. "She will," she said, "though I believe it would be honorable of King Damen to make the request himself. Just so there's no confusion."

"He will send the message immediately," Chaaksha said. Lamprophyre wondered at that, given that Chaaksha hadn't known about chalcedony artifacts before Lamprophyre had told her about them. Maybe that was just more diplomatic talk.

"So. Dragons in exchange for shields. That seems equitable," Ekanath said.

"That's not all," Chaaksha said. "King Damen requests your cooperation on another matter."

Lamprophyre's dread, which had ebbed as they spoke of dragons defending Fanishkor, rose to new and painful heights. She was certain she knew what Chaaksha was going to ask next.

"Oh? And what is that?" Ekanath asked. Lamprophyre looked at him briefly and saw his hand resting on his thigh was clenched tightly enough the tendons stood out. Maybe he knew what was coming, too.

"There is too much bad blood between our countries," Chaaksha said, "too much mutual antagonism. King Damen tires of this animosity. He wants a new era of good feeling between us, to be celebrated by the union of the royal houses."

Rokshan went very still beside Lamprophyre. Her legs trembled, and she tensed to keep her nerves from showing. Even though she'd expected it, it still left her feeling even sicker than before.

"You requested this before," Ekanath said. "The marriage of my son and Damen's daughter."

Chaaksha inclined her head again. "Indeed," she said. "And this time, King Damen has instructed me to say that he will view a refusal as an act of hostility. No marriage, no alliance. No shields. And no reconciliation."

CHAPTER THIRTY-FOUR

"No—" Rokshan began.

"That is quite the demand," Ekanath said, cutting him off. "With extraordinary consequences."

"It is a small thing," Chaaksha said, "with extraordinary benefits. A marriage between our countries to symbolize a new era of peace. And with Yalini as King Damen's potential heir, your son could rule a kingdom by her side."

"I don't—" Rokshan began again.

"*Be silent,*" Ekanath said, his voice cutting like a blade across Rokshan's words. "You understand this is not a small thing you ask. We must have time to deliberate."

"You have fifteen minutes," Chaaksha said. "We will withdraw to give you privacy." She smiled, and this time her smile was a cunning, superior expression. She knew Ekanath couldn't afford to refuse, and she enjoyed having power over him.

Chaaksha and Yalini stepped once more beneath the Fanishkorite canopy, and the canopy bearers retracted the legs and carried it to the far side of the training grounds, all the way to the path between the palace and the parkland. Lamprophyre watched them go, feeling stunned. She heard Rokshan said, “It’s insane. I won’t do it.”

“We can’t afford to indulge your whims anymore,” Ekanath said in a low, fierce voice. “This will mean the difference between life and death for thousands, maybe hundreds of thousands of people. It’s past time you shouldered your responsibilities and gave up your selfish lifestyle.”

“I can’t—” Rokshan glanced around as if suddenly aware that he had an audience of a dozen courtiers. “Get them out of here,” he said. “This is a private thing.”

Ekanath gestured. With some milling around, the courtiers retreated well out of human earshot in the direction opposite the Fanishkorite party. Lamprophyre followed them a short distance, making them back away farther, just in case any of them got any ideas about listening in.

When she returned, Ekanath was saying, “This is not a fate worse than death. I didn’t know your mother when we married, and our union has been more wonderful than I could have imagined.”

“This isn’t about whether Yalini and I would be happy together, which I assure you we would not,” Rokshan said. “I am *already married,* Father. You’re asking me to break my vows.”

“You’re not married,” Ekanath said. “A human can’t marry a dragon. You’ve deluded yourself into thinking this...this relationship of yours is equal to a human marriage. It’s just not true. And I’m damn sure you never made wedding vows, so don’t try to ride your high horse over me. Break your vows indeed.”

“We’re not married the human way,” Lamprophyre said, “but we are pair-bonded the dragon way. That’s even more binding than your marriage vows, because it’s a tangible thing.”

Ekanath made a dismissive gesture. “Not important. And not something Damen will understand. All he will see is that we’re spurning his offer. That could start a war all by itself. *Think*, Rokshan. What you want is irrelevant beside what you can do for this kingdom.”

“At the cost of my honor,” Rokshan said.

Ekanath's hand curled into a fist again. "As if you cared about honor all those years you spent wasting your time—"

"Don't bring that up again," Rokshan said. His face had paled with fury, and his jaw looked tight enough to break. "Damn it, Father, what do I have to do to earn your respect? *Yes*, I was once a wastrel, and *yes*, I haven't always made good choices. But I've changed. I've done everything I can to prove my worth to you, tried my best to make you respect me, and it's never enough. What will you demand of me next, Father? Prove myself by sacrificing my firstborn to Nirinatan? Ask me to kill my best friend because she stands in the way of the life you want for me?" He drew in a deep breath. "I won't do it. And there is nothing you can say that will change my mind."

Ekanath slapped him.

Rokshan took a step back and raised a hand to his cheek. He was breathing heavily. "Not a good counterargument, Father," he whispered.

"I no longer care," Ekanath said. "Your choice. But you will tell them the reason why. The entire reason. And when you've made this family a laughingstock—when you've let Gonjiri go up in dragon flames—we will see how comforted you are that you kept your honor."

Rokshan lowered his hand. "I won't apologize, because I've done nothing wrong."

"Tell that to everyone who will lose their homes to dragons," Ekanath said. "No, you won't be able to. They'll all be dead."

Rokshan flinched. He closed his eyes and let out a deep breath. Then he turned and walked toward the Fanishkorite party.

Lamprophyre caught up with him halfway there. "Rokshan, stop," she pleaded. "Stop and think about this."

He turned on her fiercely. "There's no choice," he said. "I'm not going to marry someone else when I'm already married to you."

"But..." Dread no longer filled her. She suspected it was because she was so overwhelmed by it she couldn't feel it anymore. "Rokshan, he's right. We need those shields. Sardonyx will come back, and there's no way we can fight her. Maybe you could...you could pretend to promise—"

"And lose my honor a different way? *No*, Lamprophyre!"

"Then promise, and tell them the marriage has to be postponed until the war is over. We'll figure out the shields ourselves before then. Then you can—"

Rokshan's jaw clenched again. "I will not be forsworn, not for anything," he said. "I hoped you would understand that."

His words struck at her heart. She lowered her head, wishing she were human to weep and weep until this misery disappeared. "I do," she said. "I just hoped I was wrong. Because it's my fault—if we weren't pair-bonded, you could give them what they want. I don't want to be the reason this alliance fails."

He put his hand on her arm. "Sweetheart, this isn't just about you. It's about the two of us together. We chose this path, and we are sworn to be loyal to each other. Suppose it were the other way around. Suppose you were the one they demanded marry one of their dragons."

"They don't have dragons."

"You understand my meaning. What would you choose?"

A sharp, hot pang shot through her. "I couldn't desert you," she said. "Even if it were possible to give up one pair-bond for another, I couldn't do it."

"Then you do understand," Rokshan said. He patted her arm. "Will you come with me? I don't want to tell them the truth alone."

Lamprophyre nodded. "So much for our secret. You know they'll tell people about the aberrant prince and his unsuitable, incompatible dragon mate."

"I know. It's not how I hoped to have it come out, but it looks like we have no choice."

They walked side by side to the Fanishkorite canopy. Chaaksha looked surprised to see them. "I didn't mean you were to announce the decision yourself, your highness," she said.

"My royal father insisted," Rokshan said. "The answer is 'no.'

There will be no marriage. And I'm to tell you why, again at my father's insistence."

Chaaksha's face went very still. "No explanation will change the outcome," she said. "No marriage, no alliance."

"It's by way of being a punishment for being responsible for the alliance's failure." Rokshan straightened his back. "The reason there can be no marriage is that I am already married."

Chaaksha's eyes widened. "Impossible. We would have heard."

"The marriage was a secret, and when I explain the details, you'll understand why."

Yalini stepped forward. "This isn't a lie, is it? Am I so repulsive?"

There were few enough people present that Lamprophyre could hear Rokshan think *you have no idea*. It would have amused her if she hadn't felt so distraught. Chaaksha's thoughts were a mass of surprise and frustration. Lamprophyre got the feeling Chaaksha's reputation was tied up in achieving this alliance. Yalini, on the other hand, was angry, like a child denied a treat. Lamprophyre wondered why she was so set on marrying Rokshan when she wasn't in love with him.

"You are lovely, and intelligent, and you should not see my refusal as a comment on your good qualities," Rokshan lied. Lamprophyre blocked all the thoughts. Hearing Chaaksha and Yalini's thoughts might be valuable, but it would mean distracting her from what was said, and she suspected that would matter more.

"About a month ago," Rokshan went on, "the ambassador Lamprophyre was the victim of a magical artifact wielded by a vengeful adept. He turned her human to make her vulnerable to his attacks. Lamprophyre is my best friend, Ambassador Chaaksha, and when she was human, that feeling turned to love. And she loves me. We were married—"

Yalini burst out laughing. "Married? I thought she was pitiful for loving you, but now I see you're even more pitiful. Feeling attraction to someone not your own species, how deviant. And disgusting."

"We were married," Rokshan continued, ignoring Yalini, "and

then Lamprophyre had the opportunity to become a dragon again. Her life was in danger so long as she was human, so she was transformed again. But that hasn't changed how we feel about each other, or the fact that we've made vows I consider sacred. So I cannot marry anyone else."

Chaaksha didn't look amused. "You can't consider yourself married when you're not the same species. It's impossible."

"I'm sorry you don't see it my way," Rokshan said, "but this is how things are. I beg you, ambassador, please reconsider. It's not my father's fault that we can't fulfill that one provision of the alliance. Please don't punish Gonjiri for my failings."

"Oh, don't worry," Yalini said, "I wouldn't have you now if you paid me. Having a husband who can be attracted to a dragon—"

"Shut up," Chaaksha said. Yalini looked surprised to be addressed so bluntly, but she fell silent. "This is disastrous," Chaaksha went on. "That marriage is key to Damen's agreement to the alliance. He wants a blood relation between our kingdoms because he's afraid if he can't hold Ekanath's posterity hostage, you'll come to war against him someday."

"Why are you telling him this?" Yalini said. "You're giving all our secrets away!"

Chaaksha made a quelling gesture in Yalini's direction. "Are you certain there's no way you'd give up this...marriage...of yours?"

"I can't," Rokshan said. "It would cost me everything I hold dear. My love, my honor, everything. I'm truly sorry."

"So am I," Chaaksha said. She gestured to the canopy bearers. "We will return to Fanishkor in the morning. Prince Rokshan, I wish you well. You and the ambassador. You're both fools, and you'll live to regret your attachment, but...good luck." She saluted Rokshan, and then Lamprophyre.

Yalini stayed behind when the canopy moved, forcing the bearers to stop a short distance away. "I can't believe I was ever attracted to you," she snarled.

"You weren't," Lamprophyre said, unable to bear it any longer. "You're greedy and selfish and all you ever wanted from Rokshan was good sex and beautiful babies. I hope you never marry, because your husband would be miserable his whole life."

Yalini's mouth fell open. Lamprophyre turned her back on the princess and walked away.

Soon, Rokshan caught up to her. "Was that true? What she wanted from me?"

"It was all true. Does it help to know she thought you were handsome and didn't care about your scars?"

Rokshan laughed. "*You* think I'm handsome and don't care about my scars. That matters far more than what some stone-faced Fanishkorite princess wants."

Lamprophyre looked ahead to where Ekanath waited. Her amusement died. "He's never going to forgive you."

"I know." Rokshan sighed. "But Darsha was right. I'll never gain his respect if I only ever do what he wants. I can't believe I took advice from a prostitute."

"Is there some reason a prostitute might not be wise?"

"Prostitutes aren't generally known for wisdom, no." He sighed again. "I think it's time I moved into the embassy. I don't want to encounter my father again for a while."

"We'll buy you a bed," Lamprophyre said.

~

THE NEXT DAY, LAMPROPHYRE HAD TO DO WHAT ROKSHAN persisted in referring to as "holding court." Petitioners came to the embassy with questions or requests, and Lamprophyre did her best to fulfill them or turn the petitioners down politely. She wished she could send everyone home, because she wasn't in a cheerful mood. But this was one of her main responsibilities as ambassador, and it did give her something to think about that wasn't Sardonyx or war or worrying about how Yalini would spread the news of Rokshan and Lamprophyre's marriage.

There was no question Yalini would tell people. And she would do it in the most negative, denigrating way possible. Lamprophyre's only hope was that Chaaksha had been serious about leaving for Fanishkor in the morning, and Yalini wouldn't have time. But it didn't matter. The secret was out, and she and Rokshan would just have to endure.

There were more petitioners than usual, and it was well on the way to midafternoon when the last one left. Lamprophyre retreated into the embassy and settled on the floor, carefully avoiding the low bedframe and mattress next to the slates. "I'm exhausted," she said.

"Nobody realizes how tiring it is to deal with a lot of people who all want different things," Rokshan said. He flung himself on the mattress, making it creak under his weight. "I bet napping has far more appeal now."

"I definitely need sleep." Lamprophyre took the blue chalcedony pendant off the wall and warmed it in her hand. "But I should talk to Hyaloclast first. Except she'll just say what she's been saying the last few days—'no contact.'"

"So wait for her to speak to you," Rokshan said. He had one arm flung across his eyes and his voice sounded drowsy.

"I don't know how you manage to fall asleep so quickly," Lamprophyre said.

Rokshan pretended to snore. Lamprophyre poked him in the side, which made him laugh. "All right, let me sleep," he said. "And you sleep too."

Lamprophyre put the pendant away and curled up beneath her spread wings. She wasn't looking forward to spring, when the weather grew hot, and definitely not to summer, when it was hot *and* rainy. Winter, though, winter in Tanajital was lovely. She fell asleep listening idly to the thoughts of her household, to Abhit and Rassika playing chase with the neighborhood children, to Bhakriya planning a shopping trip, and to Depik contemplating supper.

She came abruptly awake to someone shouting her name. "What?" she exclaimed, sitting up straight. Across the room, Rokshan stirred and rose on one elbow.

"*Lamprophyre!*" It was Hyaloclast's voice, with the odd echoing quality the pendant gave all communications. "*Lamprophyre, respond!*"

Lamprophyre scrambled to pick up the pendant. "What's wrong?"

"*Sardonyx's flight slipped past us, far to the south,*" Hyaloclast said. Her voice sounded unusually breathless. "*They are flying north along the river. We caught them at one of the southernmost cities along the river—*"

"Nishta," Rokshan said. "She means Nishta." He was already putting on his boots.

"*There was great destruction, but we forced them back,*" Hyaloclast went on. "*Unfortunately, their flight split to travel in many directions. I've set our dragons to following them, in case Sardonyx instructed them to destroy any towns they came across, but we're spread thin. I need you to come west and head off any of the dragons that continued northward along the river.*"

"They're headed for Kolmira," Lamprophyre said. "We'll stop them, Hyaloclast."

"*I fear they've figured out that humans build along the rivers.*" Hyaloclast went silent for a moment, and Lamprophyre could hear the murmur of speech, as if she'd turned aside to address someone else. "*Tanajital could be in danger.*"

"But if they're spread out, we have a better chance against them," Rokshan said. "Now's our chance to strike hard."

"*We intend to,*" Hyaloclast said. "*But they can't be allowed to roam free. Destroy them if you can, but more importantly, convince them they're in greater danger the farther abroad they go.*"

"We'll do it." Lamprophyre hung the pendant around her neck as the mist cleared from its surface. She grabbed the second pendant, the green chalcedony, and asked, "What are you doing?"

"Getting ready to go," Rokshan said.

"You're not coming with me."

"Why not? If they're attacking Kolmira, I can help direct the city's defense."

Lamprophyre shook her head. "She said they're moving in the

direction of Kolmira. I intend to intercept them before they reach that far. And I'm not risking having you with me when we encounter them."

Rokshan stood and faced her, his chin thrust out belligerently. "I'm not weak, Lamprophyre."

"You're also not immune to fire and acid. Rokshan—"

"How do you not see how much I hate watching you fly into danger? That orange dragon nearly killed you!"

Lamprophyre touched his shoulder gently. "I know it's not in your nature," she said, "but you're not equipped to fight this battle. And there's nothing wrong with that. You've already done so much! You taught the other commanders how to face dragon fire and acid, and you're working on improving the pyrite weapons. Don't feel you have to fly into battle too."

"Weapons that probably will never work," Rokshan said. "I hate being helpless."

"I know."

"And I hate that you're going into danger without me."

"I know that, too."

Rokshan sighed. "Couldn't you...no. You're right, I'd be a liability."

"Someday you'll have a dragon body, and that will change."

"Not soon enough." He shrugged. "I'll go to headquarters and see what progress they've made on the weapons."

"I'll be back soon," Lamprophyre said.

CHAPTER THIRTY-FIVE

She flew at top speed to the warehouses, where for a miracle everyone was present, even Dolomite. "Tekentriya and I flew to Suwedhi this morning," he said, "and I told her we needed a rest before going east this evening."

"There might not be time," Lamprophyre said. "We have to leave now. Sardonyx's people are headed up the Rindra River and we need to stop them before they reach Kolmira."

"Then let's go," Flint said. "Did Hyaloclast say anything else?"

Lamprophyre leaped into the air and shot several dragonlengths away from the city, followed by the clutch, before replying. "They're coming from the south. They attacked Nishta and then broke apart into smaller groups. We're trying to catch the ones that went north."

"Then we should head due west. They're too slow to have reached Kolmira already." Flint soared closer. "We can cut them off before they get that far."

"But what are we supposed to do?" Coquina said. "Even four ancient dragons are too many for the seven of us to fight."

"Hyaloclast thought they were in small enough groups for our dragons to fight," Lamprophyre said. "And at worst, we're to challenge them enough that they decide to head south again."

"That, we can do," Porphyry said with a laugh. "I'd back us against ancient dragons any day. It's all that obstacle course flying that does it."

"Don't be overconfident. Those dragons are tough," Coquina said. She and Lamprophyre exchanged looks that said neither of them had forgotten killing that dragon scout. Lamprophyre tried not to let the memory unnerve her. She had her clutch surrounding her, and there were no dragons she'd rather have facing down ancient monsters with her than them.

They flew in silence, spaced out too widely for conversation. Lamprophyre listened to their idle thoughts for a while, but everyone was thinking the same thing: when would they meet their enemy? Beneath them, parted by the pale ribbon of the road to Kolmira, the golden fields stretched out in all directions, coming up against the dark mass of the forest to the north and turning into gray-brown hills to the south. Somewhere in those hills Rokshan's dragon body waited for his transformation. The thought cheered her.

Ahead, the gleaming silver streak of the Rindra River defined the horizon. Half a dozen birds swooped and soared above it, moving like predators who'd just spotted prey. Lamprophyre's breath caught. No bird was big enough to be visible at that distance. "It's them," she shouted, thinking the words clearly in case the wind carried her audible words away.

She pushed herself faster, knowing the clutch would keep pace with her, until the darting specks became tiny dragons and the flash of fire was visible. Only five, not six, and they were closer than Lamprophyre had thought, well east of the river. There wasn't a town or even a village beneath them, just the road, but they were flying low and then soaring high. It looked as if *something* was there for them to attack, but what?

Lamprophyre considered the path she'd taken. Directly west from Tanajital, headed for Fanishkor on a straight line to Leksital.

A group of travelers, if they'd left Tanajital that morning, might have made it this far by now...

"*Stones*," she swore, and reached within herself for reserves she hadn't thought possible. In two beats she'd outpaced the rest of the clutch and was straining to see what the ancient dragons had targeted. She had to be wrong, but if she was right—*oh, Mother Stone*, she prayed, *let me be wrong*. She didn't care in that moment that her God wasn't real; the need for reassurance was too great. Five ancient dragons. The clutch was seriously outclassed.

She heard wings beating the air, catching up with her. "Something's wrong," Coquina said.

"I think that's the Fanishkorite ambassador's party down there." Lamprophyre gasped for breath. "We have to save them."

"I think it's too late. I don't see movement on the ground."

"*We have to save them*," Lamprophyre said. "I dare you to beat me there."

Coquina let out a sharp bark of laughter. "If that's how you feel," she said, and shouted, "Faster! You slugs can't catch me!" as she easily pulled into the lead.

Lamprophyre scanned the ground as they approached. Coquina was half-right; there wasn't much motion on the ground, but there were people crouched in the scant shelter of the wrecked caravan. Dead horses lay everywhere, along with dead human bodies, but Lamprophyre saw heads turn as she and her clutchmates approached. Those humans immediately shrank deeper into whatever shelter they'd found, clearly fearing another assault. Lamprophyre didn't have energy to feel bad about that.

She picked out the largest of the ancient females, a great pale blue monstrosity, and aimed herself at her. The female was hovering, drawing in breath to send another gout of fire at the caravan. Lamprophyre reversed in midair and slammed into the female feet-first, making her choke on the lungful of air she'd just drawn. Too bad the fiery contents of her second stomach couldn't burn her. Lamprophyre reversed again and raced back to her target, who'd just recovered from the unexpected attack and was ponderously turning around to face Lamprophyre.

Lamprophyre beat the air to gain altitude, keeping an eye on her target. As the female turned to ascend, Lamprophyre dropped, and at the last moment before flying past swiped at the female's face with her claws. The female bellowed in rage and pain, an atavistic sound that triggered an answering yell from Lamprophyre. It felt natural, not at all embarrassing, and she yelled again and flew past and around the female, taunting her with her speed.

To her surprise and excitement, she saw blood welling from the female's cheek and eye socket. It was a lucky hit, and she hoped she'd partially blinded the female. She told herself not to be overconfident and made another flying pass, circling the female, who spun dizzily trying to focus on Lamprophyre.

Lamprophyre looked around swiftly to see how her clutchmates were doing. Porphyry had followed her example and was looping and dodging around another bulky female, maroon like old blood, whose flanks bore signs of his claws. Coquina and Flint were dodging a bright silver male, while Bromargyrite and Orthoclase tackled another one, as purple as Lamprophyre remembered her father being. And Dolomite had closed with the third male and clung to his back, clawing at the male's wings. They were both the same dark green color, and entangled as they were, they looked like a monstrous four-winged lump.

Lamprophyre shouted a warning—getting that close could be dangerous—and pain lanced through her left leg just before the pale blue female grabbed her around the waist. "You're nothing, little female," the dragon said, and raked her claws across the base of Lamprophyre's left wing.

Agony shot through Lamprophyre, and her wing suddenly felt heavy and limp. The pale blue female let go of her, flinging her away, and Lamprophyre fell, one wing flapping desperately, the other hanging useless. Lamprophyre screamed. It was so much like her worst nightmare she was paralyzed for a few beats, her good wing fighting for altitude without direction from her. Then she shook herself free of the nightmare and focused on her injured wing. It wasn't totally useless, it just hurt when she tried to use it. And she could deal with pain.

Something grabbed her hand, and her fall stopped, became a more controlled descent. "It's not far to the ground," Porphyry shouted. "Can you fly at all?"

Lamprophyre moved her wing again. The pain was lessening. "Maybe," she shouted back. Then she looked past him and screamed, "*Look out!*"

Porphyry had just begun to turn when the pale blue female caught him around the waist and bore him to the ground. Lamprophyre's hand was ripped from his grasp, and she fell again, but in a jerky, sideways fashion as her wings fought to work together. She hit the ground and gasped at landing on the damaged part of her wing. Struggling to right herself, she shouted Porphyry's name, then ran, half on foot, half using her hands, to where Porphyry and the female fought.

The female had pinned Porphyry on his back with his wings spread painfully beneath him. Porphyry fought her off, kicking her chest and stomach, but she outweighed him. His hands gripped hers, the claws digging into her flesh, pushing back even as her head drew nearer to his throat. A flash of memory struck, and for a moment brown Corundum lay there, desperately struggling. Then it was Porphyry again, his eyes wide with terror, his teeth bared, fighting for his life.

Lamprophyre cried out his name again and ran faster. Blood from an injury she didn't remember dripped into her face, and she swiped it from her eyes, tripped over a stone, and pushed herself upright through sheer terror. Her injured wing dragged beside her, slowing her, but she was there, she was almost there.

The female roared and bore down on Porphyry, forcing his arms wide and bringing her mouth with its terrible sharp teeth within range of his throat. Porphyry screamed. The sound cut off abruptly, leaving behind a terrible silence in which Lamprophyre couldn't even hear her own screaming.

She flung herself on the pale blue female, rolling her away from Porphyry onto her back with one wing crushed beneath her. The female's mouth moved, but Lamprophyre still couldn't hear anything but that one scream, cut off, over and over again until she closed her eyes to make it go away. There was nothing but heat, and blood, and her claws in someone's throat, and still the scream wouldn't stop.

She came to herself to find Coquina shaking her, her lips moving as silently as the female dragon's had. She stared at Coquina in numb horror. Then Coquina drew back her hand and slapped Lamprophyre hard enough to make her jerk backward. Suddenly there was nothing but noise: wings flapping, voices shouting, shriller voices she knew to be humans screaming or wailing, and in the distance, barely audible, the Rindra River flowing serenely to the distant sea.

"Are you hurt?" Coquina was saying.

Lamprophyre couldn't remember. "I don't know."

"You're covered in blood. Please tell me none of it's yours."

"My wing—" Lamprophyre flexed her injured wing and hissed at the pain that shot through it. "I don't think it's bad. It just hurts when I try to fly."

"You killed her," Coquina said. Her voice shook. "You were like an animal, snarling and growling, and you tore out her throat and kept going."

Lamprophyre looked at the bloody mess nearby. Pale blue scales slippery with blood lay motionless. "She killed—"

"I know. I saw. I was too far."

They stared at each other. Lamprophyre started shaking. "He saved me," she said. "He wasn't paying attention because he was keeping me from falling."

"We scared them off," Coquina said. "Actually I think you tearing their leader apart scared them off. They flew south. We weren't supposed to chase them, were we?"

"I don't care. Was anyone else hurt?"

Coquina rotated her shoulder. "Everyone is injured. I think

you're the worst off, if you're having trouble flying."

"Then we're not going after them. If anyone else is killed... Stones, Coquina. He can't be dead. He just can't. He's the only other dragon who knows how to read."

"Lamprophyre..."

Lamprophyre shook her head. "I know that doesn't matter. It's just...he can't be dead."

Coquina stood. "Come with me."

She led Lamprophyre to where Porphyry lay, surrounded by the other males. His eyes were closed, and except for the bloody mess where his throat had been, he was unmarked. But there was no way anyone would mistake him for anything but dead. Lamprophyre knelt beside him and touched his hand. "Thank you," she said. "You wouldn't have died if you hadn't stopped to save me. Thank you."

"I'm glad you killed her," Bromargyrite said. His deep voice, normally so placid, was enraged, as if he were on the verge of violence. "I wish we'd killed all of them."

"They would have killed us first," Flint said. "Stones. We really don't stand a chance, do we?"

Lamprophyre tried to find words to stop them all wallowing in pain and despair and came up empty. "We don't," she said.

They sat together, not speaking, for a few dozen beats. Lamprophyre didn't want to listen to their thoughts, which were probably as despondent as her own. Her mind felt untethered from her body, whirling around like a kite in a spring breeze. She'd seen the masses of kites flown to celebrate the human god Meyari's return to the world and thought how sad it was that was the closest humans would ever get to true flight. Now she wished she'd never heard of flying, that no dragon was capable of taking to the skies.

"Excuse me?"

Lamprophyre looked up. A small woman in a Fanishkorite tunic that was grubby and torn and blackened down one side by a gout of acid stood hesitantly nearby. "You saved us," the woman said. "Thank you."

"We didn't save everyone," Lamprophyre said. The words tasted like bile. Porphyry had died, and so had a dozen or more humans, and most of the dragons responsible had flown away unscathed.

"That's not your fault," the woman said. "It would have been worse if you hadn't come along. Were you looking for us?"

"No. It was an accident that we crossed your path."

"It doesn't matter. We're still grateful." The woman bowed.

Lamprophyre felt the faintest stirrings of responsibility, and remembered she was the dragon ambassador. "Is Ambassador Chaaksha still alive? Or Princess Yalini? I should speak to someone in authority."

The woman hesitated. "Princess Yalini is uninjured. The ambassador was struck by acid. They think she might lose her leg."

"But she's alive. May I speak to her?"

The woman nodded. "Come with me."

The wrecked caravan showed signs of humans trying to set things right. The dead animals had been dragged to one side, and canvas-covered lumps showed where the human bodies had been moved. A couple of humans were busy repairing a wagon. It looked like the only wagon intact enough to be repaired. Lamprophyre walked carefully through the caravan, not wanting to disrupt things further. Everyone seemed too preoccupied to pay attention to her—all but one. Lamprophyre stopped next to Tarakh, whose red and white tunic was missing and whose hair and face were scorched on one side. "Tarakh," she said. "I'm glad you're alive."

Tarakh looked up at her. A faint smile touched his lips. "Oresa was killed," he said. "I wish I'd died with her."

Up until a hundred beats before, Lamprophyre would have challenged him on his words. Now she understood exactly how he felt. "My clutchmate Porphyry is gone, too," she said. "It feels like nothing will ever be all right again."

Tarakh's eyes were red-rimmed, and tear tracks made marks on his soot-darkened face. "And yet we live on," he said. "God's breath, but life can be so unfair."

"It can." Lamprophyre groped for words. "Porphyry was sort of...I don't know the human word. He loved a good joke, and he was always the first to agree to a race. Full of life, maybe. And I know, if I'd been the one to die, he would have gone on racing, and it wouldn't mean he'd forgotten me. Just like I won't forget him just because I go on living. But I can't stop thinking of the things we'll never be able to tell each other."

"That's it. That's it exactly." Tarakh wiped a sleeve across his eyes, smearing the dirt around. "We were to be married when we returned to Leksital. Such a terrible loss—and yet it only matters to me. But that's how it works, isn't it? Our personal tragedies mean nothing to anyone else."

"True, but does that make them any less important? Does tragedy have to be kingdom-shattering to be something you're allowed to mourn?" Lamprophyre rested her hand lightly on Tarakh's shoulder. "If it helps, I'll mourn with you."

Tarakh regarded her with wide, unblinking eyes. "Do you know," he said, "I think it does. Thank you."

"Oresa wasn't afraid of me. That makes her special all by itself." Lamprophyre withdrew her hand. "I have to talk to Chaaksha now, but if it's too hard for you to go to Leksital, we'd welcome you in Tanajital."

"Thank you. I'll remember that." Tarakh turned away, but she could hear his thoughts, and they weren't as despairing as before. She felt a lightening of her own spirits as well. Sharing grief did help, maybe only a little, but it helped.

The Fanishkorites had erected a little tent from the canvas formerly covering a wagon and laid Chaaksha inside. The bitter smell of dragon acid filled the air, and Lamprophyre had to work hard to conceal her dismay at seeing Chaaksha, her body laced and pitted with acid spray. A blanket covered her lower body, but Lamprophyre, listening to Chaaksha's thoughts, knew the woman's right leg hurt badly and her left leg had almost no sensation—a bad sign.

"Ambassador," Chaaksha said. Her voice was remarkably strong for someone in that much pain. "Thank you. We would have been utterly destroyed if not for you and your companions."

"I'm sorry we weren't faster," Lamprophyre said. "We thought Sardonyx's dragons were following the river, and we didn't know you were in the area for them to stumble on."

Chaaksha waved that away. "We aren't your responsibility, ambassador. I don't blame you for anything."

"I'll send word to Tanajital for them to send help. And we'll stay with you until help comes, in case those dragons return."

"Thank you, but that's unnecessary." Chaaksha fumbled at her neck and withdrew a small chalcedony pendant. "I've spoken with people in Leksital, and they're sending relief."

"Forgive me, but Leksital is at least two days away as humans travel. You can't sit out here alone waiting. We'll stay with you."

Chaaksha smiled. "It's not that we reject your help, just that my government doesn't want any confusion over our rescue."

"You mean you don't want to owe Gonjiri anything."

"You're very insightful." Chaaksha's smile faded. "Honja, Taritin, leave us," she said, waving at the two humans who stood nearby. When they were gone, and it was just the two of them, Chaaksha said, "I want you to know I disagreed with the terms of my king's proposal. If I could, I would give you the secret of the shields, and damn the consequences."

Lamprophyre shook her head. "I wouldn't want you to get in trouble with your king."

"It doesn't matter. I don't know anything about them." Chaaksha shifted her weight, and pain creased her features briefly. "But I promise you I will argue the point with Damen when I return. You saved us at a tremendous cost—they told me one of your dragons was killed."

"Yes. He was my clutchmate—do you know what that means? Closer than a brother. I've known him all my life. Humans don't have an equivalent."

"Then a terrible cost. I am sorry for your loss. Why did you do it? Fanishkor is still at odds with Gonjiri and your dragons."

Lamprophyre blinked. "Well, because we couldn't not try to save you. Because we're all rational creatures."

"You could have let us die, and saved yourselves."

"We could have. But I don't think we could have lived with ourselves afterward."

Chaaksha smiled again. "That's what I thought. Thank you again, ambassador." She extended a scarred hand to Lamprophyre, who took it gently.

She walked back to where her clutch waited by Porphyry's body, so lost in thought she didn't realize she had a companion until Yalini said, "Why did you come?"

Lamprophyre glanced at her. The princess was filthy with soot and dirt, but she carried herself as if she were perfectly groomed and walking through the halls of the palace. "We didn't know you were here. We were sent to chase Sardonyx's dragons away from Kolmira."

"I see," Yalini said.

Lamprophyre didn't say anything else. Yalini was the last person she wanted to have a conversation with. But her wing still hurt too much for her to fly, so she couldn't make an escape.

"I think it's disgusting that Rokshan is attracted to you," Yalini said. "People aren't supposed to be attracted to animals, and you're not human."

"I'm also not an animal, and I don't give a damn what you think about it," Lamprophyre shot back. "Besides, you've already made yourself clear on the subject, so I'm not sure why you feel entitled to go on criticizing and demeaning me."

"Because Rokshan was supposed to be mine." Yalini stopped and faced Lamprophyre. "We are an ideal match. I've wanted to marry him ever since I learned he existed."

Against her better judgment, Lamprophyre stopped. "Do you have any idea how many women have felt that way about Rokshan?" she demanded. "He's been treated like a prize his whole life. Why the Stones would he think you were worth loving if that's how you felt about him?"

"I respected him," Yalini said. "He's deserving of someone like me, someone of his own station. I told him I'd let him go his own way. I was even willing to let him have a mistress, until I found out it was you he loved."

Fury choked Lamprophyre, leaving her speechless. Finally, she said, "You don't know him at all if you could make such a vile proposal. He's not the sort of person who would make vows and then break them, even with his wife's permission."

Yalini shrugged. "A marriage of convenience requires compromises. That's just one of many."

Lamprophyre looked past Yalini. Coquina and Orthoclase were looking in her direction as if wondering what was taking her so long. The sight reminded her of what was really important. "I'm done discussing this with you," she said. "You're petty and small-minded and you're never going to understand why Rokshan didn't want you. Go back to Fanishkor and find someone stupid enough to accept you on your terms."

Yalini said, "I'm not—"

Lamprophyre lowered her head and let out a puff of smoke that encircled Yalini's head, making her cry out. Lamprophyre was too angry to be excited at her first real smoke ring. "I am a *dragon*," she said in a low, terrible voice. "If I choose not to be civilized, I can make you disappear and *no one* will challenge me on it. Now, get out of my sight." She turned her back on Yalini and walked away.

"What was that about?" Coquina asked when Lamprophyre arrived.

"Nothing important," Lamprophyre said. "Certainly not as important as this."

In silence, they set about burying Porphyry.

CHAPTER THIRTY-SIX

The sun was low in the sky when a group of wagons and people riding horses came into sight from the east. It had taken nearly all that time for the six dragons to dig a grave for Porphyry. By the end, Lamprophyre's wing felt as if it were being ripped out of its socket from the constant motion of digging. She and Coquina carried Porphyry to the grave and stood by while the males covered his body with earth. A memory of dead Gabbro curled in his rock cleft struck her, momentarily blinding her with grief. This was wrong, this putting a dragon into the ground, and yet what else was left to them? Even if Mother Stone had been holy, there was no way they could carry Porphyry all that way.

Bromargyrite abruptly staggered backward and sat gracelessly on his rump. "I can't," he choked, then lifted his head and let out a terrible, heartrending howl that touched some ancient nerve within her, compelling her to howl with him. It would have been embarrassing, that descent into barbarity, if she hadn't wanted so desperately to ease the pain that ate at her like acid. She didn't even care if the approaching humans heard.

She controlled herself with an effort. "Sorry," she told Flint, who'd put a hand on her shoulder. "Sorry."

"It's all right," Flint said. Across from her, Orthoclase had his arms around Bromargyrite. "I don't think anyone knows how we're supposed to grieve under these circumstances."

Lamprophyre made herself breathe normally. "I think I do," she said. "Let's finish this."

When the last bit of earth was laid, Lamprophyre stood at the head of the grave and said, "Hyaloclast told me this is what she teaches every dragon who makes the journey to Mother Stone. It's supposed to be secret, or at least private, but Mother Stone is dead, and I think we need this more than we need any more secrets." She drew in a breath, and sang:

"Born of wind and fire and stone,
To breath and ash and stone return.
I am all dragons in the bone,
All dragons end here in their turn.
My body, the stone
My breath, the wind
My heart, the fire
Let stone and wind and fire combine
Bind those who end their journey here.
Fly, heart and spirit intertwined,
Lie, body, now stone, 'til end of time,
In Mother's love rest without fear."

As she sang, she felt warmth as of a fire growing hotter and nearer. The heat comforted her, reminding her of stormy nights spent secure in a warm cave, of the closeness and love of her clutch-mates. She wasn't sure if she believed the words of the death-song anymore, but she thought of the dragons covering Mother Stone and how peaceful she'd felt surrounded by them. That couldn't mean nothing, no matter what the mountain had turned out to be.

When she finished, she sat and looked at the earth covering Porphyry. She felt wrung out and exhausted from more than just the physical labor. She couldn't bring herself to look at her clutch-mates because the moment felt so private. The warm feeling was growing stronger—and with that realization, she understood what it was, and rose in time to see Rokshan leap down from his horse and run toward her.

She hadn't told him the details of what had happened when she spoke to him because Porphyry's death was still too fresh a memory for her to bear to speak it. He stopped short when he saw the grave, and Lamprophyre saw him quickly take in who surrounded it.

"Porphyry," he said. "God's breath, Lamprophyre, what happened? No, don't tell me, just—" He put his arms as far around her as he could manage. She embraced him, not caring what anyone else thought of it, and held him while he wept the tears she couldn't. She closed her eyes and let the warmth of their pair-bond suffuse her, easing the pain that had been her constant companion all afternoon.

Then the others were there, close together as they'd been when they were dragonets cuddled together against the terror of a thunderstorm, careful not to crush their human clutchmate. Lamprophyre remembered how Porphyry had been the only one of them who wasn't afraid of thunder. "It's just noise," he'd always said, "and I bet we can make more noise than the storm if we try," and then they'd all gotten in trouble for raising an unholy racket. The memory drew a laugh out of her, startling the others.

"I'm sorry," she said. "I was thinking of Porphyry and thunderstorms."

Orthoclase laughed, a shaky sound. "Because we're huddled like dragonets?"

"No question we could out-thunder a thunderstorm now," Bromargyrite said.

That made all of them laugh. "Do you think he sees us now?" Coquina said. "We didn't bury his spirit. If it doesn't go to Mother Stone's rest, where does it go?"

"I don't know," Orthoclase said. "Maybe the death-song has it right, and his spirit flies free. If that's true, I hope he sees this and knows we won't forget him."

"We should raise a marker," Rokshan said. "If humans ever settle this way, I don't want his body disturbed."

Lamprophyre looked past him to where the wagons were drawn up near the Fanishkorites. "Chaaksha said she didn't want help."

"It's not up to her," Rokshan said curtly. "The wagons are to transport them to Kolmira, where they can wait for their people to retrieve them. And I brought seven healer-adepts, which I hope in Jiwanyil's name are enough."

Lamprophyre flexed her injured wing and hissed. When she held it still, the pain almost vanished, but any movement reminded her of the ancient female's claws. "We need to bury that female," she said, reminded too of digging Porphyry's grave and how her injuries ached worse from that. "We can't leave her lying there as a reminder of what happened to Porphyry."

"We're equipped to dig graves," Rokshan said. "You sit. All of you. I'll send someone to tend your wounds—don't think I didn't see those claw marks, Flint."

Flint reflexively put his arm behind his back. "Lamprophyre's the worst off," he said.

Rokshan laid his hand along her cheek. "Let me handle this," he said. "You should be able to fly back to Tanajital before full dark. I know you must be hungry." He ran off in the direction of the wagons before anyone could protest.

Soon a woman dressed in a healer's black tunic and trousers left the wagons and came to join them. She carried a large knapsack over one shoulder that she set down with a heavy thump. "I haven't worked on dragons before, and I hope I have enough stone," she said. "Ambassador, the prince tells me you are seriously injured. You're bloody enough—it's not all your blood? Ah, that's a relief. Let me take a look at that wing."

The healing didn't take long, and soon Lamprophyre sat watching the rest of the clutch undergo treatment. While her wing no longer hurt when she moved it, the healing hadn't done anything to cure her various aches, and sitting still was restful. She used the dust to scrub off the worst of the blood, then alternated watching the healer with watching Rokshan. He was directing Gonjirians and Fanishkorites in moving the injured to the wagons and collecting what could be salvaged from the caravan and digging graves. She knew from experience how comforting his assertiveness was, how good it felt to have him quietly but competently directing matters.

Then she saw Yalini headed his way. "Stones," she said. "I should—"

"Rokshan said rest. Listen to your mate, Lamprophyre," Coquina said.

"But that Stones-damned princess is going to harass him."

"I'm sure Rokshan can handle her," Flint said. He was lying flat with his eyes closed as Coquina rubbed the base of his neck.

Lamprophyre muttered another curse under her breath, but stayed where she was. Rokshan was just far enough away that, combined with how many people there were, she couldn't hear either his thoughts or Yalini's, but there was still enough light for her to see their faces.

Yalini looked like she'd said Rokshan's name more than once before he stopped to listen to her. He didn't look as annoyed as Lamprophyre thought he should. He said a few words that made Yalini take a step backward, her eyes wide. Then she went into what was surely a torrent of abuse. Rokshan stood still, his face almost peaceful. When she finished, he smiled, leaned forward, and whispered something into her ear. Yalini froze. Rokshan smiled again, patted her cheek in a friendly way, and walked away. Yalini came to life, her face furious, but rather than pursue Rokshan, she stormed off in the other direction.

"I wish I could have heard that," Lamprophyre mused. "I can't believe I was ever afraid he would fall in love with her."

Bromargyrite snorted a laugh. "You were afraid of that? With Rokshan as head over heels for you as he is?"

Lamprophyre blushed and shot a glance at the healer, who was deep in a trance following the trails of light her jade artifact left and wasn't listening. "I thought, he's human, I'm not—"

"I guarantee that is not something you need to worry about," Orthoclase said. "Not from what he's said."

"What he's said? What is that?"

Orthoclase exchanged glances with Dolomite. "Male business. Not for females. Right, Dolomite?"

Dolomite shrugged. "I suppose. I would really like to leave soon." He'd been the quietest of all of them, and now Lamprophyre looked more closely at him and worried. She never could guess how he'd react to anything, except that he was likely to make whatever remark was most direct and least tactful.

"Dolomite," she said, "are you all right?"

"Not really," Dolomite replied. "I was thinking of killing dragons."

Coquina sucked in a sharp breath. Orthoclase reached out to Dolomite, then seemed to think better of the gesture and withdrew his hand. "We'll do what we can," he said gently, "but it shouldn't be at the cost of our own lives."

"They killed Porphyry. I don't think they should be allowed to get away with that. Lamprophyre was right to tear that dragon to pieces. If we go now, we might still catch them." Dolomite's voice, always cheerful, was a flat monotone that frightened Lamprophyre.

She scooted forward so she could look Dolomite in the eye. "We'll stop them," she said. "I don't know how. Maybe the fight will kill more of us. But I swear we won't let Sardonyx win."

Dolomite looked at her. It chilled her to see his eyes so empty of emotion. "There has to be a way," he said. "Those pyrite weapons are useless. They're too big and they're too slow."

"They're all the humans have, though," Flint said.

"But they're useless," Dolomite persisted.

Lamprophyre felt Rokshan returning and sat up, as eager for an end to this conversation as for his comforting presence. "Is everything settled?"

"As much as we can do for now. The wagons are ready to head for Kolmira," Rokshan said. "I'm going with them, as a courtesy to Fanishkor's ambassador. I hope my presence is coals of fire upon Damen's head."

"But I wanted you to come back with us," Lamprophyre protested.

"Sweetheart, you're in no condition to carry anyone," Rokshan said. "I'll return tomorrow morning. You go back to the embassy and sleep."

"But—" Lamprophyre realized she was whining and shut her mouth. "You'll tell me when you reach Kolmira safely, all right? However late it is?"

"If that will ease your mind, certainly." Rokshan patted her shoulder. "Don't push yourself, and I'll see you tomorrow."

Lamprophyre nodded. "We have to bring stone to mark Porphyry's grave."

Rokshan nodded. "Chaaksha would take it as a kindness if you'd do something to mark her people's graves, as well."

"That's no problem," Flint said. "Let's go before we lose the light."

Lamprophyre exchanged one final look with Rokshan and followed Flint and Coquina as they leapt into the sky.

She suspected Coquina of setting a slow pace for Lamprophyre's benefit, and was grateful rather than annoyed. With the setting sun at her back, the sky to the east was a soft black spattered with stars only barely dimmed by the moon waxing toward full. The moon's light reflected off the distant Green River, giving her tired mind and body something to aim for. Shortly, she saw a handful of warmly glowing stars fallen to earth, clustered around the river. She had never been so happy to see Tanajital.

She left her clutch just past the western city gate to take a long, curving path toward the embassy. The sight of the well-known streets made her unexpectedly tired, as if her body, having carried her all this way, knew it was close to familiar territory and felt justified in giving up. She descended, yawning, into the courtyard and drew in a deep breath of lamb-scented air. "Depik, are you still awake?"

Depik emerged from the pavilion, dripping spoon in hand. "Prince Rokshan said you'd want food when you returned. It's a good thing this supper keeps warm almost indefinitely. Come in, and I'll serve you."

The embassy was quiet and peaceful as it only ever got at this time of night. Lamprophyre reflexively checked her household's thoughts and was relieved to find all of them but Depik safely asleep. "You shouldn't have stayed up," she said.

Depik shrugged. "There was something I wanted to speak to you about, anyway," he said. He lugged the enormous cauldron on its trolley out of the kitchen. "Here's a napkin, my lady."

"Thank you." Lamprophyre lifted the cauldron and downed half the yellow soup in a few gulps. She hadn't realized she was hungry until she'd smelled the soup. She patted her mouth with the cloth and said, "What was it you wanted to tell me?"

Depik leaned against the kitchen wall, a casual pose, but Lamprophyre could hear his thoughts were anything but casual. "It's about Abhit," he said. "You know the boy is smart, smarter than me or his mother, and he'd benefit from schooling at the academy."

"I was thinking that myself recently. You want me to pay his way?"

"Oh, no, my lady!" Depik stood upright. "That's more than we deserve. No, my lady, we were wondering, if you're satisfied with our work, maybe you could see fit to increasing our wages. And then we could afford to pay for his schooling."

Lamprophyre took another drink of soup to give herself time to think. Finally, she put the cauldron down and said, "What do you mean, 'we'?"

"Well, Bhakriya and me, of course."

"You're not his father, Depik. Is there something you haven't told me?"

Depik's cheeks reddened visibly even in the lantern light. "I care about his well-being, that's all. He's a fine lad."

"But he's not your fine lad. Depik, I know how you feel about Bhakriya, but if she doesn't feel the same, isn't she taking advantage of your, um, interest in her?"

Depik's face went even redder, but with anger instead of embarrassment. "It's not like that at all! She can't care for these kids on her own, not Abhit nor the girls, and I don't want to make her feel she can't count on me unless she returns my feelings."

Lamprophyre wished with all her heart Rokshan were here. He understood human social rules so much better than she did. All she did know was that regardless of how certain she was that Bhakriya loved Depik, telling him that was completely out of line. "That's not it," she said. "It's *you* I'm worried about. You shouldn't give your life to someone who doesn't love you with her whole heart. It's not fair to you."

Depik stiffened. "Not to be rude, my lady, but what I do with my life is my business. I know I owe you everything, but my pride is my own, and not you nor anyone has a right to tell me how to live or who to love."

Lamprophyre gave up. "I'm sorry. You're right. I'm concerned for you, but it's up to you what choices you make." She was going to take Bhakriya by the shoulders in the morning and shake sense into her—no, that might kill the woman, so she wouldn't do that, but she would express her irritation in the strongest terms.

She drank down the rest of the soup and set the cauldron down. "Thank you for supper, Depik. I really appreciate it on a night like this."

"What about this night is special, my lady?"

Weariness overtook her again. "I can't explain. I'll tell you in the morning. Good night."

She carried the cauldron into the kitchen for Depik and left him to cleaning. She didn't bother telling him to wait until morning, because she knew from past experience her cook would give her a horrified look and say something about sloth being the root of all evil. There were times she couldn't believe anyone had ever called Depik lazy, just because he occasionally couldn't get out of bed in the mornings. He made even the energetic Flint look like a layabout.

She settled in to sleep clutching the green chalcedony pendant. Rokshan would hate waking her, but he'd promised, and he never broke his promises to her even if he thought it would be better for her in the long run. Such a wonderful mate. She fell asleep thinking of the beautiful green and gold statue and how glorious it would be when Rokshan had that form.

A loud thump woke her, the sound of the cauldron overturning. Muzzily, she sat up and listened. More thumping, a gasp, a groan, then movement, lots of feet running from the kitchen. She blinked, coming to full consciousness, and only then thought to listen for thoughts. She heard nearly a dozen humans spreading out through the courtyard, their thoughts intent on gold and *don't wake the monster*—and one human nearer to hand, his thoughts filled with agonizing pain.

Depik.

She burst out of the embassy and flung herself at the nearest men, grabbing two and making a snatch for a third who eluded her. "You *dare* come here to steal from me!" she roared, her grief over Porphyry and her fear for Depik turning into fury. "And hurt—" She flung the two men away to lie sprawled and inert on the floor of the dining pavilion and dove after the others. Terror sharpened their thoughts, and they fled. Lamprophyre leaped into the air and followed them a few dragonlengths, pursued by the sound of Depik's pained thoughts.

Realization struck her, bringing her to her senses. They'd hurt Depik, badly by the sound of it. He needed her more than she needed vengeance.

She turned around and rushed back to the embassy, not stepping on her captives though she really wanted to. Depik lay beside the kitchen, curled in on himself, his face pinched and set with pain. Bhakriya knelt beside him with her hand on his shoulder. "He's bleeding," she told Lamprophyre in a trembling voice. "There's so much blood."

"Back up," Lamprophyre said. She gently prodded Depik's shoulders until he uncurled. Both hands covered a deep, bloody wound in his stomach. Lamprophyre sucked in a horrified breath. Even she knew this sort of wound could be fatal.

She picked him up, being as gentle as she could though she

could tell from his thoughts he was barely conscious. "No more death," she whispered. She looked down at Bhakriya, who was crying. "See if those men are still alive," she ordered. "Tie them up if you can. They had damn well better not escape, do you understand? If he—" She wasn't going to tempt fate by even suggesting Depik might die. "Send Rassika for the guards. I'll be back." With one great leap, she vaulted upwards and spread her wings wide to catch the air. She hadn't been in time to save Porphyry, and she'd be damned if she lost another person she cared about tonight.

CHAPTER THIRTY-SEVEN

Depik twitched in her arms and moaned, a weak sound that frightened her more than the blood. "Don't die," she told him. "You just have to hold on a little longer. Don't die. I couldn't bear another death. Don't die."

Depik's thoughts were incoherent, swirling around memories Lamprophyre didn't recognize. His lips moved in silent speech. "Don't talk," she told him, feeling obscurely that his life force ebbed with every word. "We're almost there." It didn't feel like they were almost there. She felt time had stretched out, making every beat last a century. She dodged a tower and kept going, following the lamps that lined the streets by law, until she saw the healing center, brilliantly lit as if they'd known she was coming.

She descended slowly, looking beneath her for humans she might accidentally crush. Why the healing center had a roof open to the sky, she didn't know, but she was deeply grateful for it tonight. The low hills dotted with benches, covered in short, fine grass, continued to confuse her—why bring the outdoors inside?—but the smell of living green things reassured her that here was a place things thrived, even people who were badly injured by greedy bastards.

She began calling out for help before she even touched the ground. "Somebody help me! Please, wake up! I need help—he's going to die!"

Most of the thoughts she heard were from sleeping people, some of whom came awake at the sound of her shouting. If they were injured people recovering from healing, she felt bad at waking them, but in a distant way, because Depik mattered more. Other people, their thoughts more alert, moved through the halls in her direction.

Lamprophyre held Depik more closely. She thought he was still breathing, but she was afraid to check. Blood still flowed sluggishly from the horrible wound, which meant his heart continued to beat. Hope threaded its way through her and she pushed it aside. Time for that when the healers arrived.

Now she heard things with her ears and not her mind: the sound of voices murmuring, the sound of feet hurrying over stone. "Help," she called out again, and doors opened and the running footsteps became louder. People emerged into the grassy space, converging on her.

"What are you—God's breath, you're a dragon," said a man in a rumpled blue shirt whose unkempt, balding head showed he'd been asleep.

"It's the ambassador," said a woman. "Ambassador, do you need healing?"

"He does," Lamprophyre said. She laid Depik at their feet, wishing she didn't have to let him go. "Please. They stabbed him—I think he's dying—"

The balding man knelt beside Depik and took his wrist. "His pulse is very weak, but he's alive," he said, and Lamprophyre's knees gave way and she sagged to the ground. "We have to hurry. No, don't move him, there's no time."

Lamprophyre heard the rest in a haze. She dragged herself away to give the healers room to work and collapsed against one of the pillars holding up the narrow roof that encircled the grassy space. Depik was invisible behind all the men and women in black gathered around him. She closed her eyes and wished she knew who to pray to. Maybe it didn't matter. If there was no God, there was no one to thank except possibly good fortune. If she hadn't been a dragon, capable of getting Depik to the healers in practically no time, he might have died. On the other hand, if he wasn't employed by her, he wouldn't have been in a position to be stabbed.

Fury swept through her again. What was *wrong* with humans that some of them felt entitled to take other people's things and kill in the pursuit of that theft? Those greedy, detestable *bastards*. She liked that human swear word. It felt good and fierce and hot with anger. She hoped she hadn't killed them, throwing them around like that, because she was going to make them pay. And if Depik died...

"My lady ambassador."

Lamprophyre opened her eyes. It was the balding healer. He didn't look happy. A pang of fear struck her. "Is he..." she managed, once more afraid to tempt fate by saying the word.

"He's alive," the healer said. Lamprophyre let out a deep, relieved breath. The healer still didn't look as happy as that news warranted. "But I feel I shouldn't give you false hope. Your friend lost a lot of blood, and while we've healed his injury, we don't have any way to replace that blood. He might still die."

"I don't understand. Don't human bodies make more blood? Dragon bodies do."

"They do, my lady, but in this case it might not be fast enough. We've done what we can to encourage the process, but it's a matter of his own recuperative power now." The healer looked suddenly very tired. "There's still hope—I don't want to discourage you—but you might want to pray to whatever God you believe in, because it could take a miracle."

"Can I see him?"

"He's not conscious, my lady." The healer laid a hand on her shoulder. He was shorter than she'd realized. "You should return to your embassy. I promise we'll send word. And if it looks bad, we'll let you know so you can be with him in the end."

That was less comforting than he probably intended. Lamprophyre nodded and flew away.

Once more the flight to the embassy felt as if it took much longer than the seventy beats it actually took. Lamprophyre's righteous fury had ebbed, leaving her cold and tired. She hoped Bhakriya hadn't let those men escape. They couldn't be allowed to get away with what they'd done, not to mention Lamprophyre intended to use them as a warning to anyone else who thought stealing from a dragon was a good idea. She silently cursed Viveki's name. How *dare* the woman spread lies for the sake of her stupid, worthless revenge?

When she arrived at the embassy, all the lamps were lit, and Bhakriya came forward from the dining pavilion to greet her. Her eyes were red from crying and she twisted her hands together restlessly, as if she didn't know she was doing it. "Is he..." she said.

"He's alive. For now. The healer said he might not survive," Lamprophyre said. Bhakriya let out a sob she muffled with her hands. Lamprophyre felt too hollowed-out with repeated grief to have any sympathy to spare for the woman.

"Did you do as I asked?" she went on. There were still two limp figures lying on the pavilion floor, but as she spoke, one of them groaned and twitched.

"I sent Rassika for the guards. She's not back yet," Bhakriya said, unnecessarily as there was a complete absence of guards in the courtyard. "Abhit and I tied them as best we could. They're both still alive. Why did they attack Depik?"

"I don't know if these ones did, specifically, but as far as I'm concerned they're all to blame," Lamprophyre snarled. "They thought there was a treasure hoard here and that they were entitled to steal it. Where are Abhit and Kavari?"

"I told Abhit to keep Kavari away. They might have—" Bhakriya's breath sobbed out of her again. "They probably wanted to keep Depik from sounding an alarm. They might have killed all of us."

"They might," Lamprophyre agreed.

She walked into the pavilion and turned one of the groaning

men over. Their wrists and ankles were tied, not very securely to Lamprophyre's eye, but it didn't matter, because with her there, they weren't going anywhere. "Wake up," she said, flicking the man in the head and making it jerk back. "We're going to have a talk."

The man's eyes opened. He looked confused, unable to focus on anything. Lamprophyre prodded him in the back. He blinked, and his gaze came to rest on her face. His face was suddenly a mask of terror. Lamprophyre ignored him and poked his companion awake. "I'm only going to say this once, so you'd both better listen," she said when she had their terrified attention. "Which of you stabbed Depik?"

The first man's confusion was evident on his face. The second was more stoic, at least on the outside; his thoughts were a gibbering mess. Neither of them had any guilty thoughts at her mention of stabbing. Lamprophyre felt a moment's regret at not being able to tear the head off Depik's assailant. But she wasn't going to let these two get away regardless.

"You came into my home and you attacked my friends because you heard there was treasure here," she snarled, breathing out a hot, fire-stinking breath into their faces and making them flinch. "What the Stones is wrong with you that you feel you're somehow entitled to take other people's things? It doesn't matter that *I have no hoard*, you fools—you're thieves, and you deserve to die for what you've done."

The first thief's breathing became rapid with fear. "We didn't take anything," he said, "wc were stupid, I swear it won't happen again."

"If you're dead, that is certainly true," Lamprophyre said.

Tears trickled down the sides of his face. "Please don't eat me," he whispered.

"Shut up, fool, dragons don't eat people," the second thief said. He still managed to hold on to his brave appearance, but inside he was composing prayers to Jiwanyil that he'd survive this. That made Lamprophyre want to laugh. She didn't know much about human religion, and she was sure Jiwanyil wasn't a god, but she didn't think gods were obliged to protect humans from the consequences of their crimes.

"No, we don't," Lamprophyre said. She extended her first claw and ran it delicately across the first thief's jawline. The scent of urine suddenly filled the air. "We do, however, eviscerate our prey. What about this evening suggests I'll be gentle with you?"

"My lady," Bhakriya said.

Lamprophyre turned to look at her. Her face was set with fear, but not of the thieves. Lamprophyre heard the terror in her thoughts and felt sick. Bhakriya was afraid of her. In that instant, Lamprophyre's anger and joy at causing these men pain disappeared. She sat back, breathing heavily. They deserved punishment, and they might even deserve harsh punishment, but torturing them only satisfied her baser instincts. And Lamprophyre never wanted the humans she cared about to fear what she might do.

"The guards are coming," she told the men. "They'll take you into custody and you will be punished for your crimes. I will make sure of that. And I will also make sure nobody else thinks stealing from dragons is a good idea." Stealing from dragons. Maybe she hadn't been the only one attacked tonight. "But I will let you live, on condition you tell the guards who else came here with you tonight. I want all of you to face justice."

The first thief nodded vigorously. "We'll do that. I swear."

Lamprophyre looked at the second thief. "Well?"

"I'm not afraid of you. Dragons don't kill humans," the man said. His defiance was tattered around the edges, but despite herself Lamprophyre was impressed.

She leaned in close and breathed hotly into his face. "You're not a fool," she whispered in his ear, "and if you continue to defy me, I'll send Bhakriya away so she doesn't have to witness what I'll do to you. I lost a friend today, and I'm in a killing mood. Do you think anyone in this city will challenge my right to make my own justice?"

The man swallowed. His eyes showed white all the way around his brown irises. "No," he said. "We can tell you who told us you had treasure. That should be worth something to you."

Lamprophyre sat back. "It is," she said, though she was sure she already knew the answer.

By the time Rassika appeared with half a dozen guards in tow, Lamprophyre was anxious and frustrated. The two thieves hadn't known much, at least not much that meant anything to Lamprophyre, but she was sure their information would matter to the guards. What had Lamprophyre anxious was her desire to get to the warehouses and make sure they hadn't been attacked. There was nothing a human could do to a dragon, but if her clutchmates were in the same mood she was, she couldn't guarantee the night wouldn't end in bloodshed.

But the guards insisted she tell her side of the story, so instead she sent Rassika to inquire. She felt a little bad about keeping the girl up so late, but Rassika's bright eyes and worried face told Lamprophyre it was unlikely she'd be able to sleep.

Remembering when she'd been interrogated by guards a few twelvedays ago, she braced herself for a long night. But the guard captain who arrived shortly after his men was alert and intelligent, asking just what he needed to know and not requiring her to repeat anything. Lamprophyre, who'd grown used to thinking of the guards as not very competent, was impressed.

Finally, the thieves, properly restrained this time, were led away out of the courtyard, and Bhakriya disappeared to check on Abhit and Kavari. Lamprophyre knew from their thoughts that they'd fallen asleep, but she was too tired to worry about them. She was too tired to haul herself into the embassy. She would just close her eyes for a bit. She could sit on the nice stone floor of the pavilion and breathe in the lingering aroma of lamb soup. Unfortunately, the lingering odor of blood overrode that delicious smell. Lamprophyre thought of Depik and wished she could cry. Crying was so comforting.

She heard Bhakriya coming back and opened her eyes. "They're asleep," the woman said. "Was Depik...I know you said he wasn't dead, but you didn't sound..." She was twisting her hands together again.

"They told me he was alive, but they weren't sure he'd survive." Lamprophyre was too tired to soften the blow.

Bhakriya let out a low sobbing breath, then visibly controlled herself. "I wish...oh, my lady, if he dies—"

"Bhakriya, I *told* you not to delay!" She was too tired for tact, too. "You were afraid to tell him how you feel, and for what? Because you thought he wouldn't care? Because you feared he wasn't the man he seems to be? How do you feel now, knowing you might have lost your chance?"

Bhakriya's eyes were wide. Her lips trembled. "My lady," she whispered.

"I'm sorry, because I know you must feel awful, but you humans live such short lives, I don't understand why you insist on not making the most of them!" Lamprophyre drew in a deep breath, reaching for calm. "No, I really am sorry. I'm just making things worse."

Tears filled Bhakriya's eyes, and she shook her head. "It's not that," she said. She reached into the neck of her shirt and pulled out a pendant on a chain. It was a small polished nugget of aventurine caged in silver wire. It was such an unexpected gesture Lamprophyre forgot what she'd been about to say.

"I had this made for him," Bhakriya said. "It was supposed to help his illness. Bring his thoughts into balance. The adept said it's not healing, there's no healing for what's wrong with him, but it's supposed to fight back the bad thoughts."

She released the pendant to dangle between her breasts. "I wanted so much for him to be well," she said, the tears spilling over. "I know he still thinks poorly of himself, even though he's not at all awful or stupid or lazy. But then I thought, suppose he thinks the pendant means I want him to be perfect so he's worthy of me? All this last week I couldn't—I didn't know whether to give it to him, or tell him first that I love him, and now it's too late!"

She slid down the pillar she'd been leaning against and hugged her knees, weeping so hard her shoulders shook. Lamprophyre felt like kicking herself. She knelt beside Bhakriya and put an arm around her, holding her against her sobs.

"We have to have hope," she said. "They told me it was all up to him, his body's own healing power, whether he survives. He has so much to live for—he has you, and the children—you know he wants you to be a family, right? He's concerned about Abhit's education, and he adores Kavari, and you've seen how he jokes with Rassika. He won't want to abandon all of you."

Bhakriya lifted a teary-eyed face to hers. "How do you know that?"

"Dragons are very observant." Lamprophyre smiled. "I didn't tell him how you feel. I thought that should be up to you."

Bhakriya nodded. "Do you think they'd let me sit with him?"

"We'll go in the morning. They promised to send word if anything changed before that." Lamprophyre released her and stood. "Go to sleep. I have to wait for Rassika to return."

Bhakriya must have been as exhausted as Lamprophyre, because she didn't argue. When she was gone, Lamprophyre settled herself against the wall of the embassy beneath the lantern and tried to stay awake. Rassika would wake her if she slept, but she felt it would look bad, like she wasn't worried about her clutchmates.

She drowsed repeatedly despite her resolution, catching herself each time she slid down the wall. Finally, she stood and paced the courtyard. Every bone in her body, every muscle from her tail to her jaw, ached with the need for sleep.

"*Lamprophyre*," Rokshan said, jerking her awake again.

She grabbed the green chalcedony pendant. "Rokshan? Are you in Kolmira?"

"*It took longer than we expected, but everyone's safely here. Did I wake you?*"

"Not really." She was too tired to tell him what had happened, and there was Rassika finally, trotting along the street toward her. "Do you want me to come for you in the morning?"

"*Yes, but sleep as long as you want. I intend to. I love you, sweetheart. Sleep well.*"

"I love you, too."

The pendant cleared, and Lamprophyre got to her feet to greet Rassika. "It was all quiet there," the girl said. "I woke Bromargyrite because he's not likely to slap me by accident if he's woken quick-like, and he said they haven't seen nothing. I guess those thieves thought one dragon was a safer target than six."

Five, Lamprophyre thought, but she was too tired to grieve. "Thank you, Rassika. Go to bed now."

"Is Depik going to be all right?" Rassika's voice trembled. Lamprophyre examined her closely and saw how frightened she was, despite hiding it well.

"I hope so. He's alive, and that's good, right?"

"I don't want him to die." *Lost my Dada before, lose another,* she thought.

Lamprophyre's heart ached for her. She put a hand on the girl's shoulder. "We'll know soon enough," she said. "Now, sleep. Depik would be so angry with both of us if he knew I'd sent you running errands during the dreaming hour."

"Guess we won't tell him, then," Rassika said with a grin.

Lamprophyre hung the two chalcedony pendants on the wall and curled in on herself, covering herself with her wings for comfort though the night wasn't that cold. She was asleep in three beats.

She dreamed disjointed images of dragons flying in formation, not Sardonyx's terrible military-like ranks, but spirals, loops, and vast sweeps of wings that divided and divided again until the sky was filled with them. Then she was flying with the rest toward Mother Stone, who in the dream was a great stone dragon whose wings encompassed all the flight. In the dream, the dead dragons were restored to life, color bleeding across their scales, and they flew to meet the flight. Porphyry was there, and it was such a joyous reunion she woke from the dream happier than she'd been in many twelvedays.

She yawned and furled her wings. It was just after dawn, and someone was crossing the courtyard toward her, someone whose thoughts she didn't recognize. She looked out the doorway and saw a man wearing a healer's tunic, but red instead of black. That meant he was an assistant rather than a healer himself. He looked stern, like he had bad news, and a jolt of fear dispelled her happiness.

She left the embassy and met him halfway across the courtyard. If this was bad news, she wanted to be the one who gave it to Bhakriya. "Yes?" she said.

The man stopped a short distance from her. "The man you brought to us last night," he said. "He's awake. And he's asking for someone named Bhakriya."

CHAPTER THIRTY-EIGHT

Lamprophyre offered to carry Bhakriya to the healing center, feeling an urgency to see Depik really was well, but Bhakriya declined. "I need to calm myself," she told Lamprophyre. "But please tell him I'm on my way."

When Lamprophyre arrived, however, they wouldn't let her see Depik. "He's weak enough we don't want to move him," the balding healer said, "and not to be rude, my lady ambassador, but you won't fit into any of the rooms." So Lamprophyre waited impatiently for Bhakriya to arrive and be ushered into Depik's room, then she shamelessly eavesdropped on the two of them until their thoughts became the wordless hum that said they were kissing. Kissing was so wonderful. Satisfied, she winged her way back to the embassy and went back to sleep.

When she woke again, it was well on the way to being noon, and she was starving. Not wanting to delay seeing Rokshan again, she bought a cow from the butcher's three streets over and roasted it outside the city, devouring the juicy meat fast enough to make her feel uncomfortably full. Then she flew to Kolmira, clutching the green chalcedony pendant as if it would lead her to Rokshan.

What led her to Rokshan, in the end, was her sense of their

pair-bond, better than any beacon. He waited for her outside the city walls, downstream along the Rindra River about twenty dragonlengths. "Bath," he said when she descended to meet him. "You'll feel better."

Lamprophyre started to protest when she realized her dust bath hadn't done more than rid her of the worst stains, and there was fresher blood smeared across her abdomen where she'd held Depik on the way to the healing center. She jumped far out into the river, sending up a great wave to swamp Rokshan, who had fortunately already shed his clothes.

Disregarding her wings' comfort, she sank beneath the surface of the river and closed her nictitating membranes so she could view the underwater world. It was murky and indistinct, not just from the membranes but from the silt she'd thrown up when she jumped in. Still, the scene was beautiful, with the early sunlight slanting through the water and the long, trailing weeds of the riverbed waving as if they wanted to fly like dragons.

She rose gasping from beneath the water and swiped water from her face. "You were right, I needed that," she said.

Rokshan was peacefully floating nearby. "I knew you wouldn't have thought of bathing, even though you were covered with that female's blood. Yesterday was overwhelming."

"You have no idea." She bobbed next to him and told him about the thieves, and Depik's injury. About halfway through the story, Rokshan sat up and began treading water. Telling the story was easier now that she knew Depik would live. Her anger of the previous night was still there, but distant, like an echo that took a dozen beats to return.

When she finished, Rokshan said, "We have to do something about Viveki. She can't be allowed to go on attacking us."

"The one thief knew she'd spread the rumor of my supposed hoard. He didn't know it originated with her, he just identified her as the person who told him the story. The other thief had heard it from his companions."

"That's not enough to convict her of a crime." He scowled, but his eyes were fixed on a point beyond her head. "Unfortunately, she's a small but persistent problem. Sardonyx's threat is far more dangerous."

"I don't even know what we could do to Viveki." Lamprophyre stretched her wings above the water's surface and flapped them hard, sending up a fresh, water-tinged wind. "Unless we caught her committing a crime. I can't believe she can't be held at fault for what happened to Depik. She was ultimately responsible."

"Human law judges direct actions. The man who stabbed Depik will be punished for it, once they catch him." Rokshan went back to floating. "I'll give it some thought. There has to be something."

"I want to spend the day swimming, but I really ought to get back. We have to arrange for grave markers for Porphyry and for all the humans who died." Lamprophyre waded to shore and shook herself. She knew she looked like an animal when she did that, but with Rokshan the only one around to see, she didn't care.

Rokshan followed her, swiping excess water from his skin and using his shirt to dry himself. "I'll come with you, but we'll need to stop at headquarters first so I can let them know what happened with the Fanishkorite caravan. I was in such a hurry I left the other pendant behind."

"I can't believe it was only yesterday. It feels like forever ago."

She was glad to fly in companionable silence. With as emotionally fraught as the past day and night had been, it felt wonderful to simply bask in the warmth of her pair-bond and let her mind drift, thinking of nothing in particular. She occasionally listened to Rokshan's thoughts for the pleasure of the added companionship, but his mind drifted too, his thoughts sharpening once or twice as he contemplated some task in his future.

"What did you tell Yalini?" she said as an idle memory struck her.

"When?"

"Last night, before I went back to Tanajital."

Rokshan chuckled. "I told her she was an attention-starved—actually, you shouldn't learn the words I used."

"I already know most human swear words from Darsha, Rokshan. You can't shock me."

"No, but I was angry, and I'd rather not relive the moment. Let's just say I called her some ugly words and told her she was a worthless excuse for a human being I wouldn't have married on a dare."

Lamprophyre gasped. "That's rather harsh."

"You didn't hear what she said about you that prompted my words. I was gentle with her. Did you really threaten to make her disappear?"

Lamprophyre thought back over the evening. "I don't remember. I think so. I was pretty angry myself."

"Well, she won't bother us again. Fortunately, she's not like Viveki, eager for revenge. I judge her self-worth is tied up in pretending I don't exist and didn't reject her. And she lives in Fanishkor, far from us and far from anywhere she might be obnoxious."

Tanajital's walls gleamed rosy-yellow in the distance. "I'm grateful for that, too," Lamprophyre said, and began the slow curving descent to the training grounds.

Soldiers in royal colors, green and yellow, thronged the field when she arrived. She alit cautiously, listening for any cries of pain or dismay that might mean she'd trampled someone, and curled her tail around herself and furled her wings to make herself smaller. Rokshan hopped down, said, "I'll be right back," and ran inside the headquarters.

Lamprophyre smiled at the nearest soldiers, who eyed her warily and hurried about their errands faster. Their thoughts weren't fearful, only uncertain, and before she was forced to block them all because of the noise, she heard one think *wish I could ride a dragon.* That was a better reaction than she could have hoped for, even if the idea of riding with a strange human made her uncomfortable.

She wished she understood the military better, to know the meaning of their marching back and forth. They either circled the training grounds or gathered into ranks and marched to the parkland and out of sight. Their ranks reminded her of Sardonyx's dragons, and she suppressed a shudder. Flying in orderly ranks wasn't anything to be frightened of, and Sardonyx's dragons would be a threat even if they were disorganized. It was just that all those dragons, all those humans even, doing everything in unison was creepy, like seeing shapes in clouds even though clouds were just water mist.

She watched the line of soldiers go around again and yawned. Rokshan had a funny idea of what "be right back" meant. She wasn't sleepy, but she was bored, and she wanted his business here finished so they could get on with more important things.

She felt him coming back and sat up alertly. Soon he emerged, followed by General Sajan and two other men bearing captains' insignia. But rather than cross the field to her, he led the way to another building, this one almost as big as the headquarters, and went inside with the other men. Lamprophyre, taken aback that he hadn't even spoken to her, walked to the building and crouched low to look inside.

Unlike the headquarters, which had a row of glass windows all down its length, this other building had only two windows flanking the door. When Lamprophyre tried to look inside, she discovered the windows were blank as if something covered them on the inside. Frustrated, she sat back and blew an annoyed smoke ring. Rokshan hadn't gone very far from the entrance, but that was all she could tell.

She settled down about half a dragonlength from the door, which would put her very close to the humans when they emerged. She didn't care if they might consider that intimidating. She lowered herself to lie so her head was level with the door, another potentially intimidating move, but also one she didn't feel bad about.

Time passed. The soldiers cleared the field, and she was alone. Still Rokshan didn't return. She felt him moving around inside the building, which wasn't big enough for her to lose her sense of their pair-bond, but none of his movements told her anything about what was going on. More soldiers marched back into the training grounds. She hadn't paid close enough attention to know whether they were the ones she'd seen leaving. She blew more smoke rings. They really were easy once you knew how.

Finally the door opened, and Lamprophyre sat up. Only Rokshan came through the door. "I have something to show you," he said.

"What took so long?" Lamprophyre replied, more irritably than she'd intended.

"It's not important. Come around back," Rokshan said.

Lamprophyre walked around the building to where General Sajan and the two captains waited. There was another door on that side, one that stood open, and as she came around the corner, another man, this one an ordinary soldier, came through the door. He held a bulky gray cylinder the length of his torso in his arms, carrying it like a human baby. Chunks of pyrite studded the cylinder's pale surface.

"That looks like a tiny pyrite weapon," she said.

Rokshan turned her way. He was smiling. "Watch this," he said. He held out his hand for the cylinder, which the soldier handed over easily. It looked heavy, but Rokshan held it as if it weighed almost nothing. Now that it was closer, Lamprophyre could see the cylinder tapered at one end, where the biggest chunk of pyrite was embedded. Rokshan tucked the fatter end of the cylinder under his left arm, gripped the narrow end with his right hand, and rested his left hand on a pyrite crystal near the cylinder's middle.

Lamprophyre was about to ask what she was supposed to watch when Rokshan braced himself as if preparing to take a punch. The air hummed, a sound that went from nothing to teeth-rattlingly loud in two beats. Then the hum stopped, the cylinder shimmered with heat haze, and a bright flash shot from the cylinder to strike the nearest tree. With a crack, the tree's upper branches shattered.

Lamprophyre stared at the tree, then at Rokshan, who was grinning like a maniac. "It worked," he said.

"You made them smaller," Lamprophyre said. "I don't understand. Why would you make them smaller if it takes a big one to kill a dragon?"

"Allow me to demonstrate. God's breath, I hope Father doesn't kill me when he sees what I've done to the trees." The hum had already built again, and Rokshan aimed the cylinder's tip at another tree. This one's trunk splintered and cracked as the light struck it. Then, in quick succession, Rokshan blasted tree after tree until an entire row of them lay fallen along the edge of the parkland.

"You still don't understand," he said as Lamprophyre continued to stare. "They fire faster, they're more mobile than the big ones—and they're only a little less powerful. This is what I was working on, Lamprophyre. They made it work."

Lamprophyre examined the weapon Rokshan held out to her. "So, are there a lot of them?" she asked. "Because it would take a lot of these to protect a city."

"They're not for mounting on the ground," Rokshan said. He offered her the weapon again. "They're for being carried into battle. By a dragon."

Lamprophyre jerked her hand away as if the thing had stung her, though she'd barely touched it. "By a *dragon?*"

"Dragons maneuver faster than the ground-based weapons. It's perfect. Here, try it."

Lamprophyre took the thing reluctantly. It was as light as she'd suspected. "How does it work?"

"You saw how I held it. Your left hand controls the firing rate. See, this crystal rotates—"

"Rokshan, don't!"

Rokshan smiled. "It won't fire unless your right hand rests *here*. That tells the weapon to be ready. Then you click the crystal once, turning it in the direction away from you, and that generates a pulse of power."

Lamprophyre hesitantly aimed the weapon at the already damaged trees. The hum was tangible with her hands in contact with the weapon. She cradled the weapon along one arm, wrapped her hand around the narrow end of the cylinder, and clicked the crystal one notch. The cylinder jolted like a bee-stung horse, and she nearly dropped it in surprise, but the flash of light flew straight at her target, sending up another cloud of splinters.

"Fly with it. See how it feels," Rokshan urged.

Lamprophyre pushed off and flapped a few dragonlengths into the air. She was starting to understand what Rokshan had in mind. She rose a little higher, then curved and sailed toward the trees. Aiming carefully, she shot—and missed. Her movement had been too fast. She flew back around and tried again. Another miss. Frustrated, she slowed her flight and tried a third time. This time, she hit a tree—just not the one she'd aimed at.

She came back to land next to Rokshan and handed him the weapon. "I'm sorry. I must not be a very good shot."

Rokshan was biting his lip in frustration. "I don't think that's it," he said. "I think coordinating flight and firing the weapon is complicated. It will take time for you to get used to it."

"But we don't *have* time." Lamprophyre's frustration equaled his.

"Maybe if we added something to let her more easily aim at a target," one of the captains said.

"That would make flying impossible. She'd have to hold the weapon to her eye," the other captain objected.

"Well, what do you suggest?"

"Make it even smaller. Less awkward."

"We already sacrificed power for size. Any smaller, and she might as well beat her enemy over the head with it."

Lamprophyre listened to the captains absently, her eyes on the weapon. Coordinating flying and firing. She'd watched the soldiers on the city wall with their crossbows, how they would run to a firing position and then hold still. If it was just a matter of getting the weapon in range—

She turned to Rokshan. "Climb up. Bring the weapon."

"What do you—" Enlightenment flashed across Rokshan's face. "Would that work?"

"I don't know. Let's try."

With Rokshan securely settled, she gained altitude as quickly as possible. "I'm going to fly past those trees, with a gentle descent," she said. "I don't want you falling off."

"Wish we had the harness," Rokshan said. "All right, *go!*"

Lamprophyre began her descent. As she neared the trees, she banked slightly, tilting Rokshan toward them. A flash of light struck the trees, then another, and another, until dark specks filled her vision when she closed her eyes. Behind her, trees toppled, bearing other trees down. She heard shouting from below and curved back around to land beside the building. The two captains were hugging each other and jumping up and down. General Sajan looked as if he'd witnessed a miracle.

Rokshan leaped down as soon as Lamprophyre landed and hugged her. "It worked," he said. "You were right. The dragon maneuvers and the rider shoots."

"It's a perfect solution," Sajan said. "Thank Jiwanyil. How soon can we bring the flight here?"

"It's not perfect," Rokshan said. "Dragons don't like flying with strangers. It will be hard to convince them to take riders."

Lamprophyre looked at her mate, whose face was alight with hope. A sick feeling stole over her. "It's impossible," she said.

Both men turned to look at her. "What are you talking about? You just proved otherwise," Sajan said.

"Because no dragon will agree to take a human into battle," Lamprophyre said. "We're immune to fire and acid. Humans aren't. And Sardonyx and her dragons won't hesitate to go after our riders. It would be a disaster. I'm sorry, General."

"But they'd know the risk—"

"She's right," Rokshan said. "We're not talking about soldiers here. We're talking about friends. We'll have to find another solution."

Sajan looked like he wanted to argue, just not with a dragon. "I really am sorry," Lamprophyre said. "Maybe, if we practice hard enough—"

"You didn't see what we did," Sajan said. "A human riding a

dragon has a better arc of fire than a dragon would. Even if you dragons master the weapon, it's still a less optimal solution."

"It will still work," Rokshan said. "And those weapons are miraculous regardless." He clapped Sajan on the shoulder. "I'll bring the dragons tomorrow morning to start practicing."

"Sooner would be better," Sajan said.

Rokshan exchanged glances with Lamprophyre. "We have another commitment this afternoon," Rokshan said. "One that shouldn't wait any longer."

CHAPTER THIRTY-NINE

The men and women at the marble quarry didn't argue with Dolomite when he explained what he needed. Lamprophyre paid, and the dragons came away with three slabs of unfinished marble. They flew over the shrouded figure of Rokshan's statue on the way out. Lamprophyre tried not to feel discouraged, as if the beautiful statue represented something she would never have. It wasn't true. It was just a matter of time before Rokshan was transformed. But after the success of the new weapons and the frustration of knowing they couldn't work, optimism felt just out of reach.

Flint led the way back to the burial site. Nothing had disturbed the graves, which lay near each other as if the humans meant to keep Porphyry company for eternity. The female dragon's grave was some distance away. Lamprophyre blessed the humans who'd known to do that. The idea of Porphyry's killer lying next to him made her sick.

The dragons set down the marble slabs and stretched fingers gone sore from carrying the stone all that way. "I told Chaaksha we would set up headstones, and her people could come back and put the names on," Rokshan said. "I know they kept careful track of who was buried where. Fanishkorites consider the grave marker an essential part of their burial rites."

"Then—Orthoclase, Lamprophyre, and Bromargyrite, why don't you cut the smaller stones for the humans, and Coquina and I will help Dolomite," Flint said in his usual decisive way. "We all want to carve part of the stone for Porphyry, right?"

"I'm not good at carving," Lamprophyre protested.

"It doesn't matter. It's more important that we all have a hand in remembering him," Dolomite said. "And I want you to write his name. You're the only one of us who knows how, and he was so proud of being able to read human writing."

That relieved Lamprophyre's mind. She set to work cutting the slabs into smaller rectangles and shaping their surfaces smooth. It was good, comfortable, mindless work, and Rokshan sat beside her, not speaking, which comforted her more. Whenever she or Bromargyrite or Orthoclase finished a stone, Rokshan took it and set it in the earth at the head of a grave. There were far too many of them. Lamprophyre hoped the stones were big enough, given that Rokshan had no trouble lifting them, but he didn't correct them, so she guessed it was all right.

By the time they finished, it was nearly sunset, and Bromargyrite handed around chunks of waste marble for a much-needed snack. Lamprophyre ate hers and regarded Porphyry's grave marker. It was made to lie flat over his body, not stand upright at the head of the grave, and Dolomite had done some of the carving already. Coquina was working on adding curves and lines crossing the curves to one corner.

"Everyone put something in," Dolomite said. Lamprophyre waited until the edges were finished, a marvelous patchwork of different shapes and artistic styles that nevertheless felt right. Then she bent over the blank center of the rectangle and traced, in her most careful handwriting, the name:

PORPHYRY

and, after a moment's thought, wrote below it the words:

RACE THE WIND

"What does it say?" Coquina asked.

"I wrote what he always used to say, that he'd race the wind if there were no other challengers." Lamprophyre carefully went over the words several times until they were deeply incised, the edges clear and sharp.

She sat back, and Dolomite leaned past her and made a last few swipes with his claws. When he finished, a stone dragon seemed to leap from the flat surface just above the writing. Dolomite had captured the essence of a dragon with those last swipes, so it both looked nothing like a real dragon and could also not be mistaken for anything else. Lamprophyre stared at it for a while. "It looks like him," she finally said. "Or—like he was at heart."

The clutch gathered around in silence. The wind had picked up, and it blew loose dirt from the graves across Porphyry's stone and on toward distant Tanajital. Lamprophyre closed her nictitating membranes against the blowing dust and watched the sun set. Through the dust, the sun's rays were orange and crimson, warmer than they'd been all day. It was a beautiful sight.

"I don't want to be sad anymore," she declared. "I'm going to miss Porphyry for the rest of my life. But sadness won't change that. It won't make his loss less if I can remember how I loved him."

The others shifted restlessly. "I was thinking—the city will mourn him, too," Orthoclase said. "You know how popular he was. I think we should celebrate who he was."

"I'd rather think about that than how we'll never argue about who's the better racer again," Flint said. "Let's go. We can eat, and plan a celebration Tanajital will never forget."

"Wait," Coquina said. "Just—wait a moment."

They all paused to look at her. She stood with her feet firmly planted beside the stone and her wings flung out behind her for balance, her eyes closed and her head tilted as if she were listening to the wind whisper. A few beats passed, and Coquina opened her eyes. "Nothing," she said. "I hoped, if there is a God, that she or he might manifest here and now. But maybe there's nothing, after all."

"We haven't really had a God in more than a millennium," Orthoclase said. "If you consider that Mother Stone never was real. And we did all right."

"I don't know that I need something to worship," Coquina said. "But if something created us, I'd like to think that something didn't just create and then walk away. I've always liked the idea of rejoining all the other dragons after my death. And more than anything, I want to believe in a God who had a purpose for us. None of that would change my instincts about how dragons should live. It would just be...nice."

"Maybe someday we'll figure it out," Lamprophyre said.

Coquina shrugged. "Let's go. Wherever Porphyry's spirit is now, it's not under this stone." She laughed. "Maybe he's finally able to beat me on the straightaway."

"Let's race back to the city, just in case," Bromargyrite said, and they did.

~

The following morning, Lamprophyre and Rokshan were the first to the training grounds. The marching humans were gone. Instead of an empty field of packed earth, bales of hay dotted the training grounds at random intervals. Head-sized circles of wood lay scattered among the bales, some of them painted red or blue, others plain. Boxes filled with more wood circles stood beside the military headquarters. It looked messy, like the aftermath of a human celebration, but without empty wine glasses or scraps of food.

Lamprophyre landed cautiously, in case the position of the hay bales and the wood circles mattered, and let Rokshan jump down. She picked up the nearest piece of wood, a blue circle, and sniffed it. As expected, it smelled of wood and paint, tangy and bitter all at once. "What is this?" she asked.

"Targets, I think," Rokshan said. "We talked about what would be the most efficient way for you to practice, without destroying most of the parkland. But now I'm having second thoughts."

"Why is that? Because these are all good targets. They're small enough that if we can hit them, we'll certainly be able to hit a dragon."

"I'm more concerned about you not hitting each other. You all move fast enough you will probably avoid most force pulses, but there are always accidents."

"Oh." That hadn't occurred to Lamprophyre. "I have an idea for that, but I'll need to talk to the others."

Rokshan nodded. "I'll let Sajan know we're here." He ran off to the headquarters building and disappeared inside.

Lamprophyre dropped the target and turned in a slow circle, assessing the field. If the new weapons weren't as powerful as the ones protecting the cities, it wouldn't be fatal to be hit by one accidentally, but it would also be harder to kill Sardonyx's people. They'd need practice in more than just hitting a target; they'd need to know where on a body to strike and how many hits were needed to kill.

She shuddered and closed her eyes. Such casual thoughts of killing. She hated Sardonyx for turning her and her friends into killers. Dragons didn't fight each other, or hadn't before now. They solved their problems through talk and understanding. The sooner Sardonyx's people were gone, the sooner dragons could be themselves again. But deep inside, Lamprophyre feared Sardonyx had opened a gate no dragons could close.

She heard the sound of wings and opened her eyes. Bromargyrite and Orthoclase were descending, their great wings filling the sky. "What *is* this mess?" Orthoclase exclaimed. "We're not supposed to clean this up, are we? Because I feel that's beneath me. That's why they have soldiers."

"No, it's for us to shoot at," Lamprophyre said.

More wings sounded, and Flint and Coquina came to join them. "Dolomite is with Tekentriya," Coquina said. "We told her about practicing with the weapons, and she just rolled her eyes and said her business was more important. Which might be true, but honestly, I think she just likes flying."

"If it keeps her from turning her crankiness on Rokshan, I don't care what she does," Lamprophyre said. "And speaking of Rokshan, it looks like it's time."

Rokshan was crossing the field toward them, joined by General Sajan and, to her surprise, Kamil. They were trailed by a couple of soldiers carrying wooden crates with gray pyrite-studded cylinders stacked inside them. "Good morning," Sajan said, saluting each dragon as if they were his own commanders. "Thank you for your willingness to help. We owe you dragons a debt I fear we'll never be able to repay."

"Dragons and humans fought Sardonyx together a millennium ago," Lamprophyre said. "We believe this union is how we'll both survive."

"But if you're worried about repayment, we all love cow," Bromargyrite said.

Sajan chuckled. "A small price to pay for survival." He took one of the weapons from a crate and held it out for them to examine. "The weapon is simple. Rest your hand here to turn it on, turn this crystal here to fire a pulse of power."

"How powerful is it?" Flint asked.

Sajan glanced at Kamil in invitation. "Less powerful in the absolute than a ground-based weapon," Kamil said, "but proportionately it's more powerful. That means it's strong enough to knock a dragon out of the sky if you hit the head," he said when the dragons looked confused. "A head shot at medium range will kill. Anywhere else, you can incapacitate your target. Multiple shots to the same location can kill as well—for example, hitting the abdomen a few times will turn internal organs to jelly."

"I didn't know you were working on this," Bromargyrite said.

Kamil shrugged. "My part of the mind-reading artifact is learning to cut kyanite small enough for personal use. I understand miniaturization better than anyone."

"Of course you do," Coquina murmured with a smile.

That made Kamil grin. "I wouldn't say it if it weren't true," he said. "It's thanks to me that a crystal the size of my fist can deliver the same amount of force we used to only get from a crystal the size of *your* fist."

"I may have to reconsider my use of the word 'obnoxious,'" Bromargyrite said.

"You should, my friend," Kamil said, slapping him lightly on the shoulder.

"Obnoxious or not, Kamil is the one to ask for details about how the weapons work," Rokshan said.

"But I haven't solved the problem of our people being accidentally hit," Kamil said, suddenly very serious.

"I have, mostly," Lamprophyre said. "Remember playing blind-my-eyes?"

The others nodded. "It's been years, though. I'm not sure how good I still am," Orthoclase said.

"It's one more thing to practice," Lamprophyre said. "It's a game dragonets play where we fly patterns around our clutchmates while closing our eyes. It—" She realized she couldn't tell them the game worked because dragons could hear each other's thoughts. "It's not complicated," she said. "And it means we know where each other are. I think it will keep us from hitting each other."

"Let's start with familiarizing you with the weapons," Rokshan said.

Lamprophyre accepted one of the cylinders and turned it over, examining it closely. The ceramic casing was lightweight enough she felt confident she could hold it in the firing position indefinitely. Without putting her hand on the activation spot, she worked the crystal a few clicks. "Will it go on firing forever?"

"Once you've used up the power, the weapon has to have its firing crystal replaced," Kamil said. "But that still gives you more than thirty pulses. Don't worry about using them up while you're practicing. It will give *us* practice at replacing the crystals rapidly."

Bromargyrite turned abruptly and aimed his weapon at a distant bale of hay. A hum, a quiet thump, and a flash of light shot from the weapon to ground itself half a dragonlength from the hay. "I know what its range is now," he said.

"That's the other thing. The range is shorter than the ground-based weapons," Kamil said, "or so I'm told. I don't know how far those can shoot. But the range on these is about three hundred feet."

"That's ten dragonlengths," Lamprophyre told the others.

"Far enough to keep us from coming into contact with Sardonyx's monsters," Orthoclase said.

"Then let's start practicing," Flint said.

Lamprophyre caught Coquina's eye. The green dragon smiled and shrugged. Well, if Coquina didn't mind being pair-bonded to a bossy male, that was none of Lamprophyre's business. Besides, Flint was smart and decisive, so what did it matter that he wasn't female?

She took a few shots at the hay bales, all of which struck their targets. She wasn't impressed with herself. Shooting while flying was far more difficult, and it would take time to master that.

After a while, the clutch took to the skies, and Sajan summoned a squad of soldiers, maybe twenty men, to toss wooden targets into the air. Lamprophyre did all right if she could hover to take her shot, but the moment she and the target were both in motion, she missed. Every time. She clenched her jaw in frustration and persisted. These weapons would keep any more of her friends from being killed like Porphyry, and she *would* learn to use them.

She'd flown back to back with the others for a thousand beats while they all worked out range and movement. Then it was time for something more complicated. "All in," she shouted, and the clutch gathered around her. "Let's see if we can still fly blind."

Blind-my-eyes was a fun game for dragonets, intended to teach them how to hear surface thoughts without listening deeper and do it on the wing. Lamprophyre closed her eyes and listened, locating each of her clutchmates by their thoughts. All of them but Bromargyrite were thinking about how hard this all was. Bromargyrite was thinking about food, a nice chunk of calcite, and Lamprophyre's stomach rumbled. The others laughed, and she opened her eyes to see Bromargyrite grinning. "Humans and their midday meals are such a bad influence," he said.

She could still sense the presence of her clutchmates, how they hovered nearby. "Everyone ready?"

The others nodded.

"Then—fly, fly!"

They split apart like a colorful seed pod, each tracking a different target. Lamprophyre shot, missed, shot again, struck the corner of a target completely by accident, and dodged Flint without looking at him. At least the blind-flying was working. She was so frustrated at her ineptitude she wanted to scream and throw the weapon at the target. She might actually hit one that way.

Finally, she thought *Time to come down* and drifted to the ground. The others alit around her. "How did we do?" Flint asked Rokshan, who'd run out to meet them.

"It was a good first attempt," Rokshan said.

They all turned on him, frowning. He held up his hands to fend them off. "All right, yes, that's the same as saying terrible," he said. "But we knew this would take time. And nobody ran into anybody else's shot, so that worked. Let's be grateful for what we have."

"I need to rest," Coquina said. "That kind of flying is much harder than racing or cross-country flight."

"And I really do think we need something to eat," Bromargyrite said. "No joking. We don't normally work that hard."

"I'll arrange it," Rokshan said. "You all wait behind the armaments building so the men can clear the field."

The armaments building turned out to be where they built the weapons. The six dragons sat in a circle in the soft grass between it and the strip of parkland and stretched cramped arms. "Do we really think this will work?" Orthoclase said.

"Archers take years to hone their skills," Kamil said from his seat next to Bromargyrite. "At least you hit things most of the time."

"You're so encouraging," Flint said.

"I think it's important to be honest," Kamil said, "otherwise how can anyone ever improve, if they believe they're already successful?"

"I agree," Coquina said. "And I'm trying to stay optimistic. But..."

Lamprophyre sat back and stared up at the sky. "And Sardonyx could strike at any moment."

"Let's hope she doesn't," Coquina said.

TWO DAYS LATER, WORD OF SARDONYX'S LATEST ATTACK CAME TO Tanajital. "Nishta again," Rokshan told Lamprophyre as they prepared to sleep. "This time, she destroyed it completely."

"Hyaloclast said the flight did almost no good," Lamprophyre said. "They were mostly a distraction. Sardonyx just flew away when the city was rubble. They couldn't afford to follow her, but she went south."

"Sachetan is south," Rokshan said. He rolled over on his mattress to stare at the ceiling. "God's breath, but I hope the Sachetanese government took our warning seriously."

"They worship Jiwanyil too, don't they? Wouldn't he have given them prophecies?"

"The trouble is that those prophecies are meaningless if you don't know about Sardonyx. Father warned Anchala, and she'll tell Torannum, and he's powerful in their government. It might be enough."

Lamprophyre settled down and spread one wing, leaving the other furled so she could look at Rokshan. "If we knew Sardonyx's plan... 'complete destruction of humanity' is a desire rather than a strategy. If we knew how she chooses her targets, we could be prepared."

"We can use scouts like she does."

"Hyaloclast does that. But even as fast as our dragons fly, by the time a scout sees Sardonyx attack a city and race back to bring the flight there, it's all over."

Rokshan let out a deep sigh. "The weapons are coming along nicely."

"You're being overly optimistic again. I still can't hit a moving target at speed. Coquina is the best of us, and even she only hits one target out of three."

"It's been three days, Lamprophyre. You're all doing amazingly well."

Lamprophyre nodded. "I suppose."

"Get some sleep," Rokshan said. "Tomorrow will be better."

Lamprophyre didn't believe that, but she didn't want to argue with her mate when he was trying so hard to cheer her up. She folded her other wing over herself and went to sleep.

Gray skies greeted her the following morning, matching her mood. She grumped her way through half a cow and all the way to the training ground, where she took up a weapon wearily. What was the point, really? She was never going to be able to do anything with the thing but make Sardonyx laugh.

She was the last to the training ground, all except for Dolomite. Irritably, she said, "When is the last time any of us have talked to Dolomite? Tekentriya takes up all of his time."

"He slept in his warehouse for the first time in days last night," Orthoclase said, "but he was gone before the rest of us woke this morning."

"Well, I don't know why she thinks she can monopolize him. I'm worried about his mental state. He was so angry over Porphyry." Lamprophyre lowered her weapon and watched

Rokshan, who'd left her without a word to go into the headquarters building when they arrived. Now he emerged and walked across the field to the armaments building. What was he up to? Something else useless, probably. It wasn't his fault that every plan they'd made had failed.

Swift motion caught her eye, and she half-turned to watch a young woman race across the training grounds to headquarters. That was so unusual—no women were soldiers—she kept on watching after the girl had entered the building and slammed the door shut behind herself. The young woman hadn't worn a soldier's uniform or royal green and yellow livery; she'd been dressed plainly, like one of Tekentriya's spies.

"Just a moment," she said absently to something Bromargyrite said, and walked toward the headquarters. When she was a couple of dragonlengths away, the door opened, and the girl came outside. She cast a startled look at Lamprophyre, then darted away to the armaments building and slammed that door behind her.

Now Lamprophyre was convinced something important was going on. How she wished she were human-sized for once! She approached the armaments building and bent low to peer through the window, which was still covered on the inside. Irritably, she listened for thoughts. There were only five people inside. The girl's thoughts were exhausted and numb because she'd run far to bring this message. Two of the others were listening to someone talk, and their thoughts reflected that. One was thinking *unbelievable, must be a trick, or sabotage*. And Rokshan's thoughts were all focused on, for some reason, Chaaksha: *she could have done it, but how? Need someone to prove it.*

Her curiosity twisted nearly to the breaking point, Lamprophyre knocked lightly on the door. After a moment, a stranger opened it. He gasped when he saw her. "Ah," he said, "yes? My lady ambassador?"

"I want to talk to Rokshan," Lamprophyre said.

The stranger backed away. Rokshan pushed past him. "Do you know where Kamil is?" he demanded.

"I—no. What's going on?"

Rokshan shook his head distractedly. "We need—God's breath, this is incredible—I don't know who was working on the shield problem, but I have to talk to whoever it is."

"Rokshan," Lamprophyre said in her most patient voice, "tell me something or I will tear the roof off this building."

Rokshan focused on her as if he hadn't seen her before now. "It's Fanishkor's shield artifacts," he said. "One just turned up here."

CHAPTER FORTY

"Turned up?" Lamprophyre said. "That's impossible."

"I don't know how else to describe it," Rokshan said. "Supposedly one of Tekentriya's spies negotiated with a Fanishkorite agent to buy it. But the message Tekentriya sent along with it said she thought someone in the Fanishkorite government was behind the transaction. As in, someone in power made it happen."

"Chaaksha," Lamprophyre said. "But how?"

"I don't know. But she's the only one in a position to do something like that who we know is sympathetic to our cause." Rokshan was running his fingers through his hair, disordering it. "And it matters that we figure out the truth, or have one of our adepts analyze the artifact, because if this is a trick—if it's set to explode, or fail at a crucial moment—it could devastate our defense."

"I'll ask Bromargyrite where Kamil is," Lamprophyre said. "Even if he isn't working on the shield, he probably knows more about it than the people who are."

"I had the same thought," Rokshan said, racing past her toward the other dragons sitting quietly together.

"Kamil intended to be here this morning," Bromargyrite said when they accosted him, "but he's not an early riser. I could go to his house, except he lives in one of those parts of Tanajital where the houses all share walls, and there's nowhere to land that I won't destroy something."

"We can wait," Rokshan said. "God's breath, I hate waiting. This is what we've been hoping for."

"I can't believe Chaaksha did it," Flint said. "I mean, I know she was grateful, but I didn't think she was in a position to help."

"Let's just be grateful that she did," Lamprophyre said. "Rokshan, what exactly did Tekentriya's spy bring?"

"A cut stone. Topaz, I think," Rokshan said. "A note with a lot of nonsense I didn't understand that I think is adept code. And another note, this one from Tekentriya, explaining where the stone came from and saying she'd be here this afternoon to find out what we made of it. Which means we have to act fast, because Tekentriya won't think twice about shredding the lot of us if we haven't made use of her spies' efforts."

"She can try," Bromargyrite said complacently. "And that's Kamil now."

Lamprophyre managed not to leap on the adept and carry him across the field to where they all waited. Kamil waved as he approached, and shouted, "Why aren't you practicing?"

"We have the Fanishkorite shield," Rokshan said.

His brevity impressed Lamprophyre, as did Kamil's stunned reaction. He came to a stop half a dragonlength away. "Is this a joke?"

"No joke. Come with me," Rokshan said.

Lamprophyre followed the two men as they raced toward the armaments building. "Rokshan, don't you dare do this indoors," she said when he opened the door. "We all want to see. And if you think I'm capable of taking the roof off this building, imagine how fast six dragons can do it."

"Fair enough," Rokshan said. "Kamil, wait here."

It took barely ten beats for Rokshan to return. He held a wooden box the size of his palm in one hand and a dirty sheet of folded paper in the other. "This is what came with it," he said, handing the paper to Kamil. He worked the lid off the box and displayed its contents. The tangy aroma of topaz rose from the box, but whatever was inside was almost too small for Lamprophyre to see, especially when her clutchmates crowded around. It was about the size of her small sixth claw and teardrop-shaped, with the fat end of the drop faceted to sparkle in full light. With the skies as gray as they were, it didn't reflect much of anything.

Kamil glanced over the paper too fast to have read it, then took the box from Rokshan and brought it close to his eyes. "I've never seen a cut like this before," he said, his voice distant as if he were thinking hard. "But all those facets, in a complete circle... yes, I can see how these would reflect force, and if..." He lowered the box and looked at the paper again, reading this time. "It would take hundreds of these to blanket a city, but it would be a perfect shield. God's breath. I can't imagine how hard this is to cut."

"So it's impossible." Rokshan's voice was flat, the sound he made when he was trying not to be discouraged.

"No, not impossible. If we got as many lapidary-adepts as are capable, start them working immediately, we could have Tanajital shielded in a week. But they'd get faster as they went." Kamil still sounded as if his voice was coming from far away. "I wonder who thought of using these to make a net. It's obviously not their original use."

"What's the original use?" Lamprophyre asked.

Kamil looked up at her, startled. "What? Oh. Probably armor. They're for personal shields. But of course it's impractical to shield a city by giving each individual one of these. Though they'd be more efficient that way."

Rokshan grabbed Kamil's shoulder and swung him back to face him. "Say that again," he demanded.

"Say what? Armor?"

"Personal shields," Rokshan said. He looked up at Lamprophyre. "God's breath. They're for shielding an individual."

Lamprophyre felt as stunned as if he'd shot her with one of the weapons. "They absorb fire and acid," she said. "They probably absorb whatever energy those weapons fire, too."

Rokshan gingerly picked up the topaz teardrop. "Is it active now?"

Kamil peered at it. "Yes. Though I'm not sure—"

Rokshan backed away. "Lamprophyre?"

"If it doesn't work, you're going to be in a lot of pain," she said.

Kamil glanced from her to Rokshan. "Wait, you aren't going to—"

Lamprophyre sucked in air and breathed out fire to engulf Rokshan.

It was as diffuse as she could make it, because she wasn't as confident as Rokshan seemed to be. But it didn't matter. As the fire struck him, a fine mesh of orange-yellow sprang up scant finger-widths from Rokshan's body. The mesh glowed more yellow everywhere the fire touched it. Rokshan raised his left hand, the one not holding the artifact, and the mesh moved with him. Fire flared and vanished, seemingly dispersed by the mesh.

When the fire disappeared, the mesh lasted a beat or two longer and then faded away. Rokshan lowered his hand. He was completely unscathed.

Rokshan and Lamprophyre stared at each other. "*Stones*," Lamprophyre breathed.

"I can't believe that worked," Rokshan said.

"There was a damn good chance it wouldn't have!" Kamil shouted. "Are you out of your mind?"

"Not anymore," Rokshan said. "Forget about shielding the city for now. I need five more of these artifacts as soon as you can manage it. No, in twenty-four hours."

"I don't know if that's possible," Kamil said.

"Now's not the time to lose your confidence, Kamil," Bromargyrite said. "This is going to change the course of this war. Or were you not serious when you said you were the best?"

Kamil looked up at him. For the first time since Lamprophyre had met him, he looked younger than his age. "What will you do with them?"

He'd been addressing Bromargyrite, but it was Lamprophyre who responded. "We are going dragon hunting," she said.

~

LATE THE NEXT AFTERNOON, LAMPROPHYRE SETTLED ON HER haunches surrounded by her clutch and watched Rokshan pace in front of the assembled dragons and humans. "Let's review," he said. "We can't afford to forget anything."

There was murmuring, mostly from the humans, but no one spoke. Rokshan held up an iron chain with links the size of his pinky nail and displayed the topaz teardrop hanging from it. "Everyone has an artifact."

The three other humans fingered their artifacts and nodded. Rokshan nudged the pyrite weapon at his feet. "Two weapons each."

Melika, sitting beside Coquina, tested the leather straps attached to hers. "We drop them when we're done, right?"

"Unless you're in a position to switch," Kamil said. "It's better if we can retrieve them to replace the firing crystal, and they're tough, but they won't survive a fall of fifty feet or more."

"Flying gear," Rokshan went on. "It gets cold up there. Coat, long trousers, gloves, boots, and eyepieces."

Lamprophyre surveyed the humans. None of them were wearing their coats, but it was too warm for that at ground level. Flint's friend Lokun looked the least comfortable, and Lamprophyre remembered he hadn't been enthusiastic about joining their flying force. But she'd listened to his thoughts, and despite his hesitation, he was determined to prove to Flint he wasn't a coward. That was enough for her.

"And the harnesses have been fireproofed, as best we can manage," Rokshan said. "You'll all need to avoid acid, because we couldn't do much to resist that."

"And the shields aren't as effective against acid the thicker the spray," Kamil said. He rubbed his ankle inside his boot. "God's breath, Bromargyrite, how did I let you talk me into this?"

"It was easy, because you secretly want to be an epic hero from the poems," Bromargyrite said with a grin. Kamil reddened, but he smiled as well.

"So now what?" Melika asked. "Do we fly around looking for enemies?"

"We are going west to patrol the Rindra River," Lamprophyre said. "Hyaloclast thinks Sardonyx will send her people north along that river, now that they've showed they can destroy a city. They've gotten bolder over time. Kolmira almost has to be their next target."

The sound of wings alerted Lamprophyre to Dolomite's arrival. Tekentriya sat perched behind his shoulders, feet securely in the harness's stirrups. The crown princess surveyed them all, her expression sour. "Which of those weapons is mine?" she said.

Lamprophyre looked at Rokshan. "Yours?" he asked.

"I want to kill Sardonyx's dragons," Dolomite said. "And Tekentriya feels the same."

"There's no way Father agreed to let his heir go into battle," Rokshan said.

"If I don't, there may not be a kingdom for me to inherit, little brother," Tekentriya said. "Now is not the time for worry over possibilities."

"You've never been a fighter," Rokshan persisted. "I know we're not friends, but you can't imagine I want to see you killed."

Tekentriya's sour expression tightened. "Pass me one of those weapons," she commanded.

Rokshan hesitated a moment before walking over and giving her his weapon. "Go," Tekentriya said, and Dolomite sprang upward, beating the air for altitude. Lamprophyre watched him soar around the training grounds until he was above the denuded, blasted trees Rokshan had demonstrated the weapon on days before. Then he dropped, speeding downward and banking past the trees. Tekentriya aimed. A hum, and a pulse of light, and another, and another, and trees fell like a row of dancers taking a bow. Tekentriya's last shot threaded between two trees to fell the one behind without so much as shaking the leaves of the others.

In silence, everyone watched Dolomite return. Tekentriya still didn't climb down. "I'm no soldier," she told Rokshan. "I am, however, a crack shot with the bow, though you're too young to remember that. And this thing is far more forgiving than a bow. I can take care of myself."

Rokshan nodded. "I guess you can."

Lamprophyre said, "We leave at first light. Be at the warehouses with your gear."

The other humans climbed up, and the dragons separated to return their friends to their homes. Dolomite came to Lamprophyre's side. "I was wrong," he said. "About not being friends with a human. I understand now."

Lamprophyre glanced at Tekentriya, who didn't pretend not to be listening. "I'm glad, Dolomite. Are you...we never see you anymore. Are you all right?"

Dolomite shook his head. "I can't draw," he said. "It's like the anger has driven the knowledge out of my hands. If we can hurt Sardonyx's people, maybe that will change."

"I'm sorry."

"I know. But it's not your fault." He stepped away and spread his wings. "I'll see you in the morning," he said, and flew away. Tekentriya looked back at Lamprophyre as he flew. For once, her expression wasn't bitter or angry.

Lamprophyre looked at Orthoclase. "Are you still willing to go into battle without a rider?"

"I can shoot this thing, and that's what matters," he said. "And I think Flint was right that we shouldn't take just any rider, simply for the sake of going into battle. I'd be so uncomfortable with a stranger, I wouldn't fly well."

"Come have supper with us. Let's pretend everything is normal."

Orthoclase smiled. "I won't turn that invitation down. Depik is a genius."

Beggars were gathering in the courtyard when Lamprophyre, Rokshan, and Orthoclase arrived. The soup smelled different that evening, but Lamprophyre didn't know enough about human food to identify the aroma.

She settled herself next to Orthoclase in the dining pavilion and watched the beggars. So many people in need. She hoped, as she sometimes did, that the people who came for soup weren't taking advantage of a free meal. There were so many who couldn't feed themselves that she didn't like the idea of capable people taking food from them. But there wasn't any way to help that, so mostly she just hoped.

The smell of hot cooked steak wafted past. She drew in a deep breath and sighed. "I love steak. I wish every meal could be steak."

"It wouldn't be special if it was every meal, my lady," Depik said. He pushed the trolley laden with steak in front of her. "I have beef butchered for you, if you'll give me a few minutes to cook it for Orthoclase."

"Thank you. I'm sorry I didn't warn you he was coming."

"I appreciate the effort, Depik," Orthoclase said.

"It's no trouble," Depik said.

When the cook had returned to the kitchen, Orthoclase said in a low voice, "Does he smell like aventurine to you?"

"It's an artifact to help his illness," Lamprophyre replied in the same low voice. "We don't know how well it works yet, because he hasn't had a bad day since he was wounded. But I have hope."

Bhakriya walked past, pushing the cauldron on its wheeled trolley for Depik to refill. Time was one cauldron of soup had been enough. Lamprophyre eavesdropped on Bhakriya and Depik, enjoying how their thoughts of each other were full of affection and love. They'd only been married two days and already the embassy felt more like home, really. Maybe she was wrong about Tanajital not being home. Maybe home was a matter of who you shared your life with.

She swallowed more steak and pushed the trolley toward Orthoclase. "We'll share all the meat. The steak isn't as good if you let it get cold."

Orthoclase nodded. Rokshan appeared from the kitchen with a plate and utensils. "Good steak," he said, helping himself. The three of them ate, contented and not needing to speak. For the first time in many twelvedays, Lamprophyre felt at peace.

Then she saw who'd just walked into the courtyard. "Tarakh," she said, sitting up straighter. "I thought he went back to Leksital."

"Who is Tarakh?" Orthoclase asked.

"Chaaksha's...I don't know. Messenger? Except I think he was more than a messenger. I told him he could come to me in Tanajital if—" She stopped speaking as Tarakh drew up close enough to hear.

"My lady ambassador," he said. "I hope I'm not intruding."

"Of course not, Tarakh. Are you hungry? You're welcome to soup, or steak...?"

Tarakh shook his head. "I went back to Leksital," he said, "but everything reminded me of Oresa. I don't know what I was thinking. I want so badly to hurt the ones who killed her, and yet I'm powerless. What can a human do against dragons?"

"Who is Oresa?" Orthoclase asked.

"She was to be my wife, my lord dragon. She was killed in the attack on our caravan."

Orthoclase nodded. "They killed our clutchmate Porphyry. I understand."

"Do you?" Tarakh sounded almost angry.

Orthoclase looked at him for several beats. "I don't know," he finally said, "what it is about grief that we never want other people to understand ours. Maybe we feel another's understanding diminishes the intensity of our pain. Maybe it's that so often people say they understand when they really don't. So I suppose saying I understand is wrong. All I know is, in killing Porphyry those dragons tore out a piece of me that I will never find a way to replace. And much as I want to make them suffer for it, no amount of killing will change the fact that he's gone."

Tarakh's angry look faded as Orthoclase spoke. "You do understand," he said.

Orthoclase sat up. "How would you like to kill the bastards who took her from you?"

"More than anything," Tarakh said.

"Then I have a way to make that happen," Orthoclase replied.

"Orthoclase," Lamprophyre murmured, "what about what you said, about riding with a stranger?"

Orthoclase extended his hand to Tarakh. "He's not a stranger," he said. "We both lost people we love to the same dragons. And we both want to see them die. Tarakh, are you afraid of heights?"

"I'm not afraid of anything," Tarakh said. Lamprophyre, listening in, realized it was true. He'd only ever feared losing Oresa.

"Then come with me, and I'll show you how we'll make that happen." Orthoclase wiped his mouth and stood. "I'll see you in the morning, Lamprophyre, Rokshan."

Lamprophyre watched the crowds in the courtyard shift to make room for the dragon and his rider. When Orthoclase was gone, she said, "That's all of us. Six dragons, six riders, against a hundred enemies."

"Not all at once," Rokshan said. "Sardonyx doesn't need to send her whole flight against us. She thinks she overpowers us. We have the advantage of her."

"I hope that's true," Lamprophyre said.

Unexpectedly, she slept a deep, untroubled sleep, filled with fragments of dreams her mind tried to connect. She drifted out of sleep to the sound of her name being called. Blinking, she focused on the misty blue chalcedony pendant hanging on the wall. Hyaloclast.

She lurched sleepily to the peg and said, "I'm here."

"*Two groups of dragons are moving north into Gonjiri,*" Hyaloclast said. "*One is headed east over the mountains, possibly toward Prabat. The other is following the river north. They passed the ruins of Nishta about fifty beats ago and kept going.*"

Beside her, Rokshan sat up, rubbing his eyes. "How many dragons over Nishta?" Lamprophyre asked.

"*It was too dark for an accurate count, but more than ten and less than twenty.*"

Fear shot through Lamprophyre. Too many. Five, maybe seven, they could handle, but twenty? She closed her fist more tightly on the pendant. "They must be headed for Kolmira."

"*Possibly. As far as we know, none of Sardonyx's scouts ever made it as far as Kolmira for her to know it's there. But even if all they intend to do is follow the river, destroying cities as they reach them, they will eventually find Kolmira. You have to stop them there.*"

"We will. Are you pursuing the others?"

"*We are. Good luck, Lamprophyre.*"

The pendant cleared. Rokshan stood. "So we're getting an early start," he said.

Lamprophyre looked outside. The sky was charcoal gray with the first light of dawn. Even Sardonyx's dragons couldn't fly in full dark. "We meet at the warehouses as planned," she said. "And then...Rokshan, *twenty dragons.*"

"No more than twenty, Hyaloclast said." Rokshan pulled on his trousers and slid his feet into his boots. "Don't let fear get to you, Lamprophyre. This is where we turn the tide."

Lamprophyre nodded. "They have no idea what's coming," she said.

CHAPTER FORTY-ONE

Another storm was coming, this one out of the west. They would fly right into its teeth. Lamprophyre cast her eye on the clouds, assessing them. They didn't look like thunderclouds, just ones heavy with rain. Rain could be as much a problem as lightning, but it would foul the wings of their enemies as well as their own, so everyone would be at the same disadvantage.

She eyed the clouds again. They looked like they were moving fast, though they were far enough away the dragons would reach the Rindra River well in advance of them. Unfortunately, the clouds' speed made it likely the storm would reach the clutch just as they met the enemy. She hoped that would be their only piece of bad luck that day.

Her clutchmates flew well spaced apart, but close enough for her to hear their drifting surface thoughts. All of them were thinking about the storm except Dolomite, whose thoughts were filled with a seething desire to hurt dragons. Lamprophyre's heart felt like cracking in two. Sweet-natured, innocent Dolomite, full of anger and pain so great he couldn't see past it. She hoped defeating these ancient dragons would make a difference. She feared she was wrong. If Dolomite had changed permanently, that was one more thing those dragons had killed.

They were moving too fast for comfortable conversation, and Rokshan, when she listened briefly to his thoughts, felt the same. *Hope it's not too soon*, he thought, and Lamprophyre added that to her list of worries. None of the humans had more than a day's training with the weapons, and Tarakh hadn't even had that. At least she was confident in their riders' safety. Worrying about Rokshan falling off would make this impossible.

Soon, the Rindra River was visible on the horizon. Lamprophyre scanned the distant landscape and the skies above it. No sign of dragons. She sped up regardless. Everyone knew the plan: see that Kolmira wasn't under attack, then fly south until they encountered Sardonyx's dragons.

Kolmira's dark roofs looked darker in the storm light, giving Lamprophyre the impression of a beast crouched astride the river, its arms and legs drawn in so it wasn't more than a shapeless blob. Again, no dragons dove and raced overhead. A little of the tension gripping Lamprophyre dissipated. They weren't too late.

She heard a shout from Flint, his words incoherent in the rising wind. When she looked his way, he was waving his arms wildly and gesturing downriver. Specks of color faded by the storm filled the sky. They were moving faster than Lamprophyre had thought possible. She thought *gather up* and flew to meet her clutchmates. The rising wind made it difficult for them to maintain position, but she hovered as best she could and let her mind fill with the sense of her clutchmates, their thoughts and, importantly, their position relevant to her. "Rokshan?" she said.

"There are twelve of them," Rokshan said. "No, don't panic," he said, more loudly to be heard above the apprehensive murmurs. "We have the advantage in our weapons, both in their power and in the dragons' not knowing we have them. We also have the advantage of mobility. Those creatures might as well be pigs in wallow with how slowly they turn. Attack from above if you can. Riders, don't waste shots, but don't be so cautious you aren't effective." He took a deep breath. "Kolmira is counting on us. Let's teach these bastards a lesson."

The rush of confidence and determination filling everyone's thoughts made Lamprophyre feel maybe they weren't all about to die. "Then—fly!" she shouted, and six dragons separated and made for the oncoming enemy.

The ancient dragons didn't alter their course as Lamprophyre and the clutch approached. Nervousness crept over Lamprophyre again, and she ruthlessly pushed the feeling aside. She'd faced Sardonyx's dragons before, she'd killed two of them, and she could fly circles around all of them. Now was not the time to worry. It was time to fight.

Something touched the top of her head, something hard and cool and bumpy. "Rokshan, what are you doing?" she exclaimed.

"Just getting into position," Rokshan shouted. "I promise I won't shoot you. But if we can get within range, and I can hit a dragon's head—"

"Be careful!" She didn't like feeling so close to the pyrite weapon, but she trusted Rokshan not to miss. The dragons were close enough to be visible as large, colored shapes, ponderous and implacable as a force of nature. Lamprophyre gritted her teeth and sped up. Time seemed to slow the faster she went, as if her eagerness to meet her foe was at odds with her fear of the future. It felt as if the dragons had slowed to a crawl; her wings took an eternity to beat. Closer. Gradually closer. They were twenty dragonlengths apart. Fifteen. Twelve.

Ten.

"*Now!*" she screamed. The weapon lifted away from her head. She heard the hum of it coming to full power, the pause, and then a thump as the force pulse shot away from the weapon, a thump that rattled her skull and made her vision go blurry.

The bright flash of the pulse struck the oncoming male, not in the head but in the throat. He jerked, his head snapping back. His wings stilled mid-beat. Then he fell, thrashing as if he were struggling for air, his wings half-furled and his tail whipping around in a desperate struggle to stay aloft. Rokshan shouted with excitement, and Lamprophyre let out an answering shout.

She dove, chasing the fallen male in case he miraculously recovered, but he hit the ground with an explosive blast of sprayed-up earth and lay still. One wing was twisted beneath him in a way no living dragon would endure. Lamprophyre pulled up and flew back toward the fight.

There were only ten ancient dragons now. She didn't have time to look for the other fallen enemy. Her friends looked slim and agile beside Sardonyx's brutes, even Bromargyrite, whom no one would ever call graceful. Flashes of force burst in the air, some of them missing, but most striking their targets. Everything was moving so fast, with the clutch darting and weaving around the enemy, the enemy shifting and taking swipes at anyone who came too close. The ones close enough to Lamprophyre for her to make out expressions looked utterly bewildered, as if they'd been hunting deer only to have the prey turn and savage them. Lamprophyre's doubt vanished. They were winning!

She beat the air for altitude and soared well above the fight, searching for a target. One of the enemy dragons had flown a dragonlength or so away from the others, gradually gaining altitude herself. Lamprophyre smiled. It was like being handed a gift.

She swung, tilting sideways, and felt Rokshan's knees grip tighter. This would be impossible without the harness, given how the humans needed both hands to fire the weapon. Instead of falling, Rokshan shifted to lean into the turn. *Pass above and across*, he thought.

"Above and across," she shouted, nodding in case her words were blown away by the wind. Not fully above, she realized, because her body would block Rokshan's shot. To the side, then.

The dragon saw her, and Lamprophyre noticed the nasty smile on the dragon's face. She hoped Rokshan would shoot that smile off. She curved, circling the dragon, and then dove just as the female let out a blast of fire that enveloped her. An air-shattering series of thumps pounded her ears, and flashes impacted on the dragon female, making her scream. When Lamprophyre could see again, she saw the female spiraling downward, one of her wings shredded and dark blotches rising up on her pale golden skin.

"Damn," Rokshan shouted. "Missed my shot."

"She can't fly, though. She's down. The shield worked!"

"It worked. I didn't even feel warm."

Lamprophyre let out another shout of excitement. Below, more bright flashes struck the downed female, and Orthoclase streaked past. The female's other wing stopped moving, and she fell without trying to stop herself, landing sprawled across the river with her head beneath its surface. Lamprophyre briefly considered having to bury all these dragons and then let the thought go. They weren't safe yet.

She again sped upward, seeking a position where she could see the battle, and gave up when she realized again how fast everything was moving. There were only seven of Sardonyx's dragons left, and the ones that remained showed the marks of the weapons, the dark bruises where the force pulses had pulverized the soft tissue beneath impenetrable dragon hide. The smell of rain filled the air, though still no drops fell. If they could win this fight before the storm came...

The enemy was getting smarter, though. Lamprophyre saw Melika aim her weapon only to have to pull up when her target put Flint between her and himself. Frustrated, Lamprophyre sought out someone to attack, and dove after a dragon the color of a day-old bruise. Just a little closer—"Rokshan, wait for it!" she shouted.

Something struck her from the side, and Lamprophyre reflexively jerked away as an enormous female whose rosy hide was so stippled with bruises she looked like a pink snow leopard slammed into her, reaching for Rokshan. Lamprophyre rolled and hoped Rokshan wouldn't fall off. The female swiped at Lamprophyre's chest, missing by scant fingerwidths. Lamprophyre kicked her assailant's stomach, and the female grabbed her foot and pulled her close.

Then the female's head cracked against Lamprophyre's, and for a moment, Lamprophyre was blind and dizzy. But there was no second blow. Lamprophyre realized Rokshan was screaming at her to pull up, realized a beat later that they were falling, and spread her wings to catch herself.

Breathing heavily with fear, she looked around for the female and found her locked in close combat with Dolomite. He was clawing and snarling like an animal, as if he'd forgotten the strategy in his lust for blood. Lamprophyre screamed his name and flew toward him, dodging what seemed like a hundred enemy dragons. Tekentriya had her weapon out, but seemed unable to get a clear shot because of Dolomite's constant movement.

Lamprophyre saw the strike coming. Time slowed again, giving her an eternity to watch the rose-leopard female's powerful right hand come sweeping toward Dolomite's unguarded belly. She saw the claws extend mere beats before the female struck, tearing five deep gouges into Dolomite's stomach and sending red blood flying like fountains.

Dolomite convulsed, and Tekentriya's weapon dropped to hang by its strap around her shoulders as she grabbed Dolomite's ruff to stay in her saddle. The rose-leopard female shoved Dolomite away to fall helplessly out of the air.

Lamprophyre realized her throat ached with screams she hadn't heard. Not Dolomite too. Rokshan was saying something she couldn't understand, but it didn't matter; she had to save Dolomite. She dove after him.

Once again her descent was slowed by having to dodge the enemy. She was still eighteen dragonlengths away when Dolomite and Tekentriya hit the ground.

She cried out and backwinged in dismay. Rokshan was still shouting things she didn't understand. Then, to her astonishment, she saw Dolomite move. How he was still alive, she didn't know, but maybe it wasn't too late.

She cast about, not knowing in her panic if she should go to help him, or kill the one who'd tried to kill him. Then she saw the rose-leopard dragon. The female was diving in her ponderous, implacable way at Dolomite, her claws extended. Dolomite shifted again. He was face down and his wings lay crumpled across his body. Tekentriya was nowhere to be seen.

Lamprophyre dodged one final enemy and was in the clear. She beat the air frantically, but she knew, even with as slow as the female was and as fast as Lamprophyre could fly, she would reach the female too late.

The female drove ever closer to Dolomite. Lamprophyre pushed herself harder than ever before. She was only seven dragonlengths away, but the female would reach her clutchmate beats before Lamprophyre did.

Dolomite's wings shifted. Tekentriya sat up from where she'd lain sprawled beneath them. She brought her weapon up and around, aimed, and fired.

The flashing pulse took the female in the center of her forehead.

She jerked, and her arms sagged, but inertia kept her dead body moving. Screaming with effort, Lamprophyre changed course just enough to ram the female's body, grabbing her around the waist and carrying her to the side so they didn't hit Dolomite and Tekentriya. She and her burden struck the earth, plowing up a great long furrow that ended at the riverside. Lamprophyre lay panting for a moment, unable to move.

"Will you for Jiwanyil's sake listen to me!" Rokshan was shouting.

"I will," Lamprophyre said wearily. "Sorry. I didn't know what to do."

"We saved Dolomite. That's more important than what I wanted you to do." Rokshan slapped her neck lightly. "Get up. It's not over."

"Dolomite could be dying."

"I know. But we have to kill the others if we want to be able to save him. Go!"

Lamprophyre pushed herself wearily to her feet and leaped into the sky just as the first fat raindrops fell.

Her worry for Dolomite distracted her, and Rokshan more than once had to shout at her to move, move, get altitude and then dive. An acid mist enveloped them once, then she dodged a gout not of fire but of actual burning stomach matter she feared was too solid for the shield to handle. Rain pelted her body and sheeted down her wings, making her struggle to maintain her speed. Rokshan shot again and again until Lamprophyre couldn't remember a time when the world hadn't been filled with thunderous echoes and the flash of pulses of force. Once she came close enough to take a swipe at a male's wings, and he turned on her, snarling, and she saw and heard his terror.

Then the moment came when Rokshan shouted, "Let her go! Don't worry about her, let her go!"

Lamprophyre watched a lone female dragon fly heavily southward, shrouded in the misty low rainclouds. "But we can kill her," she said.

"Better she return to Sardonyx with news that her dragons are no longer invulnerable," Rokshan said. "We want Sardonyx as confused and worried as we can make her."

The sound of wings filled Lamprophyre's ears. "All her dragons disappearing would be confusing and worrisome, too," Flint said. His movements were heavy with exhaustion and the pouring rain.

"True, but we also don't want her attacking Kolmira again," Rokshan said. "A total disappearance would mean sending a larger force north to investigate. This is part of forcing her to fight on a battlefield of our choosing." He sagged forward and hugged Lamprophyre around her neck. Water dripped from his soaked hair down his forehead. "Let's see if Dolomite is—" His mouth snapped shut on the rest of that sentence.

They landed a dragonlength from where Dolomite lay. The other dragons and their riders surrounded him, their heads bowed, rain pattering against them as if the sky were human enough to weep. Lamprophyre stopped. She couldn't bear knowing she'd lost another clutchmate.

Rokshan slid down her side and ran toward the fallen dragon.

Then he turned and shouted, "He's alive. It's all right, Lamprophyre, he's alive!"

Her knees trembled. She sat on the ground and closed her eyes, breathing the acid- and fire-tinged air and feeling such relief she thought she might float away. When she regained control, she walked to Rokshan's side. Kamil knelt beside Dolomite, his right hand glowing green. Two of the deep gashes were gone, and as Lamprophyre watched, Kamil ran his glowing hand slowly over a third, making it close up.

"But you're not a healer," she said.

"Any adept can use jade for basic healing," Kamil said without looking up. "Healers are just adepts who've studied their more complex uses. I hoped I wouldn't need this, but I'm glad I brought it." He started on a fourth gash.

"Lamprophyre," Dolomite said. His voice was so weak she could barely hear it.

She moved closer to his head, near where Tekentriya sat, and wiped rainwater from his face. Dolomite had his wings folded painfully beneath him to allow Kamil access to his stomach. "You nearly died," she said.

Dolomite nodded. "I think I've had my fill of revenge," he said. "I wasn't myself. I didn't like that." He drew in a deep breath and let it out slowly. "Thank you for saving me."

"Tekentriya saved you," Lamprophyre said. "I just finished the job."

"We would both have been crushed if you hadn't been there," Tekentriya said. For once, she didn't sound angry.

"I've never seen anything so brave as what you did," Lamprophyre told her. "That female was thirty times your size and you didn't even flinch."

Tekentriya shrugged. "That's just one kind of bravery. I'm afraid it's all I'm good for." She put a hand on her damaged hip. "But I wasn't about to let this fellow die. I don't have so many friends that I can afford to lose any of them."

"You just like flying," Dolomite said with a weak smile.

Tekentriya smiled back. "If that's what you want to believe."

"That's it," Kamil said. "You'll need to see a healer—we should go into Kolmira before we return, because it's possible you have internal injuries from hitting the ground."

Coquina lifted her head and turned. "I think Kolmira is coming to us."

Lamprophyre followed her gaze. Dozens of people had emerged from Kolmira's gate and were slowly picking their way across the sodden fields toward them. "I didn't realize how close we were to the city," she said. "I guess we gave them a show."

"I'll talk to the ruling prince," Rokshan said. "You let Hyaloclast know what happened."

"All right. Then what?"

Rokshan looked up at her. "Then," he said, "we should go south to join Hyaloclast. I think the rest of your dragons need to make some human friends."

CHAPTER FORTY-TWO

They reached Prabat at midafternoon, after seeing Dolomite completely healed and explaining to the Kolmirans how to dispose of the dead dragon bodies. Lamprophyre hadn't liked the humans' reaction. True, nobody wanted to have to bury eleven enormous creatures, but she and her clutchmates had saved Kolmira from absolute destruction, and surely the humans' gratitude could extend to dealing with the aftermath?

They'd taken the long way, following the river past the ruins of Nishta to the mountains before turning east, in case Sardonyx had sent more than one attacking force. But the flight was peaceful once the rain was past, the air cool and damp and smelling of water rather than fire and acid. The continuing overcast turned the light a beautiful pearly gray that illuminated the river valley only dimly, making it seem far more distant than it was. Despite the beauty of her surroundings, Lamprophyre had spent the flight chafing over how slowly they were moving. Anything might have happened at Prabat. They might arrive in time to see the last smoldering tower collapse.

But the worst hadn't happened. They saw smoke rising from Prabat's low towers, but no dragons circled the city, raining down fire and acid. There were no dragons visible anywhere, which increased Lamprophyre's worries. She sped up, passing Orthoclase, who was in the lead, and scanned the hills surrounding the city. Her heart beat faster as she saw motionless colored forms lying in clumps outside Prabat's city wall.

"Don't panic. Those are our dragons," Rokshan said.

"Yes, that's why I'm panicking. They look dead," Lamprophyre replied.

"I doubt they'd be so neatly grouped if they'd fallen where they were killed." Rokshan leaned well forward and pointed. "That's Hyaloclast there."

Lamprophyre looked where he pointed and saw the dragon queen near the city's western gate. To her relief, Hyaloclast was on her feet with her wings furled closely along her back. Leaving the clutch behind, Lamprophyre banked and swiftly descended to join her, landing so abruptly Rokshan had to make a grab for her ruff to avoid being jolted sideways.

Hyaloclast looked up from her conversation with two men when Lamprophyre arrived. "You bring news yourself?" she asked. "I expected to hear from you sooner."

"What—oh." Lamprophyre had forgotten the blue chalcedony pendant in the tumult of the Kolmiran attack and the worried flight to Prabat. "I'm sorry. I forgot. You look...that is, what happened here?"

"Heavy casualties on our side, but we drove them off. Were you forced to flee?" Hyaloclast looked past Lamprophyre at her clutch-mates, descending behind her.

"No. We killed them. Hyaloclast, the strategy worked!" Now that she knew disaster hadn't struck here, Lamprophyre's worries disappeared. They'd fought a force twice their size and nearly eliminated them!

Hyaloclast's eye ridges went up. "With none of you injured?"

"No, but there was healing. It was a close thing, but we're all right." Her mother's words finally registered with her. "Heavy casualties?"

"Thirty-two dragons of our flight killed," Hyaloclast said. "We accounted for four of theirs before driving them off."

"Yes, and that makes thirty-six giant corpses we have to deal with," one of the men said. He had a sour, pinched face and very little hair on his head, and he faced Hyaloclast with no fear, as if she were some storekeeper who'd sold him rotten fruit and he intended her to make restitution.

Hyaloclast turned her baleful red-eyed stare on him. "Lamprophyre, this is Prince Rajit," she said. "It is his city that is not now in flames thanks to us. Or am I mistaken, your highness?" The sharp edge to her voice told Lamprophyre Hyaloclast did not appreciate the prince's easy dismissal of her dead people as "corpses."

Prince Rajit took half a step back, but his sour expression didn't change. "Of course we're very grateful," he said, "but that doesn't change reality."

"What I hear you saying, Rajit, is that you don't appreciate what Hyaloclast and the dragons have done for Prabat," Rokshan said, sliding down from the saddle.

Now Rajit did recoil. "Your highness," he said. "I didn't see you there."

"Not a good response," Rokshan said. "You shouldn't need a royal prince's presence to behave honorably. Or did you think your safety could be bought with the blood of others and you wouldn't have to do anything but sit in your palace and wait for the battle to end?"

Rajit's face darkened. "Of course not, your highness."

Rokshan slapped Rajit companionably on the shoulder. "These dragons have lost many friends," he said. "They shouldn't have to labor alone to bury them. I'm sure what they want is assistance, not to turn the whole duty over to humans. Not such a burden, is it?"

Rajit shook his head. "I—my chamberlain will handle the details," he said, indicating the second man. "Is there anything else I can do for you?"

"We will need to eat soon," Hyaloclast said. Her eye ridges

shifted just enough to show Lamprophyre she was enjoying the conversation. "One cow for every two dragons."

Rajit's mouth fell open. "But that's—"

"Not at all unreasonable," Rokshan said. "I'll come with you. Lamprophyre, I'll be back soon." He clapped Rajit's shoulder again, making the prince stagger. Lamprophyre bit her lip to keep from laughing.

When the humans were gone, Hyaloclast said, "How many did you kill?"

That sobered Lamprophyre. "There were twelve. One escaped—actually Rokshan said to let her go so she could tell Sardonyx about what we did. I trust his judgment. He said it was best for our strategy."

"There were far more here," Hyaloclast said, "and Sardonyx was not one of them. I believe she's testing our resolve, looking for a weak spot."

"Did they go south?"

Hyaloclast nodded. "We could not afford to chase them far."

Lamprophyre reflexively looked south, past where her clutchmates had gathered. "I don't like to think about the destruction they're causing in Sachetan. Maybe we *should* follow Sardonyx south."

"As I said, we can't afford to chase them," Hyaloclast said, "and from what King Ekanath tells me, the dragons have done very little damage in that country. A few villages, here and there, but they have not gone far enough south to find their large cities."

"I don't understand. All Sachetan has to protect it are the prophecies warning them which cities will be attacked. Why doesn't Sardonyx destroy them?"

Hyaloclast followed her gaze. "I admit I don't know much about military strategy. General Sajan informs me that Sardonyx's approach to conquest is to defeat her most powerful opponent so she can sweep unopposed through these other countries, rather than fighting a hundred little battles in which her forces would be gradually diminished. Despite our dragons being less powerful than hers, we are still that opponent. She intends to obliterate our flight, raze Gonjiri, and then rain destruction down upon the rest of the world."

"That's terrifying."

"Given that you and your clutch have just struck a decisive blow against her, it's an intent she will have trouble fulfilling." Hyaloclast sighed. "I wish I had more confidence that your battle techniques can be extended to the rest of the flight."

"It's not hard to learn to fly with a human companion."

"You forget how much time your clutch has spent in Tanajital. You're used to humans. The rest of us, except Massicot and poor Chrysoprase—this is the first time any of them have seen a human that wasn't Rokshan. I fear it's going to take longer than we have to acclimate them."

"I choose to be optimistic."

Hyaloclast smiled. "You would. Well, it's not something to worry about tonight. We could use your help burying our dead." Her smile disappeared. "That will never feel natural to me."

"I know. I feel the same." She thought of Porphyry's grave marker and felt comforted. And Hyaloclast had referred to Rokshan by name. Lamprophyre thought that might have been the first time. "We'll help."

"Thank you. I will spread the word of your victory. We could use a boost to morale. Thirty-two dragons." Hyaloclast shook her head. "And every one of them a terrible loss."

"Is Leucite..."

Hyaloclast shot her an ironic look. "I think there was more than one question in those words, daughter."

Lamprophyre swallowed and stood her ground. "Well, is he?"

"He is unharmed. And yes, I intend to offer him a pair-bond if we both survive this. I won't ask for your approval."

"Of course not! It's none of my business. It's just been so long, and I want you to be happy."

Hyaloclast sighed. "I thought I wouldn't want another mate after Aegirine. We always knew we would be pair-bonded, from the time we were barely able to fly. That kind of connection is so rare, and so beautiful, but what I have now with Leucite is a different kind of relationship, and it is beautiful in its own way."

"I like him. I'm glad you chose him."

"He was worried you'd be upset. You might talk to him, if you get a chance. He has a very generous, caring heart."

"I will." Lamprophyre saw Coquina looking her way as if she had something on her mind. "I need to talk to my clutch about the burials."

"Go," Hyaloclast said. "And give them my thanks."

~

BY NIGHTFALL, THE FLIGHT HAD BURIED ONLY HALF THEIR FALLEN dead, and Rokshan hadn't returned. He was close enough that she could feel their pair-bond, but that only made her more frustrated: so close, and yet he didn't return to her? She tried not to worry about what might keep him away, but she was tense and exhausted from burying so many friends, most of whom she didn't know were dead until she came upon their bodies.

A procession of wagons bearing butchered cow carcasses emerged from the western gate and trundled over the uneven ground toward the dragons. They were followed by more wagons hauling barrels of clean, fresh, sweet-smelling water. Lamprophyre commandeered some for her clutch and gratefully took a long drink before pouring water over her filthy hands.

Gradually, the others drifted toward her, drawn by the scent of the water. "I'm so thirsty," Dolomite said. "I didn't notice until just now."

"Where are the others? The humans?"

Dolomite drank and wiped his mouth. "Someone sent a message for Tekentriya, an invitation to join the ruling prince. She took all the humans with her. It was meant to be a joke at the ruling prince's expense, but I didn't understand why it would be funny for him to have to feed all of them. He must have enough food for dozens of humans."

"Food," Flint said to Coquina. "Smell that? Others have started cooking their meals. You should do the same."

"Has anyone ever told you how bossy you are?" Coquina said, poking him in the side. "All right. Lamprophyre?"

Lamprophyre got heavily to her feet and retrieved one of the cow carcasses. If Tekentriya had been invited to eat with Prince Rajit, Rokshan probably had too. It irritated her that he'd desert her for human companionship—but that was stupid, he didn't like Rajit and probably only ate with him out of politeness. He would return soon.

It was full dark when the three cows were roasted, so Lamprophyre smashed two of the empty water barrels and started a bonfire. They ate without speaking, their idle thoughts dwelling on food and sleep and curiosity about where they would do the latter.

"It's too late to fly back to Tanajital," she said.

Bromargyrite groaned. "I can't believe I've become so acclimated to the human world that I'm thinking longingly of my warehouse."

"We can sleep here," Orthoclase said. He lay sprawled near the fire with his wings spread over him, already halfway to sleep. "It's uncomfortable being out in the open, but we've done it before."

"And we'd just have to fly back in the morning to finish burying our dead," Flint pointed out. "Better we sleep here."

Dolomite let out a gentle snore.

Coquina laughed quietly. "I guess it's settled," she said. "But I'll sit up a while longer. I told Melika she should come here when she finished eating, in case we decided to go back. Maybe that prince will find them lodgings in the city. It's got to be a lot worse for humans, sleeping on the bare ground without a roof overhead."

"I wish Rokshan would return," Lamprophyre groused. "He hasn't moved in over two thousand beats. I don't know what it is about human dining that it takes so long."

It was another thousand beats before Rokshan started moving, but since the motion was generally westward, toward her, Lamprophyre decided not to complain again. The moon hadn't yet risen, and the light from the bonfire blinded her to everything but her clutchmates' recumbent bodies and Coquina's restlessly shifting head. "What's wrong?" Lamprophyre finally asked.

"Nothing—that is, I don't think it's anything. I just feel uncomfortable. Probably it's sleeping outdoors that does it." Coquina settled back and coiled her tail around herself. "I feel as though trouble isn't over yet."

"Well, of course it isn't."

"I mean immediate trouble. If Sardonyx's dragons come back, they could do so much damage with all of us off guard."

"They won't fly in the dark. They likely won't even fly when the moon's up. But I can ask Hyaloclast if she's posted guards."

"That's reasonable. I'm sorry I'm so paranoid."

"Better a little unjustified paranoia than an unsuspected attack that kills us all." Lamprophyre breathed on the blue chalcedony pendant. "Hyaloclast?"

A few beats later, Hyaloclast said, "*Yes?*"

"We were wondering if you posted guards. In case they come back."

"*I have. It may be unnecessary, but I believe in taking precautions.*"

"I agree. Sorry to disturb you." She let go the pendant, which cleared so it once again gleamed in the firelight. "I wish Rokshan would come. I know I keep saying that, but I can't rest until he's here."

"It's understandable." Coquina tilted her head back to look at the sky. "I don't see pictures. Only specks. Humans have the most interesting imaginations. Did you know they actually enjoy looking for pictures in clouds? Melika told me."

Lamprophyre shuddered. "How awful. I don't know why that doesn't unnerve them. Clouds are just water mist. Why would you want to imagine them as something else?"

"I don't understand it, but Melika thought it was hilarious that dragons don't do it. Sometimes we're so different I don't know how we managed to become friends."

"Rokshan says friendship is more interesting when you're different, because you never run out of things to talk about." She yawned. "It's just now starting to hit me, what we did today. I can't believe it worked."

"I wish it weren't necessary." At Lamprophyre's inquiring look, Coquina added, "Sardonyx is an awful person. Here we have this beautiful world, with two rational species inhabiting it, and we have so much to give each other—and Sardonyx wants to destroy humans because she thinks they're a pestilence. How revolting. And how arrogant, to think her personal beliefs should apply to everyone."

"There's so much about her I don't understand," Lamprophyre said. "She has that ability to speak to minds; where did that come from? And are there any others among her followers who can do the same?"

"Didn't you say she gave that power to you once?"

"No, I said I thought that was what happened. I have no idea what it actually was, whether I had Sardonyx's ability temporarily because we were listening to the same mind, or whether it was all an illusion."

"Or maybe," Coquina said with a grin, "you've got that power yourself and you never knew it."

Lamprophyre made a face. "I doubt it. I've never spoken to anyone's mind."

"That you know of. There's scant difference between speaking to a dragon's mind and having a thought another dragon hears."

"This is a disturbing conversation, and Stones be praised, here comes Rokshan to put an end to it."

"What am I putting an end to?" Rokshan asked. "God's breath, that was the dullest meal I've ever attended."

That made Lamprophyre feel instantly better. "Is Prince Rajit boring?"

"I don't know. He might actually be interesting, but he's one of those people who's overly conscious of social rank, and he went out of his way not to say anything Tekentriya or I might be offended by. Which means the conversation was dull, and thank Jiwanyil Kamil isn't overawed by nobility, because he kept the meal from being a complete disaster." Rokshan dropped to sit leaning against Lamprophyre's side. "I'm sleeping out here. I'd rather be with you than in some stuffy bedchamber in the prince's palace. It was built about five hundred years ago, when the lords fought for dominance, and you can tell its designer was concerned about the possibility of some assassin climbing through windows, because there aren't any."

"I'm sorry it's just the hard ground."

Rokshan shrugged. "Like I said, far superior."

"Was Melika coming?" Coquina asked.

"I think so. The prince's wife was talking to her about you. She's interested in dragons and had the most unusual questions. I'm sure Melika will tell you all about it."

Lamprophyre settled down and spread her wings over herself, enclosing Rokshan beneath them. Rokshan moved to pillow his head against her shoulder. "So warm," he murmured. She drifted off to sleep feeling content and happy to have him close.

The sound of her name being shouted practically in her ear drove her upright, knocking Rokshan over. "What?" she exclaimed, looking around frantically.

"*Lamprophyre!*" Hyaloclast's voice came from the pendant just as more cries, these wordless, echoed across the fields surrounding Prabat. "*Lamprophyre, we are under attack!*"

Lamprophyre scrambled to her feet. The moon was up and sailing toward its zenith, which meant she'd been asleep for perhaps four thousand beats—almost three hours. The bonfire had died down, and its low light revealed the faces of her clutchmates, who were stirring in response to the cries. She couldn't see attackers anywhere, had no idea where the cries were coming from.

She grabbed the pendant and said, "Where are they?"

"*South. We have a few hundred beats before they reach Prabat. We must fly to them, engage them away from the city. Gather your force and join us.*"

The pendant went clear before Lamprophyre could protest that the humans were almost all in the city, that it would take time—but she didn't have time for complaining.

"Rokshan," she said.

"I'll be back. Everyone get ready," he said, calling over his shoulder because he was already sprinting for the gate.

Lamprophyre shrugged into her harness and fastened the buckles. "It's fine," she said. "The others will stop the enemy, keep them at a distance, until we reach them."

Everyone nodded except Dolomite, who had his harness on but unbuckled. He was staring southward, toward where the mountains marked the border between Gonjiri and Sachetan. "It's not fine," he said. "There are so many."

Lamprophyre looked in that direction. At first, she saw nothing with her firelight-accustomed eyes. She moved so the bonfire was at her back and looked again. Still nothing—and then movement, black against black, as if the night had wings. Gradually, the moving blackness grew, until it filled nearly half the southern sky. She caught her breath. Some of that had to be her own flight, but still...

"We'll do it," she declared. "It's not just us this time. We have the whole flight behind us. Don't let them get to you, Dolomite."

Dolomite didn't take his eyes from the oncoming blackness. "I won't," he said. "But I'm not sure they know that."

Lamprophyre didn't know how to respond. Instead, she waved at the six human figures running or in one case lurching toward them. "They will soon," she said.

CHAPTER FORTY-THREE

Moonlight silvered the ground and shone in glints off dragon bodies weaving and dodging through the air. A blast of fire, then another, turned those bodies yellow-gold briefly. Lamprophyre, in the lead, tried to count and gave up. She was too distant to distinguish between the flight and Sardonyx's people. That could wait until they were close enough to kill.

Beside her, Orthoclase stretched out his neck as if that would give him greater speed. She heard him think *fighting in darkness, good thing they're so big.* She agreed. The idea of accidentally hurting one of her friends scared her. At least they could easily tell the difference—

—and with that, a new fear struck her. There wasn't any way to blind-fly with the entire flight. "We have to be careful," she shouted. "The flight won't know to get out of our way."

"That means getting in closer than before," Rokshan said. He shouted, "Take your shots as close as you dare. It won't kill our friends to take a shot or two, but no sense being reckless." His thoughts echoed his words perfectly, extending the range of his message.

Lamprophyre heard agreement in her clutchmates' thoughts. It didn't reassure her as much as she'd hoped. She pushed those fears aside. Nothing else she could do, and the battle was coming up fast.

As they approached the wheeling, soaring dragons, Lamprophyre noted that the flight stayed well away from the enormous monsters, not trying to approach close enough to strike. It was all she had time to observe before she felt Rokshan bring the weapon into firing position. She swerved upward, found a target, and dove.

The rapid thumping of the weapon rattled her skull and neck. She swept past the enemy and, seeing an opening, swiped her claws across the creature's face. The dragon howled and dropped, his wings beating erratically. She dodged one of the flight and chased the dragon below the battle. His thoughts, when she neared him, were confused and frightened and wordless. She blocked them as Rokshan took a final shot that hit the dragon between the eyes, and wheeled away without watching him hit the distant ground.

But when she approached the conflict, she discovered the fight was over. Dragons of her flight milled about, grouped by clutches, thinking how relieved they were to be alive. She sought out her clutch and found Hyaloclast instead. The great black dragon looked silver in the moonlight. Leucite hovered beside her, his bronze body purplish under the same light. They turned to face her as she approached.

"No one was hurt," Hyaloclast said before Lamprophyre could ask the question uppermost in her thoughts. "The enemy fled in the face of our weapons. I don't yet know how many of them your clutch accounted for."

"That's bad," Rokshan said.

Hyaloclast turned her red gaze on him. "No casualties is bad?"

"No. Their fleeing so quickly. It suggests this was to test us. Sardonyx must know by now what happened near Kolmira. She probably sent this force to witness the weapons in action and return to report." Rokshan sounded grim. "I don't like the implications."

"Why?" Lamprophyre asked. "It's not as if she can defend against pyrite."

"I would not like to guess what Sardonyx is capable of," Hyaloclast said, sounding as grim as Rokshan. "Greater knowledge has to help her." She turned to look southward, where the last of Sardonyx's dragons were visible. "And now she knows what she faces."

"You're right, that's bad," Lamprophyre said. "What do we do?"

"Sleep, for now," Hyaloclast said. "We need time to recover. Tomorrow, we will make what plans we can. We need humans' artifacts to spy on Sardonyx's movements, to show us where to defend next. It's not hopeless."

Lamprophyre nodded. She heard her clutch approaching, and it comforted her. "We'll speak again in the morning." She smiled at Leucite, thinking how glad she was that he'd made her mother happy, and heard in return his relief and happiness. At least that was something gone right.

She turned to her clutch, thinking *good work*. They were all so tired and yet so elated she didn't want to mention Hyaloclast's fears. "How many?" she asked.

"Tekentriya and I killed one," Dolomite said. "And hurt two others."

"We tore up the wing of one. I'm not sure if she recovered," Melika said.

The others all shook their heads. "And we killed one," Lamprophyre said. "They ran from us."

"I like the sound of that," Orthoclase said with a smile.

This time, Lamprophyre heard Rokshan think *not tonight*. She said only, "Let's sleep. Tomorrow is another long day." But she couldn't help wondering, as they flew back to Prabat, whether it would be the kind of day any of them could predict.

~

Sardonyx didn't attack in the morning. They finished burying their friends undisturbed, and then returned to Tanajital. It felt so anticlimactic Lamprophyre became angry. So many dragons had died, and life went on, which struck her as irrational. Then she felt ridiculous for having the thought. Her friends were dead, and so many others lived, and it was those others, and all the hundreds of thousands of humans in Gonjiri and elsewhere, who mattered.

Tanajital, untouched by war, showed no sign of worrying that there was a flight of evil dragons out there somewhere that wanted all its citizens dead. Lamprophyre had to hold court the day after they returned, and the petitioners' problems were all so ordinary she felt a moment of dissociation again.

When the last petitioner was gone, Lamprophyre went into the embassy, followed by Rokshan, and sagged gracelessly to the floor. "I feel we should be doing something," she said. "Something to stop Sardonyx. Not listening to people complaining that Bromargyrite took the corner off their roof by accident."

"Sardonyx is still in northern Sachetan, according to the seers." Rokshan sat on his bed and clasped his hands loosely together. "And there haven't been any new prophecies warning of destruction. There's nothing to do but wait. And meet with Hyaloclast this evening."

"I'm excited to see the progress the flight has made in making human friends. I'll feel so much happier when it's more than just the six of us armed to destroy Sardonyx's people."

"Don't be too excited. You know the dragons aren't used to humans. It will take time."

"I know." Lamprophyre blew a smoke ring and watched it drift upward and dissipate. "It's still exciting. Humans and dragons together again, only this time we'll beat her."

"I admit that's a wonderful thought."

Lamprophyre looked up at the sound of footsteps crossing the courtyard. "Kamil!" she exclaimed. "Is something wrong?"

"Not to my knowledge," Kamil said. He wore a canvas knapsack over one shoulder, a heavy one by the way he moved. His lips twitched as if he were trying to control a smile that desperately wanted to be set free. "I wanted to show you something."

Lamprophyre sat up. His thoughts were full of excitement and pleasure, centered on— "The sodalite artifact," she said. "You did it."

Kamil scowled, but his eyes were alight with amusement. "You know listening to thoughts is rude, right? But yes, I figured it out." He set the knapsack down with a thump and unbuckled it. Rokshan stood looking over his shoulder as he scrabbled through the knapsack's contents, stone by the sound and smell, and removed something that reeked of sodalite, a rich, milky aroma tinged with the sharp scent of pine.

Lamprophyre drew in a startled breath. "It's beautiful," she said. Sodalite was one of her favorite stones to eat, but she wouldn't dream of eating this. It was a pile of rings, one large, the others smaller, linked by slender gold chains to a central disk. The rings and disc were carved all over in elaborate, asymmetrical patterns filled with gold that highlighted beautifully the white striations covering the blue stone.

Kamil picked up the artifact and began threading rings over his fingers and wrist. "The disc is the active part," he said, raising his hand to display how the disc fit into his palm. "The rings allow it to draw power from the adept to activate the artifact."

"That sounds dangerous," Lamprophyre said.

"Not really. I suppose if you used it for hours at a time, it might make you sick, but that's not how it works. It draws power once and then feeds it back into the adept, triggering his awareness of everything around him. Making him capable of remembering even the tiniest detail of something."

"And that will work?"

Kamil shrugged. "According to that madman's notes, it does. We'll have to use it to find out. It does draw power, and I tested it on myself and it has the right effect." He laughed. "It's incredibly disconcerting when you do it surrounded by people. I saw things I had no desire to be aware of."

"You said an adept," Rokshan said. "Can a non-adept use it?"

"Given the right prompting, sure." Kamil stripped it off and handed it to Lamprophyre to examine closely. "Meaning that they'd need to learn the thoughts and motions to activate it. But it's like you said the serpentine artifact is—it's no harder to use than...than learning to guide a horse."

"That's a relief," Lamprophyre said. She handed the artifact to Rokshan. "We're so close."

"I want to try now," Rokshan said.

Lamprophyre gasped. "You promised you wouldn't."

"I did not. I never promised anything."

"But they still need you. As a human."

"There's nothing I can do as a human I can't also do as a dragon." Rokshan balled the artifact in his fist. "Except be your mate. I'm tired of waiting."

Lamprophyre didn't like the look in his eyes. "I know. But you know our needs aren't as important as fighting Sardonyx. Please, Rokshan. You think I don't want this as much as you do? But—if you're transformed, that's one fewer rider. One fewer weapon."

His eyes narrowed. "That's low."

"It's *truth*." She laid her hand gently on his shoulder. "We can wait a little longer."

Rokshan looked away, his jaw clenched. "All right," he said. "A little while." He hung the artifact on a peg above his bed. "A very little while."

"Thank you." She turned to Kamil. "And thank you. What do we owe you?"

"I didn't do it to be paid," Kamil said. "Transforming a prince into a dragon, that's the stuff of legends. And Bromargyrite is right that I always wanted to be a hero out of an epic poem."

"But this must have cost so much!"

He shrugged. "I can afford it. My gift to the two of you."

"Then we really are grateful." She sniffed the artifact again. "Now I'm hungry."

Rokshan and Kamil both laughed. "Eating in the middle of the day, how decadent," Rokshan said, and it relieved her mind that he could still joke.

That evening, she and Rokshan left the city for the fields the flight had taken over. In all her life, Lamprophyre had never seen the flight assembled like this. At home in the mountains, even on sunny days some people preferred the comfort of a cave, so the flight was never wholly visible. Now, dragons sat or lay everywhere, turning the fields into a multicolored blanket like some humans put on their beds. And this wasn't even the full flight, Lamprophyre reflected, thinking of the dragons back home watching over the dragonets.

She found Hyaloclast eating at the top of a low rise that gave her an excellent view of every dragon. "Have you eaten?" the dragon queen asked. "Join me."

"Thank you." Lamprophyre helped herself to some of the cow. Rokshan declined politely. He'd eaten with Dharan earlier, though he came back from supper unusually quiet and wouldn't tell Lamprophyre what he and Dharan had talked about.

"I don't have good news," Hyaloclast said. "I'm afraid it will take much longer than we hoped to build new human-dragon partnerships."

Lamprophyre paused in her eating. "But I know the humans aren't afraid of dragons. We only accepted volunteers who aren't afraid of dragons or heights."

"I'm afraid the trouble is our dragons. Most of them don't see humans as anything but amusing novelties—certainly not as equals. And many of them have trouble blocking human thoughts when they're in close contact. Massicot is the only one truly suited to accepting a human companion, and he's mentally deaf, unable to blind-fly as you said is essential."

"I don't know. I could be wrong." Lamprophyre looked at Rokshan, who shook his head. "All right, I'm not wrong. Massicot unable to sense the rest of us would be a liability." She blew out a deep, frustrated breath. "So it will take time."

"And we may not have time," Hyaloclast said. "Sardonyx remains in Sachetan, and the adepts tell me she has destroyed a few more villages, but her movements worry me. They are the movements of someone waiting for her moment."

"I agree," Rokshan said. "I've told Sajan we need to prepare for her next attack as if we six are the only ones of our kind. And we have enough pyrite weapons...no. It will take time to teach the dragons to use the pyrite weapons themselves. We can't count on having that time any more than we can on having human riders."

"Even so, we shouldn't give up the hope of both those things," Lamprophyre said. The thought of her clutch being the only ones effective against all those dragons made her feel sick and afraid.

Hyaloclast eyed her as if she'd heard those thoughts. "We will not," she said. "And you should not fear. We will face Sardonyx as one."

"I wish we didn't have to face her at all," Lamprophyre said, bitterly remembering what Coquina had said about Sardonyx's arrogance.

"I hate to say it, because it sounds so defeatist, but it will all be over soon, one way or the other," Rokshan said. "But I don't think it's hopeless. And then—" He looked at Lamprophyre, and smiled.

"You are more hopeful than before," Hyaloclast said. "You have a solution?"

"I can be transformed as soon as they no longer need me as a military commander," Rokshan said.

Hyaloclast smiled, a sideways, ironic smile. "I find myself hoping for that day, young prince," she said.

Lamprophyre, stunned, couldn't think of anything to say to that. "We should return," she finally managed. "Rokshan needs to meet with General Sajan."

Hyaloclast saluted them with a nod and went back to eating.

In the air, Rokshan said, "Am I right that I finally have your mother's approval?"

"I wonder if she's mellowed now that she and Leucite are almost pair-bonded. Or maybe she's less dismissive of humans in general." Lamprophyre sighed. "Now I'm having trouble not planning too far into the future, and daydreaming about you being transformed into that beautiful form."

"Is it that beautiful? To dragon eyes, I mean?"

"You know how Flint is handsome? That sculpture makes him look positively homely."

Rokshan laughed. "I suppose that gratifies my vanity." He leaned out to look over her shoulder as they flew over the brightly-lit embassy courtyard. "Wait. You have a visitor."

Lamprophyre banked and curved back around. "It's a little late for that, don't you think?" But he was right. The visitor, if that's who it was, was invisible inside a plain litter with brown curtains. Lamprophyre examined the bearers as she descended, but they weren't dressed in any particular uniform or colors. Whoever this was, she or he had worked hard for anonymity.

The person also knew enough about dragons not to wait in the center of the courtyard. The bearers had set the litter near the entrance to the embassy, leaving plenty of room for Lamprophyre to land. They didn't react at all to her arrival, even though the wind her wings made stirred their short hair. Lamprophyre crouched for Rokshan to jump down, then approached the litter cautiously. It wasn't as if any human could hurt her, but the whole situation was so strange she felt wary, as if whoever this was brought danger with them.

"Can I help you?" she asked, leaning down to put her head level with the litter.

The curtain moved. "I hope I can help you," the Archprelate said.

Startled, Lamprophyre moved back to let the woman climb out of the litter. "Most Holy One," she said. "Um, is there a polite way to ask what you're doing here?"

The Archprelate laughed. Her voice, and her laugh, were the sweet peal of tinkling bells, a sound that put Lamprophyre more at ease. "I take it as a given that dragons always intend politeness. May I enter your embassy?"

"Of course." Lamprophyre stepped back farther so the Archprelate could precede her into the embassy. Rokshan followed, his expression bland, which told Lamprophyre her mate was suppressing his curiosity. She felt full to bursting of questions herself.

Once inside, the Archprelate lowered the scarf covering her hair, which was cut unusually short for a woman and tousled from the fabric. Lamprophyre knew she was older than Rokshan by about ten years, which still made her very young to be the spiritual leader of a nation. Her bright eyes surveyed the room, taking in the piles of books, the scribbled-on slates, and Rokshan's bed. "I heard a rumor," she said absently, her mind clearly elsewhere. "By what I see here...well, I'm sure not all of it is true, but now I wonder."

"What rumor?" Lamprophyre asked, though she already knew.

The Archprelate's eyes came to rest on Rokshan. "That you, your highness, fell in love with a dragon, against reason, against nature."

"You're right, that's not entirely true," Rokshan said. "I fell in love with the human woman Lamprophyre was transformed into. My feelings haven't changed even though she's a dragon again."

"That seems reasonable," the Archprelate said. Once again she scanned the room. "Isn't that what we expect of two people who marry, who swear vows of fidelity to each other? People change over the years, and our hope is that our love does not—or, possibly that it grows to encompass those changes."

Lamprophyre gaped. "That's so sensible."

The Archprelate laughed again. "Surprised to hear sense from an ecclesiast?"

"No. I just wish everyone understood the way you do."

"I'm sorry they don't. It can't be easy, loving someone not of your species. What do you intend to do?"

"I will become a dragon," Rokshan said.

"Daring," the Archprelate said. "I wish you luck." She drew in a deep breath and released it in a long, slow hiss. "But that's not why I'm here."

"You said you wanted to help me," Lamprophyre said. "In what way?"

"The only way I feel capable of in these troubled days," the Archprelate said. "I have been possessed of a prophecy, and when it was recounted to me, I knew at once it was intended for you."

Lamprophyre sat heavily, staring at the woman. "I didn't understand the last one," she said. "I don't mean to be rude, but—you know what I saw on Mother Stone. Whatever Jiwanyil is, he's not a god. And I don't trust him."

"I know what you told us. And the conclusions you drew." The Archprelate fingered her scarf, twisting its soft fabric around her fingers. "Let me ask you a question, ambassador. If, let us say, Hyaloclast...if Hyaloclast, after a lifetime of advice and guidance you knew to be good, suddenly told you something you believed not only false, but harmful, what would be your reaction?"

"You know the answer. I would want to know more."

"Yes. You wouldn't reject that lifetime's experience based on a single bad moment. Ambassador, I have been an ecclesiast for over twenty years—a blink of the eye to you, but more than a quarter of a human life. Before that, I was a faithful worshipper of Jiwanyil from my childhood. I have been possessed of many prophecies, many of which I was privileged to see come to pass. And last year I stood with my brothers and sisters and saw Jiwanyil's light fall on me, naming me Archprelate."

Lamprophyre said, mulishly, "That's all very well, but Jiwanyil made me his tool in freeing Sardonyx. And I have very few experiences like yours."

"As I have no reason to trust Hyaloclast. But you've asked the humans of Gonjiri to put their lives more or less in her hands, hers and those of your dragons." The Archprelate gripped her scarf more tightly. "I'm here to ask you to put your trust in me, and in this prophecy."

Lamprophyre glanced at Rokshan. His expression was blank again. She listened to his thoughts and heard only *so strange, why* and a sense of confusion. Rokshan was a faithful worshipper of Jiwanyil, too, and had been more shaken by Jiwanyil's actions than she. She felt an unexpected flash of anger on Rokshan's behalf. If Jiwanyil was God, why didn't he care about the people who worshipped him?

"Tell me your prophecy," she said. "I promise to listen. I don't promise anything else."

"That's enough for me." The Archprelate let go of her scarf, which was now terribly wrinkled. "These are the words Jiwanyil wants you to hear: *The voice in darkness summons you. Born of wind and fire and stone, to breath and ash and stone return. They await who bound the banded desert.*" Her voice shook. "*Your death is in the stone.*"

Lamprophyre felt numb. She realized she was sitting and that Rokshan was saying her name. "How did he know?" she whispered. "The death-song. How did he know it?"

"Take a breath," Rokshan said. "It doesn't have to mean anything."

She shot Rokshan a stricken look. "You know it does," she said. She stood heavily and towered over the Archprelate. "What does it mean?"

The Archprelate didn't flinch. "I have no idea. The prophecy wasn't meant for me. But 'voice in darkness,' that, I have heard before. In another prophecy I was possessed of, years ago. I never learned the meaning."

Lamprophyre cast her mind back to the research Dharan had done at the Hall of Visions, months back. "I remember. Shevaan. It was your name on that prophecy." She couldn't keep her voice from shaking. "But the voice in darkness...it's Sardonyx."

CHAPTER FORTY-FOUR

"That doesn't make any sense," Rokshan said. He gripped her hand tightly. "Why would Sardonyx summon you?"

"You already understand more of the prophecy than any of the ecclesiasts," the Archprelate said. "The only reference we knew was what we were told, that 'banded desert' refers to Sardonyx. But the ones who bound her a millennium ago are dead, so how can they—oh." The woman looked unexpectedly flustered.

"You mean because I'm doomed to die, and they're waiting for me to join them," Lamprophyre said. "I refuse to believe any of this is true. Jiwanyil is trying to demoralize me so I won't fight him and Sardonyx."

"That is not the intent of prophecy," the Archprelate said sharply. "It is not a guide to a future you must passively accept. It is to give you a glimpse of where your current efforts will take you."

"But's that's almost worse! My current efforts are to fight Sardonyx. Is this saying continuing to fight her will end in my death?"

"I don't know," the Archprelate said, her voice rising. "It might as easily mean aid from an unexpected source. If those who bound

Sardonyx are capable of waiting for anything, that suggests to me their power is still out there. Perhaps you should be looking for an unexpected solution."

"But they were all destroyed," Rokshan said. "The mountain swallowed them up—yes, I know that's metaphor, but that doesn't make it false."

"No—wait." Lamprophyre hadn't thought about Evart's notes in days. "Remember how Evart knew Sardonyx was bound somehow? We thought that meant she had an enemy, someone we might be able to enlist. What if this prophecy is a hint about that person?"

Rokshan held her hand tighter. "What happened to the idea that the prophecy doesn't have to mean anything?"

"You don't believe that, do you?"

His mouth made a tight, straight line. "If I believe it," he said, "I have to believe your death is a possibility."

"I know. But—" Lamprophyre closed her eyes briefly. "Rokshan, all our deaths are a possibility. I'd rather look for a more optimistic meaning. Because I hardly need a prophecy to know I'm in danger. We all are."

Rokshan sighed and released her. "Is there anything else you can tell us?" he asked the Archprelate.

"I wish I could. I can only offer my opinion that Jiwanyil does, despite appearances, want us to survive. I believe, if he orchestrated Sardonyx's freedom, it was for a reason we will eventually understand and appreciate." She hesitated, then extended her hand to Lamprophyre. "I have instructed the ecclesiasts to meditate and ponder on this prophecy. If we learn anything, we will tell you immediately."

"Thank you," Lamprophyre said. The Archprelate's small hand was cool and firm. "For everything. I'm still not convinced Jiwanyil means us well, but I'm willing to consider his words and look deeper."

"That's really all God ever asks of us," the Archprelate said. She raised the scarf to cover her head. "And, Prince Rokshan? By everything I've heard, your faith has been a light and a shield to you your whole life. It seems Jiwanyil has chosen to test your faith. I hope you will hold fast to what you know as you reach for what is just beyond your grasp."

"I'm no longer sure what I know," Rokshan said, bowing, "but I'll keep that in mind."

The Archprelate nodded. She climbed into her litter, and the four muscular men lifted it and carried it away with no direction from her. Lamprophyre watched her go. "I'm not sure what I know, either," she said. "Why would Jiwanyil give me such a warning?"

"I wish I knew," Rokshan said. "How seriously do you want to take it?"

Lamprophyre shook her head. A moth flew drunkenly into the lantern flame and sizzled briefly before hitting the ground. "If I understood it at all—as it is, taking it seriously would mean looking for my doom in every shadow. And yet all those prophecies warning of dangers to cities have been accurate. Whatever Jiwanyil is, he can see the future."

"Can see the future, and seems interested in protecting humans after setting their destruction loose on the world," Rokshan said. Then he went very still. "I wonder..."

"Wonder what?"

"We said Sardonyx had a powerful enemy. Suppose it's Jiwanyil?"

Lamprophyre laughed. "Jiwanyil wanted her freed, not captive."

"But he, or his voice, or something, was present in the cave. And—what did he say about Sardonyx? Did he specifically say he wanted her freed?"

Lamprophyre thought back over Jiwanyil's words. "He didn't. He talked about the old contract being fulfilled, and that humans and dragons should fight her together, and that Mother Stone wasn't a god."

"You see? There's nothing to indicate Jiwanyil was helping Sardonyx." Rokshan paced swiftly in front of her. "And he must be powerful to give all those prophecies."

Another moth blundered into the same lantern. Its body sent up a faint odor of scorched hair. Lamprophyre watched it fall, distracted by its death. "But there isn't anything to indicate he was keeping her trapped, either," she said, "and, again, if he *was* keeping her captive, why put the effort into having a human free her? I'm not saying you're wrong, I'm just saying it's not a theory I'm ready to base my hopes on."

"Then let's go back to the cave. If Jiwanyil is still there, he might answer our questions." Rokshan hurried into the embassy and retrieved the harness from where it lay coiled in a corner.

"But the light disappeared. He couldn't still be there."

"He certainly isn't inside me. We would have noticed that. It's worth a quick trip. If he really is gone, we're not any worse off than we were before. And if he's there..."

Lamprophyre took a step back when he approached her, offering the harness. "We can't go now. It's the middle of the night almost. And we definitely can't take off for Mother Stone when we don't know what Sardonyx intends. If we're gone when she attacks—Rokshan, see sense."

Rokshan lowered his hand and let the harness drag on the floor. "You're right. It's just if it's true that Jiwanyil is Sardonyx's enemy, his power could make a difference."

"If he's willing to use it on our behalf. He wasn't exactly forthcoming the last time we encountered him." Lamprophyre put her hand on Rokshan's shoulder. "We can go in the morning, with Hyaloclast knowing what we intend so she can summon us back if the worst happens."

"With the way my life is going, Sardonyx will attack when we're almost to Mother Stone but not far enough to have reached Jiwanyil," Rokshan muttered.

"I'm sure that won't happen." Lamprophyre prodded one of the dead moths with her toe. They were such fragile creatures, and yet they were drawn to their destruction. She wished those words didn't so accurately describe humans as well. "Do you need to speak to General Sajan?"

Rokshan fished a chalcedony pendant out of his shirt. "I do, but this will suffice. Probably better than suffice, because he can't find more work for me if I'm not standing in front of him."

"All right. I'm going to sleep. We'll want an early start if we're to make this a quick trip." Lamprophyre squeezed Rokshan's hand gently and went into the dark embassy to settle herself for sleep. Distantly, she heard Rokshan talking to the general, but she covered herself with her wings and ignored their conversation.

She slept fitfully, waking just enough to snap out of her dreams, falling into a new dream every time she slept again. Some of them shredded to nothing when she woke. Others were strange mixtures of real events and fantasy, like the one in which she and her clutch fought flying cows the colors of dragons that breathed meat-scented clouds of acid that burned her skin. In another dream, she was arguing with Jiwanyil about something Porphyry had done, something Jiwanyil insisted Porphyry had to pay for with his life. That one, she woke from with an aching head and throat, wishing she could cry.

Finally, she clawed her way out of a dream in which she was once more human and she and Rokshan were naked together, kissing and touching until she couldn't bear it any longer and made herself wake. Rokshan snored quietly nearby. The sky outside was overcast, but she could see the outline of her fingers and concluded dawn was near. She lay, breathing slowly to dispel the last vestiges of the wonderfully detailed dream, until she was calm enough to wake Rokshan.

He sat up, rubbing sleep out of his eyes as he always did, and focused on her. "You were serious about an early start, weren't you?"

"I didn't want to sleep any longer. The more I think about it, the more certain I am that no matter who Jiwanyil is, he has knowledge we can use." She tried smoothing Rokshan's hair and just made it messier.

"All right. But we should eat. It's a long flight."

Lamprophyre grumbled, but hurried to buy a cow while Rokshan dressed. She returned to find Depik talking to Rokshan in the courtyard. "You shouldn't have to do that, my lady, it's my job," Depik protested.

"I hoped we wouldn't disturb you. We're in a hurry this morning." Lamprophyre took the cow carcass to the kitchen and roasted it herself, careful not to leave any uncooked pieces. She carved off some meat for Rokshan and set to feeding herself.

"Is it another attack?" Depik asked. He sounded curious rather than fearful, but from his thoughts Lamprophyre knew he wasn't overconfident or stupid; he had faith that she would defend his family against any threat.

"We're going to see about a new way to fight," Rokshan said. Lamprophyre figured that was as accurate an explanation as anything.

"I hope you'll take care, then, my lady." Depik handed her a napkin without further comment. She wiped her mouth and hands. Trust Depik to be concerned about her manners even in the predawn hours when there was no one around to see.

In the courtyard, she crouched for Rokshan, well bundled in his cold-weather gear, to climb into the saddle. "We shouldn't be gone long," she said, and hoped she hadn't just lied to Depik.

"Good luck, my lady," Depik said, waving, and they were off.

The dragons in the field still slept, but Hyaloclast stirred and sat up when Lamprophyre landed beside her. "Is something wrong?" she asked.

"Rokshan and I have an idea," Lamprophyre said. "We're going to Mother Stone to speak to Jiwanyil."

Hyaloclast stretched her arms and then her wings. "What would be the point of that?"

Lamprophyre laid out the essence of what she and Rokshan had discussed. "At the very least, we could learn something about Sardonyx's weaknesses. And if we're right, Jiwanyil, whatever he is, could be a powerful ally."

"If Sardonyx attacks while you're away, we will be at a disadvantage." Hyaloclast looked at Rokshan, who looked uncomfortable in his heavy coat despite the coolness of the morning. "This is a terrible risk for no guaranteed benefit."

"Jiwanyil gave Lamprophyre a prophecy last night," Rokshan said. "He quoted some of the death-song of the dragons. If Jiwanyil knows that, imagine what else he might be able to tell us."

"You still have faith in your God?"

"I don't know what I believe anymore," Rokshan said, "but I intend to ask Jiwanyil for answers."

Hyaloclast nodded once. "I will tell you if Sardonyx attacks," she said, tapping the blue chalcedony pendant. "Be prepared to return immediately."

"I will," Lamprophyre said. She pushed off with her powerful legs and soon was in the air, high above the patchwork blanket of dragons. She saw Hyaloclast lift one hand in farewell before she left them all behind.

"I hope this isn't a mistake," she said after a few dozen beats. "I mean, I know the risk we're taking, and I believe it's acceptable, but there's a part of me that feels only that I'm leaving my clutch to fight alone."

"We're not so indispensable that they're helpless without us," Rokshan said. "And the other dragons aren't helpless either. I spoke with Leucite two days ago, when we were preparing the dragons to meet potential riders, and he said they've developed new tactics. Each clutch works together to target an enemy dragon, and then they take turns distracting it and attacking it. It's far more effective than individuals trying to take on the enemy alone."

"That does sound like smart tactics."

"My point is that we shouldn't think of ourselves as key to the battle. There are many dragons intent on defeating Sardonyx, and they won't fall to pieces without us."

Lamprophyre laughed. "I know you're right. It's silly of me to think otherwise. I've just been at odds with Sardonyx for so long, the two of us in opposition, I'm used to facing her alone."

Rokshan patted her neck with his gloved hand. "You aren't alone any longer."

"I do still wonder why she singled me out. Aside from bringing humans and dragons together, I don't know that I've done anything special to hurt her. It's not like I developed the pyrite weapons, or the harness that lets humans go into battle with dragons, or the shield."

"Bringing humans and dragons together was plenty," Rokshan said. "Imagine if you hadn't spoken on my behalf to Hyaloclast when I approached her for an alliance. Or if you hadn't accepted the position of ambassador. There's no reason to think Jiwanyil wouldn't still have wanted Sardonyx freed, and then humans would all be destroyed and dragons would be subjugated."

"I suppose." Lamprophyre flew higher to take advantage of an updraft. "I guess I'm just saying, why not single out you, or General Sajan, or the Fanishkorites who developed the shield?"

"I don't know, and I'm grateful she didn't," Rokshan said.

The rising sun burned off the low-lying mist, and the day was clear and cloudless all the way to the distant mountains. Lamprophyre flew high enough that the ground beneath was a featureless gray-green mass, wrinkled where it met the Green River. The other rivers shone blue-gray beneath the pale blue sky. Despite her ongoing tension over the possibility of Sardonyx attacking while she was away, Lamprophyre couldn't help appreciating the beauty of her surroundings. Flying was the most marvelous thing in the world.

Ahead, the gray line that was the mountains grew and solidified until it seemed more real than the landscape surrounding it. Lamprophyre climbed higher. They didn't have time to take the ascent of Mother Stone as slowly as was safest, so she gradually gained altitude until she'd passed the foothills and lower slopes and was skimming well above the peaks where the dragons lived.

At least one storm had come through the Handmaidens since she and Rokshan had been there last, and the tall, forbidding mountains were nearly pure white with packed snow. Lamprophyre began the long, curving ascent to the cave on Mother Stone, hoping she could still find it despite the alteration the snow had made to the landscape. She counted off beats, comparing her flight to the previous one.

But it turned out not to matter. The black patch marking the cave mouth and the ledge in front of it were as clear of snow as if a dragon had heated the stone to melt it. Lamprophyre alit on the ledge and examined the cavern warily. "I think we should fly," she said. "If we have to leave in a hurry—"

"Why? You don't think there's anything dangerous left here?" Rokshan had walked a few paces toward the entrance, and now he stopped and turned to face her.

"I was thinking more of if Hyaloclast summons us, but now I'm thinking about whether Jiwanyil has more powers than just the ability to speak cryptic prophecies."

Rokshan shrugged. "I doubt it, but I think you're right we should be prepared to move quickly. Besides, the terrain isn't easy for me to cross." He climbed back up, turned on his light cylinder, and Lamprophyre glided gently into the narrow passage.

She'd known before it was a tight fit for someone flying, but it wasn't as tight as she remembered, not now that she wasn't in a terrified rush. Even so, she winced every time she brushed the wall with the tip of her wing. She was relieved when the passage widened. Below, the jagged floor shone with its coating of ice, and soon ice crept over the walls and ceiling until every draft was damp and frigid.

The downhill slant of the passage was more noticeable now that she was flying instead of clambering over the irregular floor. She estimated they descended more than two dragonlengths before they reached the bowl-shaped chamber. It looked so different now. Huge jagged chunks and slabs of ice covered the floor, which was milky and rough from hundreds of impacts fracturing its coat of ice. The light from the chimney was almost gone now that the chimney walls weren't frozen and reflective. Lamprophyre was grateful for Rokshan's light.

The walls had shattered, revealing dozens of cubbies sized to fit a full-grown dragon. The matte-black granite of their walls absorbed the light and reflected nothing back. Looking into one of the cubbies, Lamprophyre felt momentarily confused, as if she were looking into the black eye of some creature the size of the mountain. She touched the stone, and the illusion vanished. The room still smelled faintly bitter, too faintly when one considered there was almost no air movement to clear the stink away. But then, the dragons who'd been entombed here hadn't been dead.

"I don't see the light," Rokshan said. "The floor is covered with ice chunks. Do you remember where it was?"

Lamprophyre oriented herself. "That way," she said, pointing, and slowly flapped her way across the cavern, scanning the floor. Rokshan was right; the blocks and thick shards of ice made it impossible to see anything set into the floor.

"Turn off your light," she said. Rokshan gave the cylinder a half-twist, and darkness descended over the cavern. A thin gray light showed where the chimney began, growing brighter as Lamprophyre's eyes adjusted to the dimness. And there, half a dragonlength away, was a greenish-white glow illuminating a pile of ice chunks.

"Let's go," Rokshan said when Lamprophyre didn't move.

"I don't know," she said. "The last time, Jiwanyil spoke through you. What if that's the only way he has to communicate?"

"Then he speaks through me. You know what questions to ask, so what's the problem?"

"The problem is I think you're not taking this seriously. We have no idea what he really is. What if his presence is dangerous? What if it kills you, or damages your mind like Sardonyx did Zefira?"

Rokshan slid off and staggered around the littered floor until he could face her. "No ecclesiast has ever been hurt by a prophecy."

"That's not true. Khadar has seizures when he's possessed of a prophecy, and Bhakriya's daughter Preyanka does too."

Rokshan waved that away. "Those are the aftereffects because the human body has to build up resistance to being touched by God. I mean Jiwanyil wants people to benefit from his sight and wisdom, which is why his prophecies don't kill people outright, or what would be the point? If he didn't kill me before, I don't see why he would now."

Lamprophyre's eyes were acclimated enough now that she could see Rokshan as a vague gray shape surmounted by the lighter oval that was his protective cap. She couldn't see his expression, but she knew him well enough to know when he sounded this reasonable, his mind was made up. "I don't like it."

"I know. But what was the point of coming here if we weren't going to take this chance?"

Lamprophyre didn't want to admit she hadn't remembered this detail until moments ago. "You're right. But if you start to foam at the mouth, I'm smashing the ice and hauling you out of here."

"That's fair."

They proceeded on foot, scrambling and crawling over the irregular surface. Lamprophyre occasionally gave Rokshan a hand over the rougher spots. Every time she touched him, she felt less certain that this was a good idea—but Rokshan was right, and this was no time to be a coward.

It took a few dozen beats to find the spot where the light burned beneath the ice. They had to haul away big broken chunks of ice to clear the floor, but when they were finished, the light burned as clear and green as before. Rokshan lowered himself to kneel beside it. "The ice is too thick for me to see if this is anything more than a light," he said. "Like, if there's a sculpture or a stone or something the light is coming from."

"Do you feel strange?" Lamprophyre asked.

He shook his head. "It's very bright, but that's all." He hesitated, then laid his gloved hand spread flat over the light. It cast a funny shadow on his face. "Still nothing."

Lamprophyre let out a breath. "I don't know whether to be relieved or disappointed."

"Me neither. I guess we were wrong about what this light is. It's not—"

He stopped speaking and went rigidly still. Dread struck Lamprophyre, making her as immobile as Rokshan. She swallowed to moisten a throat gone suddenly dry. "Rokshan?" she said, her voice sounding as weak as a newborn dragonet's.

Slowly, Rokshan's head rose. His eyes were brilliantly leaf-green from edge to edge. "*You return*," Jiwanyil said. "*Return, and be made one.*"

CHAPTER FORTY-FIVE

"Made one with what?" Lamprophyre managed through her tight, dry throat.

"The truth is in the stone," Jiwanyil said. *"Ask, be answered, be one."*

Everything she and Rokshan had discussed, every question she might have asked, deserted her. Seeing Rokshan possessed of Jiwanyil's voice, his face expressionless and as still as death, made her want to snatch him away, and Stones take Jiwanyil. But this was why they'd come. She swallowed again and said, "Were you the reason Sardonyx was a captive? Are you her enemy?"

"Let stone and wind and fire combine, bind those who end their journey here." Jiwanyil's voice sounded conversational, as if he'd commented on the weather. It took Lamprophyre a beat to realize he'd quoted the death-song of the dragons.

"I don't understand," she said. "Just—let me think." Stone and wind and fire—those were the elements a dragon was made of, in a poetical sense. Let those things combine and bind them, but how? Something to do with the fact that dragons died on Mother Stone, or had until recently. "Dragons," she said slowly. "Dragons had something to do with Sardonyx's captivity."

"Bind the old stone," Jiwanyil said.

"But where do you come in, if it was dragons doing it?" Lamprophyre felt as if she were feeling her way blind along an icy ledge, her wings pinned, her feet slipping and threatening to drop her over the side to fall to her death. Everything she had was a guess, and Jiwanyil's riddles didn't help.

"*To live, to follow,*" Jiwanyil said. "*Call and answer. Bind the old stone.*"

Lamprophyre blew out her breath in frustration. Time for a different question. "Does that mean you helped? You have power over Sardonyx?"

Jiwanyil didn't answer at first. Lamprophyre waited impatiently. Finally, he said, "*The old contract is fulfilled. Release the wind and fire to roam free. Human and dragon together fight to her destruction. The power is in them.*"

"But we don't have any power except the weapons and our own claws," Lamprophyre protested. "If there's anything you can do—if you're God—we really need that help."

"*Ask and answer. Call and return,*" Jiwanyil said.

"I *don't understand,*" Lamprophyre said through gritted teeth. "Why did you want Sardonyx freed? Are you our ally, or not?"

Once more Jiwanyil paused, for longer this time. Lamprophyre was about to repeat her question when he said, "*The old contract is fulfilled. The banded desert grows in power. The wind and fire roam free.*"

"I know that!" Lamprophyre let out a slow breath, calming herself. Yelling at this creature wouldn't get her anywhere. "You gave me two prophecies. What do they mean? Am I doomed?"

Rokshan's head moved side to side, so slowly she didn't at first recognize it as a gesture meaning "no." "*Return, and be made one,*" Jiwanyil said. "*They await who bound the wind and fire. Be one.*"

"You mean the people who fought Sardonyx before the Great Cataclysm."

"*Be one,*" Jiwanyil said, his voice louder. A drop of blood welled in Rokshan's nostril and spilled down his upper lip. "*Ask, and answer. Be one.*"

Rokshan convulsed. His eyes, still wide open, blazed with green light. Lamprophyre cried out and held him close against the seizure that racked his body. "Stop!" she screamed. "Stop! You're killing him!"

Jiwanyil said nothing. Rokshan's convulsions gradually calmed and then stopped. Lamprophyre eased her hold on him and felt he was still breathing, though heavily, as if he was gasping for air. The green light beneath the ice gradually faded, ebbing like liquid poured down a drain. Eventually, all the light was gone, and they were in near-darkness. "Rokshan?" she said, bending over him. "Rokshan, are you all right?"

Rokshan twitched. She could barely see his eyes open, but they weren't glowing green, and it reassured her. "Can't...move..." he whispered. "Exhausted."

"I'm taking you out of here. It's far too cold," Lamprophyre said. Gathering him up gently, she flew away from the cavern, up through the passage until they were past the ice-rimed stones. Then she heated the walls and the floor and sat in the middle of the warm spot with Rokshan in her arms. "Better?"

Rokshan nodded. He lifted his hand to wipe the blood off his face, moving so slowly he looked like a puppet whose strings were controlled by a very old, arthritic man. "He spoke?"

"He did. I don't know how helpful it was. It certainly wasn't information worth you dying for." Lamprophyre recited the conversation for Rokshan, leaving out the thoughts she'd had. "I don't know what to think," she concluded. "He withdrew his presence when I shouted at him, so I think he has *some* concern for life, but I don't know that he understands our limitations himself."

"Or he was done speaking, and it's a coincidence," Rokshan said.

"That's possible too." Lamprophyre blew out a gout of flame at the opposite wall, heating the stones again. "But I think I'm right. Stones, but I wish I'd known the right questions to ask!"

"Why do you think you asked the wrong questions?"

Lamprophyre watched the glowing stones fade to ash-gray. "I don't know. Maybe if I'd asked the right questions, the answers would have made sense?"

"They did make sense, to an extent." Rokshan shifted his weight, but made no move to sit up. "He told you dragons had something to do with Sardonyx's captivity. And we now know there was something, some contract, that released her when she was freed. Which suggests that the people who bound her in the first place never meant it to be permanent."

That hadn't occurred to Lamprophyre. "Why would they do that?"

"I don't know. In human terms, human contracts are sometimes for a limited time. Like a lease on a property, or the temporary use of a resource. The idea is that the owner of the property or resource thinks they can negotiate a better deal at the end of the term. So they benefit during the time of the lease, and then they're free to enter into another contract."

"So how does that apply here? They wanted a chance to bind Sardonyx a second time?"

Rokshan shrugged. This time, he sat up, slowly as if he ached everywhere. "We don't know enough—don't know anything—about how they bound her in the first place. But I suppose if entombing her and her dragons on Mother Stone was the best they could do—didn't you say they likely would have killed her if they'd been capable? So maybe they left a provision for someone to come along later with a permanent solution. Help me stand, please?"

Lamprophyre put her arm around his waist and steadied him on the uneven floor. "That seems like a lot of guesswork, especially since they didn't bother leaving instructions for whoever came along later. Like us."

"Yes. I'm not convinced I'm right. But it's a possibility that fits what we do know." Rokshan clung to Lamprophyre's arm a beat or two longer, then stood on his own feet, wavering slightly. "Though it doesn't explain how Jiwanyil comes into it."

"I'm even more convinced he's not God. It was like talking to someone whose mind is fragmented. Like he didn't understand most of my questions and he lacked the words to answer what he did understand." Lamprophyre tensed to catch Rokshan if he fell.

"Do you think you can ride? I want out of here. The place is unnerving."

"I think I can hang on. I almost feel myself again. It's funny, but I was thinking the opposite—that the place feels empty and nonthreatening." With a few tries, Rokshan climbed into the saddle and fastened the hip straps.

"Well, Jiwanyil appears to be gone, so you're probably right." Lamprophyre pushed off and flapped a few times to propel herself forward and up. The place did feel empty, but that was what unnerved her; there were thousands of dragons buried around the mountain, and she'd expected to feel that somehow. But this cavern hadn't been a final resting place, it had been a prison, and she didn't feel that either. She'd grown up believing she as a dragon had a connection to Mother Stone and to her ancestors, and maybe since Mother Stone wasn't a god, that belief was false all around. The thought made her feel angry and frustrated and sad, all at once.

She left the cavern behind for the fresh, freezing air and the brilliant sunlight, coasting down from the mountain heights without speaking. Thank the Stones Sardonyx hadn't attacked while they were gone, because Lamprophyre didn't feel they'd learned anything that would have justified their absence when they were needed to fight. In the distance, she heard an avalanche, the only noise aside from the sound of her wings that broke the stillness. It would have been deafening up close, but it was far enough away that it was barely louder than the sound of her stomach rumbling would have been.

"Well," Rokshan said abruptly, "it was worth trying. And at least you know those prophecies weren't meant to foretell your doom."

"But he said 'be one,'" Lamprophyre said. "Be one with what? The ones who bound Sardonyx are dead, so I don't see how I can be one with them *and* not face my death."

"I wonder if that's not something that will become clear later." Rokshan leaned forward to lie along her neck so his voice came clearer to her ear. "It is a pretty straightforward answer, but it's missing a key element. A lot of prophecies interlock like that, referring to each other, one prophecy giving information about another or a key word that makes another prophecy clear."

"The Archprelate did say the ecclesiasts will continue to try to interpret it." Lamprophyre dropped lower to skim the tops of the peaks where the dragons lived. "I've decided not to worry about it anymore. We took a chance, and either it was pointless, or we need more knowledge. Either way, we've done what we can. We should see if there's any way we can help the dragons make human friends."

"I should probably speak to Sajan," Rokshan said. "But I want to change out of these clothes first. Today looks like it's going to be unusually warm."

Lamprophyre had been so on edge the whole way to Mother Stone, fearing the chalcedony pendant growing warm and misty with the summons for them to return, she felt as tired as if she'd exerted herself beyond a simple flight. Now, she found herself incapable of fear, filled with resignation over the future. If Sardonyx attacked, all they could do was fly at top speed to meet her, and there wasn't anything she could do to change that. So she flew, not speeding along and not ambling, her mind wandering.

She caught sight of a cloud, and idly contemplated how much it looked like one of Sardonyx's monstrous dragons, bulky with spiny, ribbed wings, its mouth open to devour its victim. The thought jolted her out of her complacency, and she shivered. Humans could casually look for shapes in clouds because there was no chance they would ever encounter those shapes on their own ground.

Unfortunately, it seemed seeing that one shape triggered something, and soon she couldn't see anything but shapes: a horse's head, a trailing necklace of white beads, another dragon, this one missing a wing. The fear she thought she'd left behind redoubled, and she dropped lower, away from the unsettling clouds. Stones knew what might happen if she flew into one of those shapes. That was ridiculous, they were still just water mist, but her imagination had her in its grip and flying low made her more comfortable.

They skimmed along, following the Green River, until Tanajital came in sight. The thick clouds that had so unnerved Lamprophyre gradually dissipated until the sky was mostly clear, and Rokshan was right, it was going to be a warm day for early winter. Lamprophyre stretched her wings, enjoying how the sun's rays beat down on them. It was too lovely a day to let fear rule her. She didn't have to become complacent, she didn't have to pretend Sardonyx didn't exist, she just had to set those fears aside until they became reality, at which point she'd face them.

The embassy courtyard was as quiet as it usually was around noon on days she didn't have to hold court. Lamprophyre crouched for Rokshan to get down, which he did easily, showing no sign of the weakness Jiwanyil had caused. Abhit emerged from the embassy when she arrived, holding a book. "I forgot to ask if it was all right that I borrow this book," he said.

"You can borrow any of them you like, so long as you don't take them out of the embassy grounds," Lamprophyre said. "And you have to read Dharan's books in the embassy."

"I remember." Abhit turned and walked back into the embassy.

Rokshan had already shed his coat and gloves and was following Abhit. "Will you take me to the training grounds after I change?" he said over his shoulder.

"Of course. Then we can visit the flight and see if there's been any progress." Lamprophyre settled in the center of the courtyard and stretched her wings again, then her tail. The courtyard smelled of dust, dry and warm, and she dug a little of the hard-packed earth up with her useless sixth claw and rubbed the dust into the back of her hand, polishing her scales. Yes, this place was home—maybe not the home of her heart, but it was a place she'd grown to love.

"Lamprophyre?" Rokshan's voice sounded strange, tense and worried. "Did you move the sodalite artifact?"

Lamprophyre sat up. "I haven't touched it since Kamil brought it. Didn't you hang it on the wall?"

"I thought I had." Rokshan came to the doorway. Deep worry lines creased his forehead. "But it's not there. Abhit, have you seen a blue stone artifact? Dark blue rings with gold filling the grooves on their surfaces?"

Lamprophyre walked over to join Rokshan and saw Abhit look up from where he sat next to the pile of books, his thumb keeping his place in the one he was reading. "I saw it hanging on the wall yesterday," he said, "but I wouldn't touch any of your things, Rokshan."

"Well, it's not there now." Rokshan returned to stand beside an empty peg next to the one that held his flying coat, as if the sodalite artifact might magically reappear. "Abhit, this is important. Are you sure you didn't move it? You or anyone else in the household?"

Abhit looked grave. "I said I wouldn't touch anything that's yours, and I promise it's true. But maybe Mama or Depik took it for cleaning?"

Lamprophyre exchanged glances with Rokshan. "I can't imagine Bhakriya or Depik doing anything like that," Lamprophyre said.

"Let's ask anyway." The worry lines had grown deeper. Lamprophyre had started to worry herself.

"I don't know that I've seen the artifact you mention," Depik said when they spoke to him in the kitchen. He was preparing a noon meal for the humans and his attention was on the bread he'd just pulled from the oven.

"Depik, please, this is important," Lamprophyre said. "It's a bunch of rings of different sizes connected to a disc by gold chains. Are you *sure* you don't recall seeing it?"

Depik set the bread on the counter and wiped his hands on his apron. "No, I really don't, my lady. I'm sorry. It sounds like it might be expensive. Does it do anything special?"

"It's irreplaceable," Rokshan said. "Bhakriya, did you clean the embassy today? Did you see a blue stone artifact hanging on the wall?"

"I saw it yesterday," Bhakriya said. She held a bucket of water she'd filled from the barrel and now stood holding it as if she'd forgotten it was there in the effort of remembering. "That was about this time of day, actually. I tidied the books and made your bed, your highness, and I remember the artifact because I brushed against it and the rings made a pretty sound when they clinked against each other. But it wasn't there a few hours ago when I did the cleaning. I thought you or my lady had taken it."

Lamprophyre looked at Rokshan again. Her stomach felt sick, as if she were falling and falling and the ground was coming up fast. Rokshan's face had gone completely impassive. "It can't be gone," she said. "It just can't."

Bhakriya turned and called out Rassika's name. Soon the girl came around the back of the dining pavilion. "Did you move my lady's artifact? The blue stone one on the wall?" Bhakriya asked.

Rassika's eyes narrowed. "I never touch my lady's things, not without she says I can," she said. Then she blushed. "That ain't true for all," she admitted. "I touched it to feel the gold streaks, but I di'nt pick it up or nothing. Just put a finger on it. It di'nt fall off the peg either, so I di'nt have to lift it. Was that wrong? I di'nt think there was nothing wrong with just a touch."

"No, that's fine," Lamprophyre said hastily, seeing that Rassika was becoming distressed. "When was the last time you saw it?"

Rassika stood stiffly. "I was in the embassy putting a book back before supper yesterday," she said, "and that's when I touched it. But I swear I never moved it. I swear."

Bhakriya put her arm around the girl's thin shoulders. "We believe you," she said. "My lady just needs to find it, and anything you know about it can help."

"So it was in the embassy at yesterday's suppertime," Lamprophyre said, and stopped, struck mute. "Stones," she whispered. "We weren't here then. And there are so many beggars, and only the four of you humans to keep an eye on the place..."

Bhakriya looked horrified. "You think someone stole from the embassy, my lady? I can't believe anyone would dare! And—but we can't watch everywhere at once, and Depik's always in the kitchen, and I've got to serve from the cook pot. Oh, my lady, if we let it happen—"

"Let's not go assigning blame just yet," Lamprophyre said. "I know how busy things are at suppertime. It would be easy for someone to sneak into the embassy even if Rokshan and I were here, because we're always inside the dining pavilion, and that doesn't give a full view of the courtyard."

"But who would dare steal from a dragon?" Rokshan said.

Bhakriya absently picked up Kavari, who'd clung to her legs, her mouth open with astonishment as if she could tell things were serious. "Somebody must have seen something. We just have to ask the regulars tonight."

"Somebody bad?" Kavari said.

"Yes, sweetheart, somebody bad took the pretty blue stones," Bhakriya said.

"It was the mean lady," Kavari said.

Everyone stared at her. Kavari ducked her head at the intensity of their regard. "The mean lady," she repeated.

"Kavari, what do you mean?" Lamprophyre asked.

"She came into the hall. I was looking at pictures and I saw her," Kavari said. "She took the blue rings off the wall and put them in her pouch. I went to see if she would let me look and she pushed me down. But I didn't cry even though it hurt," she said proudly.

"Kavari, this is important," Rokshan said, gently taking her small hand in his. "Can you tell us what she looked like?"

Kavari ducked her head again. "She was big," she said. "She had very long hair she kept pushing out of her face. And her chests were round and big, too."

Rokshan's eyes blazed. "Viveki," he said.

"But Viveki is short," Lamprophyre said.

Rokshan gestured dismissively. "Kavari is four. Everyone is big to her. Kavari, did the mean lady say anything?"

Kavari nodded. "She said I was a brat and to get out of her way. And that the stupid prince owed her."

"Definitely Viveki," Lamprophyre said. "What do we do?"

"We hunt her down and retrieve our property," Rokshan said. "I know where she lives. And then I will have her taken in charge and sent to prison for at least three lifetimes."

"I completely agree," Lamprophyre said. She returned to the courtyard and crouched for Rokshan to climb up. "Should we go to the guards first? Report the theft?"

Rokshan muttered something under his breath. "You're right," he said when Lamprophyre asked him to repeat himself. "We could go wrest the artifact from her greedy little hands immediately, but if we want her sent to prison, we have to do this the right way. To the guard headquarters, then, and hope Viveki didn't destroy the artifact and sell its pieces."

Lamprophyre crouched, preparing to take flight. "*Lamprophyre!*" Hyaloclast shouted.

Stumbling, Lamprophyre grabbed the pendant. "Yes? Is it—"

"*Gather your clutch and follow the Green River south,*" Hyaloclast said. "*The seer artifacts saw Sardonyx moving north just beats ago. Her whole flight. They passed Prabat without attacking. Their goal is almost certainly Tanajital.*"

CHAPTER FORTY-SIX

Time slowed to a crawl. It took forever to find her clutchmates and forever to track down their human riders. Every beat that passed seemed to last a lifetime. It was strange, Lamprophyre reflected, because her sense of Sardonyx approaching was, contrariwise, sped up, as if at any moment Lamprophyre might look south and see a mass of colors surging toward Tanajital.

Finally, *finally*, the six dragons and their friends were in the air and flying southward. Lamprophyre brought up the rear. She tried not to think of it as hiding behind the others. She had no fear of meeting Sardonyx, but after her unsettling encounter with Jiwanyil, she wanted her clutchmates where she could see them.

She listened to their surface thoughts and heard variations on the same thing: *ready to fight, stop her, no way around it.* No fear, no reluctance. She hoped her own reservations weren't audible. She couldn't stop going over Jiwanyil's words in memory, trying to make sense of them. Finally, she gave up. She was just exhausting herself to no purpose. Jiwanyil was no help, and that meant Sardonyx's defeat was up to the flight.

The blue chalcedony pendant on her breast warmed. "*Lamprophyre, where are you?*"

She gripped the pendant. "South of Tanajital about seven hundred beats. You're ahead of us?"

"We left the city two thousand beats ago. We have not seen Sardonyx yet."

"We're hurrying as fast as we can."

"Don't exhaust yourself. We all need to be in a condition to fight." Hyaloclast sounded as calm as ever. *"And don't take on more than your share of this burden. We are prepared to take Sardonyx on ourselves."*

"I know." She couldn't think of anything else to say. "Good luck."

"And to you." The pendant stilled and went cool.

"She's right," Rokshan said. "We shouldn't exhaust ourselves. It's going to be a hard fight."

"I know, but if the flight meets Sardonyx before we arrive, all I can imagine is—" She shut her mouth before she could say the word *dying*. "No. I won't. We'll win, I know we will."

"We will," Rokshan said.

"That's far too optimistic for you. Are you humoring me?"

"Is it helping?"

Lamprophyre thought about it. "Yes."

"Then you're welcome."

The humorous tone of his voice drew a laugh from her. "All right. Thank you." Her heart didn't exactly feel light, but the burden of fear had lifted.

Now she caught the updrafts and soared, easing the burden on her wings, and watched her clutchmates do the same. Focusing on flying, on taking the most efficient route, occupied her thoughts enough that she lost track of time. There was nothing but the wind and the high, thin clouds and her sense of Rokshan perched on her shoulders.

Orthoclase dropped back and then fell behind, and she was about to call out to him to see if he was well when he surged upward and ahead, finding a wind she'd missed. She laughed and chased him. Then they were all flying wildly, laughing at how ridiculous they all looked. It was foolishness, Lamprophyre knew, but in her heart she felt they needed the release.

Then Coquina pulled up and pointed. "There they are," she said. "The flight. And I think they've met the enemy."

Lamprophyre sobered and backwinged to hover near Coquina. "All right," she said. "Let's go."

Her friends nodded. Without another word, they wheeled and darted toward the battle, taking separate paths. Lamprophyre looked for Hyaloclast and headed her way.

The sky ahead was filled with colored streaks and flashes of fire. As Lamprophyre approached, a bright yellow form hung still in the air and then fell, not trying to stop itself. She was too far away to know whose dragon that had been. She gritted her teeth and sped faster, feeling Rokshan shift the weapon across her shoulder. Now that they were here, fear was a distant impossibility.

She dove for the center of the fight, trusting Rokshan to choose a target. The thumping of the weapon didn't rattle her the way it had at first. She twisted, raked her claws against a dragon's face to distract him while Rokshan took aim, then beat the air to gain altitude. She couldn't see more than half a dragonlength ahead of her. It was like swimming through seaweed, dodging bodies and avoiding contact with Sardonyx's heavily muscled followers.

She burst through the mob and hovered above, trying to get her bearings. To her shock, five dragonlengths away Sardonyx soared as high above the fray as she did. She had the look of an owl surveying the forest floor, choosing her prey. Without thinking, Lamprophyre dove after her.

"What are you doing?" Rokshan shouted.

"Ending this," Lamprophyre shouted back.

Sardonyx saw her coming. She didn't move, didn't do anything but watch her approach. Then she turned her back on Lamprophyre and dove, taking an unwary dragon by the back of the neck and raking her claws across the dragon's throat. Another of the flight rose up between Lamprophyre and Sardonyx, and Rokshan swore and shifted his weapon. Lamprophyre forced her way past another of Sardonyx's dragons who was encircled by four slim members of the flight and came up short against a bulky female. The female snarled and reached for Lamprophyre. A blast of light skimmed over the female's head, and a second one hit more squarely.

As the female fell, Lamprophyre looked around. Sardonyx had vanished. "Lamprophyre, go!" Rokshan shouted, and she dove and felt the weapon thump-rattle, stippling a nearby shape with dark bruises.

It was madness. Lamprophyre had no idea who was winning, didn't even know where her clutchmates were despite blind-flying. She descended below the fight to catch her breath and once more saw Sardonyx. The ancient dragon seemed to drift through the fight, with each of her dragons moving to defend her as she passed. Occasionally she tore into one of the flight who came too close, shredding wings or belly or throat and tossing the body aside. Furious, Lamprophyre flung herself after the ancient dragon.

This time, she swept past and swiped a claw to strike Sardonyx's lower back. Swiftly Sardonyx turned and chased after her. Lamprophyre heard the weapon thump and rejoiced. She'd been close enough that could have been a killing shot. But Rokshan didn't shout with excitement. Lamprophyre turned to look over her shoulder. Sardonyx was flying away, apparently completely unharmed. "Didn't you hit her?" she asked.

"She's damned fast for someone her size," Rokshan said. "I think I grazed her, and she just shrugged it off. I don't know why she didn't chase us."

"Now I'm angry. She thinks we're no threat." Lamprophyre wheeled and followed Sardonyx. "We will make her take us seriously."

"Be careful. The first weapon is almost exhausted," Rokshan said.

This time, she stayed high enough to keep track of Sardonyx. The ancient dragon continued to make her way through the fight without making more than the most desultory attacks. It infuriated

Lamprophyre all over again. She beat hard to draw nearer to Sardonyx, then dove.

As she swept into an attack, she saw Hyaloclast fighting her way closer to Sardonyx. Dragons darted out of her way, and Hyaloclast's speed increased, building until she was nearly moving at full speed. Sardonyx either didn't see her coming or didn't care. Hyaloclast slammed into Sardonyx, knocking her backward, and in the next beat the two were grappling, shoving back and forth with hands clasped.

Lamprophyre pulled up a short distance away. The two enormous dragons, black and red, grunted with effort as they fought and snapped at each other like creatures out of myth. "Shoot her!" she screamed.

"I'll hit Hyaloclast!" Rokshan exclaimed. She could feel him twisting and moving, trying to find his target.

Gradually, stillness spread out from the struggling, thrashing pair, until dragons hung in the air all around, watching. Even Lamprophyre hovered, her fists clenched, willing Sardonyx to break. Rokshan lowered his weapon. Sardonyx snapped at Hyaloclast's throat, and Hyaloclast brought her legs up and kicked Sardonyx's exposed belly. Sardonyx didn't react at all, just kept driving for the throat.

Then both dragons went still, with even their wings beating slowly enough that they gradually drifted downward. Lamprophyre followed, confused that they'd both stopped fighting. Now was the time to hit Sardonyx with the weapon, but Rokshan didn't move.

She was close enough to see their faces now, and was startled that both had their eyes closed. Not fighting, not flying, not searching each other for weaknesses. Lamprophyre's dread, which had been silent since the beginning of the journey, raised its voice again. Not knowing what else to do, she listened for thoughts, hoping for some indication of what was happening.

She'd expected to be deafened by all the minds thronging the area. Instead, she heard two voices, strong enough to override the rest of the clamor, strong enough that Lamprophyre was nearly overwhelmed by them alone. The voices spoke, but neither speaker seemed interested in responding to the other. They both simply spoke, long strings of sentences Lamprophyre couldn't make out. That it was Hyaloclast and Sardonyx, she was sure, because she was intimately familiar with the sound of each dragon's thoughts. But what they were trying to accomplish, she had no idea.

Then both voices fell silent, mid sentence. For half a beat, a beat, nothing moved. Then Sardonyx shouted a wordless, silent cry of triumph. Lamprophyre felt the slicing blades of her thought slash across her mother's mind, just as she remembered from the attack on Zefira. And Hyaloclast's wings slumped, stilled, and the great black dragon fell out of the sky.

Lamprophyre screamed and dove, sharply enough that Rokshan grabbed her ruff and clung painfully tight. She was vaguely aware that other shapes were diving with her, but her world had narrowed down to that falling shape. Screaming with effort, she plunged past Hyaloclast and turned to catch her. The dragon queen weighed enough that Lamprophyre couldn't do more than slow her fall, not without crushing Rokshan. More dragons, one light blue, one bronze, caught Hyaloclast's other side and the base of her tail, and between the three of them, they carried her to the ground.

Lamprophyre instantly fell to her knees at Hyaloclast's side, feeling for a pulse, thumbing up her eyelids to see her pupils dilate. "She's alive," she told Leucite, "but I don't know more than that. Sardonyx attacked her mind, and I don't know how soon she will recover from that."

Leucite looked up. "They're fleeing," he said, his usually calm voice shaking. "The flight, I mean. They're not even trying to stop Sardonyx."

Lamprophyre looked down at Hyaloclast again. "I can't help her."

"I'll stay," Leucite said. "Marble and I will stay with her. Go." She heard him think *no use but we can't not try*, and she wished more than ever that he and Hyaloclast had been pair-bonded before this.

She nodded at milky-blue Marble, gripped her mother's hand one final time, and flew after the disappearing flights.

"They aren't just fleeing," Rokshan said. "It's a rout."

"We have to catch them and make them turn and fight," Lamprophyre said. "They can't reach Tanajital. There's no shield."

"Then go faster," Rokshan said. "The flight's already outpacing Sardonyx's dragons. We just need to get ahead of them and make a stand."

Lamprophyre nodded and pushed herself harder, speeding up until she was grateful for the harness. Rokshan's grip on her ruff was firm but not panicked, he leaned forward to make her profile sleeker, and she sped along, skimming the ground until she was beneath Sardonyx's dragons. The back of her neck itched with the knowledge that they were above her, in a perfect position to dive and attack. But they ignored her, or didn't see her—she didn't care which so long as it got her past them.

Then she was past, and the flight was visible in the distance. They looked like people in a panic, flying in a ragged group that didn't maintain any semblance of a formation. Lamprophyre saw orange and dark blue and grass-green circling the flight like a handful of dogs trying to herd frightened sheep. "The clutch will stop them," she said.

"We need to catch up to them, though," Rokshan said. "We can't be caught between the two flights. No weapons can save us if that happens."

Lamprophyre spread her wings and caught a fortunate updraft that carried her high above the ground. Alternating flapping hard and soaring, she made progress—but no, the flight was slowing, too, hovering as if waiting for her.

"Hyaloclast is alive," she said as soon as she was within earshot and range of thought, "but she's injured. We have to stop Sardonyx if we want to help her. And if Sardonyx reaches Tanajital, the city will be destroyed."

A faint ghost of a thought made her gasp. "Who was that?" she demanded. "We are *not* going to let the humans be killed just because they aren't like us. And what the Stones do you think Sardonyx will do to the rest of us when she's done with the humans? She's not going to let us survive either. But by all means, if you don't want to defend humans *the way we swore we would*, go back to the mountains. I'm sure the dragonets will welcome you."

Her dismissive, sarcastic tone elicited a lot of ashamed thoughts, but no one left. "Then we fight," she said. "Fight by clutches, surround an enemy and destroy her, do it again."

"What did Sardonyx do to Hyaloclast?" someone asked from the middle of the flight.

"Sardonyx can speak to minds, and she knows how to attack with thought," Lamprophyre said. "But I don't think it's easy, or she'd have done it to all of us. Stay away from Sardonyx—I know, I don't need to tell you that."

She looked back over her shoulder. The cloud of colored shapes was close enough that they were obviously dragons. "Rokshan, what do we do?" she asked. "What's our strategy?"

Rokshan turned in his seat. "Take the fight to them," he said. "Those with pyrite weapons take the lead, to get several clear shots before we engage with the enemy. Then, what Lamprophyre said. If you work together, those big dragons aren't maneuverable enough to take an entire clutch on. Attack from altitude when you can, don't let them get above you."

Lamprophyre drew in as deep a breath as the harness would allow and waited for the dragons to pass Rokshan's words on to those farther away. "Let's go," she said, and wheeled around. She didn't look to see who'd followed her. She knew it was all of them.

This time, the enemy dragons were moving more slowly. Their formations, always military-precise, looked a little ragged, and she counted and did a little calculating—Stones, they'd accounted for nearly half of Sardonyx's dragons! Excitement bubbled up inside her, and she suppressed it, fearing becoming overconfident.

Rokshan lifted the pyrite weapon and balanced it on her shoulder. "Not too close to my head, please, it makes me dizzy," she said.

"I remember. Don't worry, I'll move it in time."

The enemy was five dragonlengths away. Three. Rokshan lifted the weapon, and a series of staccato thumps shattered the air. More thumps nearby signaled her friends taking their shots. Dragons jerked out of formation. Two of them fell. And yet Sardonyx's people came on, unswerving and terrifying. "*Go, go!*" Lamprophyre screamed, and the front lines crashed together and everything was chaos.

Lamprophyre swerved to rise above the tangled flights. "What are you doing?" Rokshan shouted.

"Looking for Sardonyx!"

"Are you out of your mind? We tried that. She's impossible to hit."

"Not if I get close enough," Lamprophyre shouted. She scanned the melee, looking for that monstrous red shape, paler than Porphyry and dusted with gold as if she wanted to make herself a human queen as well as a dragon one. "And I'd like to see her try that mental attack on me."

"I'm running low on power," Rokshan said. "I'll save what's left for Sardonyx."

Lamprophyre nodded. Suddenly, she gasped and jerked backward, making Rokshan drop the weapon to brush the back of her neck. An enormous dirty-copper dragon shot upward past her face, clawing at her. She backwinged desperately and ducked, heard Rokshan yelp, and fought to get clear of the monster.

She never saw the second dragon, a misty green female who came out of nowhere and grabbed Lamprophyre, sinking her teeth into Lamprophyre's shoulder. Lamprophyre screamed and tore herself free, letting herself go limp to throw the female off balance. She got her feet between herself and the female's midsection and kicked, digging in her toe claws. The female jerked, dropped about a dragonlength, then beat the air, chasing Lamprophyre.

Lamprophyre pushed herself to gain altitude. Fighting this female was a distraction from her goal, and Rokshan couldn't shoot her without wasting power destined for killing Sardonyx. She swooped past the dirty-copper dragon, who half-turned to watch her pass. "Rokshan, we—" she began.

Something hit them hard, knocking Lamprophyre half a dragonlength sideways. Rokshan cried out as he was slammed into Lamprophyre's neck. She felt his grip on her shoulders loosen, his feet scrape loosely across her scales, and then he was gone, a burning brand falling away beneath her.

Lamprophyre screamed and plunged after him, slapping and kicking to get free of any dragon, friend or foe, that dared get in her way. She'd never flown faster, desperation making her fleet of wing. Her head felt swollen as she flew nearly straight down, her spine ached, but she was closing with Rokshan fast. Then she was beside him, her hands closed gently around him, and she opened her wings to slow her descent.

Breathing heavily, she landed as lightly as she could manage and laid Rokshan gently on the ground. Crouching beside him, she bent low, then said, "Rokshan, are you all right?"

Rokshan smiled. "I'm not dead," he said. "That's something."

"I don't understand. What happened?"

"That dragon slapped us with his tail. Caught me—" He coughed. When he removed his hand from his mouth, Lamprophyre sucked in a horrified breath at seeing blood on his lips. "Caught me across the back and snapped the harness. You caught me." He coughed again.

"I'll take you to Tanajital. They'll heal you."

Rokshan gripped her hand. "Lamprophyre. Sweetheart. Don't panic, but I—" He coughed a third time, spattering his hand with blood. "I can't feel my legs."

Lamprophyre felt numb. She heard wings overhead, but the sound meant nothing to her. "That's bad," she said inanely.

Rokshan nodded. "It's bad. Lamprophyre, you have to go. You have to fight Sardonyx."

"Don't be stupid. I'm not leaving you."

The nearby dragon wings stilled. and Lamprophyre turned with a snarl, ready to fight. But it was Dolomite, crouching to allow

Tekentriya to climb down. The crown princess strode forward, her usual lurch less pronounced. She took in Rokshan's condition impassively. "You can't stand," she said. "Dolomite, you'll have to carry him."

"But you have to fight," Lamprophyre said. "And I don't want to leave him."

"I've exhausted both my weapons," Tekentriya said. "We can't fight effectively. Go. I'll take care of him." She gripped Lamprophyre's shoulder. "I promise."

Dolomite picked Rokshan up. His legs hung so limply Lamprophyre felt sick. "Rokshan," she said, then didn't know how to go on. She was afraid of hugging him, afraid it would make his injuries worse. "Rokshan, I—"

"I know," Rokshan said. His voice was very weak. "I love you, too."

Lamprophyre turned and flew away. She couldn't bear to look back at the mate she was leaving behind. Her fear for Rokshan turned to anger. If he died...but that was stupid, wasn't it, because they were all in danger of dying, and threats were meaningless. What mattered was finding Sardonyx and putting an end to this. She stripped off the ruined harness, dropped it, and took off in search of her enemy.

CHAPTER FORTY-SEVEN

Immediately, Lamprophyre realized the battle was not going well for her flight. While her friends hadn't fled and were fighting as fiercely as ever, they'd been forced northward, dragonlength by dragonlength. She'd already been left behind. Her body ached and her wings felt stretched to the breaking point, but she flew after the battle, searching the air for Sardonyx. Her heart sank as she saw, far in the distance, a smudge athwart the river. Tanajital was far too close. If they couldn't stop Sardonyx soon...

And as if thinking of her had conjured her up, there the dragon was, moving through the battle as if none of it mattered to her. Lamprophyre snarled and sped up, tracking Sardonyx's movements. So many dragons lay between Lamprophyre and her prey, and she no longer— She swallowed. Rokshan would live. Tekentriya and Dolomite would see to it. She had to kill Sardonyx to make sure his living wasn't itself a death sentence.

She reached the rear of the battle and darted between huge, ancient dragons, not doing more than kick or claw to make one move, never staying to fight. She didn't bother concealing her approach. Surprising Sardonyx might be impossible, if Sardonyx was as competent at discerning thoughts from a crowd as she was at that mental attack—though if she couldn't hear Lamprophyre's thoughts, maybe Lamprophyre had a chance, after all.

Whether or not Sardonyx heard her coming, when Lamprophyre was nearly a dragonlength away, Sardonyx turned to face her. As if by magic, the dragons nearest her edged away, leaving an open space just right for Lamprophyre to fit herself into.

"You," Sardonyx said. "You're missing something."

That infuriated Lamprophyre, but she clamped down on her anger. "I don't need anything to fight you but myself," she said.

"You believe it must come to a fight?" Sardonyx's voice was as beautiful and melodic as ever. "Say the word, and my dragons will stand down."

"What?" Lamprophyre backwinged, taken aback.

"We're dragons, Lamprophyre," Sardonyx said. "We discuss things rationally. You think I enjoy bloodshed? Particularly over humans?"

Lamprophyre listened to Sardonyx's thoughts, sharp and horrible over the hum of background thinking. "You do enjoy bloodshed," she said. "All this makes you happy."

A snarl touched Sardonyx's mouth and was instantly gone. "I enjoy seeing dragons matched against each other. That it has to end in death is a side...benefit, I suppose. To me, anyway."

"Then match against me," Lamprophyre said. "Just the two of us. Let that decide our fate."

Sardonyx laughed. "You? You're barely big enough to reach my shoulder."

"That's an exaggeration. And you ought to come up with a better reason to avoid fighting me. I think you're afraid."

"What a pitiful taunt. I suppose you now expect me to fly into a rage and attack you with reckless abandon?"

"It's not a taunt," Lamprophyre said. "You can't attack me with your thoughts. You can't hear what I'm thinking. I think you've traded on that freak talent for long enough you don't remember how to defeat someone without it. And no, I don't think you've ever done anything without thinking it through. So consider this.

We will *never* stop fighting you. Maybe you'll kill us all, but we'll take more than a few of you with us. Fight me here, now, and make an end."

Sardonyx's eye ridges lowered. "Agreed," she said, and lunged for Lamprophyre.

Lamprophyre, still listening to Sardonyx's thoughts, was ready for that move and darted upward, hugging her knees to her chest to allow Sardonyx to pass beneath her. She spun and dove and got a hand on Sardonyx's tail, dragging her claws down its length and making Sardonyx let out a shriek of pain. Faster than Lamprophyre had guessed possible, the ancient dragon turned and drove straight at Lamprophyre, taking her around the waist and bearing her toward the ground.

Lamprophyre spread her wings to slow their descent and kicked Sardonyx's stomach. Sardonyx let out a whoosh of breath and let go, backwinging and bringing her own feet up to slam Lamprophyre. The blow missed as Lamprophyre furled her wings and dropped out of the way. Immediately she spread her wings and beat for altitude. Sardonyx matched her, her greater wingspan letting her edge ahead at first. Lamprophyre fought harder. She couldn't let the ancient dragon outmaneuver her.

They flew upward, neither pausing. Gradually, Lamprophyre gained on Sardonyx, first passing her head, then her shoulders, then the base of her wings. Then she was ahead, above Sardonyx entirely, and she furled her wings and plummeted straight at her enemy, willing herself heavy, like a stone. She aimed, not for Sardonyx's face, but for her wings. She grabbed for them. pinning them back, and raked the membranes with her claws.

Again, Sardonyx shrieked. She thrashed free of Lamprophyre and turned on her, and it was Lamprophyre's turn to cry out as Sardonyx tore gouges out of her chest. They broke apart again, and Lamprophyre quickly glanced around. Tanajital was closer than before, and Lamprophyre would have laughed at Sardonyx's perfidy if she'd had breath to spare. Sardonyx wasn't interested in a fair fight to determine the fate of humans. Even if she lost, which she didn't believe she would, she expected her dragons to carry out her plans.

They fought in silence for several dozen beats, darting and clawing and diving until both of them bled from shallow wounds, nothing that would decide a victory. Lamprophyre's breath came heavily, and her body ached from the sustained flying. But Sardonyx was winded, too, and her blows felt less powerful. Lamprophyre refused to despair. If they both became too exhausted to continue, that wouldn't change anything.

She stopped looking upriver at Tanajital, not wanting to see it draw closer. A lucky swipe with the edge of her wing temporarily blinded Sardonyx, who dropped half a dragonlength and didn't return to the fight immediately. Lamprophyre hovered, catching her breath. "Give up," she said. "This will only end in your death."

"Brash words from a weakling daughter of a weakling queen," Sardonyx said, and flung herself at Lamprophyre again. This time, she took hold of her by her shoulders and drew her close in an obscene parody of an embrace, her vicious teeth bared and aimed at Lamprophyre's throat.

Lamprophyre grabbed Sardonyx's shoulders and pushed, trying to free herself, but even exhausted, the ancient dragon outweighed her. Her teeth came ever closer to Lamprophyre's throat. A memory of Porphyry lying bloody in death flashed across Lamprophyre's memory, and grief struck her so hard she screamed. Sardonyx smiled, clearly believing it had been a scream of fear. "I'll make it quick," she said, her lovely voice tight with exertion.

"Think again," Lamprophyre said through gritted teeth. She listened to Sardonyx's thoughts, searching for an edge. The ancient dragon gloated, believing she'd won. Without knowing how she did it, Lamprophyre thought, *You can't touch me,* and lashed out in remembered attack.

Her thoughts tore across Sardonyx's mind, and it was the ancient dragon's turn to scream. Sardonyx turned her head away and let go of Lamprophyre, but Lamprophyre clung to her, refusing to release her grip. Then she was within the dragon's mind as she'd been once before, sinking deep into her enemy's consciousness as Sardonyx lashed out at her with her own mental attack. Lamprophyre dodged effortlessly. She felt as if she could see each attack before it struck, though there was no vision, no sound, just wave after wave of power as potent as what the pyrite weapons fired.

She thought back to that encounter several twelvedays before and made her thoughts knives, blades of all sizes, and withdrew from Sardonyx's mind, digging those blades deep. Sardonyx thrashed free finally and retreated half a dragonlength. She and Lamprophyre stared at each other, hovering, while dozens of dragons surrounded them.

Sardonyx turned and fled.

Lamprophyre, dazed by the suddenness of it, didn't at first understand what had happened. No dragon queen would abandon her flight. The dragons surrounding Lamprophyre shifted restlessly, not attacking, as if Sardonyx's abandonment had confused them too. The last traces of Sardonyx's thoughts, faint and fading as the dragon flew away, were of fear for herself—fear of a personal defeat, with no hint of concern for her flight. How typical of her, Lamprophyre thought.

Then she realized Sardonyx had headed north.

Cursing, she flew after Sardonyx, reaching deep within herself for her last reserves. Tanajital was so close, a perfect miniature city glinting in the afternoon sun, and Sardonyx by herself could do so much damage. They'd left the other dragons behind, which was odd, since Sardonyx's flight had protected her until now. It was a puzzle Lamprophyre was too tired to figure out. It was just her, streaking across the sky after the red blotch that was Sardonyx, in a chase that had already gone on forever and was likely to end only when the two of them dissolved into nothing.

Lamprophyre was still several dragonlengths behind when Sardonyx reached Tanajital. *No*, she thought, too tired to scream a warning that would be completely useless. She braced herself for the first gout of brilliant fire.

It never came.

Sardonyx didn't so much as slow over the human city. Puzzled again, Lamprophyre slackened her pace slightly and surveyed the city. It looked just as it always did, full of people staring at the red dragon overhead, open for the slaughter. But Sardonyx hadn't sent one single blast of fire to immolate the place, not even the golden-roofed palace. She was headed north.

Lamprophyre sped up, though her wings felt limp and exhausted and her chest ached with exertion. Sardonyx wasn't fleeing in terror, despite her reaction to Lamprophyre's last attack. She never did anything without thinking it through. In heading north, she had a plan, but...

Lamprophyre felt suddenly ill. The caves. The rest of the flight, and all those dragonets whose bodies weren't yet as rugged as an adult's. Sardonyx was exactly the kind of person who would take out her anger on helpless dragonets, destroy the next generation.

She flew the next several beats without seeing the world around her. She needed the flight's help, but she couldn't go back without giving Sardonyx more of a lead than she already had. She either needed to catch up to Sardonyx and fight her again—her heart wailed in agony at the thought of another battle, mental or physical—or she needed to pass her, reach the caves, and enlist the other dragons' help.

She glanced behind her. All she could see of the mingled dragon flights was a multicolored cloud that distance made appear to hover over Tanajital, though she didn't think they'd come so far already. How this had turned into a battle between her and Sardonyx, her tired brain couldn't remember. Sardonyx had attacked her first, all those twelvedays ago. But if she hadn't started the war, by the Stones, she intended to finish it.

She couldn't fly at her top speed anymore—wasn't sure how she was still flying, even—but Sardonyx had slowed as well. It was heartening to see evidence that the ancient dragon wasn't invulnerable.

But Lamprophyre already knew that, didn't she? She'd made that mental attack again, the one that had saved her when she was human and had almost been kidnapped, and it had worked. She still didn't have any idea what made it possible. She'd never done it against anyone but Sardonyx, and maybe that meant she was using Sardonyx's power against her. Maybe anyone who could hear thoughts could manage it.

Or maybe Coquina was right, and it was her own power that did it.

Lamprophyre didn't like that idea. She might be special for being the only dragon in a millennium who'd made friends with a human, but surely if she had unusual mental abilities, they would have shown up before now? On the other hand, she was also the only dragon who'd ever called on a God not her own and been touched by him. Jiwanyil's power had made her immune to Sardonyx's attack; suppose it had given her more powers than that?

Lamprophyre scowled. *That* was something she should have asked Jiwanyil, if she'd kept her wits instead of trying to force answers from a creature who clearly had only the most tenuous connection to reality. He'd nearly killed Rokshan, too—

Another sharp stab of grief hit her. Rokshan. She tried to tell herself he was alive, that she'd feel it if she lost her pair-bond, but she wasn't sure the latter was true and wasn't confident about the former, either. If he died—she couldn't finish the thought.

She was closer to Sardonyx now, though not by much. They were flying over the forest, all those evergreens and the leafy trees that were only just beginning to lose their leaves. Anger displaced her fear for Rokshan. Sardonyx had no right to try to remake the world in her image, not when everyone else wanted something different. A spark tingled up her wings and across her shoulders. She would stop Sardonyx if it killed her.

Now she flew in an exhausted fugue state, her wings beating automatically, her eyes focused on the red dragon in front of her, gradually drawing nearer. The mountains were coming closer as well, the yellow foothills giving way to the lower slopes and then to the peaks where the flight lived. Sardonyx didn't vary in her course. She didn't know where the caves were, and she'd have to hunt for them, which would give Lamprophyre time to catch up to her and stop her. Sardonyx was no more than ten dragonlengths ahead now. No distance at all.

Sardonyx swept up the slopes and soared along the rocky peaks —and kept going.

Lamprophyre blinked. She hadn't turned aside to search for the caves. Lamprophyre's tired mind couldn't make sense of it. Without thinking, she continued to fly after Sardonyx, gradually gaining ground as the ancient dragon flew deeper into the mountains.

She was sure Sardonyx knew she was there, though the dragon never looked back. The closer Lamprophyre came, the more she became aware Sardonyx was in far worse shape than she. Sardonyx's flight was erratic, weaving so much she looked like a drunk human. She seemed to remain in the air through pure willpower. The sight gave Lamprophyre a boost of much-needed strength, and she sped up.

She followed Sardonyx through the Handmaidens and to the base of Mother Stone. By then, Lamprophyre knew where Sardonyx was going, though she couldn't understand what the point of returning to that cavern was. She was a little less than two dragonlengths behind now and pushing herself to her limit. "Sardonyx!" she shouted, her words not carrying far in the thin air. "Stop now! You're beaten!"

Sardonyx didn't respond. She didn't change her speed or do anything else to indicate she'd heard. Lamprophyre caught the fleeting edge of her thoughts and was surprised, as much as her dull brain could register surprise, at Sardonyx's determination to reach the cave. All the ancient dragon's thoughts were focused on something there, something she had left behind—something that would let her defeat Lamprophyre. But there hadn't been anything left in the cave, nothing but Jiwanyil's presence. It made no sense.

Lamprophyre drew in a deep, sharp breath and plunged onward. She'd exerted herself enough that she didn't feel cold, though that would change as soon as she stopped. Whatever advantage

Sardonyx hoped to gain from the cave would not be enough to save her, not if Lamprophyre could help it.

Sardonyx flew without pausing into the mouth of the cavern, with Lamprophyre a scant two dragonlengths behind her. How the giant red dragon was able to maneuver through those first few dragonlengths when the passage was so narrow it barely fit Lamprophyre, she didn't know, but Sardonyx slowed even further, shortening her lead more.

They flew in silence through the passage as it sloped downward and gradually iced over, with Sardonyx's wings occasionally scraping the walls. When they shot out of the passage into the giant bowl-shaped chamber, Lamprophyre was almost within grabbing distance of Sardonyx's heels.

Sardonyx shot forward and skidded on hands and knees across the icy, rubble-strewn floor toward the now-familiar green glow, clambering over obstacles in her hurry to get away from Lamprophyre. Lamprophyre staggered to a halt and stood there, breathing heavily. "What are you doing?" she asked, too tired for anything but curiosity.

Sardonyx's mouth curved in a nasty smile. She drew in a breath and blew out fire that licked over the stone and melted the rime so fast it hissed into steam. Lamprophyre waved steam away from her face and squinted at Sardonyx, who'd bent to pick up something that blazed with green light. It was the size of Sardonyx's palm and shaped like a large brick with rounded corners and edges.

Sardonyx straightened. "I told you you're nothing," she said. She closed both her hands on the lighted object and snapped it in half. Brilliant green-white light exploded, lighting the chamber bright as day for half a beat. Lamprophyre snapped her nictitating membranes shut and reflexively threw up an arm to ward her eyes, and she was still blinded briefly.

The next thing she knew, Sardonyx had her hand around her throat. "This power was always meant to be mine," she said. In her other hand, she held what looked like a glowing emerald, half the size of Lamprophyre's fist. Sardonyx raised it to her lips and swallowed it. Her other hand convulsed, choking Lamprophyre, who clawed at it until it fell away. Dazed, she stared at Sardonyx, who was bent double.

Then Sardonyx straightened and slammed her fist into Lamprophyre's stomach, flinging her off her feet and into the distant wall.

Lamprophyre's head cracked against the stone, dizzying her again. Everything was murky—she still had her nictitating membranes shut. She got to her feet through force of will and staggered. Sardonyx swayed, her arms and wings flung wide for balance. She shook her head as if the blow had struck her instead. Then she lifted off the floor and headed for Lamprophyre, weaving as if dizzy, flying as slowly as anyone could without dropping out of the air. Green lights traced the phalanges of her wings and the ridges of her eyes. The sight was so unnerving Lamprophyre scrabbled along the wall for the exit, afraid to take her eyes off the ancient dragon.

She nearly fell when she reached the opening, tripping when it turned out there wasn't any more wall. Turning, she fled, certain without knowing why that her next encounter with Sardonyx would be her last.

This time, Sardonyx made no effort to avoid the walls; Lamprophyre heard her smashing chunks out of them, shaking the walls like she was a force of nature and not a dragon. Lamprophyre made it as far as the cavern mouth before Sardonyx caught up to her. Frantic, she lashed out with both feet and pushed herself harder, then dropped. She still felt warm, a terrible illusion that gave her no benefit. She soared too close to Mother Stone and kicked again, propelling herself away.

Then Sardonyx was on her, snatching at her wings and tearing a gash in a lower membrane. It didn't hurt, but Lamprophyre's flight was suddenly more erratic, less controlled. Lamprophyre furled her wings and struck at Sardonyx's face. Her claws made contact with flesh, and Sardonyx bellowed and slapped Lamprophyre's head so hard it felt as if a pyrite weapon had gone off next to her skull. Dazed, she considered how warm she was, almost hot, as if they weren't thousands of dragonlengths above the ground and surrounded by snow and ice.

Something flashed past, too fast for Lamprophyre to see it as more than a blur of color. Sardonyx screamed, and blood welled up on her flank. Lamprophyre dove away from her, taking advantage of the other dragon's attack. All she could see of him was a backlit shape against the sun hanging low in the western sky.

Then he dove, and Rokshan shouted, "Get above her!"

Rokshan. She was too muddled to think clearly. He was well, he was healed, but who had he found to carry him into battle? The harness was destroyed.

The dragon flashed past her again. "Damn it, Lamprophyre, get above her!" Rokshan screamed. His voice jolted her into action, and she beat the air for altitude. The dragon was below Sardonyx, swooping around her in a streak of emerald green and gold. No rider was visible.

Green. And gold.

Lamprophyre screamed with excitement and flapped harder. No time to find out what had happened, or how they'd pulled it off. All that mattered was that Rokshan was a dragon, and between the two of them, they could face anything.

She reached the apex of her climb, dove, and furled her wings, whipping around in midair just before reaching Sardonyx to slam feet-first into the spot between her wings. Sardonyx spun and slapped Lamprophyre with her tail, driving her sideways, but that left the ancient dragon open to Rokshan's attack on her other side, his claws digging deep into the base of her spine.

"Watch out!" Lamprophyre shrieked. Rokshan moved fast, but not fast enough. Sardonyx caught him by the shoulders and flung him at the mountainside, where he hit the rocks hard and slid, unconscious, down the steep slope.

Lamprophyre dropped away from Sardonyx and hurried to catch Rokshan, shaking him. "Wake up. Wake up! She's coming—"

A tremendous weight slammed into her, Sardonyx's full mass crushing her into the stone. All the breath whooshed out of

Lamprophyre's lungs. Gasping desperately for air and finding none, she watched helplessly as Rokshan slipped from her hold and continued his slide down the mountain. Sardonyx wheeled and backed away for another blow. "Nothing will stop me now I have my full power," she said.

How exciting. She was going to taunt Lamprophyre the way villains did in bad epics. "It's not your power, it's Jiwanyil," she wheezed. If Sardonyx was going to gloat, maybe Lamprophyre could keep her talking long enough to recover.

"No such person," Sardonyx said. "They thought he was God, before I was buried, but he was nothing more than power, available for the taking. By the right person, naturally. You used that power once, when you woke me, depriving me of it until it could regenerate. That gave you a reprieve, but now—ah, it fills me to overflowing."

Lamprophyre clung to the stony outcropping and braced herself for the next blow. "But he kept you imprisoned for a millennium. And now you want his power?"

Sardonyx hovered half a dragonlength away. The green lights played like liquid over her body. "I have no hard feelings. It's just a source. All those dragons who died on Mother Stone—I felt every death, felt them fuel his power. They won for a time, but that time is over."

She backed away and began flapping her wings, powerfully enough to generate a wind palpable even among the gales that whipped around Mother Stone night and day. "And now," she said, her voice lovelier than ever, "you're going to join them."

Join them.

Born of wind and fire and stone, to breath and ash and stone return.

Your death is in the stone.

Sardonyx flew at Lamprophyre, bearing down on her like an implacable storm.

Lamprophyre drew in a breath. "Jiwanyil!" she shouted. "I understand now! I return—*make me one!*"

CHAPTER FORTY-EIGHT

Thunder boomed out of the clear sky. It echoed off Mother Stone and the surrounding peaks, growing louder and louder until the sky rang with it. Distantly, Lamprophyre heard the rumbling of stones and ice cascading down nearby slopes, picking up the chorus.

She listened to the titanic music until the last echoes had faded. Only then did she realize she wasn't dead. Sardonyx hadn't hit her.

Sardonyx hung suspended a few handspans away, not hovering but completely frozen, her wings motionless, her mouth open in a snarl. Lamprophyre gasped and let go of the mountain, searching beneath her for Rokshan. He sprawled six or seven dragonlengths below her, also motionless. Lamprophyre pushed away from the mountain, intending to dive to retrieve him. Her wings wouldn't move. She couldn't even open her hand. It was as if she was stuck to the stone.

-Don't move,- a voice said.

"I can't move," Lamprophyre responded. She couldn't even turn her head to see where the voice was coming from.

-That is because this is a moment in time, detached from the rest. There is no time in which to move,- the voice said.

"I don't understand. If that's true, how can I speak? Shouldn't I be as frozen as Sardonyx and—is Rokshan all right? He can't die!"

-That is, of course, not true. He is as mortal as anyone. But I understand your meaning.-

Lamprophyre strained to turn. "Who are you? Why can't I see you?"

-My appearance is irrelevant. Tell me, Lamprophyre, what do you want?-

"I want to see you!"

-You called on a God not your own. What do you want?-

Lamprophyre tried to swallow to moisten her mouth and found even those muscles didn't work. "I understand the prophecy. I want to make it come true so Sardonyx and her dragons will be destroyed."

-You believe yourself entitled to choose destruction for another creature?-

Lamprophyre didn't hesitate. "I do."

-And why does Sardonyx deserve destruction?-

"Because she will never give up trying to kill every human who lives, just because they're human. She had so many chances to choose differently, and every time she went for the one that would give her power. And now it's a choice between her life and theirs, and I choose theirs."

-They're not your species, Lamprophyre.-

"Does it matter?"

-Apparently not to you.- The voice sounded amused. -You realize you choose your own death.-

This time, Lamprophyre managed to swallow. "Yes."

-You thought you'd escape that, didn't you?-

"Jiwanyil said it didn't mean my doom, but I don't think he was ever anything but a fragment. So I understand. And I accept." She glanced down at Rokshan's beautiful form and wished she could weep with longing and regret.

-Then watch, and see what your choice has wrought before you die,- the voice said.

Everything snapped into motion. Sardonyx slammed into Lamprophyre, who had just enough time to realize it didn't hurt when the sound of thousands upon thousands of dragon wings ripped the air. Sardonyx stared at Lamprophyre, confused. "What happened to you?" she said.

Lamprophyre looked at her hands. They were misty and insubstantial. "I'm dead," she whispered. "And so are you."

Darkness fell across the sky. Lamprophyre and Sardonyx looked up. Dragons, milky and colorless, streamed away from the flanks of Mother Stone, soaring and wheeling in circles and patterns Lamprophyre had only ever seen in dream. They poured away from the mountain, filling the air with their graceful dance. Lamprophyre stared at them, awestruck.

A long, long line of dragons peeled away from the flight, headed for Lamprophyre and Sardonyx. Sardonyx gasped and turned to fly away, but their graceful shapes overtook her, caught her up in their hands and carried her off. She struggled, but despite her greater size she looked like a kitten caught up by a reproachful hand. Lamprophyre watched their soaring flight until they disappeared into the far northern distance.

She turned then to look at the rest of the dragons, gliding southward. Sardonyx would have no followers left—though Sardonyx herself was gone, so Lamprophyre wondered if destroying her followers was really necessary. But despite the decision she'd made, she didn't think it was up to her. It certainly wasn't within her power to rouse a flight of dead dragons.

"Lamprophyre! Lamprophyre, look at me!"

It was becoming so difficult, moving her body, what there was left of it. She tilted her head. "Rokshan. What happened?"

"I'll tell you all about it when we're out of here," Rokshan said. It was so disconcerting to hear his voice, in a lower register, coming out of that beautifully sculpted face. "But we have to go now, understand? Can you fly?"

She was too tired even to regret being unable to cry. "Rokshan, look at me," she said. "I'm dead. I think this is so we can say goodbye."

"Don't talk like that," Rokshan said. "I barely know how I got here. Flying is much harder than it looks, you know? I need your help getting back. Just put your hand on my shoulder, and I'll help you get started."

He was so beautiful. Yes, his body was perfect, but what made him beautiful in her eyes was that he was her mate, her dearest love, and it was fitting their story should end this way. "I love you," she said. "I hope you don't regret this transformation after I'm gone."

"Lamprophyre!" Rokshan's voice cracked in the middle of her name.

She smiled. "Bury me on Mother Stone," she said, "it's not a prison anymore," and closed her eyes and fell into blackness.

"YOU KNOW," PORPHYRY SAID, "BEING DEAD IS FAR MORE interesting than I expected."

Lamprophyre examined her hands. They were blue and solid and not even a little misty. "We buried you," she said. "We didn't know what else to do."

"Well, it's a good thing you did, or we wouldn't be able to have this conversation." Porphyry stood and stretched his wings. "I'd have flown off into eternity with the rest of the guardians."

"The dragons whose deaths sealed Sardonyx into her prison," Lamprophyre said. "I figured that much out. But I don't understand what my part in that drama was."

"You knew enough to call on God." Porphyry extended a hand. "Come with me. I think it's time you had some answers."

Lamprophyre took his hand. It felt as solid as her own. "What, like in the stories of Veena, where the villain explains his dastardly plot for the benefit of the listener?"

Porphyry laughed. "I promise this person has been looking

forward to telling you the whole story for a long time. Are you going to reject that just because it happens to fit a narrative tradition?"

"I'm too curious," Lamprophyre admitted.

For the first time, she tried to examine her surroundings, but saw—nothing. At times, she and Porphyry seemed to be surrounded by shifting mists, but then the mists looked like rough-hewn granite walls, or smooth marble facings, or the black, starless sky. She was certain, by the way they switched so rapidly, that the truth was something she was incapable of comprehending, and the mists and stone and sky were her mind trying to make sense of that.

They walked in companionable silence for a hundred beats through the shifting landscape. It didn't feel the kind of place you flew through. Lamprophyre was just thinking about whether someone could end up somewhere completely different whether she flew or walked or crawled when a white light flashed in front of them, and then there was a doorway. It looked as if it had always been there, though Lamprophyre had been looking right at it when it appeared. More of the shifting mists filled it.

"You go first. You're entitled," Porphyry said.

Lamprophyre shot him a suspicious glance—entitled, how?—but walked through the doorway into a well-lit, open space that smelled of strawberries and fresh air and curried lamb. She immediately stopped and looked around for the source of the smells, but found nothing. The room—cavern, perhaps—was the size of the hatching cavern back home, but its walls were of some white stone she didn't recognize. That sent a flash of fear through her, that maybe death had made her no longer a dragon to sense stone, but she immediately dismissed the fear as unworthy. Whatever the stone was, it glowed with magical light, and that made it no stone that existed in the real world.

A white dragon, white like the snows of Mother Stone shading to pale blue in the curves of his body, sat with his back to her, drawing on the wall. Despite being male, he was the biggest dragon Lamprophyre had ever seen, and yet there was something beautifully masculine in the curve of his shoulders and the way his wings furled across his back so no one would ever mistake him for female.

Lamprophyre approached him, curious about his drawing. Whatever medium he was using, it made the lines spark and glow wherever it passed. As she drew nearer, she realized he was using nothing but his claws, and it astonished her so much she said, "How is that possible?"

"It's the way I interact with the Immanence," the dragon said. His voice was more beautiful than Sardonyx's, reminding Lamprophyre of wind through the trees and rivers rushing over stone and crackling fires, and it sounded familiar. "I arose from it, and it likes to remind me that part of me is still connected to it." He stopped drawing and gestured at the wall. "What do you think?"

Lamprophyre looked at the drawing. Tiny, perfect dragons circled a mountain rendered in exquisite detail, in patterns of circles and lines and spirals that made them seem ready to fly out of the drawing. "It's beautiful," she said. "It reminds me of Dolomite's art."

The dragon laughed. "High praise indeed." He rose and turned around, looming over Lamprophyre. His eyes were as black and featureless as a starless sky, without iris or pupil or white, but despite their ominous appearance Lamprophyre felt no fear facing him. "You know who I am?" he asked.

Lamprophyre swallowed. She now recognized the voice, though she'd only ever heard a pale imitation of it. "I don't understand," she said. "I can tell you're God, and you sound like Jiwanyil, but you look like Katayan. Katayan's not real."

"That is both true and false," the dragon said. "I am your God, yes, and this is the form the Immanence granted me, the form I gave my first and greatest creation. But in the wake of disaster, when so much knowledge was lost or warped, humans came to believe there must be a God to govern each type of creation. So they created Katayan just as dragons created Mother Stone."

"And yet humans call on Jiwanyil, and receive prophecies from him."

"I am God regardless of the name I'm given. I don't mind being called Jiwanyil or Katayan. If you need a name for me, Katayan is as fitting as any. The humans got one thing right—I have been separated from my first children for far too long."

"And...Mother Stone?"

Katayan's face stilled. "You like stories," he said. "I would like to share one with you, for all our sakes. If you don't mind."

Puzzling over that, Lamprophyre nodded. Katayan sat and folded his wings around himself, so Lamprophyre did the same, with Porphyry settling next to her in silence.

"All life seeks to perpetuate itself," Katayan said. "My mate and I—"

"Your mate?" Lamprophyre blurted out, then clapped a hand over her mouth, mortified.

"This is going to be a very long story if you interrupt," Katayan said with a smile. "My mate is far too powerful for you to comprehend, and you will never see her. But even a God cannot create alone, and we made you like ourselves, male and female. It was so beautiful seeing you grow in knowledge and love of each other. You were our finest creation.

"But we made a decision, early on, that we would not hover over you, directing your every move. We created you with the desire to learn for yourselves, only leaning on us when you chose to call on us. We could not speak to you unless you spoke first. And that was ultimately a mistake. Go ahead, ask me why."

Lamprophyre's gaze flicked to the drawing of the mountain. "Why was it a mistake?"

Katayan settled back on his haunches. "It meant that when your understanding of your creation, of God's nature, changed over time, we were powerless to correct you. And we're talking about millennia of existence. You know how stories alter in the telling as they pass from speaker to speaker. Even the prodigious memories of dragons couldn't stop that happening."

"And that led to the worship of Mother Stone."

"Not exactly." The glowing walls vanished, and they suddenly appeared to be sitting on the ledge in front of the cavern mouth leading to the prison chamber deep within Mother Stone. "That led to Sardonyx."

Lamprophyre looked around. The air smelled of snow and was freezing cold, though she felt it as if she were wrapped in Rokshan's fur-lined coat, as if it were the memory of cold. She didn't ask if it was real. That was irrelevant. "I know Sardonyx wanted to eradicate humans. You didn't say where humans came from."

Katayan tilted his head to look directly at the sun, a feat impossible for anything mortal. "We made humans on a dare," he said. "Fitting, given how they turned out. My mate and I were discussing the nature of the Immanence and disagreed as to its fundamental nature. So we decided to...encourage...the Immanence to create something given some basic guidelines. We wanted to see if such a creation would be viable. And the Immanence produced humans. Brash, daring, short-lived, but with such profound capacity for feeling joy it surprised us. We were glad to take them under our wings, though technically we weren't their creators."

"That's beautiful!"

Katayan turned his gaze back on her. "I'm glad you think so. Not everyone did. In the era when Sardonyx was born, humans and dragons knew some of the truth of their creation, enough that Sardonyx was able to willfully misunderstand the purpose of humanity—and conclude they were a pestilence unworthy of sharing a world with God's children."

A low rumble heralded an avalanche in the distance. Lamprophyre started to reevaluate her sense of their surroundings. "So why didn't—no, I see. You'd sworn not to interfere unless dragons asked you to. But why didn't they do that? I know humans and dragons fought Sardonyx together, so they wanted her gone. They could have asked for your help."

Katayan's fathomless eyes seemed to be looking at something incomprehensibly distant. "By then, dragons had forgotten their connection to their God. They believed—the details don't matter. You see, the prohibition against speaking to our creations didn't apply to humans. As part of our ongoing experiment, we decided to do the opposite with them, and gave them frequent instruction in the form of what they called prophecies. And because that only happened to humans, dragons came to believe God expected them to be completely self-sufficient. I'm afraid it made them prideful."

"And Sardonyx was the ultimate end of that line of belief."

"Precisely." With a blink, they hovered over a desert of featureless dunes extending as far as the eye could see. Lamprophyre had only ever heard stories of the desert, how its cruel heat and arid climate made it inhospitable even to dragons, but again the heat felt at a remove, as if there were invisible walls between her and the radiant sands.

"The real problem was that humans and dragons knew enough to realize they needed to fight Sardonyx together," Katayan went on, "but they believed they could do it without any outside help. Humans were used to being directed by God, but not to asking God for guidance, and of course dragons had stopped asking altogether. So they fought a series of losing battles, all the while waiting for the prophecy that would tell them what to do."

Lamprophyre drew in a breath of air that had no moisture in it whatsoever. It dried her nostrils and made her eyes feel tight and itchy. She wished she could look at Porphyry to see what he thought of all this. She'd never known him to be anything but restless during a story, and yet he hadn't moved this whole time. "Did you give them a prophecy?"

"No," Katayan said. "At least not the one they expected. Humans had only just discovered that stones are imbued with the power of the Immanence in various ways. I guided them to create what you would call an artifact that contained the power of God and left it to them to work out how to use it. If dragons had been willing to call on me, that artifact could have killed Sardonyx and her followers. As it is, the humans came up with a needlessly elaborate, fully human scheme that would bind Sardonyx in the great mountain."

Lamprophyre nodded. "Except it needed dragons as well."

"The dragons of the time agreed to let their spirits fuel the magic, and go on fueling the magic, until someone could come up with a more permanent solution. They arranged things so a human presence in the prison would free Sardonyx, knowing that no human could reach that chamber without the help of a dragon. They assumed that could only happen deliberately. What none of them realized was that the magic was so powerful it would kill everyone involved, leaving no one alive who understood the plan."

Another flicker, and they were back in the white-walled chamber. The drawing on the wall still glimmered and sparked, but Lamprophyre was sure the dragons had shifted position while they were gone—or had they been gone at all?

Katayan continued, "So that was the result of your Great Cataclysm. The humans knew Sardonyx and her followers were gone and that humans and dragons together had done something to make that happen, but nothing more. Their legends of Jiwanyil and Katayan and the rest arose out of their imperfect memories. They never saw another dragon, and concluded all dragons had died. And life went on."

"But where did Mother Stone come in?"

"You know, I really did intend to make you save all your questions until the end," Katayan said with a smile, "but I think you learn better this way, Lamprophyre. The dragons who weren't part of the magic knew only two things: dragon deaths as bound by the death-song were essential to keeping Sardonyx imprisoned, and a human presence on Mother Stone would release her. So they made up a new story, of their 'god' Mother Stone and their devotion to her. They told the rising generation nothing of the truth, just passed down the knowledge of the death-song and the warning against humans setting foot on Mother Stone. They believed they were doing the right thing."

"I see."

Katayan looked down at her, still smiling that tender, loving smile that made her feel warm all over. "No more questions?"

Lamprophyre thought over what she'd learned. "Just one," she said. "What exactly did I do? Why did I have to be involved in waking the...the guardians? Was there something special about me all along?"

Katayan laughed. "That's three questions, my child. But I won't put a limit on your learning. All along, I have had the power to stop Sardonyx, but only if I was called on to do so. You are the first dragon in a millennium to call upon God, and you did it three times. First, in asking me to purge the Third Ecclesiast of Sardonyx's taint. Second, in asking me to protect you from Sardonyx's mental attack. And third, in asking me to join you with the spirits of the dragons guarding Mother Stone."

"But I thought I was calling upon Jiwanyil."

"I did tell you it doesn't matter to me which name you use, yes?" Katayan spread his wings once, flexing them wide, and furled them again. The wings had temporarily blocked Lamprophyre's view of the drawing, and when he moved them, she was certain the tiny dragons had changed position. "Your prayer to me gave me the opportunity to act, not only removing Sardonyx's threat but also allowing those thousands of dragons to return to their eternal home. A thousand years is a long time to wait, even for a dragon."

Lamprophyre sat back. "And that's all?"

"You mean, how were you able to turn Sardonyx's mental attack back on her?" Katayan shrugged. "It's a rather dubious gift some five dragons in a hundred are born with, the ability to speak thoughts in addition to passively hearing them. Sardonyx was the first to discover its use and the first to turn it against her kin. There are at least thirty dragons living who are capable of it. But it had nothing to do with your sacrifice, or with being able to fight Sardonyx. What mattered was my protection granted you against her attack, thanks to your request. You don't need to fear turning into Sardonyx."

"You'd never do that, anyway," Porphyry said. "We'd pin your wings back if you tried it."

Lamprophyre elbowed him in the ribs. "Then what was it we encountered in the chamber? The thing that spoke with Jiwanyil's voice? Sardonyx knew it was an object, and that it would give her power."

Katayan looked grim. "That was a remnant of the artifact the humans created," he said. "It fueled the magic and was reinforced with every dragon death. But Sardonyx in her slumber found a way to tap into it, and was gradually draining it in her effort to free herself. It was me, and not-me, with some of my knowledge and the ability to speak answers to questions, but lacking any real consciousness. I am glad Sardonyx destroyed it. It has been like grit under my scales for a thousand years."

Lamprophyre looked at Porphyry. He was smiling his familiar cheeky smile, like he knew a secret she didn't. "I can't think of anything else, except...no. Thank you for telling me this story. I wish I could tell it to others."

Katayan rose to his feet. "Oh, but I intend you to," he said.

Lamprophyre couldn't help it; she looked around at the chamber, empty except for the three of them. "Is this what death looks like, then? We were always taught dragon spirits are taken into Mother Stone's rest, but I know that's false."

"It's far more interesting than that," Porphyry said. "It's—"

"Porphyry, don't taunt your clutchmate," Katayan said. "And I'm afraid I'm not done with you yet, Lamprophyre."

That made her nervous. Calling upon a God was one thing, but being his tool, or weapon—that was a burden heavier than she wanted to bear. Even so, she stood and threw her shoulders back, arching her wings above her. "What do you mean?" she asked, hoping her stance looked confident and not defiant.

"I did tell you this didn't mean your doom," Katayan said. "My mate and I have discussed the situation, and we've decided our finest creation doesn't deserve to go on in ignorance of the truth. We can't alter you to allow ourselves to speak to you unbidden, but nothing says we can't send someone on our behalf."

Lamprophyre's heart beat faster. "I'm not dead?"

"You're dead, for now," Katayan said. "But that won't last. I don't have to ask if you remember everything I told you, do I? Of course not. Tell the others. Teach them what you learned. And lead them to speak to God."

Lamprophyre realized she was clinging to Porphyry's hand tightly enough to make her scales go pale. "But they'll forget over time. They'll end up lost again."

Katayan laughed. "I think you'll find," he said, "that writing things down is far safer than oral tradition, as far as remembering goes. Write this story, and see it preserved, and your words will live far longer than you do."

"I will. I promise."

Porphyry hugged her. "And tell the others it's safe to bury us on Mother Stone now," he said. "No more trapping dragon spirits, and it's so much easier than digging a pit. Though I've seen the burial stone you made me. It's beautiful."

"I wouldn't forget you even if we hadn't done that." She hugged him back.

Then Katayan took her by the hand and guided her to stand in front of him, enfolding her in his wings so all she could see was the drawing of the mountain and the dragons. "Thank you," he said. "Now, watch them fly."

Lamprophyre watched the picture, which was now clearly in motion, spirals and curves and loops and dives as the dragons endlessly circled the mountain. She felt as if she were falling into it, very slowly, and then her fall sped up, and the dragons weren't circling the mountain, they were flying at her face, surrounding her with the sound of dragon wings—

—and she came to herself with a gasp, her eyes blinking open. The endless blue sky curved over her, pale and brilliant in the afternoon sun. She lay uncomfortably on her back with her wings furled beneath her like a couple of knobby rock protrusions. The scent of snow carried by the freezing wind enveloped her.

She lifted her head, feeling incapable of moving anything else. She appeared to lie on a narrow rock ledge covered with a damp film where her body had melted the snow clinging to it. Rokshan huddled a short distance away, his face and arms pressed to the mountainside, his shoulders shaking from his heavy breathing. She couldn't tell if he was frightened or grieving.

"Rokshan," she said, hoping she wouldn't startle him off the ledge. "Rokshan, help me."

Rokshan's head came up. His wings twitched convulsively. "Lamprophyre?"

"I can't sit up. Help me, please?"

Rokshan scrambled to her side and helped her sit, freeing her wings. He touched her face wonderingly, as if he was amazed to feel scales and bone rather than the insubstantial body she'd had when she died. "I thought you were dead."

"I was dead, and now I'm not. Rokshan, you're a dragon!"

He blinked at her. "I think you being no longer dead is far more extraordinary than me managing the transformation I've been planning for weeks."

"No—well, maybe, but my story is too long and complicated—how did it happen? You couldn't have found the sodalite artifact so quickly!"

Rokshan went from touching her face to putting a hand on her shoulder. "It wasn't necessary once we figured it out. Well, Tekentriya did. She was fairly scathing about how we should have seen it in the first place. She said if Hyaloclast didn't need it to transform you, Dolomite, as creator of my dragon body and a dragon himself, didn't need it either. It was close, though. There was no way to save my human body, and Tekentriya knew it. But we weren't very far from the marble quarry, so—Lamprophyre, you're alive!"

He threw his arms around her, holding her close. She ran her hands down his back, marveling at the feel of his scales and the sleek muscles beneath the skin.

"It feels so different," she murmured. "The pair-bond, I mean. It's bigger and more diffuse, but it's still you."

"It's wonderful," Rokshan said. "I know you said it would be, but I had no idea how wonderful." He released her, taking her hand. "Can you fly? I wasn't joking about not being sure I could manage it alone. I was sitting there, going back and forth between grief at your death and fear that I was going to die alongside you because I couldn't fly back, and not sure I cared if I did, and then..." He let out a deep breath. "I love you. I'm ready for the rest of our life to begin."

Lamprophyre smiled and rested her head briefly on his shoulder. "You know," she said, "I don't know if I told you this, but dragons have sex in midair. While flying."

Rokshan burst out laughing. "I think I need more flying practice before I'm ready to attempt that."

"It's all right. We have time," Lamprophyre said. "A whole lifetime of it."

EPILOGUE

Four years later

Lamprophyre paced outside the hatching cavern, restlessly watching the western sky. It was growing late, and the sun's rays turned the fluffy clouds pink and gold. So much could still go wrong. Rokshan wouldn't drop the egg, but what if sunset came and the egg wasn't ready? Flying at night was dangerous. What if they'd judged wrong, and the egg wasn't ready to hatch until midnight? What if the dragonet wasn't strong enough to break through the shell?

"Calm down," Hyaloclast said. "Every mother feels this way. When Aegirine made this journey with you, I was sure he would drop your egg accidentally. But fathers are always careful."

Lamprophyre cast a quick glance at her mother. "Rokshan's not an ordinary father."

"We've done everything we can to prepare him. He took good care of the egg during the twelvedays of her gestation. He'll be fine. You, on the other hand—" Hyaloclast eyed her narrowly— "appear to be on the verge of collapse."

"*You* can be calm. Your ordeal is over."

Hyaloclast shrugged. "I find, after having survived Sardonyx's attack, other things seem less terrifying. I can't explain how awful it was to be locked away inside my own head like that. The minor issue of waiting for Leucite to carry our egg here, and seeing small Mica be born, pales in comparison."

"I'm glad you only took two twelvedays to recover. The flight almost made me queen in your place." Lamprophyre shuddered and went back to pacing and watching the sky. "I already have a role to play, thanks."

"And one I wouldn't trade you for. Prophet of a forgotten God." Hyaloclast pointed. "I think that's him."

Lamprophyre had already felt the tingling warmth of her pair-bond that said Rokshan was approaching. She spread her wings and lifted half a handspan off the ground before settling back, feeling embarrassed at her show of impatience. But Hyaloclast didn't say anything. They watched together until the distant speck was clearly a dragon, gleaming green and gold against the afternoon sky. Then Hyaloclast put a hand on Lamprophyre's shoulder. "Let me know when the dragonet is born," she said, and flew away with a great flapping of wings.

Lamprophyre stopped herself jigging with excitement as Rokshan flew closer. When he finally landed, she took the egg from him and said, "You look exhausted. Are you all right?"

Rokshan nodded. His eyes looked weary and his hands shook when he let go of the egg. "I'll be fine once our dragonet is born. Which should be soon. I'm sorry I'm not a faster flyer."

The egg jumped in Lamprophyre's hands, and the click of claws against shell was audible. "Hurry, then," Lamprophyre said, ducking through the smallish opening that led to the hatching chamber.

Inside, the cave opened up immediately, becoming big enough to fit a dozen dragons without any of them touching. Purple and blue phosphorescence made delicate traceries on the walls, coloring Lamprophyre a more vivid blue and turning Rokshan's emerald scales iridescent purple. Lamprophyre hurried to the prepared nest of soft dry grasses and set the egg down. Rokshan followed more slowly and sat rather abruptly beside the nest, letting out a deep sigh. "Are you sure you're all right?" Lamprophyre said. "There's still some time—do you need a drink, or food, or anything? You've thrown your whole heart into this."

"I just need a rest, and more than four hours' uninterrupted sleep," Rokshan said. "Is that normal?"

"Yes. All fathers say the same," Lamprophyre said. "It's just that you're not an ordinary dragon father, so I thought, maybe you needed more."

Rokshan smiled. "You and the flight have done more than enough to help me. I hope it was enough. My memory is better, as a dragon, than it was as a human, but there are so many stories to remember, so many traditions to pass on to the egg, I admit to being a little worried."

The egg rocked, making them both fall silent and stare at it. Lamprophyre dropped to her knees across from Rokshan. "But you have an advantage in not knowing the stories that turned out to be false. You're the first dragon father to pass on only the truths I learned from God."

"I know. It doesn't stop me worrying."

"Me, too."

The egg rocked harder, nearly falling out of the nest. Rokshan and Lamprophyre each put out a hand to steady it. The clicking *taptaptap* of the unborn dragonet's claws became louder. Then a sharp crack rang out, echoing in the huge cavern, and Lamprophyre gasped as a jagged black line shot across the gleaming golden surface of the egg. More lines spidered out from the first, and shards of eggshell snapped off and fell to lie in the soft grasses.

A small gray form stretched within the shell, knocking off more shards as her tiny wings flexed. She kicked, sending eggshell flying, and ended up on her back with her little face screwed up, ready to cry out from the discomfort of lying on her wings. Rokshan gently righted her. She looked up at him. "Papa," she said in a clear, fluting voice. "You're so big."

Rokshan swallowed. "It's because you're so small," he said. "You'll be as big as Mama someday."

The dragonet turned liquid green eyes on Lamprophyre. "Mama

is bigger," she agreed. "And blue. And Papa is green, and I am...I don't know this color that I am."

"You're gray," Lamprophyre said, "but in a few years that will change."

"Papa told me things while I slept," the dragonet said. "About colors and animals and Katayan and dragons and humans. And that my name is Garnet. Is it a good name?"

"Of course. It's the best name," Rokshan said, gathering his daughter into his lap. "Your mama picked it because garnets are a stone filled with life, and we hoped that would bless you."

Garnet stretched her arms and legs and wings and then folded herself into a little gray ball. "I'm glad," she said, yawning, and fell instantly asleep.

Lamprophyre and Rokshan were left staring at each other in wonder. "I can't believe it," Lamprophyre said. "She's perfect. Everything is perfect."

"I'm so relieved," Rokshan said. "And now the exhaustion is setting in."

"I'll go get Hyaloclast, to welcome Garnet to the flight," Lamprophyre said. "And then I think we both should sleep for at least a day. Then the real work begins."

THEY TRAVELED TO TANAJITAL A TWELVEDAY LATER, TAKING turns carrying Garnet and the bag containing Garnet's eggshell to give to Manishi. Lamprophyre no longer worried about what Manishi might do with it. After their encounters with Viveki, she knew the difference between passive antagonism and active malice. They could endure Manishi's relatively minor self-centered malevolence.

The dragonet laughed and clapped her hands whenever Lamprophyre dove, despite Rokshan's protests that she was too little for aerial acrobatics. But by the end of the trip, he was diving with their daughter, too.

Lamprophyre gave a wave to the embassy the way she always did. She'd handed over her ambassadorial responsibilities to Cymophane when she became in egg, but she'd spent so many years there it still felt like a second home. They were too high for her to tell if anyone waved back. Her household had changed so much, between Abhit going to the academy and Preyanka returning from her training as an ecclesiast and Bhakriya and Depik welcoming an infant son and, last year, a daughter to their family, much to Kavari and Rassika's delight. They would have to stop at the embassy to introduce Garnet to everyone. But they had a more important stop to make first.

The guards at the great doors of the palace bowed as they approached, holding those doors open wide for their draconic guests. "Please tell my parents we've arrived," Rokshan told the chamberlain Mekel, who greeted them in the entrance hall. Mekel bowed, his thoughts full of *never would have guessed* and *little thing's adorable, not at all like a lizard* as he hurried away. Lamprophyre wanted to smack him, but controlled herself when Garnet said, "What's a lizard?"

"Garnet, remember humans can't help their thoughts," Rokshan said, "and it's a dragon's responsibility to be polite and not listen in."

"But I don't know how not to," Garnet complained.

"Then you have to be especially polite and not say anything about what you hear." Rokshan hitched the dragonet higher on his shoulder and said, "I hope this wasn't a mistake."

"We all agreed four years ago that if dragons were going to be more fully part of human culture, it was bad manners to eavesdrop on humans when they didn't know we could hear thoughts," Lamprophyre said. "It's not as if Garnet will give anything away. And if nothing else, it will keep your father honest."

"If he comes at all," Rokshan said bitterly.

"Who is Father?" Garnet asked. "He should want to see me because I'm adorable."

Lamprophyre and Rokshan burst out laughing. "I can see we

need to discuss more than just eavesdropping etiquette," Lamprophyre said. "Garnet, we're here to see Papa's mama and papa, remember? 'Father' is what some humans call their papa."

"Because Papa was a human first," Garnet said.

"Exactly. And—"

She heard movement at the top of the right-hand stairs and fell silent. Ekanath and Satiya emerged, hand in hand. They were alone, with no retinue or horn-blowers. They stopped and looked down at the three dragons. Lamprophyre heard Rokshan's surface thoughts of dismay and regret that smoothed into resignation. He stepped forward. "Mother, Father," he said, lifting the dragonet, "this is my daughter Garnet. Garnet, say hello."

Garnet flapped her wings idly. "Hello," she said. "You're my papa's mama and papa. I thought humans were small, but you're bigger than me."

Satiya let go of Ekanath's hand and descended the stairs, her eyes never leaving Garnet. "Oh, my," she said. "Why, you're beautiful. I didn't know dragons could be gray."

"All dragonets are gray to begin with," Lamprophyre said. "They gain their adult color when they're about five years old."

"And she speaks," Ekanath said. He hadn't moved, just stood at the top of the stairs with his fists clenched.

"I taught Garnet speech while she was in the egg," Rokshan said. He wasn't looking at his father. "Along with things a dragon needs to know."

"She's not much bigger than a human baby," Satiya said. "May I...is it all right if I hold her?"

Rokshan hesitated, then held Garnet out to his mother. Satiya took the dragonet gingerly, looking worried about dropping her, but Lamprophyre saw her relax the moment she realized how solid Garnet was. "Oh, my," Satiya repeated. Her eyes gleamed with tears Lamprophyre didn't understand. "Ekanath, come here."

Ekanath's jaw tightened. He didn't move.

"*Come here*," Satiya said, putting steel into her words. Ekanath hesitated a beat longer, then descended the stairs to join her.

"Look at her, Ekanath," she said. "Your granddaughter is a dragon."

Ekanath looked at Garnet. His jaw relaxed slightly. "I won't," he began, then fell silent.

"You don't like me?" Garnet said. She sounded curious and not at all hurt. "I thought everybody liked me. Why are you different?"

This time, Ekanath's gaze flicked briefly to Rokshan before returning to rest on the dragonet. "I like you," he said. "Stop listening to my thoughts."

"Father," Rokshan said, warning in his voice.

"I don't understand your thoughts," Garnet said, just as if Ekanath hadn't spoken. "Should Papa not have become a dragon?"

"I said—" Ekanath's voice rose dangerously loud.

Lamprophyre snatched Garnet away from Satiya and cradled her against her shoulder. "Dragonets can't control what they hear," she said, carefully maintaining her calm so Garnet wouldn't hear her anger. "And it's not as if she heard anything we didn't already know. Rokshan hoped seeing Garnet would convince you. It looks like he was wrong."

Ekanath closed his eyes and let out a breath, trying to calm himself as well. He opened his eyes and looked first at Rokshan, then at Garnet, whose liquid green eyes meeting his were the only color about her. "You rejected your birthright," he said in a weary voice. "I'll never understand that. But this...you have a wife, you have a child, you've taken on responsibilities I thought I'd never see you accept. You haven't lived your life the way I hoped. But that's not up to me."

He moved forward until he was in front of Rokshan. "Thank you for wanting me to meet your child. My granddaughter," he said. "I don't know if I'll ever understand you, Rokshan, but I honor your courage."

Rokshan's thoughts were a turmoil of pain and fear and relief. He extended his hand to his father, who clasped it. "That's enough for me," he said.

Ekanath turned to face Lamprophyre. "My granddaughter," he

said, sounding less weary. "A dragon granddaughter. Damen of Fanishkor will be green with envy."

"Can humans be green?" Garnet asked.

"Only metaphorically," Ekanath said. He held out his hands. "Come here, and let me look at you. My eyes aren't what they used to be."

Garnet reached out her hands to the king and tugged on his beard. "Humans are hairy," she said. "I like it. Being different is nice."

"You know," Ekanath said, "I think you might be right."

~

Late that night, curled up around Garnet in their comfortable warm cave, Lamprophyre said, "I told Dharan I would meet him in two days to review the last pages I dictated. Do you mind if I spend the night in Tanajital?"

"Garnet and I will be fine," Rokshan said. He straightened the dragonet's wing so it draped over her more comfortably. "I'm looking forward to seeing the book published."

"It won't be useful for a while, though teaching dragons to read is a lot simpler than I realized," Lamprophyre said. "It does make me miss Porphyry."

"You talk about him every day," Rokshan pointed out. "Part of the truth about God's relationship with dragons, and how we worship him. Though I wish Khadar weren't quite so insufferable about how humans were right about Katayan. It could only be worse if he were the Second Ecclesiast instead of the Fifth, representative of the human notion of Katayan."

"I don't mind," Lamprophyre said. "The Archprelate treats me as an equal, which means Khadar has to show me respect, and so long as he keeps his insufferableness limited to his thoughts, I can handle him."

"He might want to meet Garnet too. I think that should wait until she's a little older and better able to block thoughts."

Lamprophyre stretched. "I'll miss you, though I'm not sure Garnet will feel the same about me. Dragonets are so self-absorbed she probably sees me as a force of nature rather than as a person."

That made Rokshan laugh quietly so he wouldn't wake the dragonet. "You're right. She'll want to spend time with her clutch."

"Garnet, Mica, Jasper, and Feldspar," Lamprophyre recited. "Two males, two females, perfect for pairing."

"I'm sure Coquina and Flint would love to see Garnet pair-bonded with little Jasper. Is it usual to plan matches for dragonets this early?"

Lamprophyre stretched and laid her head on Rokshan's shoulder. Her fingers twined with his. "In a joking sort of way. Obviously we can't arrange things. But wouldn't it be sweet, the children of pair-bonded clutchmates ending up pair-bonded themselves?"

Rokshan chuckled. "Or Garnet will go the route her mother did, and find herself a human willing to become a dragon for her sake."

"I don't know how much power that serpentine artifact still has. It transformed me, and you, and Tekentriya, and who knows how many people before us."

"Tekentriya wants to see Garnet when she and Zekran get back from Kolmira," Rokshan said. "But she'll come here. Riding. I would be superstitious about riding if I were her, but she's always been braver than I."

"It's just a different kind of bravery." She'd been present the day Tekentriya's husband Zekran, aided by the sodalite artifact Rokshan had retrieved from Viveki, had transformed Tekentriya not into a dragon, but into the undamaged, pain-free body he remembered so well. Rokshan refused to tell Lamprophyre what he'd done to Viveki, and Lamprophyre didn't care enough to pry. All she cared was that it was permanent. "You were brave to change your species."

"Hah. That was easy. I had a beautiful mate waiting for me, which is all the incentive I needed." Rokshan rolled on his side to look at Lamprophyre, carefully steadying Garnet so she wouldn't be overlain. "A beautiful mate to share beautiful intimacy with." He caressed the sensitive spot at the back of her head, sending wave after wave of pleasure through her.

"Mmm," she said, leaning into his touch. "It's better than kissing."

"Better than kissing," Rokshan said, resting his chin on her shoulder so she could touch him in return, "and something we have a lifetime to explore."

Lamprophyre remembered the white-walled chamber whose details hadn't faded with time, remembered the great white dragon God and what he'd taught her. "A lifetime," she said, "and everything that comes after."

In her memory, the dragon God smiled.

ABOUT THE AUTHOR

In addition to the Dragons of Mother Stone series, Melissa McShane is the author of many other fantasy novels, including the novels of Tremontane, the first of which is *Servant of the Crown;* the Extraordinaries series, beginning with *Burning Bright;* and *The Book of Secrets,* first book in The Last Oracle series.

She lives in the shelter of the mountains out West with her husband, a daughter and a niece, and three very needy cats. She wrote reviews and critical essays for many years before turning to fiction, which is much more fun than anyone ought to be allowed to have. You can visit her at her website **www.melissamcshanewrites.com** for more information on other books and upcoming releases.

For news on upcoming releases, bonus material, and other fun stuff, sign up for Melissa's newsletter **here**.

facebook.com/melissamcshanewrites
twitter.com/mmcshanewrites

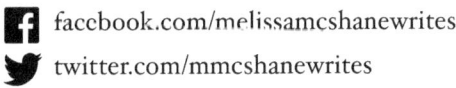

ALSO BY MELISSA MCSHANE

THE DRAGONS OF MOTHER STONE

Spark the Fire

Faith in Flames

Ember in Shadow

Skies Will Burn

THE EXTRAORDINARIES

Burning Bright

Wondering Sight

Abounding Might

Whispering Twilight

Liberating Fight

Beguiling Birthright (forthcoming)

THE LAST ORACLE

The Book of Secrets

The Book of Peril

The Book of Mayhem

The Book of Lies

The Book of Betrayal

The Book of Havoc

The Book of Harmony

The Book of War

The Book of Destiny

THE SAGA OF WILLOW NORTH

Pretender to the Crown

Guardian of the Crown

Champion of the Crown

THE HEIRS OF WILLOW NORTH

Ally of the Crown

Stranger to the Crown

Scholar of the Crown

THE CROWN OF TREMONTANE

Servant of the Crown

Exile of the Crown

Rider of the Crown

Agent of the Crown

Voyager of the Crown

Tales of the Crown

COMPANY OF STRANGERS

Company of Strangers

Stone of Inheritance

Mortal Rites

Shifting Loyalties

Sands of Memory

Call of Wizardry

THE CONVERGENCE TRILOGY

The Summoned Mage

The Wandering Mage

The Unconquered Mage

THE BOOKS OF DALANINE

The Smoke-Scented Girl

The God-Touched Man

Emissary

Warts and All: A Fairy Tale Collection

The View from Castle Always

www.ingramcontent.com/pod-product-compliance
Lightning Source LLC
Chambersburg PA
CBHW061029030726
47504CB00002B/309
9781949663686